After the Honeymoon

Janey Fraser

arrow books

Published by Arrow Books 2014

2 4 6 8 10 9 7 5 3 1

First published in Great Britain in 2014 by
Arrow Books
Random House, 20 Vauxhall Bridge Road,
London SW1V 2SA

www.randomhouse.co.uk

Addresses for companies within The Random House Group Limited can be found at:
www.randomhouse.co.uk/offices.htm

The Random House Group Limited Reg. No. 954009

A CIP catalogue record for this book
is available from the British Library

ISBN 9780099580843

The Random House Group Limited supports the Forest Stewardship Council® (FSC®), the
leading international forest-certification organisation. Our books carrying the FSC label
are printed on FSC®-certified paper. FSC is the only forest-certification scheme supported
by the leading environmental organisations, including Greenpeace. Our paper
procurement policy can be found at www.randomhouse.co.uk/environment

Typeset by Palimpsest Book Production Ltd, Falkirk, Stirlingshire
Printed and bound in Great Britain by CPI Group (UK) Ltd, Croydon, CR0 4YY

This book is dedicated to my husband and our not-honeymoon (who needs one when you live by the sea?)

> Also to Giles, who refused to go away with us (see above)
>
> Lucy and Andi (who lived it up in the Maldives)
>
> William (who loves the beach)
>
> Little Jack (ditto)
>
> My sister, whose third honeymoon (Spanish villa for twenty) was a ball

This book is *not* dedicated to

> My missed flight at Stansted
>
> Post-holiday mobile phone bills
>
> Airport luggage scales (never in my favour)
>
> Holiday rain
>
> Lost passports (why didn't I look under the photocopier?)

ACKNOWLEDGMENTS

Thanks as always to my agent Teresa Chris and our seaside business meetings. Also to my editor Gillian Holmes, Citizen Sigmund, Sarah Aratoon and all the team at Random House.

Finally, I'm indebted to ex-Royal Marine Bill McDermott for being so generous with his time; to my cousin Finni for her tales about life in Greece; to all the dinner ladies who shared their nuggets (literary, rather than chicken); friends and students who contributed real-life honeymoon stories; and to my fellow writers at the Romantic Novelists Association.

THE HONEYMOON

HISTORY OF HONEYMOONS

Norse legend has it that honeymoons used to take place before marriage. According to one version, a man would kidnap a woman he fancied (hence the meaning behind 'swept her off her feet') and carry her around on horseback for a month of moons. The couple would drink mead (a honey-based drink) while in hiding, as this was said to improve the chance of having sons. Then, when the bride's relatives caught up, they would have a marriage ceremony.

LAST-MINUTE BARGAIN!

Idyllic holiday cottage on the stunning, unspoilt Greek island of Siphalonia – suddenly available for the last week of July, due to last-minute cancellation.

Very reasonable rates!

Perfect for couple or small family. For more details, please contact Gemma Balls, head of pastoral care at Corrywood School, or leave a message with the school secretary.

Chapter One

EMMA

'So,' asked Bernie chirpily, handing her a serving of pasta curls, chipolatas and broccoli through the hatch, 'where are you going for your honeymoon then?'

Emma carefully placed the bright green plastic platter in front of a little girl from Year One with buck teeth and clear-framed glasses, before replying. Why did people keep asking her? 'We can't afford one, actually. Weddings are so expensive. Tom says we might have a bit of a break next year instead, with the children.'

Bernie, or Big-Boned Bern as she was sometimes known (though Emma, with her size-sixteen meringue wedding dress, could hardly talk), rolled her eyes. She smoothed down her Corrywood Juniors pinny and passed the next green platter over the counter that divided the cooking area from the dining room. 'Thought that was the whole point of waiting all these years before tying the knot. You know, to save up for a big do.'

Emma, who was wearing a matching yellow pinny like the rest of the team, felt a little shiver go through her: it happened every time someone mentioned the wedding. When she and Tom had first started planning all this, it hadn't seemed real enough to be scary. But now there was only a week to go and frankly she felt sick as a dog.

'That's right, love, eat up the broccoli too,' she urged. 'It's good for you.'

The kindly advice to the little girl in glasses bought her time to compose herself before turning back to Bernie. 'We've been putting aside as much as we could, but with the mortgage, it's really tight.'

5

Her friend and workmate popped a sausage in her own mouth (strictly forbidden, for hygiene reasons) and gave a sympathetic nod. 'Not easy, is it?'

She leaned across and picked out a pasta curl that had somehow got stuck in Emma's naturally wavy, honey-blonde hair. Stray bits of food on your person was one of the hazards of the job, along with the noise from the kids, which made your ears ring until you got used to it.

Emma *loved* being a dinner lady, or rather, a 'mealtime assistant', as they called it now. She liked nothing more than to help the little ones to cut up their food or sort out an argument because someone claimed to have a bigger sausage than someone else. It was even an exciting challenge to coax fussy eaters into 'just one more mouthful'.

'Mrs Walker, Mrs Walker! What happens to food when it goes into your tummy?'

It was an earnest little boy who was rather small for his age, bless him. Always asking questions. Like all the others, he addressed her as 'Mrs'. It seemed inconceivable to them that a mother could be anything else. 'It gets eaten up by your body,' replied Emma promptly, before adding encouragingly, 'Then you get big and strong and clever.'

'But *how* does your body eat it up?'

Bernie rolled her eyes and mouthed something that looked like 'Rather you than me'.

'It's all to do with digestion,' Emma began, recalling her A grade in biology GCSE.

'Die jest on.' The little boy looked as though he was memorising the words carefully. 'But *how*?'

It would be so easy to say something wishy-washy like 'It just does', but Emma always felt that when a child was bright enough to be curious, they deserved an answer. Even when it wasn't easy.

'It's like this, you see,' she patted her tummy. 'The food goes round your body and then it ends up in something called the colon.'

The little boy's eyes lit up. 'Like in English?'

Bernie spluttered with laughter behind her. Emma ignored her. 'No, although that's a good question. This kind of colon is different.'

'*Then* what happens to it?'

'I know! I know!' One of the older children was jumping up and down, arm up in the air. 'It comes out as poo!'

Emma flushed.

'Cool!' The earnest kid was nodding. It certainly hadn't put him off his food, judging from the way he was wolfing down those pasta twists.

Why was it easy to get other people's kids to obey, but not your own? It had been fine at the beginning when her son had been little, but Gawain had become much more demanding since his sister had been born.

Emma stifled a yawn as she reached for a plate of veggie nuggets to deliver to table two. She'd spent hours trying to get her eldest to bed last night. Not only had he refused to be peeled out of his Spider-Man costume for bath-time but he'd also kept swooping – arms wide out at the side like an aeroplane – in and out of the tiny bedroom that he shared with little Willow, waking her up.

It was only when she'd lain down next to him in his new bed that he'd finally dropped off. Then Tom had gone and spoiled it all by declaring Gawain was far too old for all this fuss now he was four. 'When are we ever going to have an evening to ourselves?' he'd said gently.

'He's still very young,' Emma had retorted, wondering at the same time what she and Tom would actually *do* with a whole evening on their own.

Still, the great thing about her little job at Corrywood School was that she felt wonderfully useful. Every time one of the children finished their plate or gave her an impromptu cuddle the way little ones did, she got an electric buzz. She was really appreciated here – far more than at home, to be honest.

The other big plus was that the hours fitted in with her own kids. There was just time when they finished at one-thirty, after sweeping up and stacking the little red tables, to collect Gawain from pre-school and Willow from Mum's round the corner. Tight, but just about possible.

Rather like copping out of the wedding.

Emma knelt down next to a little boy with muddy knees ('Shall we make a picture out of these sausages?'), grateful for another distraction. She'd have been quite happy not to get married at all. Mum and Dad's example had proved there was no such thing as a happy ever after. But Tom was more traditional.

For a minute, she found herself thinking about the boy she'd met at the community club disco all those years ago. Even though she'd been barely fifteen – ridiculous really – and Tom had been so much older (twenty-two!) she'd known he was the one. It wasn't just the way he'd asked her to dance with that shy smile. It was how he'd carefully asked for her number before kissing her. Her first kiss!

Picking up a squashed veggie nugget from the floor, Emma found herself blushing at the memory. It had been a rather awkward meeting of mouths, as though he wasn't sure what he was doing either, despite his age, especially when his glasses had got in the way. But she'd liked that. The last thing she'd wanted was a slick smoothie. Someone who couldn't be trusted. Someone like her dad.

They'd gone out together for the rest of her time at school. 'Don't you want to see what it's like with other boys?' demanded Bernie, who'd sat next to her in class since primary, sharing her sweets surreptitiously under the desk.

No, she didn't. It was all right for her friend, whose parents still held hands when they walked down the street. But when you'd witnessed the arguments that had gone on between *her* two, you needed stability. Yet at the same time, you were scared of committing for ever, just in case the same thing happened to you.

Only someone who'd seen their family break up would understand that.

Tom had started to talk marriage when they'd gone to Paris to celebrate her eighteenth. The hotel had turned out to be more skanky than swanky, and although she'd pretended not to be unnerved by the 'ladies of the night' who'd hung around the street outside, Emma had reached out for Tom's hand for comfort.

He'd felt awkward as well. To compensate for their unfamiliar surroundings and narrow bed with sheets that bore stains from the previous occupants, they'd had way too much to drink. Perhaps it was that which had made her forgetful.

Of course, she could have gone and got the morning after pill when they'd got back, but something inside her made her stop. After all, she'd always loved babies.

Anyway, it wasn't as though she had a proper career. She'd always dreamed of being a teacher, but then Dad had gone off, putting an end to any kind of wild aspirations like that so she'd had to leave school and get a job in a supermarket to help pay the bills.

The reality of what she'd done hit home six weeks after the Paris weekend. Tom had been much calmer than she had when they'd stared at the blue line on the pregnancy testing kit. 'I want to do the right thing by you,' he'd declared. 'Let's get married.'

Married? The right thing? Emma looked at this man with his open, honest face, greasy navy overalls from the garage where he worked, the premature bald patch in the middle of his head and those round glasses which kept misting up at the most inopportune of times. Shouldn't he be talking about passion and wanting to grow old together? Besides, he knew what she thought about marriage after Mum and Dad.

Maybe she could delay him for a bit; put it off so it didn't seem so important. It was a baby she wanted – not a wedding.

'I don't want to be four months gone when I walk down the aisle,' she had pointed out. 'It will look as though you've *had* to marry me.'

But from the minute that Gawain was born (she'd always loved that name ever since discovering his story in English class), Tom had started banging on about weddings again. 'I want a big do,' he had declared. 'Nothing can be too good for my beautiful girl.'

Emma, completely smitten and overcome with a love she had never thought possible for this crinkly, wet baby in her arms, with his shock of red hair (just like Tom's), dismissed his words. Weddings were the last thing on her mind.

As for 'beautiful girl', that was ridiculous! Emma had never considered herself to be a looker. At five foot three, she was just too short to carry off the extra half stone which had plagued her all through her teenage years and which now, thanks to post-baby weight, had crept up to one and a half. Tom, who was stocky himself, declared he liked her 'cuddly' but she knew he was just being kind. If Emma had been forced to name her best points, it would be her hair and what Bernie called her 'sympathetic, smiley face'.

'Let's think about getting married when we've settled down a bit,' she'd pleaded to Tom. 'There's enough to do at the moment as it is.'

And so there was. But Emma loved every minute of being a mum. She hadn't realised how much they'd needed their son to make them feel complete, but Tom *still* wouldn't give up on the marriage thing. 'Why bother?' she'd retort. 'It's so expensive and takes up so much time. Why can't we just stay as we are?'

Tom's face had instantly made her feel guilty. 'Don't you want to commit to me? Think you can find someone better, do you?'

'No, of course not, but . . .'

They'd been sitting on the sofa enjoying some rare couple time while Mum was out on one of her dates-that-went-nowhere.

'No buts,' he said, kissing the top of her head. 'We owe it to our son to tidy things up.'

Tidy things up? It didn't seem a very romantic way of putting it. But unable to find any more arguments, save a nagging uncertainty that she couldn't put a name to, Emma promised to look up some venues, even though they were completely out of their reach financially.

In a way it had been a relief when she'd found out that she was expecting again, just as Gawain began to toddle. Of course it meant money would be even tighter, but having another baby was important for her son. She'd always longed to have a brother or sister herself.

When Willow – a name she'd found in a poetry book – was born, she felt as though nothing could make her happier. A daughter! A little girl, with her brother's trademark red hair, whom she could go shopping with. Talk to. Confide in. It made Emma glow with pleasure to know that she had provided a lifelong friend for her son. They would love each other, she knew it – even though Gawain had already ripped up his favourite picture book on being introduced to his new sister.

But over the next few weeks and then months, Tom began to show a side of himself that she had only occasionally got glimpses of before. He started speaking shortly; behaving like someone who didn't want to talk very much or have a great deal to do with her.

'What's wrong?' she asked one night.

She'd expected Tom to say nothing, that she was imagining it. But then he'd given her a look that made her chest contract. A cold fear crawled over her. He'd found someone else. Just like Dad . . .

'I'm not happy,' he said slowly.

'Who is it?' she managed to say, her throat strangled.

Tom frowned. 'What do you mean?'

Emma could hardly get the words out.

Then his face cleared. 'You think I've got someone else? Don't be daft, Em. Though if I didn't know you better, I might wonder if *you* had someone.' He took her hands, getting down on one knee on the carpet they'd bought on credit last month. 'I'm not happy because I want to get married, and you don't. If you really loved me, Em, you'd say yes.'

She hesitated. Only for a second, but it was enough.

'Come on, Em,' he persisted. 'You know it makes sense.' My darling Emma.' He was still kneeling in front of her, blocking the television screen. 'I've asked you before but I'm

11

doing it again. Will you do me the honour of being my wife?'

Just at that moment, there was a shout from the bedroom. 'Mum? *Mum!*'

'You see,' said Tom exultantly. 'Our son wants us to get married.' He squeezed her hand, trying to stop her as she leaped to her feet to check Gawain was all right. 'We owe it to our children, Em. We owe it to them to provide a stable life with married parents.'

But we can do that without being married, she wanted to say. Yet she could still taste the fear of a few minutes ago when she'd thought he was going to finish with her. Maybe, if this was so important to Tom, she should go along with it.

'Mrs Walker, Mrs Walker! I've finished!'

The shrill little voice cut into her thoughts, bringing Emma back to the present. It was the poppet from Year One with buck teeth and glasses. Every day, the child insisted on sitting on her own, away from the other girls who were all chatting away like gossipy old women at the small red plastic tables and chairs. Poor little mite!

'Finished?' she repeated, kneeling down next to her. 'I don't think so. Look, if we move this piece of pasta next to this slice of tomato, it makes a face, doesn't it? Try eating the nose. That's right! What's that like?'

The little girl put her head to one side, considering. 'OK.'

Getting children to eat was a bit like horse whispering. You had to get them to think it was their idea. 'Now, how about taking a little nibble out of pasta man's ear?'

Somehow, Emma succeeded in encouraging the child to almost finish the plate and felt a little thrill of satisfaction.

How she loved her job! It had been Bernie who'd suggested she went for it when Gawain had started pre-school next door. Bernie was already working there herself, and she'd pointed out the notice, pinned on the board where they queued up to drop off and pick up the children. 'It's quite hard work but we have a laugh,' Bernie had assured her.

It had been a lifesaver. The supermarket hadn't wanted her

any more when she'd tried to cut her hours down after Willow was born and she needed to do *something*, especially with the mortgage. She and Tom had been saving up for years for their own place; after all, they couldn't live with Mum for ever.

Then, six months ago, they'd actually got one of those special deals with a housing association. It wasn't a big place: just two small bedrooms, a galley kitchen where you rubbed shoulders, an L-shaped lounge and a garden just big enough for Gawain to ride his trike.

As Tom said, it might swallow up most of their monthly incomings, but at least they had a place of their own. Much as she loved her mum, it hadn't been great, sharing a kitchen and bathroom. And, as she'd tried to reassure her mother, they were only round the corner.

Even so, the mortgage meant Tom had to do overtime at the garage. The dinner lady job helped a bit, but the best thing about it, to be honest, was that she hadn't so much found a job as discovered a vocation.

'See you've worked your magic again,' remarked Bernie when she left her place at the kitchen counter to help Emma and the other two mealtime assistants clear up while the children shot off to the playground, accompanied by the duty leaders. 'Little Miss Buck Teeth almost cleared her plate. That's a first.'

Emma didn't care for expressions like 'buck teeth'. Her own had a funny little gap in the middle; Tom declared it 'endearing' but she hated it. That was something she'd have liked to have had fixed before the wedding, even though it was impossible. For a start it was too expensive. And secondly, there was only a week to go.

'Have you got a second?' asked Bernie as Emma reached for her cardi to go home. 'Only the girls and I wanted to have a bit of a word.'

Her friend led her through to the back of the kitchen where the dishwasher was buzzing merrily. The surfaces were spotless and the smell of antiseptic just about took away the smell of sausages and broccoli. Emma's stomach was beginning to rumble. All she wanted was to collect Gawain and Willow and get back home for a crispbread and cottage cheese – part of the pre-wedding diet she'd been on for months now but which still hadn't made much difference.

Nor had the famous Winston King's breakfast television workout, which she'd tried to do while dishing out breakfast at the same time.

'We've got a little present for you,' said Bernie excitedly, handing her a white envelope. 'It's not just from the girls. The teachers contributed too. In fact, it was Gemma Balls' idea.'

How kind, thought Emma as she ripped open the envelope. It was typical of Gemma Balls to organise a collection. She was so nice. And bright too. Exactly the kind of person that Emma admired. Even now, she still felt a bit cheated when she thought about her old dreams of being a teacher.

She pulled out the piece of card from the envelope. It didn't look like an ordinary voucher for Boots or Marks & Spencer. This one had a picture of a beautiful little house with red and purple flowers growing up the outside with a stunning blue sky behind and a beach running down to the sea.

One week at the Villa Rosa in private cottage, said the lettering below. *Breakfast and dinner included.*

There was a photograph too of a pretty blonde woman, standing on a balcony holding a glass of wine. *Co-owner Rosie Harrison will look after your every need.*

Emma looked up at Bernie. 'I don't understand.'

'It's a honeymoon!' Her friend's eyes were sparkling with the excitement of giving someone something really nice. 'I knew you didn't have one planned. That was why I was trying to get you on the wrong track earlier when I asked if you were going away.'

Emma was still trying to take this in. 'But the children . . .'

'We've got it sorted. Your mum's going to have Willow and Gawain.' Bernie was almost jumping up and down now like the little boy in Year Three who went hyper at the whiff of

14

an additive. 'We talked to Tom about it first, of course, and he thought it was a great idea. He also confirmed you had a passport. See? We've thought of everything.'

He should have told her first, Emma thought. This wasn't the sort of thing you could spring on someone. A cold feeling of panic wrapped itself round her chest. She'd never left Willow and Gawain before. How could she do so now? 'Your mum will cope,' said Bernie as if reading her mind. 'It will do you and Tom good to go away together. He said you've never once had a break without the children.'

True. But that was because she'd become as dependent on them as they had on her.

'Honeymoons are so expensive,' she blurted.

Bernie looked smug. 'That's the beauty of it. The villa belongs to a friend of Gemma Balls who lives in Greece. The school secretary gave me the number.' She glanced at the picture. 'Posh, isn't it?'

Her eyes sparkled as though she was going herself. 'You're going to love it, Em! You've got your own cottage that's in the grounds, and in the evening, the owner cooks a meal on this gorgeous terrace overlooking olive trees so everyone can eat together if they want.' She gave Emma a knowing wink. 'Or they can have a bit of privacy, if you get what I mean.'

There was a silence during which Emma tried to think of the right words. Greece? Abroad? She'd never flown before: when she and Tom had gone to Paris, it had been on Eurostar. 'Aren't you pleased?' asked one of the other meal assistants sharply.

Swiftly she tried to gather herself. They'd all saved up for this. Gone without. Just for her. It was incredibly kind of them.

'I'm stunned.' Quickly she hugged Bernie and then the other two. 'It's an *amazing* present. Thank you *so* much.'

TV FITNESS STAR SET TO MARRY DIVORCED MOTHER OF TWO IN WHIRLWIND ROMANCE!

Charisma *magazine exclusive*

Chapter Two

WINSTON

Everything was planned, his assistant Poppy had assured him. Yes. Privacy was top priority. Details had already been 'leaked' to the press about the wedding taking place in Antigua or the Maldives, depending on which gossip column you read. Photographers were, even as they spoke, frantically booking rooms at local hotels in a bid to get the best spot.

But only five people in the world knew where Winston and Melissa were *really* going. He and his bride; Poppy (who had arranged the decoys plus the real booking); his agent; and Melissa's ex, Marvyn damn him. In case of emergency, since he was looking after the kids.

'Just one thing,' Poppy added, one of her immaculately manicured fingers poised over her iPad. 'Are you sure you don't want to do an exclusive with the *Globe*? It's a very good deal and I've got a contact there who's promised copy approval, even though it's not officially allowed. So if there's anything you don't like, you can take it out before they go to press.'

Winston King drew himself up to his full six foot seven inches and gave his assistant the look he reserved for anyone who had stepped seriously out of line. It was a stance he had mastered in the Royal Marines, where it had been drummed into them that it wasn't just physique that you needed for the job. It was attitude too. And intelligence.

'I've told you,' he said, in a voice which journalists had described as a Russell Crowe growl or a James Bond seductive whisper, depending on his mood. 'Melissa and I want complete and utter privacy. Especially on our honeymoon. We don't want to end up on a front cover.'

'Sure. Simply checking.' She gave a patronising shrug. 'And by the way, they call it a mini-moon if it's less than a fortnight. At least, that's what *Charisma* magazine says.'

Poppy gave another glance at the iPad. 'Mini-moons are either for people who can't afford a longer one or for really busy couples.'

Was that so? Still, a week was enough, wasn't it? Melissa didn't want to leave the kids for longer and he had his programme to get back to. Besides, it was all arranged, and when Winston made up his mind to do something, he never backtracked. It was part of his make-up; a birthright passed on by his haughty West Indian grandmother, who had insisted that nothing was out of his reach. Not even the elite public boys' school she had sent him to when his parents had died, a historical institution where he could so easily have sunk, instead of swum, were it not for his intimidating height, his strangely attractive bald head (a result of falling out of a tree at ten), and his sporting abilities.

'What if someone needs to know where you are?' asked Poppy, picking up her iPhone. It was amazing how people couldn't seem to function unless they were ringing or texting or emailing. Danger to them was a poor audience rating or a broken fingernail – not a burned out body on the field and the roar of gunfire.

Calm down, calm down.

Winston selected a clove of garlic from the dish in front of him and chewed it carefully. A clove a day kept you in tip-top condition; it was a tip on his website. *But clean your teeth afterwards, especially if planning close contact with someone!*

'Need to know where we are?' he repeated. 'Simply tell them we're incommunicado.' Forcing himself, he gave Poppy one of his brilliant smiles that the camera loved so much. 'And by the way, I won't always have my mobile on.'

Her eyes flickered. 'But what if I need you urgently?'

Winston took a swig of warm water with a slice of lemon and grated ginger. Fantastic for the circulation. Another tip on his website.

'Poppy, if I was in a coma, would you be able to ask me something important?'

'No, but . . .'

He felt his smile growing tight. 'Remember? No buts. Just *toned* butts.'

That was another of his *Work Out With Winston* slogans. The audience loved them.

If someone had told him a few years ago that he was going to have his very own breakfast television show, advising the nation how to tone up their pecs and abs *and* the rest, he'd have laughed in their face. He was a Royal Marine, not a fitness clown. Or at least, he had been a Green Beret until signing his release papers, just after his thirty-fifth birthday, when the horrors of war had finally got to him.

Block it out, Winston told himself fiercely. It was the only way to survive.

After getting out, he'd met up with a former batch mate who was working as a fitness instructor for an exclusive health club in London. 'You ought to do the same, mate,' said the man, who was more of a colleague than a friend. Winston didn't do friends; it wasn't good to let someone get too close. His parents' early death had taught him that. 'The money's great, and you won't believe the celebrities I come across. There's . . .'

But Winston wasn't bothered about big names. It was a job he needed. Something regular that could help him obliterate the images that had been indelibly stamped on his mind over the years. So many stories, so many lives, some of which he'd been able to save and others where it had been impossible. The little girl desperately screaming at him for help, before the sniper's crack felled her to the dusty ground. The burning shack where he had instructed his men to stay outside while, ignoring his own safety, he had stumbled in to drag out a woman screaming for her children. The kid with one leg who followed them around, pleading with them to take him home. 'UK good place. This bad.' The screaming masses who spat at them, who blew up the tanks, who would cut their throats if they could – and did.

Not to mention Nick. Always Nick. Sitting on his shoulder. Cemented into his memories.

Initially, when he'd returned to the UK, Winston had still expected someone to take a potshot at him. It took every ounce of strength not to jump if a car backfired or a siren screamed in his ear. At times, he loathed London with its crowds and shop windows full of clothes and unnecessary stuff for the house, with crazy price tags. How he despised all those self-centred people, obsessed with buying things to make themselves 'happy' when there was a whole world out there, just trying to survive.

At other times, he marvelled at the beautiful buildings; the art galleries (he was particularly fond of the Royal Academy, where his grandmother used to take him during school holidays); and the parks.

As luck would have it, his physical instructor friend broke a leg the week after their conversation. 'Any chance of you taking over for me, King? I don't want them to get anyone else in case I lose the job altogether. It's only for six weeks, but it will give you experience.'

Winston was grateful for the tailor-made opportunity. Luckily for him, the gym was only half an hour away from the two-bedroom flat in Kensal Rise he'd bought using his grandmother's legacy, which gave him just enough space between work and home. Winston had had enough of living on the job. Some men, when they left the Royal Marines, missed the noise and banter of everyone around them.

After Nick, he just wanted peace.

Rather to his surprise, Winston took to his new life like a duck to water. 'You're doing well,' said his supervisor after one particularly demanding overweight woman had told him that Winston was a 'real asset'. 'Keep going like this and you could stay on if you want.'

'Not if it means kicking my mate out of his job,' he retorted, fixing the bloke with what his mates used to call 'His Majesty Look'. 'But I'd appreciate a reference.'

He got it. Four weeks later, he moved on to another gym

where he was equally successful. There were even more celebrities here, although to Winston, each client was the same.

'Would you consider private sessions at my house?' one of his clients, whose agency had instructed her to lose a stone before the next film, had asked. 'I'll make it worth your while.'

She named a figure that stunned him. Why not? Even though his grandmother had left him enough money to buy the Kensal Rise flat, he still needed an income. Besides, it wasn't as though he had a girlfriend to moan about him working all hours. And it helped to block out everything else.

It was at this actress's house that he got his big break. By chance (his grandmother always used to say he was lucky), a TV producer friend called round with a script. 'We could do with someone like you,' he said, eyeing Winston in his black lycra leggings and bare chest. 'Ex-Marines, you say?'

'*Royal* Marines,' Winston had replied, gritting his teeth.

'How old, if you don't mind me asking?' The producer sucked in his breath at the reply. 'Might get away with it. Take my card. Give me a ring.'

Quite how it happened so fast, Winston wasn't sure. All he knew was that the television world worked very differently from anything he'd known before. If he'd still been in the corps, he'd be doing his morning pyhs (the name for the gruelling dawn workout) and then heading for morning prayers (the daily briefings) before going out on ops (operations).

Instead, here he was under the hot studio spotlights, doing a five-minute stint every morning on breakfast television. He earned more in a month than he'd done in a year. If he wasn't careful, he'd end up like the Londoners he'd loathed when he'd first come here. To ease his conscience, Winston made some substantial donations to the Royal Marine Benevolent Fund.

Meanwhile, the nation loved him and the emails were pouring in, praising the lithe Marine – he was always having to add the *Royal* bit – who appealed to everyone from teens to grans. All the nationals wanted to interview this rising star who insisted on cycling instead of using the studio car. Even *Charisma*, not to mention *The Times* and *Tatler*.

'You've got to do it,' squealed the producer when *Work Out With Winston* became so popular it was offered its own half-hour slot. So he did, making sure that he only allowed the interviewers to get so far before pulling the covers over his personal life.

Then one day he came into the studio to find a different make-up artist from the usual jolly, grandmotherly Carole. Winston took one look at the gorgeous woman waiting for him and suddenly found it hard to breathe.

It wasn't just her striking height (five foot eight at a guess). Or her glorious shoulder-length mane of wavy dark hair, black eyes, creamy complexion and high cheekbones. Nor was it her rangy, boyish build, accentuated by the clingy top she was wearing over stretchy jeans and little red boots. It was the combination of all of them.

Nick, he thought immediately.

'Hello,' she said shyly, although behind her eyes he was certain he detected a certain toughness. 'I'm Melissa Greenwood.' Her voice was surprisingly deep and gravelly. 'Carole's not well so she asked me to cover at the last minute. We used to work together years ago, before I had kids.'

At this point, she glanced at the mobile in her hand before slipping it into her blue suede bag. 'I hope that's all right.'

The resemblance to Nick was striking – or was it because it was four years to the day since it had happened, and he'd been thinking about it all morning?

The post-traumatic stress counsellor had assured him it was natural to 'see' Nick because it gave him hope. It was a bit like when you went on holiday, she'd told him. You thought you saw people you knew on the plane or in the resort because it made you feel secure. The difference was that coincidences might well happen like that in real life.

But not when someone was dead.

He sat down on the chair, ready for her to start work. Don't be so ridiculous, he told himself firmly. He had to get a grip, otherwise he'd go back to the way he'd been during those crazy months after it had happened when his sanity had been, very seriously, on the line.

Luckily Melissa Greenwood was talking, so he used the opportunity to stop his hands from shaking through sheer will power. He wasn't sure what she was saying but that gravelly cadence was soothing. Restful. Peaceful. Something that Winston hadn't experienced for a very long time.

Out of the corner of his eye, he could see her glancing at her phone again and then delving into her bag. 'I've bought you a pot of honey, as a sort of thank you. For letting me do your face, that is.'

She was stammering: maybe she was less tough than he'd initially suspected. 'I mean, I'm sure you get lots of presents from fans, but my next-door neighbour keeps bees and I just thought you might like it.'

Somehow Winston found his voice. 'Thank you. That's very kind.'

'I adore your programme,' she said, biting her lip as though confessing a deep secret. As she spoke, there was a shrill ring from the blue suede bag. Instantly, that creamy white complexion developed two little red spots on each cheek. 'Whoops. I've just got to take this.'

He stood up and moved to the window to give her privacy but could hear words like 'in the fridge' and 'homework'.

'So sorry,' she said, making a point of switching off the phone and putting it in her bag. 'Is it all right if we start now?' She was speaking, he observed, with a mixture of amusement and irritation, as though *he* had delayed *her*.

Then Melissa sat down on the chair next to him and examined his features with a completely different look on her face. The rather nervous woman was replaced now by the professional. Without looking, he could feel her taking him in.

'A bit of shading here, I think,' she was saying, opening one of her palettes. 'And a touch of foundation on the neckline.' She locked eyes with him in the mirror. 'Broad, generous lips. I like that.'

Carole liked to work in silence but this one clearly enjoyed a chat. Normally it would annoy him but he found he didn't mind Melissa's chatter.

'Tell me, Winston. It is all right if I call you that, isn't it?' She was talking while working with her pencil, her tongue showing slightly between those small white teeth in concentration. 'What did you really want to do when you were little? Did you have a big passion in your life?'

To his surprise, he found himself telling this pretty woman with a pale white space on her wedding finger that he had dreamed of being an artist like his mother, who had died along with his father in a train crash in India.

'I used to love watercolours,' he added.

'Wow! I do a bit myself, with my children in the holidays, to keep them amused. Do you still do it? Paint, I mean?' She added a touch of brown to his eyebrows.

Briefly, Winston thought of the times when the only comfort in his tent had been to sketch what he had seen on the field in his notebook. They hadn't been pretty pictures but it had helped to release the horror. 'Sometimes.' Then a dreadful thought struck him. 'You're not going to run off and sell all this to the *Globe*, are you?'

Melissa stopped. Bending down, she put her face next to his in the mirror. To his dismay, he saw that he had offended her. 'I wouldn't dream of it.' Then she made an expression that suggested she was cross with herself rather than him. 'I'm sorry. I'm asking too many questions, aren't I? It's just that I'm nervous, because usually at this time I'm doing the school run – not talking to one of the most famous people on television!'

She glanced at the bag. 'That's why I have to keep checking the phone. I know it's not very professional, but I'm worried because I've left my daughter – she's thirteen – in charge of getting her little brother off to school.' She bit her lip again. 'Not sure if I should have done, but it was the only way I could be here so early.'

Thirteen? Winston thought back to himself at that age. He wasn't just getting his own breakfast in the holidays. He was travelling to the other side of the world on his own to see his grandmother. 'That's old enough to cope, surely?'

She laughed: a pretty, tinkly laugh, as though he'd just said something highly amusing. 'You'd think so, wouldn't you?' Then she gave a little sigh. 'I probably shouldn't tell you this, but this is my first job for ages. I used to be full-time, but then I had my children and turned freelance.' To his horror, he could see in the mirror that her eyes were growing misty. 'It worked out well. I took on as much as I needed to but turned down anything that clashed with family commitments.'

She looked down at her ring finger. 'But then you got divorced,' said Winston softly.

There was a little nod. 'Is it that obvious?'

'I've been taught to notice things,' he replied evenly.

Another nod. 'Of course.' Then her voice grew brighter in the way that Winston recognised; she was making herself sound stronger than she felt. 'My decree nisi came through two days ago. It's probably why I'm feeling a bit . . . well, wobbly. My husband . . .'

There was a short pause before she continued. 'Marvyn got together with someone from work and now they live round the corner, which is really awkward in one way, but in another it's good, because he sees the children quite a lot.' Suddenly, she picked up her pencil. 'Oh dear. I'm so sorry. I really shouldn't be telling you all this. It's just that, well, you're very easy to talk to.'

'So are you,' Winston heard himself saying. Don't do it, screamed the voice in his head. You said you'd never love anyone else again. Have you forgotten?

'Look,' he added, ignoring the voice. 'I've got to go now. I'm on in a minute.'

'Wait.' Her voice was strong now. Commanding, even. She was so close that he could smell her perfume, a mixture of roses and lily of the valley that reminded him of his mother. Funny how he could still smell her even though he could barely recall her face. 'I've just got to cover up that scar.'

25

Winston froze.

Don't touch it, he wanted to shout, but she was already running her finger over it questioningly. Carole had noticed it too but he'd told her in no uncertain terms to steer clear of the long jagged line on the base of his neck. Now he tried to do the same thing but failed. Her touch was so soothing! As though hypnotised, Winston found his eyes closing as she smoothed something cool onto it.

'It's a special oil that I make myself with herbs from the garden. Helps to make scars look less red.' She smiled wistfully. 'My mother taught me. She was Spanish, you know.'

So that explained the dark looks. As for the scar, it had been troubling him all morning, burning, as though it was still open and raw. Was it reminding him of the date, as if he needed any prompting?

'How did you get it?' she was now asking tenderly.

There was a flash of fire in front of his eyes. A scream. The smell of burning flesh – just like bacon – which had turned him vegetarian overnight. He pushed back the chair and leaped to his feet. Enough was enough. Who was this woman who thought she was some kind of psychotherapist?

'It's none of your business.'

She was looking at him now with a stricken expression. 'I'm so sorry. I didn't mean to be nosy. It's just that I'm talking out of nerves. Please don't complain about me or they won't ask me to do any more.'

God, he felt like a heel now, even though it had been her, surely, who'd stepped out of line. There was a knock on the door.

'Three minutes, Winston,' Poppy called out.

Melissa actually had a tear running down her face. This was awful. How could he go before the cameras and do *Work Out With Winston*, knowing that he'd upset this woman who had somehow, on the strength of half an hour's acquaintance, affected him more than anyone had in years, right where it mattered?

'Look,' he said urgently, leaning forwards. 'I've got to go now, but how about a coffee afterwards?'

He'd expected her to be grateful but instead she was texting on her phone, brushing away that tear as though it was an inconvenience.

'I can't. Sorry.' She was frantically texting while speaking. 'I'd love to but . . .'

'It's OK.' He headed for the door, hot with embarrassment. 'You don't have to make excuses.'

'No, really.' She ran a hand through that glorious black mane, shaking it like a wild pony. 'My son has left his homework behind so I've got to get back and take it in to school. If I don't dash now, I'm going to be horribly late. There are only two trains an hour back home.'

There was another knock on the door. Louder than the first. 'Two minutes, Winston.'

Damn that. 'Where's home?' he asked brusquely.

She was still texting. 'Corrywood. It's about an hour away.'

'Wait there.' Winston heard his voice barking like an order. Her face jerked up, startled. 'I mean,' he continued, in a softer voice, 'I'll get my PA to sort out a car for you.'

'Really?' Now Melissa was looking anxious and relieved at the same time.

'Sure.' He could feel his chest tightening with apprehension at what he was about to say. 'But on one condition.'

Her dark eyes searched his, just as Nick's had done at the end. 'What's that?'

Winston heard his voice coming out of his mouth without his brain having given it permission. 'That you have dinner with me one night.'

'One minute, Winston.' Poppy's voice was edged with panic.

There was another toss of that wonderful black mane. Nick's had been much shorter, of course, but the colour and texture were almost identical. Winston held his breath as his words came back to him, words which he'd tried so hard to bury all these years. *I'm trying, Nick. I'm trying.*

Then Melissa smiled. A lovely smile which made him weak with relief. 'I'd love to – providing I can get a babysitter.'

That had been three months ago. 'I loved you from the moment you walked in,' he confessed during his proposal, which he'd blurted out while they were walking along the canal near her home. He'd been more nervous than he'd ever recalled, far more scared than when he'd run into that burning shack.

'But will you love my children too?' she had asked urgently.

Winston thought of the girl – Alice – with her sharp, distrustful eyes: thirteen was a difficult age. He remembered it all too well. Freddie was friendlier; they'd already played a bit of footy together. No problems there, as far as he could see, especially if he could persuade her to put them into boarding school – something they hadn't discussed yet.

'Of course I will,' he had promised, ignoring that little voice inside his head. *Kids? What do you know about them?* Nothing, he told himself firmly, that he couldn't look up in some manual or work out for himself.

'And you don't mind living in my house,' she'd continued, entwining her fingers in his, 'so the children can stay at the same school? They've been through so much. They need continuity.'

He'd put his arm around her, deciding that this wasn't the time to discuss the boarding option. 'Anything. Just as long as I make you happy.'

After that, with her agreement, he'd arranged everything. The wedding at a registry office near her home. And the honeymoon destination: a simple rustic taverna in Greece which Melissa had cleverly found through someone at school. Provided no one spilled the beans, they'd be guaranteed privacy. Marvyn, the ex, was having the children and they would have a week together, just to themselves, before getting back to filming.

Of course, the papers had a field day. A whirlwind romance, they all called it. One had run a cruel piece with a headline that had made his agent shudder: 'Is Bachelor Boy Winston King Getting Married to Disprove Gay Rumours?'

Still, if Melissa had seen the article, she hadn't mentioned it, and Winston certainly wasn't going to.

Meanwhile, he privately swore on his life to protect this beautiful woman who could be so vulnerable one minute and so unreachable the next. She mesmerised him. If he went for more than a morning without talking to her, he felt as though part of his chest was missing. When they'd made love for the first time, he had silently cried in a mixture of relief and self-loathing.

'I love you,' he'd whispered.

'I love you too.' She'd turned towards him. 'The last few months have been so difficult,' she'd confided, biting her lip. 'But now I feel safe.'

Her words had filled him with both love and terror. Safe, he'd repeated, running the word round his mouth. He hadn't been able to save Nick.

But maybe now, Winston told himself, as he strode out of the television studio and unlocked his bike from the underground car park, he might finally be able to erase the past.

TRUE HONEYMOON STORY

'We had one night in a really expensive hotel with marble floors. To our horror, confetti fell out of our clothes as we undressed and we spent the entire night scrubbing off the pink and blue stains from the tiles.'

Jo, who got married last year

Chapter Three

ROSIE

Rosie woke, blissfully aware of the warm Mediterranean sun streaming in through the half-open white wooden shutters. If she opened her eyes just enough, she could see it dancing off the glittering aquamarine sea outside, in little sparkly lines. It was going to be a scorcher, she thought, sleepily stretching out like one of the stray cats who would, no doubt, be lazily licking themselves on the terrace outside.

Even after sixteen years of living on Siphalonia, she still found herself counting her lucky stars. Paradise! That's what the wide-eyed tourists called it – at least the ones who were adventurous enough to stray off the beaten track and find them.

And it really was. Long, sandy beaches with clean, fine white sand. Whitewashed cottages with bougainvillea clambering up the walls and terracotta roofs, nestling next to each other like cloves studded on an apple, on different levels, leading up to the mountains above. Locals with gappy teeth and wrinkled leathery skins who grinned at strangers.

But Rosie was under no illusions. It took at least two generations to be fully accepted here. Jack's children might just make it, if they were lucky.

Jack. Oh God. Rosie sat upright in bed, stark naked in the liberating knowledge that her bedroom was built in such a way that no one could see her through the window. Perhaps it wasn't a good idea, after all, to leave him. Running her hands through her short curls, bleached over the years by the sun, she suddenly panicked now that the time had come. Was she mad to leave Jack for three whole days on his own in charge of the Villa Rosa?

31

It wasn't too late to change her mind.

'I can do it, Mum,' he had insisted when the subject had first been raised, weeks ago. 'Don't you trust me?'

Yes, she did. Jack wasn't like the fifteen-year-old boys you read about in the English newspapers. He was reliable. Solid. Practical. Older than he looked with a wise head on his young shoulders. Much taller than she was – which wasn't difficult, given that she was barely five foot two. He'd had to grow up fast. They both had.

But every now and then, her son made the odd slip-up, like that booking last year which he'd forgotten to write down. 'It won't happen again, Mum,' he'd assured her. And it hadn't. At least, as far as she knew.

Now Rosie slipped into her pretty cotton rosebud dressing gown that her friend Gemma had sent her for Christmas (they were both suckers for Cath Kidston) and padded across the room to turn off the noisy air conditioning. She needed to keep an eye on the bills but a/c was an essential at night when it could get unbearably stuffy. Glancing in the mirror, with its bright blue driftwood frame decorated with shells, she tilted her head to one side, looking at what her old drama teacher had described as her 'delicate elfin features and mischievous eyes' which had earned her the role of Puck one year in the school play.

Opening the shutters, she leaned on the window sill and gazed out across the water. It was a view that never failed to enthrall her. Today there was a large white liner on the horizon and, closer to the shore, a fishing boat returning with the morning catch. It looked like Greco's, the *Siphalonian*, with its jaunty red and white bow and little cabin beneath.

Rosie felt a small smile creeping across her face along with a tremor of misgiving as a tall, lean, tanned man with the hint of a beard, wearing shorts and nothing on top, leaped easily out onto the shore, hauling the boat in.

It wasn't Jack she needed to worry about. It was Greco, with his broad chest and mass of curly black hairs sweeping down to his navel.

'You're going to Athens?' he had exclaimed when she'd casually mentioned that she needed to visit suppliers. Over the years, Rosie had learned to speak Greek fairly fluently, but Greco usually spoke to her in English. 'It so happens I have some business there myself. I will go with you, yes?' He'd laid a hand lightly on her arm, as he did to any woman under ninety. 'A beautiful woman like you should not travel alone.'

She had laughed him off, pointing out that she'd been independent for a very long time and was quite used to looking after herself, thank you. Anyway, she'd added with a slight edge suggesting she didn't fully believe his story, what kind of business did he have out there himself?

'You still think after all these years that I am just a fisherman?' he had replied, his eyes twinkling. 'I will surprise you, Rosie. Just you wait and see. Besides, it will be good to have some time alone together, will it not?' His face grew serious. 'Away from the island and all those prying eyes.'

He had a point.

What had got into her? Rosie asked herself, stepping into her shower and shuddering as the cold water spurted out, suggesting that the hot had run out again. Greco, of all people! When she'd arrived, all those years ago, pregnant with Jack, she had been warned, almost immediately, by Cara who had run the villa at the time.

'That Greco, he bad boy.' The old woman, whose command of the English language had been shaped by visitors to the island, had waggled her short brown index finger. 'You do not fall for his charms, yes?'

Back then, Rosie wasn't falling for anyone's charms. She'd already made one grave misjudgment, and look where that had got her.

Now, slipping into a pair of white cut-off trousers and her favourite turquoise halter-neck top which (according to Greco) brought out the colour of her eyes, Rosie grabbed the suitcase she'd packed the night before, shut the door behind her (it had taken a while to be convinced there really was no need

33

to lock up in Siphalonia) and made her way over the cobbled stones.

Every now and then, she paused to stroke one of the cats and to say *'Ti kanis?'* ('How are you?') to her loyal band of women who were already hard at work, scrubbing the stone floors of each cottage and changing the linen so there were crisp white sheets ready for the next batch of new arrivals.

As she did so, Rosie's mind wandered back to her old life in the small seaside town on the borders of Dorset and Devon where she'd been at school with her old friend Gemma. The pair had been inseparable. In fact, it was Gemma in whom she'd confided when she'd first suspected she might be pregnant.

'You can't be,' Gemma had gasped, despite the fact that they weren't meant to talk in the school library. 'Surely you haven't actually *done* it?'

But she had. It had only been the once and Rosie wasn't quite sure how it had happened. All she knew was that it was done, Charlie was gone, and that the result, confirmed later by the pregnancy kit which Gemma bought with her, proved her worst fears were true.

The strange thing was that although Rosie was terrified, she also felt oddly calm. When her father had yelled 'Get out of my house and never come back', she wasn't that surprised. Dad had never been the same since Mum had died. He'd always had a short fuse for small things like running out of tea bags or leaving a light on. But they faded into insignificance compared with an unmarried, pregnant seventeen-year-old daughter.

So she'd packed her bag, hugged Gemma goodbye and hopped on the next ferry to France, feeling sick with nerves and pregnancy. If only Charlie had answered her letter . . .

Rosie soon discovered, when she got bigger, that a lone pregnant woman in a foreign country elicited a certain amount of empathy and incredible generosity. A kindly mother of two in France had given her a job in her bar for a while, plus a room at the top of the house. And a couple in Spain had taken her on temporarily, to help the chef in their restaurant.

But by the time she had pitched up in Siphalonia, after waitressing her way through Italy, she was ready to stop. Her earlier, naturally bright attitude to life was fading as her bump became more and more pronounced. Only now was it really coming home to her. She was expecting a baby. And she had neither home nor security to offer it.

One of the older boatmen, who had taken her from the mainland to the small Greek island, detected her exhaustion and directed her to a small white house close to the harbour, with the sign 'Villa Rosa' on the outside. 'Cara,' he had said, nodding understandingly. 'She will take care of you.'

Rosie stood there, shaking with exhaustion and trepidation. Villa Rosa? The baby lurched inside her; suggesting that the name, so like her own, was a sign that she would be all right here. For a while, at least.

'*Ti yinete?*' said the speckle-faced woman who came to the door. (Rosie later found out that this meant 'What's up?'). The older woman's eyes passed over her, taking everything in. Then she took her arm, in a motherly fashion. 'You stay here.'

Rosie discovered that the Villa Rosa was a small, run-down equivalent of a B&B in England. To her embarrassment, Cara refused to let her pay for her hospitality. 'I can waitress for you,' Rosie had protested, but Cara would hear none of it.

'I had daughter like you once,' she had said with a wistful look in her black eyes. 'Now I think maybe you are her, coming back to me.'

The poor old thing had lost her marbles, thought Rosie, but the lure of a clean bed with proper sheets was too much. Jack clearly felt the same, for he arrived two weeks early, with the help of Cara and the local doctor. After that, it became an unspoken agreement that Rosie would stay on to help at the villa, which Cara had owned for years but which had got too much for her since her husband's death.

Rosie hadn't been wrong about Cara not being quite right

in her head. Although she declared herself to be 'not a day over fifty', she seemed much older. Often her mind would ramble or she would tell her tales about the daughter who had been 'lost at sea', although the details were clearly too painful for Cara to recall.

For a while, Rosie carried on looking after Jack, who was a model baby, and helping Cara. Eventually, at Gemma's instigation through increasingly persistent letters, she forced herself to write to her father, telling him where she was and enclosing a small picture of his two-year-old grandson. There was a gap of a month before he wrote back to say that her maternal Scottish grandmother had died and left her a fairly large sum of money.

The tone of the letter was grudging, implying the legacy was more than she was entitled to. To her disgust, there wasn't a word about Jack or even a question about how they were getting on so far from home.

Rosie had put the letter carefully back in the envelope and gone to find Cara, who was chopping aubergines in the kitchen and yelling at the small boy to take the next lot of orders 'before you're old enough to start shaving!' Today was a good day, from the look of things.

'I wonder,' asked Rosie, looking out of the window to where Jack was asleep in his pushchair in the shade of the olive trees, 'how you'd feel about having a partner?'

And so the Villa Rosa was reborn. With Cara's agreement, Rosie used her grandmother's money to build two cottages near the villa, in order to take on more guests.

They advertised through the classified pages of *The Lady*, and of course the local tourist board. By the time Cara decided it was time to retire with a nephew on the mainland, leaving Rosie in charge, the Villa Rosa had earned a good reputation and attracted a small number of select holidaymakers from all over Europe who returned again and again.

Cara wasn't great at communicating, apart from the odd poorly spelled letter. But Rosie never forgot the lessons her mentor had taught her. 'Always trust your gut instinct about people you don't know. And look out for that Greco.'

Still, Rosie told herself as she made her way into the main house to check that the cook had started to make breakfast for today's departing guests, people changed, didn't they?

When she had first arrived on Siphalonia, Greco wouldn't leave her alone – perhaps because she was one of the few young girls who refused to fall for this impossibly handsome Greek with the bold nose, almond-shaped brown eyes and deep, hypnotic voice.

'Forget it,' she would tell him when he brushed against her, reeking of lemon cologne, or asked her once more if she would share a carafe of wine.

'You do not mean that, I think,' he had laughed, raising his eyebrows in that quizzical, *how can you turn me down?* fashion. But eventually he got the message, becoming instead a good friend. Rosie soon came to realise that Cara had perhaps been rather unfair in her criticism of this man, who was always happy to carry shopping or mend a leaking pipe at the Villa Rosa.

'May I go fishing with Greco?' Jack kept asking when he was eight. And because she knew that the man was a respected fisherman who never took chances with the tides, she allowed it. Her son needed a masculine figure in his life, she told herself. It wasn't good for him to be surrounded by women all the time.

Over the last few years, Rosie had noticed that Greco had matured and become more responsible, while still bearing an innate charm that made her insides flutter, in a way they hadn't when they'd first met.

Or perhaps it was because she was just plain desperate. It wasn't as though there was anyone else available. Most couples got married around here in their mid-twenties. Rosie was nearly thirty-four now.

Greco was virtually the only man left. But *what* a man!

'He makes me melt,' she confided to Gemma during their last Skype conversation. 'But you have to be so careful here. No one misses anything in Siphalonia, so I'm not going to commit, until I know it's right . . .'

'You won't know if you don't give him a chance,' Gemma had pointed out. 'Besides, it's been ages since . . .'

Her voice tailed off but she might as well have said the name. Charlie. Rosie's first love. Her only love. However hard she tried to block him out, he still kept coming back into her head, even though he had let her down so badly. Was it surprising? After all, her beloved Jack was a daily reminder.

And now, here she was. Ready and packed, despite her huge reservations. Breathless with anticipation and excitement and fear, although of course she tried to hide all that.

Greco was already waiting for her in the kitchen, wearing a crisp white shirt and freshly pressed blue jeans. He took in her bare shoulders approvingly. 'So! You are ready?'

The transition from friendship to possibly something more had been so slow that it had taken her a while to recognise it. Such was his generally flirtatious nature, that she wasn't even certain he felt the same. Besides, nothing physical had happened. Yet.

'I'm still worried about Jack,' she whispered, hoping that no one else was listening in. The problem with living on the job was that there was never any privacy.

'Nonsense.' Greco shrugged, stroking the hint of stubble around his chin. As he picked up her little navy blue case she couldn't help noticing his muscles rippling. Rosie tried not to remember the three children – sometimes it was four – he was rumoured to have scattered around the Greek islands. 'Your Jack is a big boy. A man now. I was his age when I owned my first boat.'

Rosie wavered. 'I'll be away for the new intake of guests.'

Greco touched her right shoulder lightly, sending electric waves through her. 'If you do not give the boy responsibility, he will never learn.' He was very close to her now. 'Nor will you.'

Rosie stood back just in time as the cook – an elderly man about to retire – appeared from the larder. He gave her a knowing look, making her blush.

'Are you off now, Mum?' Hastily, Rosie broke away from Greco as her son strode into the kitchen. If it wasn't for the fact that he had her smile and blue eyes, they might not be taken for mother and son. Jack, with his mop of black hair just like his grandfather, was the colour of a native with his tanned complexion, and spoke the local dialect as fluently as he spoke English. Everyone loved him for his happy nature, polite manners and willingness to please. She was so lucky.

'You don't mind, do you?' Unable to stop herself, she hugged him, even though she could barely reach his shoulders. How was it possible that boys could grow so tall? Hungrily, she breathed him in. He smelt of pine; to his delight and her shock, Jack was one of those boys who'd needed to shave from the age of twelve.

''Course I don't!' Jack wriggled away with a twinkle in his eyes. 'Besides, if you don't get the boat, you'll miss those supplies you're after.'

Rosie flushed. Her son was no fool. He could sense the vibes between his mother and this man whom he'd known all his life. It was almost embarrassing, but something in her warned that if she didn't take this leap of faith, she might regret it.

'He's right,' said Greco firmly, placing his hand on her shoulder again. 'We must go.'

Rosie stood there for a moment, looking from the older man to the younger. 'You'll look after the new guests when they arrive tomorrow? They're newly-weds. It's their honeymoon. So don't forget the rose petals on the bed and the heart-shaped chocolates and—'

'Mum.' Jack's voice had an edge to it that she'd never heard before. 'I'm not a kid any more. Give me a chance. Please. Besides, you need to enjoy yourself. See you in three days.' He hugged her. 'And have a great time.'

TRUE HONEYMOON STORY

'My husband flaked out at the reception so I put him to bed and then went back to the party. I had a great time.'

Anonymous, now divorced

Chapter Four

EMMA

'Mummy! What's a hornymoon?'

Gawain's blue eyes stared trustingly up at hers, with that clarity and utter belief in another person that only came from a child. 'Granny says you and Daddy are having one – without us.'

Emma knelt down on the floor of the village hall, flicking away a piece of pink horseshoe confetti which had got caught up in the folds of her off-white taffeta bridal gown, and took her son's small, warm hands in hers.

'Actually,' she said, ignoring the titters around her, 'it's called a *honey*moon.'

His eyes widened. 'Is that cos it's made of honey from the moon?'

Carefully, she tried to find the right words that would be truthful without denting the wonderful image in her son's head.

'What a lovely idea, but the moon is really made of rocks.'

He was frowning now. 'But what *is* a honeymoon?'

Emma tried to sound bright, brushing away her own misgivings. 'It's a holiday when two people who have just got married go away for a few days on their own.'

There was a sniff from a passing great-aunt. 'Usually people do it *before* they've had kids. Still, better late than never.'

Ignoring the barb, Emma gathered her son to her, breathing him in. God, she felt awful – and not just because she'd finally done it. Given Tom the wide gold ring that they had chosen together. Received one in turn – just as Gawain, all done up in his pageboy costume and flashing-light trainers, had called out, 'Mummy! I need a wee-wee!'

Everyone in the church had roared with laughter, including Tom, but Emma could have wept. Didn't that prove that her children needed her? How could she possibly leave them for a whole week?

Ever since Bernie and the girls had sprung the surprise wedding present on her, Emma had felt horribly uncertain and wobbly. She and Tom had never once left the children overnight: even when Willow had been born, she'd made sure she was out of hospital and back home before Gawain's bedtime so they could all be together.

Now, just because others had decided that a honeymoon was the thing to do, she was being torn away from the two people who meant most to her. Even more, she had to admit, than her own husband. Of course she loved Tom. But it was a different kind of love from that all-consuming, unconditional passion that meant she wouldn't think twice about running in front of a car to push her children to safety.

Would she do the same for Tom?

Of course.

Maybe.

'Can we come too, Mummy?' Gawain's voice came out muffled against her too-stiff skirt, making her heart twist in pain. How handsome her little man looked, with that jaunty red bow tie, even though he'd insisted on wearing his Spider-Man costume underneath. How vulnerable. So, too, did Willow, fast asleep in Tom's arms now, thumb in mouth, orange juice spilled down her bridesmaid's dress. They needed her. She needed *them*.

'I'm sorry, poppet.' She scattered light kisses over her son's downy head as she spoke. 'Hornymoons – I mean honeymoons – are just for mummies and daddies. You and Willow are going to have a lovely time with Granny instead.'

Gawain broke away from her arms and glared. 'But I want to go with *you*.'

See, Emma said silently, shooting an *I told you* look at Tom. She knew this would happen. The children didn't want them to go away any more than she wanted to leave them. How dare Bernie interfere? Tom was no better.

42

'You should have discussed it with me first,' Emma had snapped on the day that Bernie and the girls had given her the honeymoon envelope.

Tom had looked uncertain, giving her one of his owlish looks behind his thick-rimmed glasses. 'We thought it would be a nice surprise.' He shifted awkwardly from one leg to the other. 'The lads and I were talking in the pub and I just happened to mention to Phil that we couldn't afford a honeymoon. He said something to Bernie and that started the ball rolling.'

'It wasn't just that we couldn't afford one,' Emma had sniffed. 'It was because I didn't want to be away from the kids.'

Tom had put his arm around her then. 'I know,' he said quietly. 'But don't you think we need some time on our own? It's only for a week, and your mother is used to looking after Willow when you're at work.'

'That's for two hours a day, Tom. We're talking about a whole week.' Emma's eyes had filled with tears. 'What if they want me at night? What if my mother doesn't watch them properly and they have an accident? I'd never forgive myself.'

Or you, she had silently added.

'That could happen any time.' Tom, normally so compliant, had a firm edge to his voice. 'We deserve some couple time, Em. Besides, it's all arranged and paid for. You'd upset Bernie and the girls who saved up for this out of their earnings.' He bent down to kiss her. 'You'd upset me too.'

He was right. She had no choice but to go along with the girls' generous gesture. It would, she knew, have made a big dent in their pay packets.

To make herself feel better, she'd made a list of all the things that her mother might need reminding of, for a long-term stay. Gawain hated any food that was orange or green (which ruled out quite a lot of vegetables). His spare Spider-Man tee-shirt was in the storage bag under his bed. Willow's fluffy blue comfort blanket was kept in the second drawer down. The brake on the pushchair was a bit stiff. And so on and so on. The list was endless.

43

'I know most of this,' her mother had said, glancing at it dismissively. 'Besides, I did bring *you* up, you know. Stop fussing.'

But she couldn't help it, especially as it was time to go now. Inside Corrywood Hall, the guests were still bopping along to the loud disco which they'd got for a discount rate because one of Tom's friends knew the DJ, and picking away at the cold buffet which she hadn't been able to touch, thanks to nerves. All that money they'd been saving up for years had been blown. And to show for it, she had a shiny gold wedding ring on her left hand, and a piece of paper which tied her to her husband for life.

Divorce, in Emma's book, wasn't on. Not when you'd suffered like she had, from her parents' bitter break-up.

'Better get going or we'll miss the flight,' said one of Tom's friends chirpily. 'I've got the car ready outside.' He winked at her. 'The boys and I did it up. Tin cans, foam and everything. Wait till you see it!'

Gawain caught hold of her skirt and, as if on cue, Willow began to whimper as Tom prised her off his neck and handed her over to Emma's mother.

'I can't do it,' whispered Emma. 'I can't leave them.'

'Nonsense.' Her mother's voice was sharp, hissing in her ear. 'You're a wife now. Not just a mum. Don't make the mistake I did. Tom's a bit dull but he's a good man. Just make sure you hang on to him.'

Emma stared at her mother, shocked. It wasn't the 'dull' bit, which Mum had come out with before. No. It was the 'Don't make the mistake I did.'

The divorce had been Dad's fault for going off with that tart in the office. Was it possible that Mum blamed herself for not giving him more attention? If so, that was ridiculously old-fashioned.

Frankly, she'd expected more from her mother. At fifty-two, she was still a very good-looking woman. Even her name, Shirley, suggested a certain *joie de vivre* which, despite her single status, Mum possessed all right. Sometimes she was

44

mistaken in the street for a taller Barbara Windsor. She had the same blonde looks and warm, welcoming face, with a throaty laugh that made you feel good about yourself. Certainly, if it wasn't for Mum looking after Willow, Emma couldn't do her dinner lady job.

Maybe Tom was right. She ought to trust her enough to go away. After all, you only had one honeymoon.

'Mummy and Daddy won't be long,' she said, giving both children one more kiss and hug. 'Be good, won't you?'

Oh no. Willow was beginning to wail even louder and Gawain, with a grip that was incredibly strong for a four-year-old, adamantly refused to let go. 'They're just tired,' her mother said crisply with an authoritative air. 'I'll take them home now.'

Somehow, Emma managed to extricate herself from her son's grasp, feeling like a traitor. 'Mummy,' he called out desperately as Tom took her hand and led her to the car outside. A group of friends were already gathered there, confetti in hands; broad grins on their faces. 'I can't do this,' she cried, the tears rolling down her face as she threw her bouquet into the little gathering. 'I really can't.'

'They'll be fine.' But her new husband's voice was tight and she could tell from his tone that he had doubts too.

'What if the plane crashes?' she whispered as Tom's friend's car, with its silver and purple 'Just Married' pennant fluttering from the aerial, slid through the night on the way to Heathrow. 'We wouldn't be around to bring up the kids. What if . . .'

Tom's hand reached out for hers and held it firmly. 'You can't go down that road, love.'

Oh, but she could. 'We should have changed before we left,' added Tom, adjusting his suit trousers uncomfortably. 'There'll just be time at the airport if we don't get held up.' His arm wrapped itself around her. 'How does it feel to be Mrs Walker?'

Wonderful, she wanted to say. Perfect. But she couldn't. All Emma could think of, as Phil's old Vauxhall Cavalier approached the bright lights of the airport, was that she'd left her children behind and that if she had a choice, she would gladly have swapped them for Tom here on the back seat.

'The temperature in Siphalonia is approximately twenty-six degrees and counting.'

The pilot's enthusiastic voice sent a ripple of appreciative murmurs through the plane. Emma woke up from an uneasy sleep, hazily recalling the events of the last few hours, and felt her stomach lurch with fear all over again as she thought of the children. She glanced at Tom, whose face was lit up with excitement. I hate you for not understanding, she thought. I hate you.

But it was too late to turn back. They were here. And if anything did happen to the children, they could just fly back like Tom said, providing there was a flight available.

'I also have another notice,' said the pilot's voice, crackling slightly on the loudspeaker. 'We have a newly married couple on board. Mrs and Mrs Walker! Let's give them a round of applause, shall we?'

And to Emma's embarrassment, Tom stood up and made a mock bow, pointing to her. Everyone began to turn round in their seats: for a minute she wished they hadn't changed out of their wedding finery and into jeans and sloppy sweat-shirts. Then there was a wave of clapping and someone thrust a glass of something bubbly into her hand. Even though she didn't particularly like the taste, she knocked it back for Dutch courage, as Mum would say.

'Here's to married life,' declared Tom excitedly, clinking his plastic beaker with hers. 'Feeling better now?'

She nodded, tucking her arm into his. Of course she didn't hate him, she told herself guiltily. That had just been because she was tired and upset.

'Look,' Tom said, pointing out of the window just as he'd done when they'd taken off at Heathrow. But this time, instead of lights in the darkness down below, she could see a vast expanse of blue sea and then the outline of an island in the early-morning light. It was like the toy car mat that Gawain had at home, with a network of tiny roads and a garage and shops and houses.

'Which one of those is the Villa Rosa, do you think?' she asked, caught up in the euphoria of seeing the tiny white houses with little patches of brown and green around them.

'Maybe that one.' Tom sounded like a child. 'The L-shaped one with the pool.' He gripped her hand tighter. 'Hang on. We're going to land.'

It was much smoother than she'd expected, even though there was a terrible noise and a feeling of real speed, like being in a sports car, perhaps – though she'd never been in one. Then they stopped. At last! Emma jumped up before the seat belt sign had been switched off. 'You've got to wait,' said Tom, as if he was an experienced flyer. There was a ping. 'Right. We can go now.'

Almost unable to believe she had got through her first flight, Emma watched her husband(!) heave her hand luggage out of the overhead locker and gesture that she should go ahead.

Nervously, she made her way past the stewardess and then clung to the top of the steps as the dry heat hit her.

She was actually in Greece! Gawain and Willow felt so far away now that they might almost be in another world. Part of her wanted to dive back into the plane and beg for a flight home. But another part of herself, a part she didn't recognise, was excited. Curious.

'We're here,' said Tom unnecessarily as he shepherded her onto the airport bus behind a very pretty, tall, dark-haired woman holding hands with an even taller, well-built, bald West Indian with large sunglasses who kept looking nervously around. Now where had she seen him before? The woman looked a bit familiar too.

'We're here,' repeated Tom, as though he could hardly believe it either. 'We're on our honeymoon, Em! Isn't that amazing!'

47

TRUE HONEYMOON STORY

'We drove to Wales but it rained so much that we went home.'

Jo, still happily married after twenty years

Chapter Five

WINSTON

Had they been spotted? Winston looked swiftly around the airport bus, taking in the passengers, using his training to home in on anyone who looked suspicious.

There were no obvious candidates. Even so, he ran through the options around him. There was that other honeymoon couple who'd had that tacky announcement on the plane which had made him cringe. *She* looked quite sweet despite her rather simple moon face and a body that needed to shed at least a stone. But her husband wore clear-rimmed glasses and a thick grey sweatshirt, despite the heat, with 'I'M ON MY HONEYMOON' written on the front in big bold red letters. How naff was that? He shuddered at the thought of ever wearing something like that.

There were a couple of Greeks staring out of the window with no particular interest in anyone else. And there was a family of five who were making a right old racket because one of the kids had lost a toy on the plane and wanted to go back for it, even though the bus had already set off for the terminal.

The high-pitched whining reminded him of Melissa's girl, who was always moaning about something. Neither she nor the boy had bothered to hide their resentment at his intrusion into their mum's life. In fact, there had been a number of times in the last few weeks when Winston had been worried Melissa was going to call off their wedding altogether just because the *children*, as she insisted on calling them (even though the older one was a teenager), were still feeling 'unsettled'.

But somehow, Winston had won her round. With carefully thought-out arguments and – dare he say it? – a smattering of charm, he had persuaded Melissa that Alice and Freddie would benefit from a permanent male presence in the house, instead of a father who was always away, doing some big deal in Singapore or Hong Kong or banging yet another secretary (he hadn't voiced that last bit, obviously). And indeed, he really did believe it himself. All the children needed was a firm but kind hand. Starting with a break from their mother.

Besides, it would do them good to be with their father for a week. Winston would have given anything, at that age, to have had that opportunity.

As the bus rattled its way across the airport to the terminal, Winston put his arm around Melissa and pressed his lips against her hair, breathing in her smell. 'Did you enjoy the wedding?' he whispered.

She nodded, sinking her head into the broad dip in his shoulders. When she'd first done that, it had felt like someone had slotted a missing jigsaw piece into his body. 'It was perfect,' she murmured.

It had been, too. For a few brief seconds, Winston allowed himself the luxury of closing his eyes and recalling every precious minute. That tense wait inside Corrywood registry office (a nondescript dark red building near the post office), waiting for Melissa to arrive. Desperately willing her to come – there was a pit of fear in his solar plexus, in case she'd changed her mind. Casting questioning looks at his assistant and agent, to check that there weren't any photographers about.

That had been one of Melissa's stipulations when she'd accepted his proposal. 'I don't want to get caught up in all that publicity,' she had insisted. 'It wouldn't be fair on the children. Or on us.'

She was right. Winston didn't like it himself, though he knew there had to be some price for all the money he was paid. Still, he was as keen on a private ceremony as his bride was, despite the lucrative magazine and newspaper offers which had come pouring in.

And somehow, thanks to all the false trails that Poppy had laid, they had achieved it! Melissa had arrived, looking stunning in an Amanda Wakeley dress and a little black sequin jacket because, as she said later with her beguiling smile, you didn't get to her age without earning a few black marks.

They'd said their vows and recited a poem each (which they'd made up themselves), despite Melissa's daughter giving him the evils and the boy continually kicking his sister during the ceremony amidst loud 'ouches'.

Afterwards, they'd sneaked out of the back entrance, giggling like a pair of school runaways, and into his agent's Mercedes with tinted windows. Then they'd taken the children and Melissa's sister, who'd travelled from France, out for a late Italian lunch.

The difficult bit had been the evening when the husband had turned up to collect Alice and Freddie. Amazingly, since the man only lived round the corner in Corrywood, Winston hadn't met Melissa's ex before; partly because he'd taken care not to be around when he came to pick up the kids for weekends and partly because the man was always away working. But Winston had built up a mental vision of him, accrued through jealousy and the odd family photograph that was still in the house.

When Marvin turned up at the restaurant as arranged, Winston had been a bit taken aback. His predecessor was taller than he'd realised. More good-looking too, with a suave assurance that made Winston feel he'd been the one who was in the wrong.

'Dad!'

Alice and Freddie had flung themselves at him, and Winston was surprised to find himself experiencing a slight pang of resentment as he watched the man ruffle the kids' hair and then – bloody nerve! – place his cheek against Melissa's.

She had flushed like a beetroot.

'Congratulations,' Marvin had said, in what sounded to him like an over-jovial voice. Then as he walked past Winston he had muttered, 'Good luck. You might need it.'

What do you mean? Winston had almost said. Conscious that his fists were clenched inside his pockets, Winston watched his new bride's anxious face as she kissed the children goodbye. 'It's only a week,' she kept saying, but they didn't need any reassurance – couldn't she see that? The turncoats were happy as Larry, skipping along with their dad towards one of those ridiculously big people carriers where a tarty-looking peroxide blonde was waiting in the driver's seat.

'It will be all right,' he'd murmured to Melissa on the way to the airport. 'It's *you* they really love.'

She'd given him one of her sad but amazing smiles which made him feel both protective and alive. Really alive; as though she'd just opened a huge shaft of light in his head. 'Thank you,' she'd replied softly. But nevertheless, she'd been quiet all through the flight and as soon as they'd landed, had checked her phone. 'They promised to text as soon as they got back,' she'd fretted. 'But the reception here is awful.'

The little buggers were probably having too good a time to bother with their mother. 'We'll call from the villa.' His eyes were still distracted; darting everywhere; checking, as they got off the bus and made their way into the small, cool terminal, that there wasn't anyone around with a camera.

It wasn't just Melissa's privacy he was worried about. It was the other thing too. There was only so much that the world was allowed to know about Winston King. It wouldn't do for anyone – including his bride – to get too close. She might not understand.

'Isn't it pretty?' exclaimed Melissa as the car turned the corner and stopped outside a smallish white house with the sign 'Villa Rosa' outside.

Winston's sharp eyes took in the position. Perched on the seafront as the ad had said. Surrounded by hills which would be perfect for the ten-mile jogs he liked to take every day. A slightly faded Mediterranean-blue veranda running along the front, and the glimpse of the promised holiday cottages, also in white, at the back.

'It is,' he agreed. 'You did well to find it.'

When Melissa had first mentioned the notice at the children's school, advertising the Villa Rosa, he'd got his assistant to check it out. Yes, she'd assured him. It was very quiet and they didn't have any other English bookings.

Great. Then there'd be no one to spot them.

So he'd instructed Poppy to book under a false name. Luckily, she wasn't asked for passport details. At the same time, he'd got his assistant to book some more high-profile destinations in other spots to throw snoopers off the track; the privacy would be worth the cancellation fee.

Hang on. Another car had stopped close behind them. It was the other honeymoon couple. 'Feeling any better, Tom?' he heard the bride saying in one of those little girl voices that set his teeth on edge.

So they were staying here too? An English couple who might recognise him – just what he hadn't wanted! Hastily he put on his shades again. If necessary, he'd keep them on for the whole holiday. Inside and out.

'I still can't get any reception,' Melissa was saying, checking her phone again.

Winston fought back the impulse to tell her that she had to get over this. That for one week only, she needed to let the children go. 'As I said, we'll ring from reception,' he reminded her briskly. 'Let's make a move, shall we?'

Slinging one suitcase on his back, he picked up the other and marched ahead, conscious of the admiring glances both from his wife and the moon-faced bride. 'He must be strong,' he heard the latter mutter. Instantly, he reproached himself for doing something that stood out. Wasn't the whole point about this break to have some privacy? To look after Melissa? To make an amazing start to their life together?

They reached the small reception desk before the other couple. To his irritation, there was no one there, although there was the sound of scurrying behind a door leading off the little hall. Winston rang the tinny bell that was on the reception desk. No answer. He tried again.

This time, the door opened and a young man walked in. On closer look, Winston realised he was more of a boy and that his older appearance came from a smooth, unblemished skin uncommon in adolescents, plus a very polite, assured manner.

'So sorry to have kept you,' he said in impeccable English with a very slight Greek accent. Good. So there wouldn't be any communication problems here then. Winston bent his head in acknowledgment.

'It's Mr and Mrs Walker, isn't it?'

That wasn't the false name he'd instructed Poppy to use! 'Actually,' he said quietly, 'we're booked under Churchill although the real name is King.' Swiftly he looked behind to check no one else was listening. '*Winston* King.'

If this kid recognised the name, he wasn't showing it. Instead, there was a flurry of page-turning. 'Ah, here we are. Churchill.'

Winston's heart soared with relief.

'But it looks as though it's been cancelled.'

No! Winston felt sweat trickling down his back – and not just because of the poor air conditioning. 'That can't be right.'

The boy gave him a look, the type you got if you returned something to a shop and were told that no one else had ever complained. 'Do you know who you spoke to when you first made the booking?'

Of course he bloody didn't. 'My assistant did it.' He was struggling now to remain polite. 'Are you sure it was cancelled?'

'Look.' The boy pushed the diary across the desk. Winston stared. The booking had a big red line through it. Someone had cocked up big time. Either his assistant or someone at this end. No prizes for guessing who his money would be on. Poppy was never wrong.

There was a hand on his back. Melissa. Every time she touched him, he wanted to melt. She looked so beautiful in her halter-neck red cotton dress, which set her dark hair off to perfection, that he could hardly believe she was his.

Nick. Forgive me.

'Is everything all right?'

He nodded, desperately trying to collect himself. 'Sure. Why don't you go and sit in the cool? We won't be a minute.'

He turned back, gritting his teeth. 'Please find me your manager.'

The boy looked him straight in the eye with what seemed like more than a whiff of arrogance. If he'd been one of his men back in the Royal Marines, he might have got a warning.

'I'm afraid she's away for a few days. Would you like to wait on the patio? We can give you a complimentary drink while we try and find you another place to stay.'

Winston's voice was low and steady. 'I don't want a complimentary drink. And I don't want alternative accommodation either. I want the cottage for my wife and myself. The cottage that we booked. We've been travelling all night, and frankly, we want to rest. Is that clear?'

There was the sound of someone retching behind him. Great. The man with the honeymoon sweatshirt was actually vomiting on the ground.

'I'm so sorry.' The blonde woman was hastily mopping up with tissues from her bag. 'I'm afraid my husband isn't feeling very well. Do you think we could go straight to our cottage? The name's Walker.'

Winston let out a silent groan. So this couple had got their rooms! He waited as the woman filled out the registration form while the man was sick again, just by his feet. Thank God Melissa was on the patio, still trying to get reception. It might give him time to sort out this mess.

'What are you going to do about us?' he growled to the kid. As he spoke, Winston willed himself to calm down. There was something about this place that he liked. It had an air of peace about it, despite that man throwing up. Nice position, too – right on the sea, which always soothed him. Close to the hills so he could climb high and lose himself. He didn't want to have to find somewhere else.

'Please.' The boy was picking up the phone. 'Give me a moment and I will see what I can do.'

He carried the handset through the door but Winston could hear the odd word. 'Not sure whose fault it is. Really, Mum? You're sure?'

Then he returned, his young face revealing a dark flush. 'The manager apologises for any mistake. Unfortunately we've had a leak in the main house guest rooms so they're out of action.'

What kind of dump had they come to?

The boy, as though sensing his annoyance, hurried on. 'So she has suggested that you have her room. It has a luxury en suite, a terrace and a stunning view over the sea. There will, of course, be a discount.'

'Thank you,' he said firmly. 'I appreciate it. There's something else. My wife needs to make a phone call and she can't get any reception.'

The lad shrugged. 'Rather hit and miss, I'm afraid.'

In one way, that was good, Winston told himself, although he didn't like the casual attitude. 'In that case, I presume there's a phone in the room.'

The boy's face suggested he'd asked for the moon. 'Sorry. The only landline is in reception.'

'Then may my wife use it? She needs to ring her children.'

Immediately, the boy looked sympathetic. 'Of course.'

His wife didn't need telling twice. 'Thank you so much,' she said to the boy.

'Pleasure. Mr and Mrs Walker, would you like to come this way?'

Meanwhile, Winston picked up one of the tourist magazines in the little hall and pretended not to listen in to his wife's conversation. But it was difficult not to.

'Really? Why? I see. No, Marvyn. That's fine. I mean, if there's no option. Yes, I know they're my children too. No, Winston won't mind.'

Something was up.

'Marvin's been urgently called out to Hong Kong for work.' Melissa's face was fixed on his with a mixture of hope and uncertainty. 'He can't have the children any more. He's rung around their school friends but everyone has gone away, and my sister's gone back to France. So he's booked them on the next flight here.'

She leaned on his shoulder and he felt his body melt, even though his head was beginning to throb. 'That *is* all right, isn't it?'

HONEYMOON FACT

The Queen took her corgi Susan on honeymoon to Balmoral.

Chapter Six

ROSIE

'Problems?' asked Greco quizzically, when Rosie dropped her mobile back into her bag.

'You can say that again!' She sighed, running her hands through her hair as she was prone to do when stressed. 'Either Jack has messed up – I'm pretty sure it wasn't me – or one of our clients has got it wrong. It would be pretty bad at any time but this one is with some wedding guests who have requested absolute privacy. Apparently, they booked one of the cottages in a false name, but in the book it's been cancelled. Now they don't have anywhere to stay.'

Rosie took a deep breath, steadying herself. 'So I've given them my room. Jack's going to have to tidy it up and put my stuff somewhere. And on top of that, Cook's decided to leave this week instead of next month – something to do with his arthritis – so Jack's having to hold the fort until Yannis arrives.'

Yannis was a distant cousin of Greco's who had been working on the mainland but had applied for the position of cook back on the island. Cara had been inexplicably opposed to Rosie employing him, but, as Rosie had told her, they desperately needed a cook and there were no other decent candidates. It was always worrying when someone new started, in case they didn't fit in, and now she had this extra problem to deal with.

Couldn't the villa cope for five minutes without her?

'It sounds,' said Greco soothingly, 'as though you need a drink.' Sharing the rest of the carafe between her glass and his, he gave a lazy smile before moving his chair closer to the table just as a motorbike zapped by. The wine felt good. Rosie could feel it sinking in as she stretched out in her chair, enjoying the buzz of the pavement cafe around her with its smartly dressed women in tailored skirts and sunnies talking animatedly to their girlfriends or men in dark suits.

Greco had been right. This break was exactly what she needed. Much as she loved Siphalonia, it could be too quiet and insular at times. Of course, she missed the sea. Without it, she felt dry inside. It was odd without Jack, too, although not quite as odd as she'd thought it might be. Maybe Greco had been right on that one too. A mother needed her space, just as a teenage boy did.

'Anyway,' added her companion, his eyes on hers as he signalled to the waiter for another carafe with an authority that suggested he had lived here all his life, 'why the hush-hush over this booking?'

Rosie shrugged. 'I've no idea. In fact I don't know their real name – not until I see their passports, that is.'

'Aren't you curious?'

'Yes and no. More flattered really, that they've chosen to come to us, whoever they are.' She shook her head. 'It was a last-minute booking through the ad that my friend Gemma put up at her school in England, apparently.' She groaned. 'Such a nuisance about the flooding in the main guest rooms, or we could have put them there.'

That was one of the infuriating things about living in a small place. Simple plumbing parts weren't always available. Greco gave her a reassuring smile, his hand brushing hers as he handed her the topped-up glass. 'I'll see if I can get those washers while we're here.'

'That would be great.' Rosie had planned on trying to source them herself but DIY had never been one of her strengths. She felt a sudden warm surge of gratitude, which helped to ease the annoyance at having to give up her room at home.

'They're only here for a week,' she added, as though reassuring herself. 'I'll just have to find some corner when I return.'

'Or stay with me?' There was the flash of a cheeky smile that could be interpreted as jokey or serious.

'Not so fast,' she said lightly. 'We don't want to spoil a good friendship, do we?'

His strong brown hand reached out and clasped hers around the wrist, sending little unexpected – but not unpleasant – electric tremors down her arm. 'But you don't rule out something more?'

She hesitated. 'No. Not exactly. I don't know.'

Was that the wine talking or herself? she wondered. Maybe it was because they were somewhere different; somewhere where no one was watching them, interpreting every move and nuance. It was like that in a small place, whether Greece or England, which was one of the reasons she had chosen to flee all those years ago. If she'd stayed, she'd have had to put up with the neighbours gossiping about her unmarried state along with her father's snide comments.

But now what?

Rosie drained her glass, knowing she'd had far too much for the middle of the day, closed her eyes in the warm sunshine and tried to imagine herself in ten years' time. Jack would be in his mid-twenties then, perhaps with a family of his own.

There would be some benefits in that, surely, she thought guiltily. She'd be able to do what she wanted without worrying about him. She could enjoy life on her own; after all, she wasn't the kind of person who needed others around her all the time to make her feel complete. When it was quiet at work, there was nothing she liked more than to find a shady patch on the terrace and read a book, or to go for a swim before drying off on the beach, grateful that she didn't have to make conversation with anyone, unlike some of the couples she saw struggling at the dinner table.

Then again, she thought, glancing at Greco lying back in his chair, eyes closed in a post-lunch haze, there were times when she desperately craved some male company. There were also times when, even though it made her blush to admit it, her body needed it, as well as her mind. And there was far more to Greco than she'd realised.

That reminded her.

'Don't you have a meeting soon?' she asked.

His eyes snapped open as though he hadn't been dozing after all. 'Right. Thanks.' Sitting up, he heaved a large bag onto his shoulders. 'Want to come along?'

When Greco had first admitted at the airport that his check-in bag contained 'stuff made from driftwood', she hadn't taken him very seriously. There were a lot of artisans in Greece, mainly amateurs who sold to holidaymakers keen on bringing back a souvenir.

It wasn't until he'd opened it up that she realised how good he was. Stunned, she'd taken in the beautifully crafted jewellery boxes and small figures. 'Did you really make these with your own hands?'

He had looked down at his broad brown fingers as though seeing them for the first time. 'No one else's.' Then an uncertainty flitted across his face. It was a look she had never seen before on this man who generally acted as though he told the world what to do, rather than the other way round.

'Thought I might see if anyone was interested in buying them,' he'd added casually. 'Not on the island. But in Athens.'

Instinctively, Rosie guessed why. If these beautiful pieces didn't sell on the mainland, then no one on Siphalonia would be any the wiser. Whereas if they flopped at home, Greco might lose face. It was a measure of trust in her that he'd confided this much.

To her surprise, he'd already made some firm appointments with a couple of shopkeepers whom he'd found, he said with just a touch of embarrassment, on the net. She'd been impressed.

'Have you worked out your profit margins?' Rosie asked as they made their way down the street to the first meeting.

'Not really.' Greco shrugged. 'Just wanted to see what they thought first.'

Rosie's own business experience set alarm bells ringing. 'Don't undersell yourself,' she said quickly, moving to one side as a pair of teenagers strode towards her. 'I don't want to interfere, but do you actually want me to go into the meeting with you?'

He gave her an amused smile. 'Hold my hand, you mean? Like you do Jack's?'

That wasn't fair. 'I've left him in charge of the villa, haven't I?'

Another shrug. 'Then let him sort out this room problem without worrying about it.' He touched her arm briefly. 'Meanwhile, you're welcome to come with me, Rosie, but please don't say anything. I know what I'm doing.'

Did he? Unable not to fear for him, Rosie followed Greco into the shop, looking around. It was one of those upmarket gift places with security guards on the door and some rather nice ornaments with pricey tags. Her friend had set his sights high. Rejection would hit him hard and, to her surprise, Rosie found that she really didn't want that, even though she'd often thought, back home, that he needed to be taken down a peg or two.

'Mind waiting here a bit?' whispered Greco as the manager approached.

Apprehensively, Rosie pretended to busy herself by picking up a pair of jade earrings and then putting them down again. On the other side of the display, she could glimpse Greco laying out his wares and could hear low murmurings taking place between him and the manager. How she cringed for him! These shopkeepers were used to dealing with sharp-suited reps, not fishermen. Poor Greco had no idea what he was doing.

'Utterly exquisite!' exclaimed an American voice, slicing through her worries. 'How much is that?'

Peeping through the display, Rosie could see a tall, elegant woman in a pair of tapered cream trousers, leaning over the jewellery box she'd admired earlier, made of driftwood and shells.

'It's not for sale, madam.' The manager's voice was smooth. 'This gentleman is simply showing me his goods.'

'Then may I buy it from you direct?' The American, to

Rosie's astonishment, was opening her purse and handing over a fistful of notes to Greco, who promptly pocketed them with a satisfied smile. 'Here is my card,' he replied, extracting a slip from his wallet. 'Let me know if you are interested in anything else on my website.'

He had a website? That was something he hadn't mentioned earlier. The manager was now looking distinctly edgy. 'You have more of those jewellery boxes if I place an order?' he was saying now.

Greco gave an easy smile. 'Only two.'

'But there are four in your bag.' The manager was pointing. 'I can see.'

Her friend shrugged. 'I need to keep them for my next appointment.'

The manager's voice grew terse. 'I will buy them all.' He then named a price which nearly made Rosie drop the china pot she was 'admiring'.

'I'm afraid that is not enough.' Greco then named a higher figure. Mesmerised, Rosie overheard the manager agree. A few minutes later, Greco walked straight past her and out of the shop as though he didn't even know her. Rather cross, she hurried after him.

'That was amazing!'

He nodded briskly. 'Hang on a moment. It is not finished.' He strode on and she had to run to keep up with him. Where was he going? Then he stopped suddenly, took a right into a little lane and then went down another on the left, into a small wine bar.

'Haven't we had enough . . .' Rosie began to say before stopping. There was the tall American woman in the cream trousers. The same one from the shop.

'Thanks,' he was murmuring, giving her a brief kiss on the cheek. 'I appreciate it. Sure I don't owe you anything?'

The woman, a well-preserved forty-something, was almost purring. 'Only the usual.'

Greco glanced back at Rosie, who was waiting awkwardly by the door. The wine bar was almost empty so she was able to hear nearly every word. 'Sorry. My circumstances have changed. See you around, maybe. Keep the box.'

Then he walked back to Rosie jauntily, took her arm and steered her out into the street. 'It was a set-up!' Rosie exclaimed. 'I don't believe it. How did you manage that?'

Greco shrugged. 'Let's just say that an old friend owed me a favour.'

Should she be shocked or impressed? Rosie wasn't sure, especially since that last glass of wine. Like many of the locals, she could hold her own when it came to drink, but she never usually had anything at lunchtime. Not when there was work to be done.

Just as well that her own appointments with the factories that sold her linen, and also pots and pans, weren't until later.

'It is time for a siesta, I think.'

Greco's words reminded her that they had yet to check in to the small *pension*, where she'd booked two rooms on the strength of Trip Advisor reviews. They'd better not lead into each other, she suddenly thought. She should have checked that at the time.

'Goodness. It's quite nice, isn't it?' She was surprised, as they made their way under an archway into a little courtyard. Around them stood a squat, homely grey stone building with pale blue shutters, wrapped around the square. Greco opened the big green door in the middle to let her through first and she looked around curiously.

Like anyone else who ran a hotel, she was always keen to see how others did it and pick up some tips.

It might be a busman's holiday but it was useful.

'Two rooms,' confirmed the girl at the desk. 'Credit card, please.'

Greco got there first before taking the two sets of keys. The white iron staircase was quite elaborate and there was an air of nineteenth-century history along with a contemporary feel. 'Connecting rooms, I see,' commented Greco, as he helped her in with her case.

No!

'Only joking.' He grinned.

'I hope you're not playing me, like the manager in the shop?' she shot back.

He didn't laugh. 'Don't get the wrong idea, Rosie. That was business. When it comes to . . . to other things, I have changed. I need you to understand that.'

For a minute, they stood there, facing one another. I could let him kiss me right now, Rosie thought, amazed at herself. It would be so easy. So natural.

Then the moment passed and he turned and went into his own room. Rosie almost had to fight back the disappointment. Don't be so ridiculous, she told herself, hanging up her clothes and then lying down on the bed. You must be crazy to even think of it.

For a while, Rosie lay there, wide awake. Usually, at siesta time, she was out like a light. It was such a civilised custom – there was nothing like a power nap to gather your energy before tackling the rest of the day, especially if you worked late into the evening as she did at home.

But this wasn't home. This was Away. Perhaps this was why nothing seemed as it should. Tossing and turning on the cool, crisp cotton sheets, she eventually got up to look out of the window. The square below was deserted, apart from some pigeons. Everyone else was asleep too.

Everyone else was married.

No, that wasn't true. But there were times when she couldn't help wondering if she was ever going to find someone. At home, she could brush these thoughts under the carpet by concentrating on work. But now she was away from it, all the old doubts came crowding in. It wouldn't be that long until Jack left home, and what would happen to her then? Would she end up as lonely as Cara, but without a kindly nephew to take her in?

'So you are still awake?' The voice came from the window next to hers. Leaning out, with the pigeons cooing above, was Greco, his black hair wet, suggesting he'd just showered.

She laughed, awkwardly. 'I can't sleep.'

'You want to come here?'

It was said in such a way that for a moment, Rosie wasn't even sure if it was Greco speaking. This wasn't the usual cocky, arrogant face he presented to the rest of the island. This was someone who seemed nervous; shy, even.

Hardly knowing what she was doing, Rosie found herself nodding. As though in slow motion, she made her way to the room next door. Greco was waiting for her, naked from the waist upwards. She'd often seen him like that before, of course, on the beach while dragging in his boat from a morning's work.

But she'd never before felt him. Never experienced the warmth of his body as he drew her to him, wrapping his arms around her.

'I don't go in for one-night stands,' she began.

His hands were moving as though they had been there before. 'I know,' he whispered. 'Nor do I, any more.'

Then he stood away from her for a second, his eyes locking with hers. 'I won't ever hurt you, Rosie. I give you my word.'

His mouth was bearing down on hers now, making her heart beat wildly. Oh my God, thought Rosie, this man could kiss! It was like being taken into another world, one that she had never glimpsed before. What was she doing? If she did this, they could never be friends again . . .

But then his hands began to unbutton her shirt and as his palm closed around her right breast, Rosie Harrison knew she was lost.

After her appointments, they went for an evening walk, his imprint still inside her. His hand held hers firmly. It felt good, even though it was crazy. When they got back, it would be so awkward! Still, if you couldn't get to your mid-thirties without going off the rails once or twice, it would be a pretty boring life, wouldn't it?

Rosie shivered. Who was she kidding? If only she could be the kind of woman who could dismiss the two hours they'd spent together before she'd had to reluctantly get dressed for business. But when you'd shared the kind of intimacy they just had, it was hard to forget it.

'You want a paper?' asked Greco smoothly as they stopped by a stall on the street. 'Or a magazine? Look, they do some English ones.'

Briefly, she was distracted. Rosie had always been a sucker for the glossies. Gemma was the same; sometimes she sent her copies of their favourite magazine, *Charisma*, even though the postage from England was more than the cover price.

Then she caught sight of something.

'You like this?' Greco handed her the latest edition of the *Daily Express* with a large photograph of a man holding up a pair of weights. 'This man has muscles,' he said lightly. 'But not like mine.' He squeezed her bottom meaningfully. 'I hope you agree.'

But Rosie was staring at the picture with a strange flutter in her chest.

BRITAIN'S FAVOURITE EXERCISE GURU GETS HITCHED AT LAST

Winston King, former Marine and the nation's keep-fit darling, has got married in secret! His bride is a make-up artist and a divorced mother of two whom he met while filming. They are thought to be holidaying in the Maldives at a secret location.

Rosie stole another look. There was something about the man that reminded her of Charlie, though he was fuller in the face, with more lines around his eyes. It could be his older brother, if he'd had one – although Charlie had been an only child, like her. Maybe she was just imagining it. Of course, it had been a long time ago. Even so, at night, when she couldn't sleep, she saw her first and (until just now) *only* boyfriend's face so clearly that she might as well have had a photograph of him next to her bed.

'Do you recognise him?' asked Greco, noticing her expression. 'From television, that is?'

'No, I don't.' Rosie's mouth was dry. Buying the paper and stuffing it into her bag, she hurried on ahead of him, stepping into the road and narrowly avoiding a car. Suddenly she needed to put space between herself and this man whom she'd foolishly allowed to come too close. 'Sorry,' she called out over her shoulder, 'I've got one more appointment. See you back at the hotel, OK?'

MORE HISTORY OF HONEYMOONS

Honeymoons were only taken by wealthy people until the 1930s, when it became more commonplace. During Victorian times, the whole family often accompanied the happy couple during a month-long, post-wedding tour, frequently in Europe.

Chapter Seven

EMMA

Emma's jaw had been dropping ever since they had left the dusty road leading from the tiny airport and headed out into the countryside. All around them were clusters of trees – olive trees, the driver told them with a delightful toothy grin – with white houses slotted in between. Some were really posh-looking, with pools at the side. Others were more run-down, with goats tethered in adjoining fields.

But wherever you looked, there was always the sea, sparkling at her. 'This ees coastal route,' added the driver, noticing her expression in his mirror, which was festooned with pictures of saints and a silver crucifix on a beaded chain. 'Very beautiful, yes?'

Beautiful? It was stunning, although she wished he wouldn't take his eyes off the road to look at her in the mirror like that, especially with these hairpin bends. She needed to stay alive to bring up the children.

'Amazing, isn't it?' she said, breathlessly turning to Tom. Only then did she notice how pale he looked. 'Are you OK?'

'Not great, to be honest.' He hung onto the back of the driver's seat in the absence of a seat belt. 'These roads are really turning my stomach.'

That was odd. Tom wasn't normally car sick. It was usually Gawain. Suddenly Emma had a vision of their son's white little face, when they'd driven down to Margate last year. Oh dear. She'd forgotten to tell Mum not to take him on any trips. It wasn't just that he might be sick. What if they had an accident? Mum wasn't a very confident driver.

Suddenly the view outside didn't seem so wonderful after

all. 'I think I've got some travel sickness pills in my bag,' she said, rooting around. 'They're for children but they might help. Yes. Here they are.'

Her husband looked at her plaintively. 'Got any water?'

'No.' She swallowed back her irritation. Why was it that men could be so childish when they were under the weather? How on earth would they cope with periods or childbirth? 'Can't you swallow them without? They're not very big.'

Dutifully, he did as he was told, just as the driver screeched to a halt. 'We are here,' he announced triumphantly.

Emma gasped. The villa was like something out of one of the children's fairy-tale books! For a start, it was built on a slope, set into a hill, which gave it a really sweet charm all of its own. The first floor jutted out slightly and there was a terrace wrapped round the side with parasols fluttering over the tables. It was white, just like many of the houses they'd already passed, but there was a brilliant purple and scarlet plant winding its way up from a huge tub by the front door. The sign outside had a flamboyant rose, below the name.

Villa Rosa.

It was perfect. At least, it would be if the children were here too. But as they weren't, she'd make the best of it. Maybe Bernie and Mum were right. She had to put Tom first, just for the next week. After all, they were here now. She might as well enjoy it.

'Come on,' she said excitedly, helping her husband out of the car. 'You'll feel better when you've had a bit of a lie-down.'

Emma had hardly been able to believe her eyes when the boy had led her to what he called 'the cottage'. It was a mini version of the villa, except this one was on one level. If only Mum were here to see this! Staggered, she tried to take it all in. Whitewashed walls; purple plants around the door; deep-blue and scarlet rugs over the flagstoned floor; a squashy, sunset-yellow sofa next to a coffee table laden with magazines; an enormous bed with a high wooden headboard and a turquoise and cream patchwork quilt, which looked invitingly snug. But best of all, a stunning view to the sea outside. In fact, they were virtually on the beach! The kids would have loved it. She would have brought a bucket and spade and they could have set to, making a sandcastle.

'How are you?' she asked, sitting down next to the bed with a plastic bag at the ready, just in case. It had been so embarrassing when Tom had thrown up. Then there had been that awkward argument between the other couple and the young lad at reception.

The bald West Indian man, who looked so familiar, hadn't seemed too happy. Even though Emma felt a bit guilty that they didn't have a cottage, she also couldn't help feeling grateful that it wasn't them.

'Do you think you're going to be sick again?' she asked, turning back to Tom. It wasn't that she was unsympathetic. It was just that she didn't want him to ruin the beautiful carpet. If they'd been at home, she'd have had the sick bowl out, the one she kept specifically for the kids when they were poorly.

Tom nodded wanly. 'Maybe.'

'Hopefully the tablets will work soon,' she told him. But inside, she was feeling nauseous too. Nerves, Emma told herself. It wasn't just the worry of leaving the children. It was the fact that 'It' was done. That they were married. Was it her imagination, or had their relationship already changed? Tom seemed to be relying on *her* now.

How ironic that she had left two children at home, only to acquire another!

No, she reprimanded herself sharply. To love and to cherish through sickness and health. Wasn't that what they'd said only yesterday in church? But when Tom still didn't feel any better by lunchtime, a selfish part of her began to feel a tiny bit cheated. It looked so lovely out there, but with Tom ill, how could she abandon him and enjoy it?

Never had Emma seen a sea with a colour like that. Such a deep, deep blue with light dancing off it like fairies carrying sparklers. So close. She could get there in a couple of minutes, just by walking out of the door and down the sandy slope. It was very private, the boy had told them when he'd pointed everything out.

'I'll be all right, love,' said Tom, turning over with his face to the wall. 'Honestly. You go and ring the kids. Check they're all right. You might get a better reception on the beach.'

'Sure?' she asked hopefully, unpacking her faded sundresses and noticing, to her dismay, that toothpaste had leaked onto them. She'd have to wear that old pair of shorts she'd thrown in at the last moment. Pity, too, that she hadn't brought some fake tan. Still, with any luck, her horribly white legs might get brown before too long. Especially if they got some sun right now.

Kicking off her flip-flops, Emma walked barefoot over the sand. It was all so beautiful, with the waves lapping hypnotically at her feet and that glorious sun – how she loved the heat!

But it was also horribly quiet and empty without the kids. If they'd been here, thought Emma, undoing the button on her too-tight shorts (must try to lose some weight!), she'd be holding little Willow in her arms and making sure that Gawain didn't rush into the water without his water wings.

Motherhood gave her a job. A purpose. Now, as Emma switched her phone on, she was beginning to wonder what she was going to do with herself for a week, especially if Tom was off-colour.

Yes! You could get reception here. It would be horribly expensive but it would be worth it, just to hear the children's voices.

'Mum? It's me. Em.' She felt a shot of excitement at actually getting through. 'Is everything all right?'

'Not really.' There was the sound of grizzling in the background.

'What's wrong?' As she spoke, Emma jumped out of the way of the next wave before the phone got wet.

74

Mum's voice was weak. 'Loads of people have been sick, including me. Did Willow and Gawain have those chicken vol-au-vents?'

Her mind raced. 'No. They hate chicken. But Tom's been sick too. Why?'

'Looks like they might have been off.'

Was that why Tom was ill? 'How serious is it?'

'The doctor's told us to give it three to five days.'

That didn't sound good. 'Shall we come home?' she asked, wondering whether the plane would even allow Tom on board if he was being sick.

'Don't be daft. I can manage, and Bernie said she'd help out a bit. Luckily, she's just started a no-protein diet so she's all right. *Gawain!* I've told you once already! Stop sucking Willow's dummy. You're a big boy now. And blow that nose of yours. It's all snotty again.'

He's not very good at blowing, Emma was about to say, but Mum cut in before she could get a word in. 'Now you just leave the kids to me and concentrate on your husband. Make sure he has plenty of water to drink and nothing fancy to eat. Just dry toast. By the way, did you know your son's been hiding his crusts in the toy box? *Gawain, I said no!*'

Emma's heart sank. It sounded like chaos at home.

'Still,' her mum added, 'we might get some money back. I've left a message on the caterer's answerphone, telling her just what we think.'

You had no right without talking to me first, Emma wanted to say. The caterer was a friend of Bernie's who'd done them a discount as it was. But that was Mum all over, always thinking she knew best.

'Can I talk to the children?'

'Better not. Might unsettle them. No, Gawain. No chocolate right now. Maybe later.'

Emma felt as though her chest was being pulled like a long elastic band down the phone. Perhaps Mum was right. Willow was too young, and it might upset her son to hear her voice:

he still couldn't work out how someone could be at the other end of the phone without his being able to see them.

'I'll ring again tomorrow, Mum. Hope you feel better soon. And thanks once more. I really appreciate it.'

Walking back up to the cottage, making footprints in the sand (how Gawain would have enjoyed doing that with his little feet!), she peeped in through the bedroom door. Tom was fast asleep, his chest rising and falling slowly. She'd have to wait until he woke, to find out about the chicken.

Meanwhile, perhaps she could just sit outside the cottage on one of the blue-and-white-striped loungers. Or test out the hammock that was strung between two trees near the beach. She could tie her hair back – it was too warm, to wear it loose – slap on that coconut sun cream which Bernie had recommended and lose herself in Katie Fforde's latest, stamped inside with *Corrywood Library* and protected by its clear plastic covering. Every Saturday morning, she and Tom took the children down to the library for the under-fives storytelling session. There she went again! Always thinking about the children.

This is *my* time, Emma reminded herself, recalling her mother's no-nonsense advice during the reception. *If you don't give yourself time – and your husband – then your marriage won't work out. Take it from me, love.*

Emma hadn't realised she'd dozed off over her book until voices began to punctuate her dream. In her sleep, she'd been fighting with Gawain over one of those stupid chicken vol-au-vents; telling him that he couldn't have one because they'd make him sick.

'They're my *children*. You knew I had responsibilities when you married me.'

Slowly Emma opened her eyes, realising that the voice came from a tall, extremely beautiful woman with long dark hair and a flimsy blue beach wrap. It was the strikingly good-looking couple from the plane and reception.

'Marvyn can't just announce he's going away,' the man was saying. 'He'd promised to have them.'

The woman was taking his hand now, twisting it in what looked like a conciliatory gesture. 'But it's his work. He can't help it.'

Then they were out of earshot. Hitching herself up on one elbow, Emma watched curiously as they walked along the beach. From their expansive hand gestures, it didn't look as though they had resolved their argument.

So that lovely dark-haired woman had children too! But who was this Marvyn? A male nanny, perhaps. There were quite a few male au pairs in Corrywood now. Still, thought Emma, getting up to check on Tom, that wasn't any of her business.

'How are you feeling?' she asked softly.

Tom gave a groan, causing Emma a stab of panic. It was all very well for the doctor at home to advise giving it a few days. But out here, it might not be so easy to get help.

'Mum says some of our guests have been sick,' she said nervously. Tom could be a bit of a hypochondriac at the best of times. 'Might have been the chicken vol-au-vents. How many did you have?'

'Just a couple.' There was another groan. 'But it could be travel sickness. I had this before when the lads and I went to Ibiza before we met.'

He could have told her!

'Excuse me,' said a voice at the door. It was the boy from reception. 'Just checking you've got everything you need. I forgot to give you this, too.' He handed her a leaflet. 'It tells you about the various activities we have here.'

'Actually, my husband isn't well. It might be food poisoning. Or maybe travel sickness.'

The boy made a sympathetic face. 'We've got a great remedy for that. Hang on a minute and I'll bring it over.'

He returned within minutes, holding a small blue bottle without a label. 'You just take a spoonful every four hours,' the boy said confidently. 'It's one of Cara's old recipes. She used to own this place before Mum became her partner.'

Really? Emma had wondered exactly how you got to start a place like this.

Tom glanced at the bottle through half-closed eyes. 'I'm not taking that stuff. They don't have the same rules and regulations as we do. It could be anything.'

Emma coloured up with embarrassment and sent a *sorry* look to the boy, who kindly gave her a reassuring *don't worry* glance back. 'Let me know if you want anything else,' he added. Goodness, he seemed very confident for his age. What was he, Emma wondered, fifteen, sixteen or seventeen? It was hard to tell because he was so tall, but his face looked young.

'The doctor,' groaned Tom, sitting up and reaching for the bowl Emma had found. 'I'd like to see the doctor.'

Mortified, Emma mopped up her husband. 'I'm so sorry,' she said to the boy, who didn't seem fazed at all: indeed, he was opening a cupboard to find clean towels. 'I think my husband's right. Can we make an appointment?'

The boy shook his head. 'You don't need one. You just queue up.'

'Where?'

'At the town hall. He's there every Friday.'

Friday? But today was Sunday.

Emma's heart was beginning to race. 'Isn't there any way of getting him here faster?'

''Fraid not.' The boy glanced at the bottle. 'Like I said, take this. It works every time. Well, usually.'

After he left, Tom began to nod off again. A sleep would do him good. It would also, thought Emma guiltily, give her a chance to return to the sun, while listening out for her husband.

Stretching out on the lounger, she looked at the leaflet the boy had brought. It had a pretty drawing of the Villa Rosa on the front. There was some practical information, including instructions on not putting lavatory paper down the loo. Oh dear. Too late for that. You couldn't drink the tap water either unless it was boiled.

Emma turned the leaflet over. A pool! She hadn't realised there was one. There was early-morning yoga too. She'd always wanted to try that out. Goodness, for a small place with only a few rooms, the Villa Rosa seemed to have a lot going on.

There were even art classes in the afternoon. How she'd love to do those too. But she couldn't leave Tom here alone, could she? He might choke on his vomit, and she'd never forgive herself.

It was like being in a sweet shop without being allowed to touch anything.

Putting the leaflet in her bag, Emma caught sight of the bundle of wedding cards which she and Tom hadn't had time to open before leaving.

She ought to wait until Tom was better to enjoy them, Emma told herself. But then she caught sight of a large beige envelope with a sloping handwriting that she hadn't seen for many years. Her skin began to crawl.

Nervously, Emma took out the letter from inside a gaudy glittering wedding card, inviting them in silver writing to be 'Happy Ever After'.

Don't read it, she told herself. It will only upset you. But, unable to help herself, her eye was drawn to the opening paragraph.

Dear Emma,
By the time you read this, you will be a married woman. You may not think I am qualified to hand out advice but there are still some things which I feel I must tell you.

Advice? Who was he to talk?

When I first met your mother, we respected each other. Respect is more important than love. It is, or should be, the foundation of all relationships. But it has to be nurtured or else it can so easily get lost.

Hah! Had her father shown respect when he'd gone off with that woman?

I am aware that you think badly of me but that is

79

because you are young. One day, you might know why
I acted as I did. One day, you might know the truth.
  With all my love,
  Dad

How dare he? As for the truth, she already knew it! Emma's mind went back to that horrible day when, as a fifteen-year-old, she had listened through her parents' door to the arguing. Words like 'that woman' and 'if you'd shown me more affection' were still indelibly printed in her mind, along with Mum's hysterical weeping.

Did her father honestly think she could ever forgive him for the pain he had caused her mother? Despite this, she quickly found a pen and wrote down the address on the card before furiously swinging her legs over the chair and running down through the warm sand to the sea. Standing in it, with the water splashing her ankles, she tore up both letter and card into tiny little bits and threw them into the air. They floated down like cheap pink glitter confetti, only to lose their sparkle as they hit the water.

Too late, Emma realised she'd committed the sin of pollution. She tried to scoop up the bits of paper but a wave came in and took them out of reach. Had anyone seen what she'd done? She glanced down the beach. That striking couple from the plane were sitting down now on some rocks. They were some way off but she could see, slightly enviously, that they were kissing. Clearly they'd made up.

It was more than she was going to do with the writer of the letter. In fact, Emma told herself, walking back to the villa, there was no need to tell anyone she'd received it.

Let alone reply.

TRUE HONEYMOON STORY

'When my parents got married in 1939, they spent their
first night in a thin-walled room next to a spinster
great-aunt.'

Carol, happily single

Chapter Eight

WINSTON

'But where will the children *sleep?*' protested Winston when Melissa had announced that her kids were on their way out here, right now. For a moment, he had visions of Alice and Freddie sharing their room, which wasn't even theirs at all.

The absent owner, he'd decided, was one of those weird bohemian types. You could tell that just by observing the large collection of floaty coloured scarves hanging from the back of the door; a tacky shell mirror which was far too low for either of them (suggesting she was short) and a strange blue and green ornament on the window which, his wife had exclaimed approvingly, was called a dream catcher.

Dreams? The whole idea of his stepchildren (he was still getting used to that phrase) coming over to share their honeymoon, was a complete bloody nightmare.

Then, as if that wasn't bad enough, Melissa had accused him of not being sympathetic. 'It's not easy for them,' she'd said with an edge to her voice that he hadn't heard before. 'They've been used to having me around for themselves. You knew you were taking them on when you asked me to marry you.'

They'd been walking along the beach to 'discuss' it, although Winston had tried to calm things down when he realised that the plump, pretty, moon-faced bride was outside her cottage (which would have been *theirs* if the kid at reception hadn't got it wrong), staring curiously at them.

Then Melissa had burst into tears and said that she was sorry, but if Winston didn't want her children, that was the same as Winston not wanting *her*. Maybe, she'd added tearfully, all this had happened too fast and perhaps it was better if she just went home with Freddie and Alice.

That had scared him. Already, he couldn't imagine life without Melissa. At least, he didn't think he could. Or was it, Winston asked himself uncomfortably, because he didn't do failure?

You couldn't have much more of a failure than a marriage that had disintegrated on day one of the honeymoon. The papers would love it.

What was needed now was a plan of action. Damage limitation, as they'd called it in the corps. So he'd sat his bride down on the beach, which was rather picturesque, in a basic Mediterranean way, and folded her into his arms. 'Of course I want your children,' he had said, before adding silently to himself, but only because I can't have you without them.

And then she'd put her head into that little space below his arm and they'd nestled up together. It hadn't been long before their lips homed in on each other's and they were well and truly locked together. Not in *that* way, of course, even though it was a private beach, but pretty damn near it.

'The children will have to sleep on the floor,' said Melissa suddenly, breaking into his thoughts. 'Well, there's nowhere else, is there?'

Instantly, he sat up. 'We'll have to think of something. Besides, Alice is virtually a woman.' He felt himself reddening. 'It wouldn't be right for her to see us in bed.'

Melissa shrugged. 'I suppose so. But you are her stepfather.'

For a grown woman, his new wife could be very naive. Maybe she didn't realise just how scathing the press could be. Winston shuddered. He could just imagine the headlines: '"Work Out With Winston" Shares Honeymoon Room With Teenage Stepdaughter'. No way.

'We'll talk to the kid at reception.' His mouth set. 'If he hadn't messed up our booking, it wouldn't have been a problem.'

Melissa stroked his cheek. When previous girlfriends had

done that in the past, it had irritated him. *Possession,* it had screamed. Now he found it soothing. Reassuring. 'You can't blame him. It might have been our fault.'

No. Winston didn't do mistakes *(Nick, Nick)* and nor, by default, did his staff.

'Let's go and find him – see if he's sorted something out.' Standing up, he stretched out into the warm sun before reaching down and pulling Melissa up, gently slapping her bottom. She giggled. That was better. They'd make this disaster work out somehow.

'You're just used to all those smart five-star places they put you up in,' Melissa added teasingly as they ambled up the beach, arm in arm. There was something in that. For the last Christmas special, the television people had sent him to St Lucia, where he had performed a morning workout session on the white sandy beach for the viewers back home. The hotel had been amazing, with an enormous round bed, facing the veranda. Now that would have been a *real* honeymoon destination.

Still, at least they'd managed to avoid any paparazzi here. No one would have expected them to have pitched up at a two-star taverna on a mediocre Greek island; especially one where they'd been allotted staff quarters.

'Look. There's our young man from reception,' said Melissa, pointing. 'How sweet. He's feeding the chickens.'

Winston marched right up. 'Look, I know we talked about this earlier, but we've got a problem here. As you know, my wife's children are coming out and they need somewhere to stay. I believe you suggested putting a mattress on our floor, but frankly, that's not good enough.' He shot a look at Melissa that read, *Don't say anything. Leave this one to me.*

The boy stood up, dusting the corn off his shirt, and shrugged. 'There isn't anywhere. I'm sorry. Unless . . .'

'Yes?' said Melissa quickly.

'Well, unless they're willing to share the stable block with me.' He shifted awkwardly from one foot to the other. 'There's one room free opposite mine, although it's pretty basic. It's next to the cook or at least it will be when he arrives. The old one had to leave unexpectedly.'

Great! So there wasn't any decent food here either!

'I need to confirm it with Mum – she's one of the owners.' The kid spoke hesitantly as though he was working all this out in his head. 'But it's not easy to get hold of her at the moment.'

Melissa clutched his arm. 'The stable block will do for a bit, won't it, darling? The children will be here by teatime. In fact, we need to send a taxi to meet them. Marvyn's text said that—'

'*Mum, Mum!*'

I don't believe it, thought Winston, watching a black car screech to a halt at the bottom of the slope where the Villa Rosa's grounds met the dusty lane. They were here already.

'Dad got us an earlier flight,' panted the boy as he ran up and flung his arms around Melissa's waist. 'And he arranged for a car to bring us here from the airport. Said it would be a nice surprise for you to have us early.'

I'll bet he did, added Winston to himself. Couldn't Melissa see what was going on here? Marvyn was trying to sabotage their honeymoon, for whatever reason. Jealousy? Maybe. He'd seen the way the man had looked at his wife, as though he hadn't realised until now what he'd thrown away.

Well, it was too bloody late. She was his now! Winston folded his arms, grappling with the emotions that were rippling through him. OK. Compromises had to be made. If Melissa's children were that important to her, he, Winston, would have to show willing. That scene earlier, when she'd talked about leaving him, had unnerved him.

'Welcome,' he said stiffly as the girl came tottering up the slope. What was she wearing? Those heels were totally unsuitable for her age – she was thirteen, not twenty-three – and she was actually wearing make-up.

Alice shot him a look that was made up of pure hostility. 'Welcome?' she repeated. 'It's my mum we've come to see. Not you.'

Say something, he wanted to tell Melissa. Tell your daughter not to be so rude. But Melissa was hugging both of them as though she hadn't seen them for weeks instead of hours and there was a look on her face that made him realise something. Melissa was overjoyed they were here. In fact, she was a completely different woman. So he wasn't enough for her . . . Not on his own, at any rate.

'Isn't it wonderful?' she exclaimed, all shiny-eyed. 'We're here together as a family.'

Family? The girl scowled at him from under her mother's arm, clearly thinking along the same lines. There was no way they could ever be a family. Who was she kidding?

'You're going to love it here,' continued Melissa, unaware of the faces her daughter was making at him. 'There's a lovely swimming pool and there's a banana boat and lots of little places to explore on the beach.'

The girl's eyes were rolling now and she was muttering something that sounded like 'Boring'. Winston could read her like a book. Much as he hated to admit it, there was something in her that reminded him of being that age himself.

There was a small, polite cough beside them. 'There's a disco, too, in town, with special under-eighteen nights.'

Winston had forgotten that the owner's son was still there. Was there no privacy in this place? Then he became aware of something. Alice had stopped rolling her eyes. Instead, she was extricating herself from her mother's arms and adopting a lolling position on the boulder by the villa sign.

'I'm Jack, by the way,' said the boy in that casual way which boys adopted at that age when they were trying to impress a girl. (Oh yes, Winston could remember that one all right).

'I'm Alice,' squeaked the girl in a contrived voice that was so ridiculously artificial that Winston almost laughed out loud.

'Cool.' Jack was edging from one foot to the other. Meanwhile, Freddie was staring up at the older boy with admiration all over his face.

This might not be so bad after all, Winston suddenly

realised. With any luck, Jack might come in handy, if only to distract his stepkids.

Catching Melissa's eye, he smiled. Instantly she visibly relaxed. 'Thank you,' she said, tucking her arm into his as they followed the kids up to the villa. 'Thank you for being so good about all this.' She gave a little sigh. 'I thought it all seemed a bit too convenient when Marvyn said he could have them.' Winston gave her a comforting hug, then stopped briefly to brush his lips against hers. Instantly, as if through some magic detection radar, Alice whipped round and shot them a *how dare you kiss my mum* glare. He felt Melissa stiffen with embarrassment.

'Give them time,' she whispered softly.

He nodded, but inside, Winston was seething. This was their honeymoon! He was entitled to show some affection, wasn't he? Anyone would think that *he* was the one who shouldn't be here, not the children.

Uncomfortably, he recalled a statistic he'd happened to spot in the paper on the plane out here. Something about one in two second marriages failing, because of existing children. Well, that wasn't going to happen to them. He wouldn't let it.

As he looked down at the bay he thought he saw a light. Just a flicker, as though someone was taking a photograph.

Every nerve in his body tightened. It was like being in the field all over again.

'What is it?' asked Melissa.

Winston didn't answer for a second. Each one of his senses was focussed on the spot where he'd seen the light, close to the second holiday cottage. The one with the drawn curtains that he'd glimpsed this morning, next to the place where the plump blonde and her husband were staying.

Had he imagined it? Was it just the sunlight glinting through the trees?

Maybe.

Maybe not.

'I was just looking at the sea,' he replied evenly. 'By the

way, Jack, who's staying in that second holiday cottage?'

The boy, who'd been walking shyly alongside Alice and Freddie, shrugged. 'Some French couple. They're on honeymoon too.'

So that was the end of his photographer-in-hiding theory. Winston shook himself. He was getting too bloody paranoid. 'Shall we go and find some lunch?' he said, changing the subject. 'I noticed a place on the beach that might be worth checking out.'

'Great, Mum,' said Freddie, swinging from his mother's arm as though she had made the suggestion and not him. 'I'm starving!'

Bloody hell, thought Winston crossly as he watched his wife run along the sand with the kids in some giggly, silly game of Catch.

He might as well not be here at all . . .

FOR BETTER OR WORSE

One in five couples have doubts about their other half
during their honeymoon.

Charisma bridal special survey

Chapter Nine

ROSIE

She'd break it off, Rosie told herself firmly, after negotiating a rather satisfactory deal with a shrewd crockery manufacturer. It was all very well letting your hair down away from home, but, as Cara had warned her years ago, you couldn't have a love affair with someone on this little island unless it was serious. And she wasn't ready for that.

Not with Greco.

But then she'd found him waiting for her back at the Athens hotel, standing at his bedroom door with that look on his face. He'd gently pulled her towards him and she'd been lost all over again.

Now, as she lay in his arms in the wide, comfortable bed overlooking the square outside, with the gentle trickling sound from the fountain, they seemed so right together that she wondered why she'd resisted his advances for so long.

'I knew you'd be beautiful,' murmured Greco as they lay on their sides facing each other, with the late-afternoon sun streaming through the shutters. 'But I hadn't realised just how gorgeous.'

He bent down and took her right nipple in his mouth, twisting it with his teeth. Rosie let out a little yelp, partly because it actually hurt and partly because the movement was so unexpected.

'I never understood why you didn't take a lover long ago,' continued Greco, moving to her other breast. Rosie braced herself but then realised he was gently licking her with small, darting actions. Practised actions.

'I wasn't ready,' she began but then stopped as Greco moved further down her body. Oh God.

She could feel bits of herself twitching that had nothing to do with the parts that Greco was . . . well, investigating. Heavens! She was jerking like a puppet. Part of her felt rather silly – none of it felt very real. But another part, that she hadn't known she even possessed, didn't want him to stop.

Oh God.

He *had* stopped.

'Why?' she asked, confused, as he rolled away. Had she done something wrong? It wouldn't be surprising if she had. Sex wasn't like riding a bike. It was easy to forget the script. Especially if you'd never had much experience in the first place.

He ran a finger teasingly down the side of her face. 'Because it's even better when we start again. That's why.' He leaped out of bed and Rosie had a flash of that sleek brown body slipping into a pair of pale blue jeans. 'Until yesterday,' he said, tossing over her white shorts, 'I always thought you were a bit of an ice maiden.' His eyes glinted. 'I used to wonder if Jack was an immaculate conception.'

Rosie wasn't Catholic but she knew that Greco went to mass every Sunday, and his flippancy shocked her. 'Of course he wasn't.'

'So what's the story there, then?'

His question, so swift on the heels of her disappointment (was she *really* so useless in bed that he simply couldn't be bothered to continue?), took her by surprise. Usually, she had her answer carefully crafted, as protection against those guests who were forward enough to ask about Jack's father. The locals were already well aware of the tale she'd put about via Cara. Whether they believed her was another matter.

Greco clearly didn't.

'You know what happened,' she said curtly, ignoring the shorts and heading for the shower. All the earlier intimacy had now disappeared, replaced by anger at his question about Jack.

Why had she been so stupid as to fall for the local lothario, who would probably now go home and tell everyone that

Rosie was a lousy lay? Was it just because of being away from the island? If so, she had been daft – really daft – to let down her guard.

'I told you before. Jack's father is dead. I'm a widow.'

'Yeah. Right.' Greco was coming towards her now, his eyes serious. 'So why don't you have any pictures of him?'

When Jack had asked that, she'd brushed him off with something about leaving everything in England, but Greco wasn't so easily fooled.

'You were only eighteen when you got here. Only just old enough to be a bride, let alone a widow. Come on, Rosie. We were man and wife just now. You can tell me the truth.'

Man and wife? The phrase had a peculiar – but not unattractive – ring to it. Nevertheless, still cross and embarrassed, Rosie turned away, shutting the shower door behind her. Immediately she was aware of it opening. He was behind her, naked again. Cradling her body as though he had never left it, cupping her breasts with both hands and pushing himself into her from behind.

For a minute she could hardly breathe. 'It is the truth,' she moaned. 'He is dead.'

So was she. Greco was pinning her now against the shower wall, so that she had to grab the pipe in order to stay upright. Every part of her was exploding into tiny pieces; including any remnant of common sense.

He'd been right, Rosie thought as everything washed over her. It *was* better when you started again. Indeed, Greco's own moans indicated that perhaps she wasn't as hopeless as she'd thought.

The realisation gave her a sense of empowerment. A little bit like the last time. Sixteen years ago.

She'd been known as Rosemary then. Not Rosie.

'Coming to the youth club disco on Saturday?' her best friend Gemma had asked hopefully as they'd ambled back from school together, hoisting their heavy book bags from one shoulder to the other. It had been the year before A-levels and the pressure was on. 'If you carry on like this,' the English teacher had told Rosemary with an excited edge to her voice, 'you can apply to Oxbridge.'

Mum would have liked that. So too would Dad, although he rarely let his emotions surface. Even when Mum had died, he'd muttered something about 'getting on with it' and that's just what they had done. As she got older, Rosie learned to keep house for her father and have dinner ready for him when he got back from work.

'I'd like to,' Rosemary had said wistfully, 'but I need to finish that essay on the Romantic poets.'

Gemma, who was normally as conscientious as herself, gave her a little nudge. 'Treat it as romantic research! Apparently, that new girl is bringing her cousin and some of his friends from the Marine training base. Could be fun.'

'Fun' was a word Rosemary's father viewed with deep suspicion, although she was pretty sure that her mother had had a different approach to life. She might only have been nine when she'd died, but Rosemary had a distinct memory of her mother – who'd been blonde, just like her – whistling tunefully to the radio.

Then again, maybe that was just her mind playing tricks on her.

'You need to lighten up, Rosemary,' her friend had insisted. 'Remember what they say about all work and no play.' They'd stopped now, outside Gemma's house. Inside she knew that Sally, Gemma's mother, who used to be a good friend of Mum's, would be waiting, keen to find out about her daughter's day. There'd be a cup of tea and a slice of warm raspberry sponge cake, a treat which Rosemary was often invited inside to share.

'Want to come in for a bit?' asked Gemma. She was so nice, thought Rosie. Such a good friend. But there were times when it hurt too much to have a glimpse of a proper family home when you knew that afterwards you had to go back to a cold, silent house with a resentful dad and photographs of a mother you could barely remember.

Maybe that was why she, Rosemary, was always smiling; something else that infuriated her father. Her mother used to smile, according to Sally. And anything that her mother had done, she wanted to do too.

'Not tonight, thanks.' Rosemary patted her school bag. 'Not if I'm going to finish this essay early so I can go to the disco.'

A delighted beam spread across Gemma's face. 'That's great. Tell you what! You can wear my new skirt if you want. The one that Mum got me from town.'

That was so typical of Gemma, to offer an outfit which she had hardly worn herself. Of course, it was because she knew Rosemary's dad rarely gave her anything for new clothes. Until recently, both girls had had a Saturday job – she'd worked at the local stables where she was allowed to ride – but at the English teacher's suggestion, Rosemary had given up to concentrate on her work.

'It's all right, thanks.' She gave her friend a quick hug. 'I'll find something to wear.'

When she got back to her own house, a little voice inside told her to go to Mum's wardrobe – breaking another of Dad's rules – and leaf through the curious array of jumpers, blouses, trousers and dresses which her mother had left behind so suddenly when that vicious cancer had torn through her body, giving little notice.

It was surprising really that Dad hadn't just bundled them all up and sent them to a charity shop. Maybe he was more sentimental than she'd given him credit for.

Instinctively, Rosie buried her nose in a lavender-coloured dress at the back. A mixture of talcum powder and roses drew her back through time, recalling a dim memory she didn't even know she possessed. 'Mum,' she murmured, drawing the dress out of the wardrobe and holding it up against her as she stood uncertainly in front of her mother's old barley twist mirror on the wall.

Mmm. It might look quite good if she took the sides in and maybe shortened the hem. One skill that Rosemary had inherited from her mother was the ability to sew and make something out of nothing. Even her father, who was so fussy, always handed her his shirts when they needed mending.

She'd just have to see what she could do with this dress, thought Rosemary, shutting the wardrobe door behind her and going back into her bedroom to tackle the Romantic poets essay. It might just work.

When Rosemary came downstairs the following Saturday, ready to meet Gemma, her father was sitting as usual in front of the telly. She'd already cooked his supper (pork chops and mash) which he was eating now on a tray in front of a quiz programme that he loved to revile. Usually, they ate at the dining-room table, but Saturday nights were an exception. It was the one evening off when Rosie was allowed out, and that was only because the youth club was run by the local church. The same one where her mother had been christened, married and buried.

Unfortunately, there were far more girls than boys where they lived, which meant that so far neither Rosemary nor Gemma had managed to get a boyfriend. If they didn't hurry up, they often told each other, they'd be left on the shelf.

'I won't be late, Dad,' she'd said lightly, dropping a kiss on the top of his head and hoping that he wouldn't look up from the telly.

Just her luck. 'What's that?' His eyes took in the lavender dress which now had more of a waist. It was set off too by the matching tights that she'd found in a drawer and by the little mauve ribbons, twisted in her hair as a last-minute thought. The shiny black shoes looked good, too, even though they were a bit high. It hadn't surprised Rosemary to discover that she was the same size as her mother.

'It's a dress,' she faltered in answer to her father's question.

His eyebrows met in a frown. 'I can see that. It was your mother's, wasn't it?'

Rosemary nodded, waiting for the cutting criticism that would follow. How dare she go through her mother's wardrobe?

What right did she have to mess about with something as sacred as her clothes? Didn't she have any respect for the dead?

Then the frown seemed to melt away. 'You look . . .'

Rosemary waited, holding her breath.

'You look very pretty,' continued her father. Then he actually reached into his pocket and handed her a note. 'Buy yourself a fizzy drink with that. And have a good time.'

His eyes were wet. Overcome with emotion, she bent down and gave him a cuddle. There was no response. At the same time, the doorbell went.

'You'd better go,' her father had said gruffly. Then he added something as Rosemary went out of the room to get her coat from the hall. It sounded something like 'Your mother would have been proud of you.'

Rosemary could hardly contain her excitement as she and Gemma made their way through town to the youth club building, a rather boring looking red-brick hall during the day which took on a far more exciting air at night when there was music inside and boys(!), sauntering casually past the wide-open doors.

When you went to an all-girls school, it seemed weird to have people of the opposite sex around, thought Rosemary, shyly making her way towards the cloakroom. Usually, there weren't that many: only a couple of boring ones from her old confirmation class and a gaggle of youths who hadn't stayed on for A-levels, with whom she had little in common.

Still, as Gemma often said rather wistfully, they would hopefully find someone when they finally got to university.

Tonight, however, was different. Gemma had been right! There were lots of new boys here: clean-cut, tall ones who looked more like men. 'Just look at those muscles,' nudged Gemma.

Rosemary began to feel nervous. She and Gemma might snigger in private at the confirmation lot who hogged the ping-pong table, but there was something comforting and non-threatening about them. This new lot were more like men. They were looking at her and Gemma in a way that made her feel a bit shivery inside, a peculiar mixture of nerves and also excitement.

Rosemary felt an elbow in her ribs. 'I like the look of him, don't you?' Gemma was eyeing up a very tall boy who was talking to his friends on the other side of the room. He was what Dad would have called 'coffee-coloured' and – amazingly – quite bald. It was difficult not to stare. Rosemary had never met anyone, apart from an old man at church, who had a head that was shiny all over. Yet, perhaps because it was brown, it seemed inexplicably attractive, as did his bold, handsome, striking face which reminded her of a picture of a Greek god in her Classics textbook.

Briefly, as the music stopped, Rosemary heard a deep laugh, an infectious sound which made her automatically laugh out loud herself.

As she did so, he looked up, caught her eye, looked away and then back again at her. Rosemary felt a tingle travel down from her neck to the base of her spine. 'He's coming to ask you to dance,' Gemma whispered excitedly.

Rosemary's mouth went dry as this impossibly good-looking boy strode confidently across the room. Maybe it was Gemma he was interested in. But no. He was actually stopping right in front of *her*.

'Would you like to dance?' he asked, his eyes on hers as though they'd already met.

Unable to talk, she nodded. His hand was large and warm as he led her out to the floor. Rosemary was aware that all eyes were on her, and not just because they were the first couple to dance. Very tall, bald, coffee-coloured young men weren't particularly common in this part of the world.

Oh my goodness! The music had changed now. Instead of the loud, jaunty tunes, it was a slow record. That meant you had to move closer instead of jiggling with a safe distance apart. 'I like your dress,' said her partner, looking down at her.

She blushed. 'Thank you.'

Then they proceeded to move round in small circles, his arms around her. Thanks to her diminutive height, she barely reached his chest. It was tempting to bury her nose in his shirt, simply for comfort, but of course that would have been far too forward.

Rosie could hardly breathe with the newness of it all. A man! So close! A man she knew her father would never approve of because of the colour of his skin. A man who seemed to draw her in as though she had no choice.

'My name's Charlie,' he said when the music ended.

'I'm Rosemary,' she volunteered nervously.

He smiled. 'I know. I asked someone who you were when you came in.'

Rosemary hardly knew where to look. So he'd actually noticed her, even though there were so many pretty girls around. Unused to compliments, Rosemary didn't know what to say. Luckily, he was talking instead.

'I'm only here for a month,' he said, feeling in his pockets and bringing out a small piece of paper and a pen. 'But I'd like to see you again – that is, if you want to. May I take your number?'

Then he held her hand and Rosemary knew she never wanted him to let go.

Looking back, as she did again and again over the years, Rosemary couldn't explain why she had allowed herself to break all the rules that she and Gemma had set for themselves – including nothing above the waistline unless you'd been going out with a boy for at least six months. (As for below, that was inconceivable!)

The only excuse she could come up with was that being with Charlie felt so right that it couldn't possibly be wrong.

It wasn't just that she felt physically drawn to him. It was the way he talked to her that made her feel special: something that she hadn't experienced since Mum had died. He felt the same.

'Sure you don't mind me being bald?' he'd asked one evening

when they'd been sitting on the beach, their arms around each other, watching the waves edge further out. He took her right index finger and ran it over his head. 'I've always wanted to ask girls,' he added tentatively, 'but never had the courage to do so until now. Yet you . . . you make me feel I can say anything.'

His head did feel odd, all smooth and shiny. But it was part of him, and frankly, anything that was part of Charlie was fine as far as Rosie was concerned. More than fine, in fact. 'You wouldn't be the same if you had hair,' she offered.

'Thanks.' He began to tickle her, which made her scream with laughter. Together they rolled on the pebbled beach like puppies before catching their breath. The mock play-fighting was, she instinctively knew, a distraction for both of them. Otherwise they might so easily do something else, something that should be saved for marriage.

'You know,' said Charlie, gently positioning her so that she sat between his legs, 'I lost my hair by falling out of a tree at prep school when I was ten. The shock made my hair fall out.'

He said all this in such a matter-of-fact manner that she almost didn't take in the significance.

'How awful,' she breathed.

'Better than being paralysed, which is what the doctors said might have happened.' His arms encircled her, pulling her gently backwards into his warm body. 'My grandmother, who brought me up, told me that I could either spend the rest of my life feeling insecure about being bald or I could make it into one of my strengths. So I did. When I came back to school, one of the kids said something spiteful.'

His voice was hard, harder than she'd ever heard it before. It spoke of pain and also anger. 'So I took him by the scruff of his neck and told him that my baldness gave me a special strength. If he wasn't careful, I could make him lose his hair too.'

The gleeful way he said this disturbed her. It didn't fit with the kind, warm Charlie she'd come to know in the last few weeks. 'What happened after that?'

Charlie grinned down at her. 'I got made head boy. The same happened when I went to senior school.' He shrugged. 'Ended up as head boy there too.'

Then he began to massage her neck, so deftly that she felt herself melting.

Somehow, she managed to keep their relationship hidden from her father, with the help of Gemma and her mother, who both thought it was very romantic. Her English teacher wasn't so approving. 'You're going to have to do better than this,' she told Rosemary disappointedly when her next essay – on Shelley this time – was a week late and not up to its usual standard. 'Is everything all right at home?'

Rosemary would have liked to have confided in her young English teacher, but something held her back. What she and Charlie had was precious, something that she didn't want to share with anyone else. Besides, how could she describe that feeling adequately? That fear in the throat if he was a few minutes late for a secret meeting. That hot wave that passed through her when he kissed her, making her feel as though she hadn't lived before they'd met. That awful heavy anticipation because he was going to be sent away soon.

They'd agreed to spend their last evening together, sitting quietly in the park. It was summer: a wonderful warm July when it was acceptable for her to make excuses to Dad about needing 'a breath of fresh air' and slip out after dinner. Purposefully, she wore her mother's lavender dress, to remind him of their first meeting.

'I'm going to miss you so much,' said Charlie, his arm around her waist as they got up from the bench and walked down to the harbour. But as he spoke, she could see that his eyes were fixed on the cluster of boats bobbing around on the water and she knew he was also desperate to go.

'I'll miss you too,' she murmured, burying her head in his chest. They stood there for a few moments, rocking gently back and forth. She could feel a hardness against her. Was that what she thought it was? Suddenly she felt very bold.

Naturally, they'd kissed. And his hands had explored her breasts – initially above her jumper and then next to her skin, which made her go all hot to think about. Once he had suggested that he explore down below her waist but she had guided his hand away and instantly he had apologised.

But tonight, it was the other way round. Right now, it was *her* hand which was guiding his, as though it belonged to someone else. 'You are sure?' asked Charlie, his voice thick with surprise.

She nodded: shocked, herself, by her blatant daring; prompted perhaps by the bottle of wine they had shared and the awful searing pain of their imminent separation. He was being posted to somewhere in Europe, he'd confided, although he wasn't even meant to tell her that. He certainly wasn't allowed to reveal where, exactly. Meanwhile, the clock was ticking. They had to make every minute count.

'There's a boat, down at the harbour.' Charlie was walking alongside her, his hand stroking her arm and giving her electric tingles. 'On the west side.' He sounded embarrassed. 'Some of the men use it . . . It might not be empty.'

But it was.

She should have – could have – said no. But that night, another girl was in her body. One that didn't heed rules any more because, as Mum had shown, you didn't live for ever.

'Oh God,' he breathed as he sank into her. 'You're so beautiful.'

The day after that, his ship sailed. Two months later, she and Gemma had nervously gone into a chemist on the outskirts of town where no one knew them, to buy a pregnancy testing kit.

'You're up the duff?' her father had roared when she'd summoned the courage to tell him. 'With that coffee-coloured sailor you've been seen out with?' He slammed his fist down on the kitchen table. 'Don't think I didn't know, but I'd hoped you'd come to your senses. I suppose you expect me to allow you to stay here with some black kid, do you?'

'No.' Rosemary heard her voice sneer with a strength she

hadn't known she possessed. 'I'm not living here a minute more than I have to.'

Within a few minutes, she was downstairs again with a suitcase and her savings book, which contained just about enough to buy a ticket on the overnight boat to France. Europe, Charlie had said. With any luck, she'd find him.

In the meantime, she'd write to him, asking him to reply to Gemma's address. She'd call, she assured her friend, to see what he said.

'Penny for them?' said Greco, looking down on her in bed.

Rosie shook herself. 'I was just thinking, that was all.'

'Too much is bad for you.' He smiled. A warm, jaunty smile. 'Let's hit the city, shall we? It's our last night in Athens, after all. Tomorrow we go back to the island.'

His words filled her with foreboding.

'I'm hoping it won't change things, my beautiful Rosie. We are special together. Do not you think?'

TRUE HONEYMOON STORY

'We bumped into my old boss at the airport on our way
to our honeymoon. I decided not to tell my new husband
that we used to date.'

Sylvia, about to celebrate her silver wedding anniversary

Chapter Ten

EMMA

So! That glamorous couple on the plane had actually had their children flown over. Or rather, *her* children, judging from the overheard conversation on the beach.

Even if she hadn't eavesdropped on their argument, Emma would have guessed that the cheeky-faced boy and the rather precocious girl (strutting along in high-heeled sandals and face plastered with make-up) belonged to the woman, just from the body language.

Emma prided herself on understanding 'movement psychology', as Gemma Balls called it, especially during staff meetings. It was something you learned to recognise in the school canteen when one of the kids was sitting away from the others or was muttering, eyes fixed on the ground, that they'd 'forgotten' to bring their packed lunch in. Much more likely that they didn't want it or that a parent hadn't bothered to make it.

The handsome bald man's body language (arms folded and tight lips) suggested that he wasn't very happy about having his wife's kids around.

'I'm sure I've seen him somewhere before,' Emma said to Tom when she returned to the cottage with a bowl of salad. 'I just can't think where, that's all. *She's* vaguely familiar too.'

Tom gave a little moan. 'Are you still feeling awful?' sympathised Emma, immediately feeling guilty that she'd been thinking of something as trivial as the other couple.

There was an affirmatory groan. 'It might be the sun.' He put his hand across his eyes and turned over, burying his face under the pillow.

It was true that Tom, with his pasty complexion, wasn't a great sun-lover. When they occasionally got a scorcher at home, he was the one who stayed inside while she liked nothing more than to lie outside on their little patio (until one of the kids needed her, of course).

But that's what Greece was, wasn't it? Sunny.

'It makes me sick,' he added, still under the pillow.

'I thought it was the travelling,' said Emma edgily. 'Or the vol-au-vents.'

He groaned again. Louder this time.

'Then why come away at all, if you don't like the journey or the weather?' she found herself demanding rather tersely.

'Because it was a present.' Tom sounded almost irritable, which wasn't like him at all. 'And you love the heat. So I just went along with it.'

Emma's heart melted. He'd done all this for her without saying a word. Yet in a way, she wished he hadn't. What good was a honeymoon if your husband was flat out in bed, unable to get up and share things with you – like the lovely white sand outside and the swimming pool where she'd just seen the new kids messing about?

They'd have been better off walking the hills at home or maybe taking the children down to Tom's sister near St Mawes.

The children . . . The mere thought of them punched a hole in her stomach. When Emma had seen the glamorous woman's kids by the pool, her insides had curled up with jealousy. How she would have loved to have her lot here too: cuddling up to them and knowing exactly where they were.

On the other hand, there was so much here that wouldn't have been safe. The shiny terracotta floor tiles in the villa which might have made Gawain slip. The swimming pool which could have been lethal for little Willow. The heat, which might well have brought them out in a rash.

'Don't mind me.' Tom was still buried under the pillow. 'You go outside and enjoy yourself.'

Emma hesitated. 'I can't, without you. Besides, you ought to eat something. Look, I've brought you a salad.' She held it out, knowing as she did so that Tom wouldn't be very impressed. He was a steak-and-kidney man: lettuce and tomato wasn't 'real food' in his book.

But, hang on, he was actually coming out from under the pillow and casting a suspicious eye at the bowl.

'What's that stuff?' He was pointing at the white cubes of cheese.

'It's feta cheese.'

'Haven't they heard of Cheddar?' moaned Tom, his head dropping back on the bed. There was another groan.

'Have some water,' she urged. 'It doesn't matter if you don't eat anything as long as you get your liquid in.' That was better. Mind you, they were almost out of the complimentary bottles that had been left in the fridge. How weird not to be able to drink out of taps. As for the toilet (something she needed to clean after Tom's last bout of sickness), it was downright dirty having to put the paper in the bin at the side.

'Please go,' Tom murmured. 'I need to sleep.'

'You don't want me?' Emma couldn't help feeling hurt, but at the same time, there was a tinge of relief. 'I'll just be outside then,' she added. No answer. He was already snoring with the funny adenoidal sound that had taken some getting used to when they'd first started living together.

Maybe, thought Emma as she stood outside the cottage, listening to the new children splashing in the pool on the slopes above, she'd go up there herself for a dip. She might also try to ring home again if there was enough reception for the phone up there.

'Mum? It's me. Everything all right?'

'*Get off!*'

'Sorry.' Emma shielded the phone with her hand to try and block out the noise of the precocious girl and cheeky-faced boy who were trying to push each other into the deep end. 'I didn't catch that.'

'Piss off, or I'll tell Mum!'

'Then give me back my phone – you'll get it wet!'

106

'Hang on a minute.' Those two were making such a racket she couldn't hear properly. Still, she'd seen it all at school before.

Walking up towards the villa, Emma tried again. 'Mum. It's me again. Yes, I know. I couldn't hear you either but it's better now. Is everything OK? Can I talk to the children?'

Her heart pounding, Emma sat down on the slope. The grass felt rougher than the type at home. Almost rubbery. 'Gawain? Is that you?'

There was a silence. Emma could just picture her little boy, his blond fringe, which had been trimmed for the wedding, no longer flopping over his forehead.

'Say something to Mum,' she pleaded. Normally, Gawain didn't need any encouragement to talk on the phone. In fact, he usually grabbed the receiver as soon as it rang and had to be coaxed off it. 'Are you having a lovely time with Granny?'

No answer.

She tried again. 'What are you doing?'

Still no response, although she could hear the blare of the television in the background. 'He's gone, love.' It was Mum again. 'Got a bit tongue-tied.'

With his own mother? Emma felt her stomach dip with rejection. 'What about Willow?'

'Just fallen asleep. There's no need to worry, you know.' Her mother sounded a bit tense. ''Sides, I told you. It disturbs them to hear your voice.'

'But how are *you* feeling?'

'A bit queasy. Hang on . . .'

There was a long pause before she returned. 'That's better.'

'Have you been sick again?'

'Stop fussing, Em. It's driving me mad. Now you go and have a good time.'

But how could she, if Mum wasn't well? She knew what it was like to feel poorly and look after the kids.

'Tom on the mend, is he?'

'Not really.' As she spoke, Emma heard voices. It was the glamorous woman coming back. She had the kind of figure

107

that looked as if it had never given birth. Emma suddenly felt frumpy in her baggy tee-shirt and pink shorts.

'Just make sure he has enough water and then leave him to sleep it off,' said Mum dismissively. Emma felt hurt on behalf of her husband. She knew her mother found Tom boring, but that was better than a man who couldn't be trusted, wasn't it?

Dad's wedding card flashed into her head. For a minute, she considered telling her mum about it but then, almost instantly, changed her mind. No point in upsetting her.

'Make the most of your holidays,' added her mother tightly. 'No, Gawain, don't poke your sister like that. You'll wake her up. You'll soon be back to the real world, love. So have a break. You deserve it. Gawain, I said *no*. Hang on. I need the bathroom again.'

'I'll ring tomorrow,' promised Emma desperately, but the line had already gone dead. As she slipped the phone back into her shorts pocket, Emma caught the eye of the glamorous mother. There was a warm smile, the sort that said *I know what it's like.*

'Don't I know you from somewhere?' asked the woman, dipping her head to one side.

'I've been thinking the same,' admitted Emma, blushing, admiring the other woman's gold sandals which made her own flip-flops look really boring.

'Where do you live, if you don't mind me asking?'

'A small town called Corrywood.' Even as she said it, Emma felt a longing to be there right now, safely with the children and with a doctor round the corner to take a look at Tom. 'It's near . . .'

'I *know* it!' There was an apprehensive edge to the other woman's voice. 'We live there too. Are your children at the school?'

Emma nodded, glancing at the boy and girl who were still shoving each other around on the side. 'My daughter's too young – she's only two – but my son will be starting in reception after the summer.' She blushed again. 'I work there as well.'

108

For some reason, the woman seemed really twitchy now. 'You're a teacher?'

If only! 'Just a dinner lady.'

Don't say that, Tom was always telling her. 'Just' was one of those words that did you no favours in life. Besides, dinner ladies did some great work.

'Then maybe you've come across my lot.' The woman gave a little sigh.

'I don't think so. I'm in charge of the infants, although I did help out with the after school club last term when one of the others was ill.' She'd quite liked that, she almost added. It was a bit of extra money and Mum hadn't minded baby-sitting. But then the woman she'd covered for had come back, and although Emma had made it known she'd like to be considered again, nothing had happened.

'Maybe that's where we've seen each other,' said the woman thoughtfully.

Come to think of it, Emma *could* remember a brother and sister – the same sort of age as those two – squabbling over the computer. Their argument had got quite heated until one of the other after-school club helpers had divided them.

Emma's thoughts were interrupted by a loud splash followed by a screech. 'He pushed me in! Tell him off, Mum. And he's taken my phone!'

The woman rolled her eyes. 'My daughter is addicted to the wretched thing – not to mention her laptop. I've tried putting her on a digital detox but she just went mental.' She gave a little confiding look. 'I know this is going to sound a bit strange, but I didn't really want anyone to know we were here. My husband is quite famous. You might recognise him . . .'

She stopped, hand clasped to mouth as though she'd said too much. 'What I'm trying to say is that we want some privacy. So do you mind not telling anyone from home that we're here – not until we get back, that is?'

How odd, thought Emma. It wasn't even as if she knew their names, so how could she tell anyone? Quite famous, she'd said. So that was why his face had looked familiar. Why oh why couldn't she recall who he was? That was motherhood for you. It shrivelled up your brain.

Meanwhile, her new friend was looking so worried, twisting her shiny gold wedding ring round and round, that she didn't feel it was her business to ask any more questions. 'Sure. That's fine.' She tried to make a joke out of it. 'Mum's the word.'

There was a little sigh of relief. 'Thanks. I really appreciate it. We've had enough problems already. It's meant to be our honeymoon, you see, but my first husband couldn't have the children. To make it worse, there's been a mix-up over the rooms.'

Emma didn't want to say she'd gathered that from the fuss when they'd arrived. It might have sounded as though she was eavesdropping. Mind you, she hadn't realised they were on honeymoon too. Was that why they wanted privacy? A secret wedding?

'I've left my two kids behind,' she said, feeling a lump rise in her throat as she spoke. 'It's the very first time I've been away from them.'

There was a rather sweet smile of sympathy. 'I remember that stage so well. It's like missing a limb, isn't it?'

Emma's head bobbed up and down. 'Exactly! My mum's looking after them but . . .'

'But you never feel that anyone else can look after them quite like you!'

Got it in one. So she *wasn't* being fussy, like Mum and Tom said. That made her feel a whole lot better.

'You know,' the woman was now whispering, 'I'm secretly quite glad the children are here with me now, because I don't really trust my ex to keep an eye on them. Still, on the plus side, at least you'll be able to relax a bit without yours, won't you?'

'My husband's feeling sick,' Emma heard herself saying. 'So we're not exactly having the most amazing time at the moment.'

110

Oh dear. She hadn't meant to moan but, despite being so glamorous, this other mother was surprisingly easy to talk to. Really sympathetic, even though she did sound posh. 'Poor him!' She touched Emma's arm lightly. 'I've brought some stuff with me that might help.'

Not another lot! 'That's very kind but I'm not sure that Tom will—' she began to say. However, the woman was nodding vigorously. 'Honestly. It's no trouble. I'll just go and get it. Mind keeping an eye on my two while I'm gone?' She smiled. 'Otherwise they'll only try to kill each other again.'

'Fuck off, Alice!'

'Shitface!'

Emma gasped but the woman just rolled her eyes again. 'I'm going to pretend I didn't hear that. Sometimes it's easier.' She held out her hand. 'My name's Melissa, by the way.'

What gorgeous nails! Her own wedding polish had already begun to chip from cleaning out the bathroom after Tom had been ill again. 'I'm Emma.'

'Great to meet you, Emma!' Her new friend gave a little gasp, putting her hand to her mouth. It was something she seemed to do a lot. 'I've just thought of something. Is that how you heard about this place – through that advert at school?'

Emma nodded. 'Sort of. At least, a friend did. She got it for us as a wedding present, you see.'

'How sweet!' Melissa's voice dropped. 'Tell me, is it what you thought it would be? I mean, we wanted somewhere private but it *is* a bit basic, isn't it? The pool's *tiny*. There's not enough hot water and the food is pretty average. I know they're waiting for the new cook, but you'd think they'd have it sorted for the season, wouldn't you?'

What on earth did she mean? It was all lovely, as far as Emma could see – although it would be a lot better if Tom wasn't sick. 'I like it,' she shrugged. 'I can't wait to do the yoga tomorrow morning.'

Then she stopped. How selfish. That would mean leaving Tom, which wouldn't be fair, would it? On the other hand, maybe he'd be a bit better by then. That reminded her. 'I'd better go.'

Melissa grabbed her hand. 'Sorry. I got carried away; I can be a bit scatty at times.' She blushed. 'I still can't believe all this is real, can you? Getting married and all that. Now just wait there and I'll be back in a second with my magic medicine. Trust me. This stuff always works.'

For someone she'd only just met, Melissa was very forthcoming, thought Emma. Still, it was nice to make friends, especially as there was still no sign of life from the holiday cottage next to theirs. Was anyone actually staying there? It really was very quiet down by the cottage.

Then again, wasn't that what you wanted on your honeymoon?

'You've got lice, you've got lice!'

'No, I haven't!'

'Yes, you have! Just take "A" off your name and you get l-i-c-e . . .'

'Piss off, Freddie!'

Those two needed a good telling-off. She would never, resolved Emma firmly, allow Gawain and Willow to get away with language like that when they were older.

Sitting down on the lounger to wait for her new friend to return, Emma closed her eyes in the gorgeous sunshine and automatically twiddled her new ring. Except that it wasn't there . . .

Oh my God! Her eyes snapped open. No. She wasn't imagining it! Sweating with fear, she leaped to her feet and began frantically searching the ground. 'My ring!' she called out desperately. 'Someone help me! I've lost my wedding ring!'

TRUE HONEYMOON STORY

'My then-husband abandoned me on a Scottish mountain during our honeymoon. I should have seen the warning signs then.'

Liz, now happily remarried

Chapter Eleven

WINSTON

Winston heard the commotion from the top of the hill above the villa, where he'd been working out. He'd found the spot soon after they'd arrived. It was perfect for some privacy – Winston didn't like exercising in front of anyone else unless he was being filmed – and at the same time, there was quite a nice view of the bay.

The villa might be basic but there was something about this place that was very appealing.

'My ring! My wedding ring!'

It was, he could see, marching down the slope, the plump blonde bride. She was running round the pool area in a pair of tight shorts that didn't do her any favours. Oh God. Alice and Freddie were there too, shooting him hostile looks. Winston was tempted to turn round and tear back up the hill again.

'I've lost my wedding ring!' The woman's eyes were shiny with tears and her face was all red and blotchy. Winston's heart went out to her; the poor woman really was in a state. 'Look!' She thrust out her hand at him as if he needed proof. 'I had it this morning when I woke up. I'm sure I did.'

Her breath was coming out in short puffs, as though she was having a panic attack. Automatically, his training kicked into action. 'Inhale,' he instructed firmly. 'Lean on me – that's right – and take long, deep breaths.'

It was working, even though the kids were giving him funny looks. The woman's fingers were beginning to relax now; a few seconds ago, her nails had cut into his back. 'Better?' he asked.

She nodded.

He led her to a bench by the side of the pool. 'Sit down. That's right. You've lost your ring, you say?'

Her eyes filled with tears again. Quickly, before she could have another panic attack, he continued, using the low, steady voice they'd been taught, right at the beginning of their training. It was a voice to fool someone – usually a comrade in trouble – that everything would be all right, even if there wasn't a cat in hell's chance of making it.

A voice which he'd used on Nick.

'When exactly do you last remember seeing it on your finger?'

'This morning, in the cottage.' Her voice came out in gasps, as though she was making a huge effort. Probably embarrassed. He knew about that, too. 'I remember waking up and giving it a little twist.' She gave him a sad smile. 'I can't help doing that – couldn't, I mean. It feels – felt – so new.'

He knew exactly what she meant. His own ring felt like an impostor. In the registry office, it had taken a while for Melissa to slide it onto his finger; something that had made her giggle with nerves. The recollection gave him a funny pang. Had that really only been two days ago? He hadn't even considered the possibility of their honeymoon being hijacked then by two spoilt brats.

'Right.' He forced himself to concentrate on the drama in front of him. 'So you had it when you woke up. Then what did you do?'

'Had a shower.' She blushed. 'That didn't take long because the water was cold . . .'

Tell me about it, Winston almost said. Not that the inadequate plumbing system bothered *him* but he so wanted everything to be right for Melissa. And frankly, tepid showers in a cubicle that wasn't even big enough for one (not someone his size, anyway) weren't what he'd had in mind.

'Then I had to clean up after Tom.' The woman was going red again. 'He keeps being sick, you see. At first we thought it was food poisoning – the chicken vol-au-vents were off at our wedding reception – but now he reckons it was the plane or the sun or both.'

She lowered her voice. 'In fact, he's asleep right now. I crept out of the cottage so I didn't wake him. I'm hoping a rest will do him good.'

The woman was talking as though her husband was a baby. 'When you cleaned up after your husband,' Winston said thoughtfully, 'did you wear rubber gloves?'

There was a nod. 'I did, actually. There were some in the kitchen in our cottage. It's got everything, hasn't it?'

Winston snorted. 'I wouldn't know. We're in the owner's room.' He stood up from the bench. 'This is just a thought, but why don't you go down to the cottage and take a look inside your gloves?'

'Fuck off, Freddie!'

'*You* fuck off!'

Winston shot round. 'Enough of that. You two can come with us. That's right. Four heads can be better than one. Where's Mum, by the way?'

'Gone to get some medicine for my Tom.' The woman was twisting her hands. 'I'm afraid we're causing a lot of trouble for you.'

'Not at all.' It's good to have a project, he almost said. Besides, it would give him an excuse to check out that cottage next door; the one where he could have sworn he'd seen a light flashing the other night. 'Now why don't you take us to your place? We need to go back exactly the way you walked up here. Keep your eyes peeled on the ground, everyone.'

Even if the plump blonde hadn't been leading the way, Winston would have known where to go from the sound of the snoring. Bloody hell. That man wouldn't have lasted two minutes on the front line. Those adenoids would have alerted the enemy within seconds.

'He's still out for the count.' The woman sounded exasperated. Not surprising. A noise like that would drive him nuts.

'Cool place,' exclaimed Alice behind him. 'You've even got a television!'

'Leave it alone,' warned Winston.

'I wasn't going to touch it, anyway.' The girl's voice was sulky. 'You don't have any right to talk to me like that. You're not my father.'

The bride shot him a sympathetic look.

'I know I'm not,' said Winston in a low voice. 'But since he has managed to get out of looking after you, I'm doing so instead.'

The pained look that shot across Alice's face, coupled with the disapproval in the woman's eyes, made him wonder if he'd been a touch too hard then.

'I washed out Tom's sick bowl in the sink.' The plump bride's voice reminded him of why they were here. 'Look. There are my gloves.' She held up the left one and shook it. Nothing.

'Put your hand in,' he suggested.

She did so, hopefully. Then her face fell. 'It's not there!' Her cheeks reddened again and tears rolled down. 'I've lost it.'

Winston looked around for something long and thin. A barbecue stick with a kink at the end. That might do. 'Let's take a look at the bathroom.'

The woman was blustering behind him. 'I'm afraid it might smell a bit.'

Not as much as rotting corpses in Afghanistan, he almost said.

'Ugh.' The girl was giggling. 'Did you make a smell, Freddie?'

'Piss off.'

'Stop it, both of you.' Winston handed the stick to the boy. 'Hand this to me when I say.'

'Please,' said the girl sharply.

Winston stood up. 'OK. You do it. Go on. Put your hand down the loo bowl and see what you can find.'

The girl glared at him. 'Fine.'

He had to give her credit. She wasn't squeamish.

'Freddie, push the stick down from the top. That's right.'

117

'I've got something!' The girl's voice had a squeal to it. 'Shit. It's gone again.'

Deftly, Winston unscrewed the waste pipe. A bit stiff but it was coming . . .

'Will you be able to put it back?' asked Freddie worriedly. Clearly his father hadn't taught him any DIY.

'Sure.' Kneeling, Winston tried to put his hand in. 'You do it,' he instructed Alice. 'Your fist is smaller.'

Amazingly, she didn't need asking twice. The girl had more guts than he'd thought. 'I've got it,' she shouted. 'I've got it!'

Triumphantly, she withdrew a small, dirty-looking band of gold. Emma gasped. 'Thank God!'

She flung her arms around Winston and then both the kids. 'How can I say thank you?'

Winston shrugged. 'We're just glad we can help. Aren't we, you lot?'

The girl's face had gone all stony again. '*We?* I'm the one that found it.' She turned round and started washing her hands.

'Alice, that's not fair,' began Freddie.

'Hey,' interrupted Winston. 'It doesn't matter. What's important is that this lady's got her ring back.'

'Please call me Emma.'

She waited as if expecting him to give his name in return but he couldn't. It was too risky. There was a low mutter from the girl. It sounded suspiciously like, 'Pity Mum can't lose her ring too.'

Winston felt a ridiculous pang of disappointment. For a minute, when they'd all been working together, it had felt rather good. How stupid he'd been to think that he'd managed to mend fences. Whatever he did with these two was never going to be enough to win their approval. He'd suspected as much before the honeymoon, but now it was written, clear as day, on Alice's face and, to a lesser degree, Freddie's.

Meanwhile, Emma had washed the ring and was now dancing around like an overweight fairy. 'I'll never, ever lose it again. Thank you, thank you.'

118

If she wasn't careful, she was going to wake up Mr Adenoid there.

'We'd better go back to Mum,' said Alice sulkily. 'She'll be wondering where we are.'

Winston walked to the door, looking out through the patch of trees to the blue-and-white wooden cottage next door. 'Met your neighbours yet?' he asked casually.

Emma shook her head. 'Someone said they were French. Maybe they keep different hours.'

She was quite sweet really, Winston decided. A little irritating but her heart was definitely in the right place. Pity about her husband not being well. Never flown before, she'd said. Incredible. Some people led such insular lives. Then again, was that such a bad thing? Sometimes he wondered if he'd have been better off having fewer expectations in life.

'By the way,' she added brightly. 'I was talking to your wife earlier and discovered why your face looks so familiar!'

He stiffened. Surely Melissa hadn't told her the truth? He'd warned her not to get too close to the English woman in case she twigged about his identity. At times his new wife was like a child: trusting those who clearly weren't to be relied on.

'It's through the school, isn't it?' She was still twisting her ring as though to reassure herself that it was back in place. 'I must have seen you pick up the children.'

There was a snort from Alice's direction and a dismissive glance that suggested he knew nothing. 'He only collected us once and even then he went to the wrong entrance. 'Sides, we either walk home or else Mum or our real dad picks us up.'

That was telling her! And him. The poor woman realised she'd put her foot in it now, not that it was her fault. Meanwhile, Winston told himself as he walked back to the pool – the kids racing ahead to meet Melissa, who was waving at them – he had to do something to get his stepchildren off his back.

They were driving him bloody crazy.

*

Winston waited until dinner to carry out his plan. Unwittingly, Melissa helped by suggesting that they had dinner at the villa instead of going out.

'It would be nice to show some support, don't you think?' she'd said, taking his arm. She only showed affection, he noticed, when the children weren't looking. Yesterday, when he'd been kissing her on the beach, she had suddenly sprung away from him when Freddie had come along. But they were married now, he'd wanted to say. Surely they were entitled to show each other some affection!

'That nice young man, Jack, asked if we wanted a table and I said yes.' She squeezed his arm lightly. 'I hope that's all right.'

'But they're still waiting for the new chef.'

'Exactly!' Melissa, who had been making a rather gratifying fuss of him after the ring-rescuing mission, gave him one of her melting looks which always reduced him to submission. 'I was talking to Jack when I went back for that medicine and he was telling me that they're a bit down on numbers this year.'

Hah! Maybe they ought to sort themselves out a bit then.

'They're desperate to make things work, so he's doing the cooking himself until the new chef arrives. If we can tell the manager that the food was good, it would really be a feather in Jack's cap, don't you think?'

She could be so sweet, his Melissa. Always thinking of everyone else, even when it was a boy she hardly knew.

So they'd gone to dinner, which was served on the patio overlooking the olive grove, and found that they were the only ones there apart from Emma, who kept telling the whole story of the ring over and over again. 'I don't know whether to tell Tom or not,' she was saying to Melissa. 'He's asleep again now, you know, otherwise I wouldn't have left him to come up here.' She gave a little simper. 'It's so nice to have someone to talk to.' Then she looked worried. 'Just as long as I'm not intruding.'

Don't worry about that, Winston only just stopped himself from saying. The kids were doing a great job of that without any help from anyone else. While the two women were nattering on – mainly about school stuff and someone called Gemma Balls – he finished eating (the stuffed vine leaves were surprisingly good) and slipped out towards the kitchen.

Jack was chopping up watermelon with a large knife as he came in. 'Everything all right, sir?' he asked.

Maybe it was time to put the room argument behind them. Just until the owner got back. 'Sure. Great food, by the way.'

The boy flushed with pleasure and then glanced at the watermelon. 'I'm afraid this is all there is for pudding. I ran out of time and there isn't anyone else to help.'

So he had to do all the prepping and washing up too? Winston was impressed. He couldn't see Freddie or Alice doing that. 'What happened to the French couple, the ones in the other cottage?'

'They ate earlier.'

Really? If they were here to spy on him, they'd have made sure they were here at the same time. For God's sake, he had to stop this paranoia stuff.

'Look, I was wondering,' he began. 'You mentioned some kind of club or disco when we arrived.' He felt in his pocket. 'The thing is that I'm concerned my stepdaughter might be a bit bored without anyone else of her own age. Any chance you might like to take her there this evening?'

Jack's eyes widened. 'I've got to finish up here first.'

'Sure, I understand that. We don't mind if she's out until midnight or so, just so long as you're with her.' He brought out a couple of notes and laid them casually on the side. 'This might help towards drinks. There's only one thing. Please don't tell her that I suggested it or she'll think I'm interfering.' Winston held his breath. 'Is that all right?'

'Well . . .' The boy looked as though he wanted to say something.

'Go on,' instructed Winston.

'I just wondered if you could do something for me, sir. I saw you working out this afternoon, at the top of the hill.'

Shit. His cover was blown. He'd been recognised. How bloody stupid he'd been.

'The thing is that Mum got this local chap in to do yoga classes every morning, but he's cancelled on us. She doesn't know that yet. I don't suppose you could run tomorrow's class for us, could you? Only we've already had a couple of bookings and I don't want to let anyone down.'

Winston liked this kid. He had initiative. 'That wasn't yoga I was doing. It was a general workout.'

Jack's face fell.

'But it so happens that I'm a trained yoga teacher too.'

'Really?'

The relief in his voice said it all.

'And you won't tell Mum?' He was flushing furiously now. 'She'd go mad if she thought I'd asked a guest to help out.'

'Hey. It's fine. It will be just between us. Both things.' He glanced at the notes still on the counter and held out his hand. 'Deal?'

The boy's handshake was firmer than he'd expected. 'Absolutely, sir, although I don't really need any money.'

'Please.' Winston was sure on that one. 'I insist.'

'Don't be late!' Melissa said again and again when Alice had finished dolling herself up. If he had a daughter, thought Winston, there was no way he'd let her go out dressed like that. Her skirt was more like a scarf tacked on to her knickers.

Melissa was turning to him worriedly. 'I'm still not sure we ought to let her go. She doesn't even know the boy.'

'*Mum!*' Alice scowled with that same condescending look and tone that she'd used on him earlier. The one that said she was in the right and everyone else was an idiot. How could his wife put up with it? 'I'm nearly fourteen. Stop fussing. Jack says he goes there every week.'

'Jack says! Jack says!' taunted Freddie.

'Piss off, twat-face!'

'Alice,' said Melissa mildly. 'That's not very nice.' Then she hugged her daughter. 'You look lovely. But please be careful.'

There was a knock on the door. Flushing, Alice ran to it. On the other side stood Jack. Winston had to admit that he scrubbed up well. He hardly recognised the boy who'd been chopping up watermelon a couple of hours ago. Instead of an old apron, he was now wearing a crisp white shirt and his hair was combed back neatly.

'I promise I'll look after her, sir,' said Jack, looking straight at him and then at Melissa.

Alice flushed again. 'See you later, Mum.'

No goodbye to him, noticed Winston. Still, it was wonderfully peaceful after she'd gone. Freddie was much better when his sister wasn't around, Winston noticed. He was quite happy playing on his phone.

Melissa was quiet too. Good quiet or bad quiet? It was difficult to tell. In fact, he was beginning to realise how little he knew about his new wife, especially since the children had arrived. She'd been . . . well, quite distant with him. Maybe what they needed was a quiet, romantic evening on their own. It was only ten o'clock, after all. Plenty of time for a walk along the beach.

'I don't want to leave Freddie,' frowned Melissa when he suggested it.

'But he's perfectly happy in his room with that new gadget of his,' he'd pointed out. 'It's not as though we'll be far away.'

Melissa had made an *I'm not sure* face. 'It's OK when he has his sister. I'd rather we stayed here in case he needs us.'

How would they ever learn to be independent? thought Winston crossly. But he could see that Melissa wasn't to be moved. So instead, they snuggled down and listened to the iPlayer, her head in his lap. It was rather cosy, really. Maybe, Winston told himself, this was what it was all about. Quiet, married bliss . . .

'Winston, Winston!'

Dimly he was aware of Melissa shaking him, her long dark hair brushing his face as she leaned over his side of the bed. He must have fallen asleep. 'Wake up. It's nearly two o'clock. And they're still not back. I'm really worried. Something must have happened to Alice.'

TRUE HONEYMOON STORY

'My first husband and I got locked in our bedroom on our first night and had to be rescued by the B&B owner.'

Author (first time round)

Chapter Twelve

ROSIE

Had they really been away for just three days? Incredible to think it was only Tuesday. So much had happened. So much that *shouldn't* have.

Rosie waited at the harbour, shivering slightly, not because of the breeze whipping across the water but because she really wasn't sure what was going to happen now.

If they hadn't gone away to the mainland, this would never have happened. Greco would have just carried on flirting in his easy manner and she'd have continued ignoring him and getting on with what she did best. Running the Villa Rosa. Making sure that everyone was happy. Trying to find new business in the recession (hopefully, the new direct flight path from the UK would now attract more custom). Keeping an eye on Jack. Not allowing herself the luxury of thinking too much about herself.

And now, just because she'd had a little break, she'd thrown caution to the wind and embarked on a relationship which not only couldn't work – they were so different! – but was bound to cause problems in their day-to-day lives.

Rosie could just see it now. The nudge nudge, wink winks at the taverna, where Greco would be bound to tell everyone about his conquest. The sly little pinches of her bottom when he passed her in the street. The melting down of professional distance which she'd worked so hard to maintain.

Why had she done it? Rosie asked herself, as she watched Greco stroll back towards her on the deck, carrying two cups of coffee. He was a simple fisherman, for heaven's sake, albeit a very sexy one.

Hadn't she learned her lesson before? A lesson which had been brought home – as if it needed to be – by the article on that man who had reminded her so much of Charlie. Rosie shivered again. Her one and only love seemed like another world away, now. Never again would she allow someone else to change her life like that. Somehow she had to extract herself from this mess.

'I was thinking,' said Greco, handing her a cup of coffee, deliberately brushing her hands (or so it seemed). 'It might be difficult when we get back, mightn't it?'

Her mouth went dry. 'What do you mean?'

Greco laughed. She rather liked the way he laughed; it was a deep, throaty love-of-life laugh with a flash of white teeth – beautifully straight, without any need for the braces of her own youth. Then he began to trace the outline of her face with his finger. 'You are an intelligent woman, Rosie. You know precisely what I mean.'

He swigged back his coffee and tossed the cup in a bin. Then, putting both his arms around her waist, he forced her to face him. 'We had something special in Athens but I'm no fool, Rosie. I know we were taken over. We were not in our own territory. I think we both did things we might not have dared to do at home.'

Both? Rosie felt a wave of embarrassment crawling over her. So Greco had his doubts too? How humiliating!

'You regret what happened then,' she said curtly, turning away.

Immediately, she felt his body close in on hers, behind, his arms wrapping around her. Pulling her in. It felt good. Warm. Reassuring. Her pulse quickened.

'I didn't say that, Rosie.'

She kept her eyes steadily on the horizon: a thin grey-blue line. Across the water somewhere was the island. A place she had learned to call home. Safety. Yet now, because of what she had done, it didn't feel quite so safe after all.

There was a loud hoot from the white funnels which made her jump; the boat had started. Within a few hours they would be back. 'It certainly sounds like that,' she replied, trying to keep her voice light.

He spun her round without warning. His face was so close to hers that she could smell the lemon cologne; observe the way his dark eyebrows joined together; drown in his deep blue eyes even though she fought to look away. 'I am simply giving you a chance to forget that any of this happened,' he said softly. 'I do not want you to think that you have committed yourself if you do not want to.'

His eyes were so tightly locked on hers that Rosie felt hypnotised, unable to move.

'I am aware that you are a mother first and foremost, but also a successful businesswoman in your own right.' He shrugged. 'You might not want to carry on with a simple fisherman.'

Weren't these the same words which had been pounding round her own head? Yet when *he* said them, they made her feel selfish and shallow. Yes – he had made the first move. But she could have said no.

'I've really enjoyed the last few days,' she said, blushing furiously. 'And besides, you're *not* a simple fisherman.'

It was true, despite what she'd told herself only a few minutes ago. Greco, she'd discovered over the years, was a great reader. In fact, this had been a contributing factor in the slow cementing of their relationship. He often borrowed her books and when he began to order his own through Amazon, would suggest one or two authors she had not come across before.

His taste had surprised her. Poetry. Short stories by a Canadian writer. A rather clever crime book, too, by an author whom she'd skipped over in the past. 'I like to read on my boat when the water is still,' Greco had told her, shrugging. 'It calms the mind and fools the fish.'

Right at this moment, she was beginning to feel fooled herself. So what if she had fallen for a fisherman with a past? Yes, he had a reputation, but that was when he had been younger. Now he seemed responsible. Mature. Loyal.

There had been plenty of admiring glances in his direction from women over the weekend in Athens, including some rather well-dressed ones. Yet Greco had, to his credit, failed to give them a second glance or even show that he was flattered.

She could, Rosie told herself, do a lot worse than throw her lot in with a solid, reliable man who also happened to press the right buttons in bed. Besides, she thought, glancing at an older woman sitting on deck with a small white dog for company, this could be her last chance.

'It's up to you.' Greco's hands were cradling her head, his eyes still locked on hers. 'You can forget this happened if you like and I swear on my mother's soul that I will never tell anyone. Or we can continue back home, regardless of the gossip that you and I will undoubtedly create.'

His eyes twinkled yet his voice was serious.

'What about Jack?' she said.

Greco gave another of his big shrugs. 'He is almost a man, Rosie. It will not be long before he goes to college and flies the nest.' He looked a little wistful for a moment. 'Besides, it might be good for the boy to have me around more. I would have liked a son like that. It is a shame his father died before his time.'

Rosie looked away. Conversation about Jack's father was never something she wanted to encourage, especially when it was founded on a lie. It made her feel uncomfortable. Yet Greco had a point when he said that Jack could do with a male figure. At fifteen, it was becoming even more important than when he was younger. Could this be a good thing, her and Greco? Not just for her but for her son too?

'We could see what happens,' she said, taking a deep breath.

Something flickered in Greco's eyes. 'See what happens?' he repeated. 'That sounds very modern to me.' He put a finger under her chin, tilting it up to him. 'Do you know why I haven't committed to anyone before? It is because I wanted to be certain.'

His voice dropped so that she had to strain to hear it over

the scream of the gulls. 'And I am certain with you, Rosie. But I need you to be sure of me.'

Her lips were so dry that she could barely reply. 'It's very soon,' she managed to say. 'I mean, all this has happened so fast. But I do care for you, Greco. And I would always be true to you.'

His eyes flickered again. 'That is all I ask.' Then he bent down and his lips met hers. Every bone in her body vibrated; and not just because her back was pressed against the ship railings. Sometimes, she told herself, you just had to take a risk . . .

Greco held her hand as they got off the boat and continued to do so as he waved his other hand in greeting at one of the local boys who had arranged to pick them up from the harbour.

The excited look on the boy's face as he took in the hand-holding was an indication of what was to come, thought Rosie with a rush of panic. He'd be on his mobile now within minutes, alerting the rest of the island. The English woman from the Villa Rosa had finally succumbed to the charms of Greco the rogue. All it had taken was a 'business trip' to Athens.

'So,' said Greco jauntily as the boy started the car up. 'How has it been during our absence?'

He spoke from the back with his hand on Rosie's knee, a gesture which the boy could see, from the way he kept grinning inanely in his rear mirror. 'Good. Very good, although we had some trouble at Andidavies last night.'

Rosie mentally tuned out. Andidavies was the local nightclub. There was always trouble there, usually involving bored kids or holidaymakers who had had too much to drink.

'It is to do with Jack,' added the driver casually.

Rosie started. 'What do you mean?'

He turned round briefly with a grin and then back again to take a sharp corner which sent his crucifix swinging from the mirror. 'Your boy took a girl there. But there was an incident with a motorbike.'

Rosie's mouth went dry. 'Are they all right?'

'I don't know the details, but . . .'

They were here now. Rosie scrambled out of the door almost before the car had stopped. Leaving Greco to sort out the cases, she tore up the path to reception. No one was there. Oh my God. She should never have allowed Jack to be on his own. Fifteen was too young. She'd been an irresponsible mother . . .

'Jack!' she called out, racing towards the pool. There was a plump blonde woman sitting there on a lounger.

'Are you looking for that boy at reception?' she said, leaning on one elbow and peering over her paperback. 'He's gone to the market to get some fresh fish for lunch.'

So at least he was safe. 'I heard there'd been an accident with a motorbike,' stammered Rosie.

'Not exactly an accident.' The woman looked excited. 'But he took a girl out on one of those scooter things, without telling her parents. Well, her mother. The father's actually her stepdad. They're staying here. And when they found out, they weren't too pleased.' Suddenly, she flushed. 'Whoops, here they come now.'

Rosie stared at the slim, extremely beautiful woman with long dark hair floating towards her. Straggling behind was a sulky-looking teenage girl and a younger boy with freckles.

But it was the man Rosie couldn't take her eyes off. A very tall, handsome man, possibly of West Indian extract. Bald. Rather like the man in the newspaper she'd seen in Athens, although of course that was impossible.

Wasn't it?

Numbly, she absorbed the intimate way he had his arm around the woman and their low, urgent conversation. As they approached, he glanced up at her, his eyes hardening.

Rosie stopped breathing.

Had he recognised her? Yes. No. Why should he? Sixteen years was a very long time. Then again, maybe she was mistaken. Lots of people looked like others, didn't they?

If it wasn't Charlie, this man *did* look very like the celebrity in the newspaper. Her head went into a spin as she desperately tried to recall the words from the headline. A honeymoon in the Maldives. Not Greece.

'May I help you?' asked Rosie, gathering herself and holding out her hand in a cool greeting. 'I'm Mrs Harrison. I run the Villa Rosa.'

The man's brows knitted. He did not look pleased. 'Jack's mother?'

She nodded, heart pounding.

'My name's Winston King.' He spoke in a quiet voice, although Rosie couldn't help noticing that the plump blonde guest on the lounger was listening intently. 'We need to talk.'

TRUE HONEYMOON STORY

'We went camping for our honeymoon but a storm blew the tent away. Best orgasm of my life.'

Lally, now divorced

Chapter Thirteen

EMMA

Winston? Winston King?

Emma hadn't intended to listen in to the conversation between her new friend's husband and this small, blonde woman with elfin features who had come running up the path from the taxi below.

Despite being curious she had forced herself to lie still, nose in her book, touching her ring every now and then to check it was still there.

But it had been impossible not to hear Melissa's good-looking husband.

'My name's Winston King,' he'd said. 'We need to talk.'

Of course! She hadn't recognised him from the school gates; she'd recognised him from the telly! How stupid had she been – although to be fair, he looked different in the flesh. Skinnier (they said telly made you look chunkier). And he wore sunglasses all the time here, which could make a person look quite different.

To think that she'd been within touching distance of the very celebrity who appeared on her telly every morning, encouraging her to do buttock squeezes while dishing out breakfast to the kids. *No flabby butts! Just great butts!* It was her mantra – and Mum's too.

Emma was so excited that it was all she could do not to jump up and tell this god how amazing he was and how she'd been trying, really hard, to follow his routine *and* to eat less. But it was so difficult, what with the kids leaving so much on their plates (such a waste to leave it) and not having enough time to do his 'Five A Day' exercises.

Mum had bought her Winston's *Get Fit for Summer* DVD in an effort to inspire her for the wedding, but there hadn't been time to use it. Instead, it had sat next to the telly, with a picture of Winston grinning at her encouragingly.

And now, here he was, standing only a few feet away from her! It was all she could do not to whip out her mobile and text Mum or Bernie from work.

But it wouldn't be right. People like him needed his privacy. Oh my God! So that's why Melissa had asked her not to tell anyone they were here. And maybe that's why her new friend hadn't divulged her surname when introducing herself. She'd been worried that Emma would do exactly what she'd just thought of doing – ringing everyone at home.

Well, of course she wouldn't. They might only be casual acquaintances, but she had more loyalty than that. Besides, she felt honoured to have been taken into Melissa's confidence. Emma glowed. It was almost like being 'one of them', although it couldn't be easy being famous and trying to live a normal life.

Quickly, she sneaked another look over her paperback at Winston. He was listening to the woman who, from what she was saying, was the villa's owner. Mrs Harrison. She didn't look old enough to be Jack's mum. Perhaps she was one of those lucky people who didn't look her age.

Regretfully Emma thought of the tired eye bags which had sprung up soon after Gawain's birth. Winston and Mrs Harrison were moving away now. Melissa was with them too. and their voices were rising. Oh dear. Emma hated arguments.

''Snot fair.' The sulky-looking teenage girl was stomping around the pool, pouting and kicking her feet in the water every now and then as though to make her point. 'We weren't that late. And it wasn't our fault the bike broke down.'

So that's what had happened! Emma had been aware of some kind of problem when she'd come out for breakfast earlier on. Melissa had been sitting quietly, toying with a bowl of fresh fruit. Her son was at the table too, but not the daughter. Then Winston had arrived and they'd hardly spoken to each other, and they both ignored Jack, who was serving. When they stood up to go, Melissa had given her the briefest of smiles.

'You know you weren't even meant to be on a bike,' the younger brother was saying now. 'It's against the rules. Mum always said so. Dad too. Ouch, don't splash me like that.'

'I'll do what I like.' The girl scowled. ''Sides, Dad isn't here, is he? Only that stupid bloke that Mum's married.'

The boy began kicking a pebble about on the ground. 'Winston's OK.'

'You just think that cos he plays football with you.' The girl was sitting on the edge of the pool, splashing the water angrily. 'Dirty suck-up.'

'No, I'm not!'

'Yes, you are!'

Uh-oh. They were having a real water fight now! Emma gasped as she got splashed in the face. Her book was soaked through too. Leaping off the lounger, she grabbed her towel to cover up (maybe a bikini had been a bit too ambitious) and moved to the other side of the pool.

It wasn't their fault, poor kids, she told herself. It wasn't easy when your parents split up. She knew that. In fact, Alice wasn't much younger than she had been when her dad had left. 'You've ruined my life,' she'd screamed at the time. She still believed it.

Winston and Melissa were walking back to the pool now, holding hands. The owner was nowhere to be seen. Had they sorted it out? She hoped so.

'What was all that noise about?' Winston was saying to the kids, looking from one to the other with a displeased look on his face.

'Nothing.' The boy glanced at his sister who, in turn, was sending him daggers. 'We were just mucking around.'

Winston was looking at her now. Emma wondered again how on earth she hadn't recognised him before. But you didn't expect to bump into someone like that on holiday, did you?

When someone was on television, you sort of assumed they had a different kind of life from yours.

'I hope these two haven't been bothering you?'

The girl winced. Emma's heart went out to her. He shouldn't talk like that, not when he wasn't her father. If she'd been that girl, she'd have been upset too. 'No, not at all.' As she spoke, she slipped the wet paperback under her towel. 'In fact, it's really nice to hear children having a bit of fun.'

She felt herself colouring up. 'I really miss my own kids. 'Course, they're a lot younger, but watching your two – I mean your wife's two – well, it shows me what it's going to be like when my Gawain and Willow are older.'

There was a low mutter from Winston's direction. It sounded something like 'Good luck'. That wasn't very fair. Melissa, she noticed, was shifting anxiously from one foot to the other. 'How's your husband doing?'

Instantly, Emma felt guilty. She should be worried about Tom, rather than someone else's private life. 'He's stopped being sick, thanks,' she said, suddenly aware that her towel had slipped and that her tummy was poking through. Quickly, she sat up straight and rearranged herself. 'Thanks very much for the medicine. It worked a treat.'

She didn't add that she'd slipped it into Tom's water without him knowing.

Melissa looked pleased. 'I got it from this alternative health shop just outside town. So is your husband going to be well enough to join us?'

Emma thought of Tom, whom she'd left sitting up in bed, next to the fan which the boy at reception had found for them.

'Actually, he's finding it a bit too hot.'

Melissa's eyebrows lifted.

'Yes, I know,' continued Emma hastily, feeling rather silly. 'Greece is . . . well, it's a hot place, but I don't think Tom realised quite how warm, if you see what I mean. But now he's come out in this funny little pink heat rash, so he's playing safe and staying inside.'

Melissa's eyes were wide with sympathy. 'Poor thing. I've got something for heat rash too, if you like.'

The girl rolled her eyes. 'Mum's got something for everything. She's a walking medicine kit.'

Winston visibly stiffened. 'There's no need to be rude to your mother.'

'I'm not. And it's none of your business anyway.'

'Alice,' murmured Melissa weakly.

Oh dear. This was getting awkward. Clutching her towel, Emma tried to get off her lounger as elegantly as possible without revealing any more. 'I think I'd better go and check on him,' she said quickly. 'Have a good afternoon. By the way, are you two doing the morning yoga?'

Winston looked awkward. 'I'm helping them out, actually. I, er, do a bit myself, and the instructor has let them down.'

He was really staring at her, as though wondering if she'd guessed who he was. Should she come clean and say that she wouldn't tell anyone? Maybe not.

'That's great.' Emma began to shuffle off. 'See you then. If not before. Bye!'

Walking back down to the cottage, Emma passed a woman selling shell necklaces from a basket with a baby sling round her neck.

'You want?'

Emma shook her head, hungrily taking in the baby. She reminded her of Willow at that age, deliciously plump and small. Almost edible! 'I've got two children at home,' she said, feeling an urgent need to tell this woman that she was a mother too.

But from the look on her face, she didn't understand. 'You want necklace?' she repeated, and somehow Emma found herself buying one, even though she didn't particularly want it, just because of the baby. Still, maybe Mum would like it.

When she got back, Emma noticed that the cottage next door had its front door open. That was a first. Glancing up, she saw a young woman sitting on the balcony with her face up to the sun. French, someone had said. Rather chic in those black shades. Emma gave her a little wave but the woman didn't respond, which made her feel a bit silly.

Some people liked to keep themselves to themselves, she supposed. Like Tom. To be honest, she'd felt pretty hurt this morning when her new husband had said he felt a bit better but didn't want to go out into the heat. *You* go, he had told her, so she had, but it wasn't the same. Honeymoons were meant to be for two people. Not one. Still, it wasn't his fault he was ill.

'Are you OK?' she said softly, putting her head round the door.

Tom was sitting against the pillow, eyes closed, headphones on and nodding as if in time to the silent tune. So he was well enough to listen to music! Emma felt a wave of irritation as she dropped a kiss on top of his head. He jumped.

'You startled me.'

'Sorry. There's no need to snap.'

'I'm not snapping.'

What had got into him? Maybe the heat was affecting him more than she'd realised. 'How's the rash?'

'Still there.' He was scratching.

'So you don't want to come outside then?'

'And make it worse?'

'No, but it doesn't seem much fun if you're going to stay here all day.'

'I can't help that, can I?'

It was as though someone had given her a different husband. She'd never known Tom to be like this before. 'Do you think you'll feel well enough to come up to the villa for dinner tonight?'

Languidly, Tom made to put his headphones on again. 'I don't know. I'll see.'

'Fine.' Emma heard the words snap out of her mouth. 'Then I might go for a walk on my own. OK?'

Crossly, she strode out of the cottage and down to the beach. This was weird! Usually she had so much to do that there wasn't time to think. There was always someone who wanted her.

But now, with her husband like this and the children far away, she just had herself. How often had she yearned for a bit of peace and quiet? But now she had it, she didn't know what to do with it. She felt useless.

As she gazed out at the sea, it seemed impossible that Willow and Gawain were so far away; that they weren't just round the corner at nursery or Mum's house. Seeing the baby just now had got her all upset again.

Unable to stop herself, she rang Mum's number. 'Just me. Is everything OK?'

'You on the phone again? If you keep calling, love, you won't give the kids a chance to settle. I told you before. They're fine. Gawain slept right through the night.'

Really? But he didn't do that for her. Instead of being pleased, Emma felt slightly resentful that her mum had succeeded in doing something she hadn't been able to.

'All I had to do was let him grizzle for a bit. Doesn't do to pander to their every need.'

'Can I talk to them?'

'Best not, love. They're both glued to this DVD. Bernie brought it over with some of her home-made flapjacks.'

That didn't sound good. Either the DVD or the sugary flapjacks.

'Tom any better?' Mum cut in.

Emma decided not to go into too much detail. It would only give Mum a chance to have another go at him. 'Getting there, thanks.' Swiftly, she glanced around to check no one was listening. 'By the way. You know Winston King, the bloke who does the morning exercises on telly?'

''Course I do. Why?'

It was so tempting to say he was here! Emma paused, her pulse quickening in her throat. 'I just wondered. Has he got married?'

'Funny you should say that! Bernie was jabbering on about it. Then it was in my paper. Turns out he's got hitched to one of the mums from school. He's going to live right near us, he is. Well, at the posh end anyway. Gone to the Maldives, according to the paper.' Her mother, who was always a sucker for celebrities, hardly paused for breath. 'Why do you ask?'

'I . . . I just wondered.'

'Well, you must have had a reason.'

The Maldives? Now it was beginning to make sense! They'd just have said that to get some privacy. But she, Emma Walker, was one of the few people who knew the truth. It gave her a superior glow inside. 'Look, Mum, I've got to go.' She crossed her fingers. 'Tom's calling for me. I'll ring tomorrow.' Turning off the phone, she strode back along the beach past the cottage where the French woman had been sunbathing.

Except that her neighbour wasn't doing that now. She was leaning nonchalantly against the balcony. Right next to her was the man.

Both totally naked.

As if oblivious to her presence, the bloke was spinning the woman round so her back was facing him. Then she got down on all fours as if about to do one of Winston's exercises. The man remained standing. Emma tried to look away but she couldn't. Oh my God! Surely they couldn't really be doing *that*, right here, in full view of everyone else?

Giving a little gasp, she hurried on, although she couldn't stop herself from looking back. The two bodies had merged as one now; it was like an acrobatic show for adults only. Emma's eyes widened. How on earth did the bloke manage *that*, while still standing up? Was that really what everyone else did when they made love?

A vision of Tom on top of her, quietly pumping away with a little gasp at the end, came into her head. Which was more normal? That display on the balcony or the blink-and-you'll-miss-it in their own bed?

Sex wasn't the kind of thing she talked about to friends, although she suspected Bernie might have a few views.

'You'll never guess,' she began excitedly as she went back

into the room. But Tom was asleep again, headphones on the sheet next to him, humming merrily away into the silence.

Emma sat down on the edge of the bed, feeling empty inside. This was their honeymoon! It should be Tom and her making wild, passionate love. Not some French couple next door.

'Are you all right, Tom?' she said, gently.

Nothing. Just a loud snore.

Emma stood up and looked down on her new husband. Tom had never, as her mother had declared on more than one occasion, been much of a looker. But from this angle, with his mouth open and the snores and that red rash, he seemed particularly unattractive.

Of course, looks weren't everything. But there was a great deal to be said for giving someone attention. At home, most of that was lavished on the children.

But now they weren't here.

And apart from the kids, Emma was beginning to wonder what else she and Tom had in common. Maybe losing her ring had been a horrible omen . . .

MISSING MUM

Sixty per cent of brides on honeymoon ring their mothers at least once. Ten per cent of grooms do the same.

Survey from a bridal magazine

Chapter Fourteen

WINSTON

'I think she's recognised us,' said Winston, worriedly massaging oil into his new wife's shoulders. The action felt reassuringly intimate; at least, it would have done, if Alice wasn't shooting him filthy looks as though he had no right to touch her mother like that.

'Who?' asked Melissa, leaning back into his chest, eyes shut; unaware of her daughter's hostile expression.

'Emma. The plump woman.'

'Winston!' She opened her eyes in shock. 'You shouldn't say things like that.'

'Yeah, Winston. You shouldn't.' Alice scowled. 'Some people can't help being podgy. It's their DNA. Everyone's different. Of all people, you ought to understand that.'

Was she alluding to his skin colour? Hah! If so, she'd soon learn that it would take more than that to rattle him. 'The point is,' he continued, ignoring Alice, 'that I think your new friend knows who we are. She's been giving me some really funny looks.'

Melissa moved away and, seemingly aware now of her daughter's disapproval, adjusted her top self-consciously. Having those kids here made him feel as though he and their mother were a pair of teenagers, trying not to get caught. 'It's all right. I had a word with her. Don't look so worried, I'm sure she won't tell anyone. She's really sweet.'

He almost choked. 'You told her who I was?'

'Not exactly. I just said I'd rather she didn't mention we were here to anyone. She lives in Corrywood. Such a coincidence!'

This was getting worse. Of course the woman would have put two and two together. She was probably ringing up *OK* or *Hello!* or *Charisma* magazine right now.

Swiftly, Winston tried to think damage limitation. If Emma had blown their cover, there was nothing he could do about it. After all, it was Melissa who had been worried about publicity when he'd proposed. She'd wanted the children to have a normal life, or so she said.

For himself, Winston was used to the fact there was a price to be paid for fame. Yet at the back of his mind, all the time, there was always the fear that the rat pack might dig up the one thing he didn't want anyone else to know. Including Melissa.

Meanwhile, he was still mad about last night. 'Haven't you got something else to do?' he said, glaring at Alice, who was watching them like a Victorian chaperone.

'Winston!' protested Melissa, frowning. 'She's entitled to sunbathe, isn't she?'

'It's not as though there's anything else to do,' scowled Alice. 'When Dad used to take us away, there was always a proper teenage club. Not some hole like this place.'

'Then don't bother staying,' he retorted.

'Winston!'

Melissa's furious face forced him to mutter an apology. Maybe he *had* been a bit sharp, but they were all a bit twitchy still after last night. When Melissa had woken him to say that Alice and Jack still weren't back, he'd reluctantly gone out to look for them. It had been pitch-black out there; if he hadn't had his special head torch, he might never have found them. In fact, they were only a mile or so down the lane, walking back up to the hotel and pushing the kid's bike, which had broken down.

Frankly, he was just relieved he'd found them safe and sound. But Melissa didn't view it that way. Instead of seeing the bright side (the kids were in one piece, weren't they?), she was almost hysterical when they'd all trooped back. 'You know you're not allowed on a motorbike,' she'd wept. 'Your father and I always made that quite clear.'

Then she'd turned to him. 'Aren't you going to say anything?'

So he'd torn a strip off the boy, because that's what Melissa seemed to expect, although deep down he felt quite sorry for him. He seemed quite nice and genuinely remorseful for having got his stepdaughter back late. After all, a snapped cable could happen to anyone.

Winston had said as much to Melissa when they'd finally got to bed, but she'd accused him of not understanding because he didn't have children. Somehow it all escalated into a bit of a row which, thankfully, had ended with some pretty passionate make-up sex.

Today – amazingly – Melissa seemed to have forgotten that it was her daughter who had broken the motorbike rule. Instead, she was giving poor old Jack the cold shoulder, which wasn't very fair. She'd also (despite the make-up sex) gone back to being cool with him too, as though this had somehow all been his fault.

Well, excuse me for being here on my own honeymoon, he almost wanted to say. Couldn't Melissa see that the little monkey was twisting her round her little finger?

'Why didn't you tell Emma that you weren't going to do the yoga any more after what Jack did?' asked Melissa, referring to Winston's all-too-hasty promise last night in an attempt to appease his wife.

Winston shrugged, watching her move away from him to the sun chair next to her daughter, as though trying to put as much distance as possible between them. He hadn't realised until the honeymoon just how stubborn his new wife could be. 'Because I'm still thinking about it. I know you're cross with the boy, but he didn't mean any harm.'

Alice shot him a reluctantly grateful look.

'And besides, your new friend is looking forward to the class,' he added. 'It would be a shame to disappoint her.'

Melissa nodded thoughtfully. 'I was thinking exactly the same myself. And maybe you *are* right about Jack. He seems quite a sweet lad.'

That was more like his wife; the one he had met three months ago. A real softie, although every now and then he glimpsed a flash of defiance underneath.

Just like Nick.

'In fact,' said Winston, leaping to his feet, 'I thought I'd go and find Jack now. Sort out a few things.'

Alice looked alarmed.

'About the yoga. I need to check my emails too, and the reception's better up there. See you later, OK?'

It was so good to get some time on his own. Every time he spoke now, he was waiting for his stepdaughter to jump down his throat. Melissa was different too when her kids were around – not so affectionate with him, only interested in her children. She also, like her daughter, kept referring to previous holidays, stirring him into jealousy. 'Remember the Seychelles where we went scuba diving with Daddy?' she'd said to Freddie only that morning, forgetting – or so it appeared – that her previous husband had behaved appallingly. In fact, her tone had been decidedly wistful.

Not for the first time, Winston began to feel a tremor of misgiving. Had he jumped in here a bit too soon? When Melissa had first told him about her kids, he'd wanted to look after them too, make up for the pain they'd been through.

What he hadn't realised was that they still seemed to love their father. Instead, he, Winston, who hadn't done anything wrong, was the enemy.

Now, however, he had a plan. It was quite simple really. Befriend the enemy. Fool them into thinking that you're onside.

In other words, do something that would make Alice like him. All he needed to do was find . . . ah. There she was.

'Mrs Harrison?'

The small, slim woman scattering corn to the chickens swivelled round. There was something about her heart-shaped face, framed with wispy bits of blond hair, which seemed vaguely familiar.

Then again, maybe it was just that common need to

'recognise' strangers in order to feel secure when you were away from home. He and his men had felt the same during those long six-month tours. Sometimes, the more you looked at someone, the more you thought you knew them – even when you'd never clapped eyes on them before.

Now Winston forced himself to smile; to put on what his assistant Poppy called his camera face. 'I just wanted to say that I'm worried we got off on the wrong foot about your son and my stepdaughter. Jack seems a very nice boy.'

She was staring at him, hands on hips, waiting defensively.

'He *is*,' she retorted coolly.

'I wouldn't want him to get into trouble,' he added.

'Why should he be?' Turning her back on him, she scattered more corn so that the chickens' squawks almost drowned their conversation. 'He didn't do anything wrong. All the kids have motorbikes out here. It's how they get around. If your stepdaughter isn't allowed on one, it's up to her to say so. My son can't be held responsible.'

So defensive about her son! Just like Melissa over her kids. What was it about parents and children? His own father had never stood up for him and he wouldn't have expected it.

Winston shuffled uneasily from one foot to the other, wondering how to phrase the next bit. 'There's something else too. It was very good of you to give up your room for us. I'm concerned that we've put you out.'

Her tone was softer. Friendlier. 'You don't have to worry about that. Sounded like it was our mistake.'

Despite her conciliatory words, Mrs Harrison was eyeing him strangely. She'd definitely recognised him. He could see that. Might as well come clean. 'We appreciate the anonymity,' he said crisply. 'Thanks. It's important to my wife that our honeymoon is as private as possible.'

Mrs Harrison raised an eyebrow in a rather imperious manner. She was possibly a little younger than he was, yet there was something about her which made him feel she had the edge. She seemed to know it too.

'All honeymoons should be private.'

Winston found himself beginning to stutter, something he hadn't done since school. 'All I'm saying is that if any . . . if anyone should ring, asking if we are here, I'd be grateful if you could put them off.'

Another scornful look. 'Mr King, I can assure you that I never reveal the identity of any of my guests, even if they're famous.' She flashed a short smile at him, leaving Winston feeling even more confused. Had she recognised him? Or was she just talking generally when she'd mentioned the 'famous' bit? It was hard to tell.

'Now,' she added with a sharp look, 'if there's nothing else I can do for you, I'm afraid I have work to do.'

And with that, she turned and left.

There was something about this ballsy woman that both infuriated him and yet – if he hadn't been married – was curiously attractive. Was there a *Mr* Harrison? Surely it couldn't be the Greek oik she was always hanging around with. (For some reason that he couldn't put his finger on, he really didn't like the look of the bloke.)

Winston considered this as he wandered on through the ground floor of the villa, admiring the bold watercolours on the walls, the blue and orange rugs on the stone floor and the huge white pitchers, bursting with pink flowers that he couldn't put a name to. No, Mrs Rosie Harrison was probably one of those self-assured English divorcees, who had come over here to make a new life and take a lover. What was wrong with that?

'Hi there.' Entering the kitchen with its huge gleaming range and copper saucepans hanging from the ceiling, he smiled reassuringly at the boy, who was prepping the veg. Nice movement, observed Winston. The kid could certainly use a knife.

'It's OK. Don't look so worried. I've come to apologise.'

The boy frowned. He looked a bit like a startled hedgehog with his hair ruffled up like that. When was it, wondered Winston, that young boys lost that rather sweet expression? Thirteen? Fourteen? It depended on what life had thrown at them, he supposed. For him it had been much younger. Maybe that explained why he was as he was. Independent but needy, as Nick used to say.

'About the bike business,' he continued, pulling up a chair next to the kid. 'Reckon I was a bit tough on you last night. My wife too. I want to make it clear we don't hold you responsible.'

The boy's face cleared. 'Really?'

'Sure.' Winston tried to sound casual. 'Tell me, do you like my stepdaughter, Jack?'

The poor kid was blushing as red as the tomatoes on the wooden board in front of him.

Winston gave him a reassuring pat on the back. 'It's natural if you do.' For a minute, he thought back over some of the girlfriends he'd had as a young man. There had definitely been one or two whom he would have liked to have seen more of, but it wasn't easy when you did his kind of job.

'The thing is,' he went on, 'my stepdaughter is a bit bored. So's her brother. I was wondering if you could get them involved with your mates.'

'Sure.' The kid was flushing even more.

'I don't mean take them out on bikes. Just for some beach volleyball or whatever it is you do round here.'

Jack's eyebrows were raised, reminding him of his mother's steady gaze just now. 'We do a lot of fishing. And football.'

Fishing? Great. That would really get the kids out of his hair for a good two or three hours. With any luck, he might persuade Melissa it was all right if Freddie was there as well. 'Fantastic. Now all I need you to do is suggest it to Alice. It would look better if it came from you.' He delved in his pocket and brought out a couple of notes.

The kid's face tightened. 'I felt bad about you giving me money last time, sir. I don't take money for friendship.'

Instantly, Winston realised he'd stepped out of line. 'Sorry. I just thought we might make some kind of regular arrangement. A boy like you could probably do with some pocket money.'

'It's why I help out here.'

Good honest labour. Mrs Harrison had brought him up well. 'Sure. Sorry.' Now it was Winston's turn to feel like a gauche teenager. 'So, I'll leave it up to you, shall I? Oh, and by the way, I'd appreciate it if you didn't let Alice know that the day out suggestion came from me.'

The boy's eyes narrowed. 'You want me to lie?'

'Of course not. But that yoga instructor . . .'

Winston was fishing here but his instinct told him he was right.

'He didn't really let you down, did he, Jack? You forgot to book him and you'll be in trouble if you don't find a replacement.'

Jack nodded reluctantly. Just as he'd thought. It was the kind of thing Winston might have done himself at that age. 'So we have a deal then? I'll still do your yoga, provided you entertain my stepkids.'

The boy shrugged in agreement, giving him a look that made Winston feel rather dirty. Wishing he could have put it a bit better, he turned away just as his mobile rang.

Unknown.

Winston's antennae, fine-tuned through years of survival, prickled. He knew it. The blonde bride had alerted the press! It would be a journalist, wanting to ask how his 'secret honeymoon' was going.

'Winston King?'

The voice down the line was vaguely familiar. 'Marvyn here. Melissa's husband. Her *first* husband.'

This was said as though a first husband was the only real kind.

Winston stiffened, conscious that Jack was probably listening behind him. 'Marvyn.' He tried to sound as though it was perfectly natural for the ex-husband of his wife to call during their honeymoon. 'What can I do for you?'

'I've just been talking to my daughter and I'd like to know what the fuck you think you're up to?'

Swiftly Winston walked out of the kitchen, past Mrs

Harrison, and waited until he had some privacy. 'What are you talking about?'

'My daughter said that you allowed her to go out with some kid from the village on a motorbike. How bloody irresponsible is that?'

Little minx! So Alice thought she could cause trouble, did she? 'Actually she—'

Marvyn cut in furiously. 'Don't make excuses, Winston. You might think you've got a new family but they're mine. Don't ever forget it.' There was a nasty laugh at the other end. 'Melissa's still in love with me, you know. You'll find that out one day. You might think you're a big shot, Winston King. But if I were you, I'd watch your back.'

Then the line went dead. The bastard had rung off.

TRUE HONEYMOON STORY

'I didn't see my husband during our honeymoon. It was 1962 and he was watching the World Cup on telly.'

Margaret, still a 'football widow'

Chapter Fifteen

ROSIE

He still hadn't recognised her! Somehow, Rosie thought he would have done by now. It was the day after she'd got back from Athens; time enough surely for him to have observed her more fully.

To have twigged.

She might be a Rosie rather than a Rosemary; her hair was shorter; she'd lost her West Country accent; and she was skinnier (ironically) after Jack than she had been before – but she wasn't *that* different, was she?

Besides, there was no doubt now that Winston really was Charlie. After that shock encounter outside the villa, she'd raced to the office and shakily looked up the photocopy of the passport that Jack had made when the Kings had arrived (at least her son had managed to do that right).

And there it was. Charles Winston King. Clearly he was using his middle name for some reason. Just in case there was any doubt, his date of birth matched. She'd remembered it because it was the same as her mother's: 17 March.

Get real, she tried to tell herself while making up the beds in the annexe. He was twenty-three when you knew him. How many other girls do you think he's had since then? Is it surprising he doesn't remember you?

In fact, she reprimanded herself fiercely while tucking in the crisp cotton sheet corners the way Cara had taught her, she ought to count her lucky stars that he *hadn't*.

Just think of the trouble it would cause! Her skin began to crawl with the implications. If Winston knew Jack was his child, he might try and get custody; might attempt to take her son back to England with him. Oh God. What a thought. Maybe she ought to see a lawyer. But there was only one on the island, and although Rosie had never needed to see him, she wasn't sure how discreet he was. Discretion wasn't considered a great virtue around here, where gossip was an integral part of day-to-day living. True, she could go to the mainland for legal advice, but that would mean leaving everyone again so soon after getting back; it was both impractical and risky. Winston might work out the relationship himself while she was away.

Anyway, she couldn't abandon Jack again. Look at what had happened during just three days! She was lucky that the girl's mother hadn't caused more trouble about that motorbike. Jack knew he wasn't allowed to date guests; it was why she'd had to get rid of a former waiter when he'd made off with a married woman who was staying with her husband. (They'd actually got married themselves later on, although that was another story.)

What a mess! Rosie smoothed down the white broderie anglaise duvet cover – what an irony that Winston and his bride were in *her* bed – and glanced in the mirror at her tousled blonde layers. She couldn't help smiling wistfully at the memory of Charlie running his hands through her (then) long hair.

'I'll never find anyone else like you,' he'd said . . . Rosie shook herself. Yeah, right. That's why he hadn't answered her letter all those years ago. He'd abandoned his responsibilities. Still, it was his loss. He was the one who had missed out on having a child.

Dusting down the dressing table, Rosie's heart glowed as she thought of her son. That was true love, she reassured herself. Not the love between a man and a woman, which was as fickle as the sea: strong one minute and retreating the next.

No. A love between parent and child was always there, even if you pretended to ignore it. Even if you had a father like hers who renounced you for getting pregnant at seventeen.

Rosie began to fold Winston's wife's black satin nightie to put on the scented lavender pillow case. How galling that now, here she was, looking after the wife of her son's father. Talk about complicated!

There was only one person who would understand. Rosie glanced at her watch. Gemma was sometimes free at this time. Glancing round the room once more, in case she'd missed something – unlikely, since Cara had taught her the art of perfection – Rosie made her way to the little room at the back of the annexe where she was sleeping in the emergency put-you-up bed.

This wasn't the first time she'd had to give up her room for a guest. Business was tough at the moment, and you had to take whatever custom you could get. All the hoteliers agreed about that round here. She was lucky that both cottages were occupied: next week, only one was booked.

Sitting down on her bed, Rosie switched on her laptop. Yes! Gemma was online.

At times, Rosie couldn't help feeling slightly jealous of her old friend. Gemma had done things the *right* way round. She had finished her A-levels, got a degree, trained as a teacher, found the man of her dreams, and now had three lively children, with a fourth due in the spring.

She was desperately hoping for a girl, although, as Rosie kept trying to tell her, there was a lot to be said for teenage boys.

Skype was ringing now – a real lifeline when you lived so far away – and Gemma's pretty face was coming into view. 'Rosie! I was just thinking about you.'

'Really?' Rosie felt a thrill going through her. The only time she ever missed the UK was when she heard her friend's voice. It was almost like being round the corner from her again.

'How are your new guests getting on? The ones who saw your notice on our school board. Stunning looking, aren't they?'

Rosie's mouth went dry.

'Rumour has it,' continued Gemma excitedly, her face

beaming from the screen, 'that Melissa is on her honeymoon and that she's married this really famous fitness guru who's on television all the time.'

Sweating, Rosie glanced at the door to check it was closed. 'Gemma, I'm going to tell you something that you simply can't tell anyone else, OK?'

Her friend's smile wavered. 'What? You're scaring me.'

'You . . . you remember Charlie.'

There was a second's pause, during which Rosie wondered if the sound had failed. 'Yes. Of course I do.'

'It's *him*. The groom.'

There was a small gasp. 'But it can't be. He's called Winston.' There was a little wobble in her voice. 'What was Charlie's surname again?'

Rosie felt her nails dig into her palm. 'King. According to his passport, he's using his middle name. I don't know why, but it's him all right.'

She could see from Gemma's expression that her friend was still trying to take this in. 'Has he recognised you?'

'No. At least, I don't think so.'

'And are you going to tell him?'

'No way.' Rosie felt a bit sick. Maybe she should have kept this to herself. Even though she trusted Gemma more than anyone else she knew, she was still taking a risk. 'No one must ever know I had his baby. This is so awful, Gem. What am I going to do?'

'Poor you.' Gemma's sympathetic voice brought a lump to her throat. 'Is it difficult seeing him with someone else? I mean, I know it's been years but . . .'

Her voice trailed away. She understood, thought Rosie gratefully. Understood that you never forgot your first love, whatever else happened afterwards – especially if it had led to a child. Rosie froze. What was that noise? It sounded like someone was stifling a sneeze outside the door. Jumping up, she flung it open. No one. Was she imagining noises on top of everything else?

'I feel so guilty,' she said returning to the screen. She lowered her voice. 'I mean, Jack thinks his dad is dead!' She put her head in her hands briefly as the enormity of it all began to sink in. 'What am I going to do? Do I tell him? And if I do, what if Charlie – or Winston – denies it? It would break Jack's heart to be rejected.'

Gemma let out a little sigh. At the same time, her face began to blur. That was Skype for you. The reception could be very unpredictable around here. 'I don't know, Rosie. I wouldn't want to say one way or the other. It's a decision only you can make.'

'What would *you* do?' Rosie asked suddenly.

'Not sure. Maybe . . .' There was the sound of yelling in the background. 'Sorry, I've got to go. Thought it was too good to be true. Little one has just woken up.'

Instantly Rosie felt guilty for having hogged the conversation. 'How are *you* doing?'

'Fine, thanks. Just getting over the sickness bit.'

How chirpy she sounded! Briefly, Rosie reflected on her own pregnancy, when Cara had taken her in out of the goodness of her heart, clucking around her in a language she didn't understand but which had sounded reassuringly comforting. Until then, the world had seemed so scary, so uncertain. But with Cara's help and, she had to say, her own initiative, she'd managed to carve out a life for herself and her son.

I'll be damned, Rosie told herself sternly, if Charlie, or Winston, or whatever he calls himself now, is going to mess it up for me.

'I'll call later in the week,' Gemma sang out. 'Oh, I almost forgot. Mum mentioned that your dad had to have an op. Nothing serious apparently – he's out of hospital now – but I thought you ought to know. Chat soon. Bye!'

Dad had had an op? What for? Rosie felt a flutter of unease, followed by hurt. Dad had only written once since she'd left; even though she'd sent him the odd letter and snapshot of Jack now and then. How was it possible, in today's day and age, for a parent to disown you for having a child out of wedlock, as he'd put it?

If Mum had been alive, she'd have understood.

Sometimes, Rosie toyed with the idea of taking Jack back to the South-West to see his grandad. Maybe then he'd change his mind when he saw what a lovely grandson he had.

Then again, who was she kidding? Her father was a selfish man who had made her mum's life a misery when she'd been alive. At least, according to Gemma's mum.

Her head now reeling with everything that had gone on, Rosie got up and looked out of the window. By the pool, she could see Emma Walker talking to Winston's bride. Her heart did a little flip. So that was the kind of woman who had finally captured Charlie's heart. Not surprising really. Melissa King was gorgeous.

Even so, two children was quite something to take on. Winston would have his hands full. How ironic that his own son was here and he didn't even know it . . .

Heavens! Rosie let out a gasp as she suddenly found herself being swung around in the air, strong dark hands round her waist. How long had Greco been there for? And had that been him before? 'You can't just sneak in like that,' she said, noticing that the door, which she'd shut, was now ajar.

He gave her a broad grin as his deep blue eyes bore down on her. 'I like to take you by surprise. It is romantic, yes?'

Yes. No. She wasn't sure. To be honest, ever since they'd got back, Rosie hadn't felt comfortable about the new footing they now found themselves on. Everyone seemed to be watching them, including Jack.

'We must be discreet,' she said, steadying herself.

Greco looked disappointed. 'You have changed your mind about me?'

'No.' Rosie glanced out of the window again. Winston was by the pool now, sitting on the edge of his new wife's chair, his arm casually slung around her with an air of ownership that made her chest tighten. 'I just haven't had a chance to talk to Jack yet, that's all.'

Greco put his head on one side quizzically. 'About me or his father?'

Rosie froze. 'What do you mean?'

'Come on, Rosie. I know.'

'You were listening through the door,' she said furiously. 'You had no right. That was a private conversation I was having.'

There was a conciliatory shrug. 'You should have learned by now that there is no such thing as a private conversation on the island.'

That was true enough. Frantically, Rosie tried to recall exactly what she'd said to Gemma.

'So Jack's dad isn't really dead at all,' mused Greco thoughtfully.

Blast. Had she really said that?

'So who could it be?'

Clearly he hadn't heard everything, then.

'Let's think. It can't be the pale Englishman with the travel sickness. It might be the Frenchman who insists on making love to his mistress on the veranda, even though they pretend to be on honeymoon.' Greco was stroking his chin. 'But my money is on the big man who is running your yoga class.'

What?

'You didn't know?' Greco clearly found this rather amusing. 'I gather your son has arranged it.' He put a finger under Rosie's chin, tilting it up so she had to look straight into his eyes. She felt her heart lurch. He'd got her, dammit. What was it about chemistry that threw two such unlikely people together?

'It seems, Rosie, that there is quite a lot going on at the moment that certain people don't know about. But do not worry. Your secret is safe with me.'

Then he gave her a little look, suddenly surprisingly vulnerable. 'I presume this old boyfriend of yours did not come here to find you.'

Rosie spluttered. 'No. It's . . . it's just one of those awful coincidences.'

Greco smiled wryly. 'There is no such thing as coincidence in life. These things happen for a reason.' He glanced out of the window at Winston, who was poised, ready to dive into the pool. He looked pretty good, Rosie couldn't help thinking. Really fit.

'Perhaps it is the universe giving you a little nudge, Rosie. Maybe now you have to face up to some tough choices.' He patted her bottom lightly: an action which Rosie didn't know if she liked or not. 'Including your decision about me, my lovely English rose.'

TRUE HONEYMOON STORY

'We ran out of coins for the electric meter in our B&B on honeymoon. We cuddled up instead. Still do.'
Pam, still cuddling but with more cash now

Chapter Sixteen

EMMA

Emma woke with a start, trying to remember which day of the week it was. Wednesday? Thursday? When she was at home, she knew exactly where she was, right down to the minute. Everything was organised: it *had* to be when you had two small children, Tom to get up for work, and a little job yourself.

Emma was so used to her family's frenetic routine that she never stopped to think how shattered she was. But right now, as she stretched out in the heat next to Tom, it all felt like another world.

Willow and Gawain were her life. Yet after four whole nights away from them, she was actually beginning to get more accustomed to their absence.

There was no one here yelling 'Mum!' Or wanting her to wipe their bottom or give them something to eat or hold their hand or mop their tears. In one sense it made her feel redundant. In another, she felt strangely liberated. For once, she had time to do things for herself . . .

Then she remembered. Early-morning yoga! Her heartbeat quickening with excitement, Emma slipped out of bed, leaving Tom snoring for England, mouth open like a goldfish and his hair all sweaty. That was his own fault. Last night, he'd insisted on the air conditioning being turned off because it was 'too noisy'.

Squeezing into her pink shorts – the only thing she had that was suitable for yoga – Emma searched for her flip-flops, which had got kicked under the bed. Maybe, if Tom was still asleep when she got back, she'd hire one of those bicycles she'd seen outside the villa.

She cast another look at her new husband. Now the sickness had stopped, there was nothing wrong with him – just a reluctance to get out into the sun because it brought him out in a rash. 'You go ahead and enjoy yourself, love,' he'd said to her yesterday in a weak voice, which, she was surprised to find, deeply irritated her.

Emma thought of the French couple in the cottage next door, who'd been 'making out' (as Bernie would have put it) so loudly and obviously. So far Tom hadn't even bothered to kiss her properly! It was understandable when he'd been sick, but he was so much better now. And it was, after all, their honeymoon . . .

A picture of the Frenchman next door doing unmentionable things with his legs swam into her mind, making her feel surprisingly moist below. Had she been missing out on something for all these years?

'Reach up to the sun!'

Emma felt a hand lightly touching her shoulder; gently adjusting it a little way to the right instead of the left. That felt so much better. He was good, really good.

If only she could tell Mum right now that she was actually doing yoga on the beach with Winston King and that he'd touched her bare arm to ease her into the correct position! But she'd made a promise, hadn't she?

'Now down.'

Keeping her eyes fixed on his body – you could see those muscles moving like fish! – Emma placed both hands on the sand as instructed, desperately trying not to wobble. There were some small brown children going by, including a little girl she'd seen the other day with her hair braided with pink and yellow beads. It gave her a pang to think of Willow at home without her. Unable to help it, Emma gave her a big smile. The little girl gave a shy smile back. What a poppet! Enchanted, Emma tried to wave without falling over.

Glancing to one side, she could see Melissa doing the moves in a serene, smooth way. There was the French couple too, which made her blush – hopefully they hadn't seen her prying! – and a couple of others whom she didn't recognise.

On the edge of the group was Jack – just the kind of boy that she'd like Gawain to grow into one day.

'Salute the sun!' Winston was now commanding. Emma found her body stretching out in an almost cat-like pose. It seemed much easier to do this on the beach in the warmth than at home on the kitchen floor with Gawain tugging her hand or Willow crawling all over her.

'Thank you.' Winston was sitting on the ground cross-legged wearing long white shorts, with his hands clasped together as though in prayer.

Melissa was doing the same next to him, her eyes closed and hair swished back in a glossy ponytail. She didn't look as though she was wearing any make-up at all, yet she still seemed as lovely as ever.

Was the class over now? Emma didn't like to move until everyone got up. She'd just have to sit here, pretending to meditate like some of the others. Up on the slope, she could hear the sound of ping-pong and a shout, 'That's *my* point!'

'No, it's not, you moron!'

Melissa opened her eyes, rolled them as though to say 'Kids!' and then gave Emma a wink before closing them again.

It was no good. She was going to giggle. Serious occasions always did this to her: she'd almost got going at her own wedding and had stopped purely through concentrating hard on the altar flowers.

But there was no stopping the silly laugh which was escaping through her mouth. Winston was giving her a disapproving glare. Oh dear. She'd really blotted her copybook now.

'Sorry,' chirped Melissa as they all drifted apart on the sand amidst the 'Thank yous' and 'See you tomorrows'. 'That was my fault for setting you off.'

Emma couldn't believe how nice she was. The wife of someone famous like Winston was actually apologising to her! Not, of course, that Melissa knew that *she* knew.

'No, it was me. I'm afraid your husband is going to think

I'm not taking the yoga seriously. But Mum and I always try to do his – I mean our – exercises at home.'

She looked down at her body ruefully. 'Not that it's done much good.'

'Nonsense!' Melissa's voice had that slightly artificial ring to it that people had when they weren't quite telling the truth. 'I think you're great as you are.'

'Give me back my ball!'

'It's my turn to serve!'

'No, it's not!'

Melissa laughed. 'There we go again! Better go and sort those two out.' She gave Emma a conspiratorial smile. 'Winston thinks I'm too soft on them, don't you, darling?' Then she lowered her voice. 'But they've been through so much with the divorce that I don't like to be too hard. And now they've got a new life to get used to . . .'

As her voice tailed away, Emma squirmed with embarrassment on behalf of her new friend. Should Melissa really say so much to someone she didn't know – and in front of her new husband too?

There was a cough from Jack. He was addressing Melissa, rather than her. 'Er, I was wondering if your children would like to come into town with me. There's an afternoon gig in the square and one of my friends is playing.'

He was twisting his hands rather nervously as he spoke. Maybe he fancied the girl. They were quite young, of course, but then again, she'd met Tom at fifteen . . .

To Emma's surprise, Melissa greeted the idea with enthusiasm. 'I'll check with them, but I'm sure they'd love to come.'

Jack looked pleased. 'Does anyone want to rent a bike?' he went on. 'They're on special offer at the moment.'

'Great exercise,' said Winston, looking at her pointedly.

Emma flushed. She'd give anything to look like Melissa.

'I can find you something right now, if you like,' added the boy, keenly.

Emma followed Jack up to the villa and the bike rack behind. What else did she have to do?

Looking back quickly, she observed Winston taking his bride into his arms and giving her a long kiss.

A pang went through her. When had Tom last snogged her like that? Even after the wedding, he had just given her a quick peck with his dry mouth.

Perhaps, she resolved, it was time for *her* to take the initiative when she returned from this bike ride.

Wow! It had been years since she'd done this! Emma stood on the top of the hill catching her breath. She'd cycled halfway up, which wasn't bad. Not bad at all. And now she had this fantastic view as a reward, along with her aching legs, which had to mean that she'd done some good. No pain, no gain. Taking off the helmet, which Jack had insisted she wore, Emma felt the light breeze play with her hair. That was better. Still, she'd better put it on again before making her way down. In fact, she couldn't wait to tell Tom how she'd cycled for a good hour now, and not just on the flat, either. Mum would be impressed too, when she made her evening phone call.

'Lovely view, isn't it?'

Emma whipped round to see a very tall, lanky, olive-skinned man walking towards her. Instantly she made to move on.

'Hey, it's OK!' There was a broad grin with perfect white teeth. 'I've seen you before. You are staying with my friend Rosie at her villa.'

A brown hand was thrust out in front of her to shake. 'They call me Greco.' His grip was strong. 'I have lived on this beautiful island all my life. If there is anything you want to know, then I am your man.'

Emma took in this vision of a Greek god in front of her and then looked away, shocked at herself.

What was getting into her? Just because Tom wasn't . . . well, wasn't doing what a man should be doing on his honeymoon, didn't mean she had to eye up every other male around her.

Trying to gather her wits, Rosie realised that she recognised Greco now; he was the man whom she'd seen holding hands

166

with Rosie the other evening. It had surprised her at the time. Somehow the two didn't quite go together; the Englishwoman was more conventional, Emma suspected. She might have lived out here for years, but she still served proper loose tea in teapots with floral china cups and saucers. That didn't seem to go with this unshaven man with the red frayed shorts and rough brown hands that were gesticulating wildly.

'Anywhere you want to go, I take you! You are on your honeymoon, yes?'

Was there anything that these people didn't know?

'Then I will whisk you and your new husband on special trip to magic island.'

Emma was intrigued. 'Magic island?'

Another broad white grin. 'You have not heard? We have a very special island near our own, that is hard to reach unless you know the waters.' Greco's teeth were brilliantly white, she noticed, and he had such a nice smile. 'Luckily I am the man. We will make a trip, yes? Maybe with the other couple who have got married.'

It was certainly an idea, but only if she could persuade Tom. 'I'll let you know,' she promised, beginning to move her bike. She didn't want to look rude, but she'd been gone for long enough. It was time to get back and check on Tom.

'I will see you soon, then.'

He stood at the top of the hill, waving at her as she went down, almost as though they were long-lost friends. The locals really were a bit pushy. Yet the man had a charm about him. He had looked at her in what was, yes, an admiring way, without seeming to notice her lumpy thighs under the shorts or her red, puffy face. Of course, these men had a reputation for being Romeos, but even so, it was still quite flattering.

'Tom,' she said breathlessly, wheeling the bike back to the cottage. Fantastic! He was actually sitting up in bed. 'You'll never guess—'

'Shh.' He was waving her away, his ear next to the small transistor radio that had been supplied in the room. 'I've just managed to tune in to the game.'

Man U again! Tom might have lived down south for years but his parents had come from the north and he was inordinately proud of it. Still, there was a time and a place. It was as though, now they were married, he couldn't be bothered to try so hard.

'If you're busy,' she said coolly, 'I'll see you later. I'm going up to the villa to get some lunch and then I've signed up for an art class.'

'Great.' He wasn't listening to her, she could tell. Just like one of the kids. 'See you.'

TRUE HONEYMOON STORY

'Our car broke down during our honeymoon drive from Yorkshire to Bath. It was 1952 and we couldn't afford to get it repaired so we got the bus back.'

Tina, still happily married with three grandchildren

Chapter Seventeen

WINSTON

His plan was working! Jack had taken both Alice and Freddie off to a local gig after lunch. Amazingly, Melissa had unwittingly gone along with it, declaring it would be good for the children to have some fun. Watching Jack and Alice together, Winston had felt an unexpected twinge of nostalgia. How well he could remember being in love at their age. And how lucky he was to have found it again. He turned to Melissa. 'How about,' he murmured, squeezing his bride's bottom lightly, 'spending the afternoon in bed?'

Melissa gave a throaty giggle. He loved it when she did that. Sometimes she seemed too young and giddy to be a mother. 'What if they come back early and find us?'

That was just the kind of thing that Alice might do, which was why he'd slipped her a handful of euro notes and told her to 'enjoy herself'. With any luck, it might buy him a bit more time.

'They'll be out for a while,' he said confidently, taking her hand. 'Come on.'

An hour later, they were lying on their sides, facing the window that looked out onto the sea. Melissa was pressed against his back, her arms around him. 'It's fine,' she murmured reassuringly. 'This kind of thing happens.'

Winston stiffened, but not in the right parts. Her sympathy made it worse. Sure, he knew that men were, at times, unable to . . . well, do what a man was meant to do on a honeymoon. It wasn't as though they hadn't already, as the Victorians might have put it, consummated their marriage.

But in the last day or so, there had been something about the way that his stepdaughter glared at him that had put him off making love to her mother. He wanted to, of course he did. But the message didn't get across to the bits that mattered.

Winston heaved himself onto his elbows, looking round the room. This place didn't help. It would have been all right if they'd had one of the cottages – they would have had privacy then – but it was difficult losing yourself in passion when you were in the owner's bedroom with all her paraphernalia around them. It was rather like being a teenager again and making love in places that you shouldn't.

'Did you see Mrs Harrison with that Greek man?' Melissa asked, cuddling up to him. 'I wouldn't have put her with a man like that. He seems a bit, well, rough and ready for her. Nice cheekbones, though.'

'Maybe they're not married,' he remarked. 'She strikes me as a divorcee with a lover.'

Melissa pretended to look affronted. 'Thanks. That was me until last week.'

'Ouch!' He winced as she began to tickle him. It was the one thing he couldn't cope with. Stop! he wanted to gasp but she wouldn't listen. So then he began to tickle *her* until she gave in and they both lay back, laughing like children. That was better, he thought. That was more like him in pre-Nick days when, like all the other Royal Marines, they went in for stupid tricks and tomfoolery in order to block out the horrors.

But after Nick, he hadn't been able to do any of that.

'Emma's a pretty woman, isn't she?' continued Melissa. Her hand was tracing his body now. Nice. But it still didn't achieve what they were both hoping it might, dammit. 'She's got gorgeous eyes, but I'm dying to tell her that she ought to use brown mascara and not black.'

Winston kissed the top of his bride's head. 'She needs to lose at least a stone,' he said firmly. He glanced at the wall on his left, which had a large framed poster of an English country lane in autumn, complete with gold and red leaves.

Maybe Mrs Harrison missed home. Still, the grass was always greener on the other side, wasn't it?

'Maybe.' Melissa was nodding. 'But sometimes people suit being plump.' She moved away, stretching herself out and arching her back against the bed. God, she was beautiful. Something began to stir. If he didn't think about it, it might be all right.

'You do think the children will be OK, don't you?' She was lying on one side, looking at him through her mane of dark hair. Winston began to run his hands through it.

'Definitely.' He was burying his head in her hair now, working his fingers down her neck: something, he was discovering, that she really liked.

'You don't think I was irresponsible letting Alice go with Jack after last time?' Melissa's voice sounded uncertain. 'She was so desperate to hang out with him that I couldn't say no.' She smiled sweetly. 'I remember that stage myself when I was her age.'

Winston's head was moving down her body. 'Isn't that why we sent Freddie with them?' he asked huskily. 'To make sure they behaved themselves.'

God. She smelt wonderful. Yes. It was definitely beginning to happen now. His breath began to quicken, in tune to Melissa's. Any minute now and . . .

DING, DING, DING, DING. DING, DING, DING, DING.

'My phone!' squealed Melissa, her hand shooting out to the handset by the bed. She kept it on night and day, just in case the kids needed her – even when they were in the same house. Silently Winston groaned.

'Hello?' Melissa's voice was edged with a panic he had grown to recognise. It usually meant nothing. Maybe some homework that had been left behind. Or the pressing need to be dropped off somewhere or collected. Sometimes it was Marvyn declaring he couldn't have the kids after all. But that was at home. What did they want now? Hadn't he paid both Jack and Alice enough euros to keep them both quiet for a bit? Winston turned away, feeling his body subside. The moment had really passed.

'It's for you.' Melissa handed the phone over. 'Your agent. She's been trying to get hold of you but your phone has been off.'

Yes, Winston almost said, because it's our honeymoon and I don't want to be disturbed.

Reluctantly, he took the handset, eased his legs out of the bed and padded towards the window overlooking the sea. He could concentrate that way, without being aware of Melissa watching him. Life always worked better when it was compartmentalised. If nothing else, his work had taught him that.

'Winston!'

Tara, a savvy woman he'd hired for her networking contacts and reputation rather than her crisp bedside manner, was wearing her no-nonsense voice. 'I wouldn't have called, darling, but this one is urgent.'

There was a fishing boat on the water, he could see, bobbing closer and closer to shore. Some people had such simple lives. Maybe he should have taken that path himself.

'Darling, someone's spilled the beans, I'm afraid. I've had a phone call from *Charisma* magazine. They've got wind of your little Greek hideaway and wanted a quote.'

Winston slammed his hand against the window pane in anger. *Charisma* had just been voted the top weekly glossy celebrity magazine. So far, all their articles about him had been gushing with admiration, but Winston was very aware that the press was a fickle beast. It was, as his agent kept reminding him, why he had to keep them sweet.

'Don't worry, sweetie. I didn't give anything away. In fact, I've promised them an exclusive when you get back, providing they don't send anyone out there.'

Really? Winston's gaze was riveted on the fishing boat as it drew closer. Any minute now, and some bloody journalist would be leaping out, complete with photographer.

'There is something else, though.' Tara's voice had something in it that he'd never heard before; a flicker of apprehension. Tara didn't do apprehension. She dished it out.

'What?' Winston hadn't taken his eyes off the boat. It was a trick he'd been taught years ago. When in a crisis, focus on something that makes you feel calm. For some reason, this simple fisherman – not a photographer at all, as it turned out – made him feel exactly that. There was something about his easy manner, the way he slung his catch over his back and walked up the beach, that made Winston feel the world was a simpler and more manageable place after all.

'Have you got Internet access in that place?' Tara's crisp voice sliced down the phone.

'Every now and then. It's patchy.'

The fisherman was grinning now. Holding up his catch with pride as though he was a caveman returning with his kill. He was calling out to someone. Winston's eyes narrowed. It was Mrs Harrison. She was coming down to meet him. Of course! It was the Greek that he and Melissa had just been discussing.

Bloody hell. That was some kiss: more on the Greek's part than hers, from what he could see. Mrs Harrison, who had pulled away first, seemed to be looking around to see if anyone had noticed.

Winston turned from the window, embarrassed. Then he stopped. She was looking up at him. How awful. She thought he was spying! Mortified, he walked back towards Melissa, who was sitting up in bed, her long dark hair strewn over her breasts.

'Winston?' Tara was shrilling down the line. 'Are you still there?'

'Sure.' What was wrong with him? Normally he was far more on the ball than this. It was this place, that's what it was. And the people around him.

'You might want to check out the *Globe* this weekend.'

Her voice definitely had an edge to it now.

'Why?'

'They're running a piece on you, apparently.' Tara's tone

was dangerously light. 'Nothing to worry about. You know what these journalists are like. Goes with the business. Must go, darling. I've got another call coming in. Have a great honeymoon.'

She was gone. Almost immediately the phone rang again. Melissa snatched it off him. 'Alice. Are you all right? No, I'm not fussing. All right. Have a lovely time.' She turned to him, her eyes dancing. 'The children are fine.' Then she grabbed his hand. 'Shall we go for a swim? Maybe we could try some skinny dipping in that little cove we found, before they get back?'

He loved it when she was carefree like this. Once more, Winston felt an overwhelming urge to protect her and make up for her miserable first marriage.

'Was everything all right?' she asked as they made their way down the wooden staircase. 'With your agent, I mean?'

Anyone else might have asked this sooner, but actually Winston was glad she hadn't. It helped him to block out the rest of the world from his head, including this wretched newspaper piece.

An hour later, Winston walked smugly back up to the villa, arm in arm with Melissa; their hair wet and their bodies drying in the late afternoon sun.

'I've got sand inside me,' giggled his wife as she leaned her head against his bare chest.

Winston was light-headed with relief. So he'd been right. It *had* been the room that had put him off, with those posters of the countryside and the blue and red Junior Gymkhana rosettes on the mirror, suggesting that the owner used to ride as a child.

'Mum!'

Winston's heart sank as two figures flew towards them. Alice, as usual, was in the lead. 'Where have you been? We've been looking all over the villa for you.'

Crossly, she took in her mother's flushed appearance and her bikini top with its right-hand strap falling loose on one side. His stepdaughter knew what they'd been doing, Winston realised. And she didn't like it. Not one little bit.

'Where were you?' she repeated angrily.

Melissa was flushing and stammering. 'We . . . we just went for a walk, didn't we, Winston?'

He eyeballed the girl. 'Sure. Did you all have a good time?'

She shrugged. 'It was all right until we ran out of money.'

The little so-and-so was looking right at him. What was she trying to do? Blackmail him for more?

'Didn't I give you enough?' asked Melissa, worried.

So his wife had stumped up too!

'No, but Winston did.' Alice was hanging on to her mother tightly, to establish clear ownership. 'Didn't you, Winston? You gave me quite a lot, just as long as Freddie and I gave you some peace for the afternoon.'

Little cow!

'Those weren't my exact words,' he began, but Melissa gave him a disappointed look and moved away.

'Mum,' puffed Freddie, running up. 'I'm bored. Alice and Jack ignored me all afternoon.'

'Didn't!'

'Did!'

'Didn't!'

Didn't those two ever stop?

'I just wanted us to have some time on our own,' he whispered, brushing Melissa's cheek, acutely aware that the girl was taking in every word.

His wife glared. 'You paid them to give us some "peace"!' When she put it that way, it didn't sound great. 'How could you?' Then her eyes hardened. 'Please tell me it wasn't your idea that Jack took them out for the afternoon.'

Winston hated lies. But sometimes they were necessary. 'Of course not. Look, I've got to go and check my emails. I'll see you for dinner in an hour, shall I?'

Quickly he headed back to the room, grabbed his iPad and went down to the terrace below where, if he was lucky, the Wi-Fi would kick in. Yes. He was in luck.

'Had a good day?' Annoyed at the interruption, he looked up at Mrs Harrison. Not for the first time, he was struck by her piercing blue-green eyes. There was something about them that reminded him of someone.

'Fine.' He looked down at his iPad again. 'I've just got to catch up with some work.'

'Of course.' She ran her fingers through her short blonde hair. 'I also wanted to thank you for running the yoga session. It's very good of you. A couple of guests from another taverna have joined up too, so it's great publicity. I'm grateful.'

Please go away, he wanted to say. 'It's a pleasure,' he heard himself saying instead.

'My son tells me that you work out every morning.' He could feel her looking at the screen while he scrolled down. 'A bit of a hobby, is it?'

Was she having him on or was it a genuine question? Perhaps she honestly didn't know that he was *the* Winston King. After all, he wasn't on Greek television, as far as he knew. 'Sort of.'

Surely any fool could tell he didn't want company, but she wouldn't take the hint. 'Would you like a coffee?'

'No, thanks.' Winston's eye was drawn to the words on the *Globe* site. His skin began to crawl as he started to read.

EXCLUSIVE SERIES, STARTING AT THE
WEEKEND

TWENTY THINGS YOU DIDN'T KNOW ABOUT
WINSTON KING!

THE REAL TRUTH ABOUT BRITAIN'S FAVOURITE
FITNESS GURU!

HOW WINSTON WOOED MY WIFE, BY HER
FORMER HUSBAND.

WHAT WINSTON'S LIFE WAS *REALLY* LIKE IN
THE MARINES.

WHY I'M HANDING IN MY NOTICE –
BY POPPY, WINSTON'S RIGHT-HAND WOMAN

DON'T MISS THE NEWS THAT EVERYONE'S
TALKING ABOUT!

TRUE HONEYMOON STORY

'Our honeymoon loo didn't have a lock on it. At eighteen I found that really humiliating.'

Sandra, now married for sixty-three years

Chapter Eighteen

ROSIE

Rosie had long ago made it a rule not to tune in to guests' conversations. The Villa Rosa, Cara used to tell her, needed to be a place where people could relax. But even so, she hadn't been able to stop herself from glancing at the iPad screen that Winston was reading so intently, with that worried crease on his forehead: 'Twenty Things You Didn't Know About Winston King!'

The sentence might have an exclamation mark, but in Rosie's head, it was a very big question. Could one of those twenty things have anything to do with her? she wondered with a shiver.

She'd already glimpsed the first at the top of the 'teaser', which gave a flavour of what was to come.

> *Winston's real name is Charles, but his agent persuaded him to use his middle name because it was more distinctive – and because 'Winston's Workout' had a better ring to it!*

So that explained it. She could hardly criticise him. After all, hadn't she been a Rosemary at school? It wasn't until she had left home and her pregnancy had begun to show that she'd decided to become Mrs Rosie Harrison (the surname had been her mother's maiden name). It was a new start. How ironic that Winston had done the same.

Uncertainly, Rosie had glanced again at the screen, but it was difficult to see more without looking obviously nosy. Trembling, she headed back into the kitchen on pretence of checking the new cook had got everything under control. But her mind was not so much on Yannis (a rather good-looking man with a handsome aquiline nose who reminded her of Greco), as on the letter she had sent Winston all those years ago.

'Write to him,' Gemma had urged when the second test – just to make sure – was positive. Her sweet face had shone with the conviction that the rest of the world was as decent as she was. 'I'm sure that if you did, he'd come back and marry you.'

Marry her! The idea of getting married at seventeen had seemed unreal, yet at the same time, what else could she do? She was pregnant, and she loved Charlie with an ache that was like a transparent hole in her chest. Rosie felt sick and excited and terrified all at the same time.

So she did write. In fact, she could remember the words as clearly as if they were in front of her right now on the scrubbed pine kitchen table in Greece.

> *Dear Charlie,*
>
> *I've got something really difficult to tell you. I'd much rather talk face to face, but I don't know where you've gone, so I'm hoping that if I send this to your base, you will get it before too long. There's no easy way of saying this . . .*

Her pen had trembled here, but dear Gemma, with a comforting squeeze of the hand, had helped her find the next paragraph.

> *I'm pregnant. And I'm scared. I need you here with your strong arms around me, telling me it's going to be all right. Dad is going to go absolutely mad when he finds out. He wants me to go to university and I want to go too. But I can't get rid of your baby, Charlie. I just can't.*

She'd stopped here for a little cry against Gemma's shoulder. Both girls had discussed this endlessly and reached the same conclusion. Gemma had said she couldn't have had an abortion either; not when it came to it.

If I don't hear anything back from you, I'll presume you don't want anything to do with me. But I know you're not like that. I know you'll do the decent thing.

She'd crossed that last line out. It had seemed, as she'd explained to Gemma, too forceful. If Charlie was the decent man she'd thought, he wouldn't need any prompting.

And if he wasn't, she didn't want anything to do with him.

Six weeks later, there was still no sign of a letter in reply. There was nothing else for it. Even now, Rosie could hardly bear to remember the details: only the stark facts. Eventually, she'd had to summon up courage and tell Dad. There had been a furious argument and, despite Gemma's tears, Rosie had packed her bags and left.

The rest was history.

'Mum! I prepared the vine leaves exactly as Yannis told me but he's having a go at me for not doing it right.'

Jack's newly gruff, almost-grown-up voice brought Rosie sharply back to the present. She glanced at the rows of plates with the vine leaves and the tomato salad carefully placed in the middle, ready to be rolled up into the Villa Rosa's signature starter dish.

They seemed quite passable to her. Yet when Jack had pleaded to work at the villa and get paid for it, she'd decided he had to take his place in the pecking order. As the kitchen assistant-cum-general run-around boy, he had to take criticism – even when it wasn't fair.

'Yannis is in charge of the kitchen, Jack. I'm sorry but that's how it is. You can learn from him. He's good.'

He was, too. He also happened to be Greco's cousin, but then again, wasn't everyone related around here? Including one of the guests and her own son . . .

Rosie shivered. Supposing Jack found out? This was her

worst nightmare. Back in the early days, it had seemed easier to pretend she was a young widow. This, of course, had led to several sympathetic but inquisitive questions and before she knew it, Rosie had found herself spinning a story about a tragic motorbike accident in the UK, when she was only two months pregnant.

Over the years, the tale had become so vivid and real in her head that when Jack had become old enough to ride a bike himself, she had been quite distressed.

'I don't want to lose you in the same way as your father,' she'd declared, realising, as she did so, how some people got their lives in a real old muddle thanks to lying.

'I'll be careful, Mum,' he'd insisted. 'But I can't be the odd one out.'

She could see that. All the kids had these little mopeds which didn't, after all, go that fast.

Now, looking across the kitchen at Jack and Yannis working side by side, rolling up the vine leaves (they seemed to have resolved their differences), Rosie couldn't help wondering what her life and her son's would have been like if Charlie, or Winston as she should probably think of him now, had bothered to respond to her letter.

Her son certainly wouldn't be living a life on a Greek island with mopeds, working in a kitchen to earn pocket money. He'd have been at a good school, like the one where Gemma and her husband taught, perhaps, near London. She would be married to Charlie/Winston and they'd have had at least another child. Maybe two.

The image was so real that Rosie almost had to grab the edge of the table to steady herself. She'd always wanted a daughter, but another son would have been just as wonderful. At times, her heart ached for Jack as an only child. Hadn't she sworn as a teenager that her own children would have the brother or sister that she herself had always craved?

Grabbing one of the kitchen knives from the block, Rosie sliced through a watermelon with an anger that wasn't like her at all. Both Yannis and Jack stared as she proceeded to chop it up furiously in the way that Cara had taught her.

'What's got into you, Mum?' asked Jack, raising his right eyebrow. Rosie started. Her son had always done that all his life: raise his right eyebrow without lifting the other. It was something she'd never been able to do herself. But in the last couple of days, she'd seen someone else do exactly the same thing.

Winston.

'Nothing,' she said crisply, arranging the slices into a fan shape. 'Nothing at all.'

Blast. The phone. Normally she'd have left it to the receptionist, but she'd given Anna extended time off to visit her sick mother on the mainland, insisting that Jack could help during the school holidays.

'I'll go,' offered her son, clearly eager to do something that didn't involve vine leaves or melon.

Rosie nodded, glad to be left with her thoughts. Winston's arrival had shaken her to the core, and now she had to put up with him mooning over that tall, dark, pretty woman who was so hopeless at dealing with her own kids. As if on cue, the girl – Alice, wasn't it? – walked past, looking through the kitchen window, clearly searching for Jack.

Rosie felt a tremor of apprehension. This girl might only be thirteen but she acted much older. Maybe she ought to have a word with Jack and tell him to be careful. Girls nowadays could be so forward.

Then she stopped, appalled at the irony. Was that what Winston had thought? Had he considered her forward because she had so foolishly given herself to him? Was that why he hadn't respected her enough to come back and do the decent thing?

Reaching for the corkscrew, Rosie opened a bottle of red and took a deep slug. Yannis was watching but she didn't care. Normally she never had a drink until the guests were settled with a meal in front of them. But the events of the last few days had knocked her rules for six.

Jack was coming back through the door now. He had a

bounce in his step, she noticed, and a slightly awkward air about him. 'Everything all right?' she enquired.

He nodded. 'Sure.'

'Who was on the phone?'

Jack looked as though he'd forgotten that he'd gone out to get it in the first place. 'Someone for Winston.'

The headline from the *Globe* leaped into her head. 'Who?'

'Didn't say.' Jack was buttoning up his shirt, which seemed to have come undone during his brief absence. 'Just wanted to speak to him.'

Rosie experienced a pang of alarm. 'And what did you say?'

Jack flushed. 'Alice was in reception and she said Winston had gone back to the room with her mother. So the woman at the other end said she'd ring back.'

Alice had found Jack then, which explained why he was looking so red and flustered. 'I've told you before. You can't give out details about guests without their permission.'

Jack's face was shining with indignation. 'That's not fair. I didn't tell them anything.'

Rosie began to slice another watermelon even though it wasn't needed. 'Yes, you did. You confirmed he was here.' She lowered her voice. 'Apparently he's some keep-fit star in the UK.'

Jack shrugged. 'I know, Alice told me, but so what? He might be a bigwig over there, but he's hardly royalty. These people don't know what it's like to live real lives, like us, do they?'

At times, her son astounded her. He really was an old soul, as Cara used to say. Rosie would give anything for Cara to be with her right now. How she missed her wise advice. Still, that was the wonderful thing about this part of the world. Instead of ending up in an old people's home, as so many did in the UK, your own family looked after you out here. Cara was being treated like a queen, according to her letters, by her extended family just outside Athens.

'You're right,' she said slowly, laying down the watermelon

knife. There was no point, she added to herself, in complicating things by telling Jack the truth. He would be hurt by Winston's betrayal and he'd be upset by her lies as a teenager. Kids could be so judgmental.

As for the phone call, if it was a journalist – and something made her think it might be – then there was nothing she could do about it. That was Winston's problem. Not hers.

Rosie began to lay the tables outside on the terrace, ready for dinner. Perhaps, she thought, placing the pretty green and pink salad bowls out on the crisp cream tablecloth, it was time for Winston to get his comeuppance. Indeed, the thought of her old flame getting his just deserts was surprisingly agreeable.

Just as long as it didn't affect her and Jack.

Dinner went well that night, mainly thanks to Emma. Rosie loved it when her guests began to visibly relax after a few days. Cara used to say it was part of the villa's magic, and she was right. Her heart was really beginning to warm to this pretty, unpretentious, plump blonde who had had just a bit too much to drink and was making them all roar with laughter.

'So there we were in WH Smith and Gawain – he's my four-year-old who never keeps still, bless him – was rushing round and I was trying to keep up with him as usual.'

There was an 'I remember those days' murmur from Melissa who was sitting, Rosie observed with a pang, on her husband's knee. That had been *her* place, sixteen years ago . . .

Emma took another slug of wine and giggled. 'Then I called out after him. I said "*Will* you hold my hand?" in a bit of a cross voice because, to be honest, I'd had enough.'

Melissa nodded enthusiastically. Winston's smile, Rosie noticed with interest, looked decidedly forced.

Emma gave another little giggle. It was clear that the punch-line was to follow. 'So this voice said, "Hold your hand? Very well. If you insist!"' Emma beamed around the table. 'It was one of the staff. He was pretending that I was talking to him,

186

you see, to make me feel better about yelling at my son! And he even pretended to take my hand!'

Melissa laughed delightedly but Winston definitely didn't get it. Rosie could, however. Jack had been a little monkey when he'd learned to walk, always running here and there. The difference was that on the island, there was always someone to look after someone else's child. No one got upset when a child played up in a shop. It was considered normal behaviour.

'I do not see you as a woman who shouts at her children,' observed Yannis, who was perched on the edge of the patio, smoking a cigarette.

Rosie always encouraged her staff to join the guests after cooking. It was something that Cara had taught her. Even so, she'd have to have a word with Yannis about the smoking later on. It was sometimes hard for the locals to understand that the British didn't always care for the habit at table (or near it), even though dinner had finished.

'I'm not.' Emma blushed. Her burned pinkness had faded now; in its place, she'd developed a rather lovely sun-kissed look. Her fuller figure seemed more attractive in the floaty blue waistless dress she was wearing. In fact, she looked every inch the lovely bride – except that her husband still wasn't with her. He'd gone to bed early, Emma had explained, rather too quickly. Still feeling a bit under the weather.

Did Yannis realise she was married? Rosie felt a catch of alarm in her throat. Her new chef certainly seemed rather interested in her guest, judging from the way his brown almond-shaped eyes were continually fixed on her.

'Sometimes kids make you do things you shouldn't,' Emma explained, as Yannis passed her the carafe of rosé. She hesitated. 'I cut down on my drinking after the kids.'

Yannis gave a wolfish grin. 'But they're not here now.' He was pouring it for her. 'Just one more won't hurt.'

The new Mrs King had had too much to drink too: you could tell that from the way she was babbling on and from the high colour in her cheeks. 'The other month, my two were having an awful argument in the car on the way to school so I pulled in to sort it out. We were all yelling at each other, so much that a man came down his drive to find out what the noise was about.'

Winston frowned. 'Really? You were *all* yelling?'

He gave his bride a disappointed look and Rosie felt a quiet thrill of satisfaction.

'It's not easy shtaying calm when you have kids,' said Emma, who was beginning to slur her words. Oh dear, thought Rosie. Perhaps she ought to have intervened earlier before Emma had had another top-up. Still, her guests were grown-ups; not children . . .

'By the way, Rosie, I'm loving the art class, I really am. I mean, I'm no good, but it's so nice to do something for myshelf for a change.'

Rosie buzzed with the compliment. The art class had been something she'd wanted to get off the ground for a long time. Then an Italian watercolourist had moved into town and Rosie had persuaded her to give some lessons. It all helped to make the Villa Rosa a little different.

'I mean, I mish my kids, I really do. But I'd forgotten whash it's like to be me again, without them.'

'Isn't that sweet!' Melissa was grabbing Emma's hands in maternal solidarity. 'I must say, I am rather enjoying having mine here. I hate being away from them, don't I, Winston? But it won't be long, Em, until you're back home with them.'

Her new husband's lips tightened. Interesting! It wasn't the first time Rosie had suspected that he wasn't that keen on having his stepchildren on honeymoon with them.

'D'you want to see shome pictures of my two from the wedding?'

Emma was passing round her phone now and there were various 'ahhs', even from the French couple, who'd been unable to keep their hands off each other, both below and above the table.

'He's very cute,' gushed Melissa, passing the phone over.

Rosie gazed at Gawain in his pageboy outfit and blond

curls. He was, too. In fact, he reminded her of Jack at that age. So winsome. So sweet. So fatherless.

Suddenly she wanted them all to leave. Jumping up, she began to clear the table, gesticulating to Yannis that he could give a hand. Jack had disappeared, even though he was meant to be on duty. Was he with Alice, who had also disappeared, leaving her brother to play with one of the ginger cats, scouring the patio for leftovers? Too late, she realised she should have kept her eye on him.

'Let me take this,' she said, reaching over for Melissa's plate and then Winston's. As she did so, his hand went up to help. Their skin touched and she almost fell over with the heat that surged through her.

At the same time, she felt a pair of arms around her waist. 'So, you are still here?'

Greco's body was behind her, claiming possession and attracting curious looks from around the table. Rosie blushed. She'd already warned him that they mustn't be intimate in front of the guests. It didn't look professional.

But Greco had seen her hand brush Winston's. She was pretty sure of that from the way his eyes were shooting daggers. Rosie's mind went back to the Skype conversation with Gemma earlier when Greco had overheard too much for comfort.

'You are on your honeymoon, yes?'

Rosie froze as Greco addressed Winston directly across the table.

Winston gave a curt nod.

Don't mention that he is famous, prayed Rosie, trying to remember exactly what she had told Gemma when Greco had been on the other side of the door. That had been confidential.

'Rosie here, she tell me . . .'

No. No.

'She tell me that some people, they would like to go on a fishing trip.'

Phew! Rosie almost audibly exhaled with relief.

Greco was leaning against the patio wall now, his arm

firmly around her shoulder in case there should be any remaining doubt about their relationship. Embarrassed, she pretended to pick one of the purple flowers growing in between the bricks. 'We do not have long left,' continued Greco meaningfully, looking round at them all.

There was a nod from all but the French couple, who were staying another week.

Greco leaped up and clapped his hands high in the air, as though he was a performer rather than a fisherman. He had, Rosie was forced to admit, real presence with that aristocratic-looking hooked nose and olive skin. He was also wearing a crisp new white cotton shirt that suited him. 'Then we go on Saturday night, yes? We fish by the light of the moon.' He winked at Rosie. 'Very romantic, I think.'

Melissa was swaying slightly. 'What about my children?' she was saying. 'Can they go too?'

Greco was nodding, probably totting up the extra euros in his head, thought Rosie. 'Why not?'

Winston's face almost made her laugh. He was muttering something as he went past. It sounded like 'Great'.

'I want them to come,' Melissa was saying, tugging at his shirt.

So! They were beginning to have marital disagreements already! Rosie felt another quiet thrill of satisfaction.

'You like him.' Greco jerked his head towards Winston as the couple made their way across the cobbled stones towards Rosie's old room. His upper lip curled in a slight snarl. 'If I am not mistaken, you are still in love with him.'

Rosie looked around sharply to see if anyone was listening. Only the French couple – who had started pawing each other again. Everyone else had gone, including Yannis. 'Don't be ridiculous. I knew him a long time ago. That was all.'

Greco gave her a searching look. 'Do not play games with me, Rosie. I heard you on the phone, remember? That man Winston, he is Jack's father.'

She gasped at his indiscretion. 'You mustn't say that out loud. Do you hear me?'

'I am surprised the idiot has not recognised you.' He ran his right index finger slowly against her cheek. 'I would not have forgotten someone as lovely as you.'

Flushing, she turned to one side. 'I was different then. My hair . . . everything about me.'

'Hah!' Greco was snorting like a proud stallion. 'It is because he has had so many women since, I think. He looks like that type of man.'

Takes one to know one, she almost said.

'He is like Jack too, is he not? Your son, he has your eyes. But his forehead and his frown, it belongs to his father.'

So *he'd* noticed that too.

'Do not worry.' Greco made to gather her into his arms. 'I will not say anything. But I need your word on something, Rosie. You have to tell me if you still have feelings for this man.'

Niftily, she stepped backwards. 'Don't be ridiculous. I've told you, I was no more than a teenager then.'

As she spoke, something caught her eye, down on the beach. It was a light – a motorbike light. But it wasn't moving. Next to it, was a couple kissing. A young couple. Jack and Alice? It was impossible to tell from here. Impossible, but not out of the question.

'So he means nothing to you now?' repeated Greco, coming even closer. Very deliberately, he placed a finger under her chin so she was forced to face him once more.

It was hard to lie when you were looking at someone.

But not impossible.

'Nothing at all,' she murmured. 'I promise.'

HISTORY OF HONEYMOONS CONTINUED

The actual word 'honeymoon' gets its origins in sixteenth-century English literature, and it did not start out as an encouraging phrase. The author Richard Huloet referred to the period after a marriage as a 'hony mone' to represent the waning of the feeling of true love as the moon shifts from one phase to the next.

Chapter Nineteen

EMMA

Emma woke with a taste in her mouth that reminded her of her teenage days – a time when there had been nothing to stop her going to a club and dancing until two in the morning. Drinking far too much, she remembered guiltily, recalling the double Bacardis she used to treat herself to, so long as she kept the rest of her wages for Mum.

It was what everyone did. Besides, letting her hair down once a week had helped blank out what was going on at home.

Poor Mum had floundered, unable to cope after Dad had left. She'd hardly known what day of the week it was, let alone how many glasses of cheap wine she'd got through every night. It was all Dad's fault. Emma would never forgive him. Never. And she certainly wasn't returning any of the calls he'd made.

In fact, if it hadn't been for Tom with his sweet, mild manners, Emma would have thought all men were total bastards.

Of course, as soon as she'd got pregnant with Gawain, she'd stopped drinking immediately. Nowadays, she and Tom would share half a bottle of wine on Saturday night, but no more.

Yet last night, just because the children weren't here – and also because it had seemed rude to say no – she'd had more than her usual glass. Far more.

Emma sat up in the soft, wide bed, which was far more comfortable than their own at home, and tried to remember exactly what had happened.

They'd all had dinner on the patio together, she recalled. It had been really nice. Lots of laughter and jokes, although she had to keep pinching herself every time Winston said something. Imagine her, Emma, having dinner with the Fitness King of TV!

He'd made some lovely comments when she'd got out the pictures of the children on the phone, as though he was genuinely interested.

Someone else had been interested in her too . . . It was beginning to come back now. If she wasn't a married woman, she might have thought that the new cook Yannis was pretty keen. Guiltily, even though she didn't have anything to be guilty about, Emma glanced down at Tom.

Honestly. All he'd done on their honeymoon was sleep! 'So your new husband, he is not with you?' Yannis had said after dinner last night, his thick dark brows raised with apparent curiosity.

Emma had tried to make light of it. 'He's been ill. Food poisoning and then travel sickness. Nothing catching,' she added hastily.

Melissa's eyes had widened across the table. 'I thought he was better now.'

'He is, sort of, but now it's sun-sickness, so he didn't fancy getting out of bed for dinner.'

Emma didn't think it was wise to elaborate on her husband's exact words, which had been something along the lines of not wanting to eat 'any of that Greek oily stuff'.

In fact, the stuffed tomatoes had been delicious. But she couldn't help feeling a little cross, rather than sympathetic, with Tom. Just because they were married now, didn't mean he could stop making an effort.

Yannis certainly had! All those compliments about her 'beautiful' hair and how she looked 'far too young' to have two children!

After the French couple (who'd virtually been having foot sex all evening under the table) had announced they were going for a moonlit 'promenade' along the beach, Emma had decided to make a move too.

'We'll walk back with her, won't we, Winston?' Melissa had chirped.

But then Yannis had stepped in. 'I am going that way myself. I will be honoured to make sure that you reach your cottage safely.'

Emma had flushed deeply, hoping no one else had noticed. Luckily Rosie had been deep in conversation with her Greek boyfriend (she'd agreed earlier with Melissa that they were an unlikely combination) and didn't even say goodbye when she'd left in Yannis's company.

What exactly had she done? wondered Emma now, sitting up in bed and hugging her knees as she tried to piece together that walk down the hill and along the beach to her cottage.

She'd been flattered by his attention, there was no denying that. Yannis was tall and dark like his cousin Greco, but a bit stockier, which she liked (even though she wasn't so sure about the mermaid tattoo on his right arm). He was a good talker, too. He'd trained at one of the hotels in Athens, he'd told her, but had missed his childhood home. So when Greco had told him about the job vacancy at the Villa Rosa, he had jumped at it.

'I am so glad I did,' he had said in a low voice when they reached the cottage. 'I have met many wonderful people as a result.'

Including her. Of course, he hadn't actually said that, but she'd been dimly aware, despite her alcoholic stupor, that the insinuation was there.

She had a vague memory, then, of him stepping towards her when they reached her veranda. But again, that might have been to give her the keys that she'd foolishly dropped in the sand.

Apart from that, nothing else had happened. She might have had too much to drink, but not enough to forget something like that. Just as well. She could never be unfaithful to Tom. So why, Emma asked herself crossly as she got out of bed and turned on the shower, did she have this feeling of disappointment? Hadn't she always declared that there was no excuse – none at all – for playing around?

Yet, as Emma began to soap her breasts (which had a rather pleasing suntan line), she was uncomfortably aware that there had been an attraction there.

If she hadn't been married, something could definitely have happened . . .

'Did you have a nice time last night?' murmured Tom from his side of the bed when she returned from the shower.

Emma froze. 'It was all right. You wouldn't have liked the food, though.' How guilty she felt, saying that! Hadn't she had seconds? 'Stuffed tomatoes and lamb in oil,' she added with emphasis.

Tom shuddered. 'Don't. You'll set me off being sick again.'

Whatever happened to the so-called stronger sex? With an annoyed sigh, Emma turned away to slip into the slinky beach sarong that Melissa had lent her.

'You know what?' She rounded on him. 'I really wish we'd stayed at home. At least then we'd have spent some time together.'

Tom's dark brown eyes regarded her with disappointment. 'I told you. I didn't want to let you down.'

Emma ignored him, aware that this wasn't like her. Then again, what was she like? Ever since they'd arrived in Siphalonia, she'd felt different.

'I'll try to do something with you today, Em,' Tom pleaded, adjusting his pillow. 'We'll go for a little walk, as long as it's not too hot.'

'Well, it is.' Emma adjusted Melissa's sarong in the mirror and gave a little twirl. 'It's very hot and you won't like it. I'm just going off for yoga now and then I'm having a swim. I'll pop back after that to see if you're all right.'

Tom's voice was weak with self-pity. 'You're angry with me.'

'No, I'm not,' she said sulkily.

He reached out for her hands. His limp grasp, she couldn't help noticing, was so different from Yannis's strong grip as he'd helped her down the hill. 'I can tell you are.'

'Put it this way, Tom. If *I* didn't feel well, I'd make more of an effort to be with you on our honeymoon. I'm sorry for you, of course I am. But you men just give in to things, don't you? When you're a mother, you can't afford to be ill.'

Tom's eyes flickered with hurt. 'That's not fair.'

'Isn't it? Think about it. Look, I've got to go or I'll be late for yoga. ' Grabbing her big blue-and-orange-striped bag, Emma left before she said anything she shouldn't.

Sometimes, she thought, catching sight of the French couple wrapped around each other on their balcony, it felt like she was the only one around here who wasn't getting any sex.

Those once-a-fortnight duty fumbles in bed hadn't seemed much of a problem before. But now, in this island paradise where everyone else was a proper couple, Emma couldn't help feeling that she'd really missed out.

And now she was married it was too late. Or was it?

'What are you going to do now?' asked Melissa chummily when the yoga class had finished. 'Want to join us by the pool? The children are playing football with Jack,' she added, touching her arm lightly in a girly fashion. 'They're really excited about the fishing trip tonight.'

She'd forgotten to mention that to Tom. Still, there was no point, was there?

'Will your husband come to that?'

Emma snorted. 'Shouldn't think so.' A picture of Tom's hurt expression swam into her head. Maybe she'd been a bit tough back there in the cottage. On the other hand, didn't it serve him right for not making the effort? 'I don't know if I should go on the boat trip,' she began.

'Why not?' demanded Melissa. 'It's your holiday too.'

Her new friend was right. All that anger which had been building up inside began to gather momentum. Just because Tom was being so wet didn't mean she had to go along with it.

'You're right. I'll go! Think I might have one of those massages on the beach today.' She'd not had the idea until

197

the words came out of her mouth. It wasn't cheap, but blow it! She deserved a bit of pampering.

'It's lovely.' Melissa sounded dreamy. 'Had one myself yesterday.' Then she gave a shy little glance at her husband. 'Mind you, Winston's massages are the best. He touches all the right spots.'

I bet he does, thought Emma with a flash of jealousy. It wasn't that she fancied Winston; it was Melissa's allusion to the physical bit that had made her envious. Everyone around her appeared to be doing it.

'Sometimes,' added Melissa wistfully, 'I wonder if the sex is almost more important than it should be. We don't actually have a lot in common, Winston and I. He doesn't have kids, you know, so it's hard for him to understand. But after my first husband went off with someone else, it was very flattering to find that someone else wanted me.' She put a little hand to her mouth. 'Oh dear, I'm probably saying too much again.'

Yes, she was! Melissa kept using Winston's name. Did she think Emma wouldn't recognise him? Or was she just hoping that there were other dark, bald men out there, also called Winston King, who weren't famous?

If so, she was pretty naive.

Nevertheless, Emma felt the need to reassure her. 'When you're away from home, you need someone to talk to,' she said.

But secretly, she felt uneasy – not just because of the confidence but because of the sex bit. Emma's thoughts went back to the jokes that Phil, their best man, had made at the wedding. Smutty jokes with all kinds of innuendos about what she and Tom would be getting up to on their honeymoon.

Tom had sniggered along with the rest of them, she remembered, but the truth was that sex had never been a big part of their relationship. Even when they'd first met, she'd found his kisses rather, well, wet and coarse. After she'd finally gone on the pill, after putting it off for as long as she could, she'd been quite disappointed.

Was that *it*? she'd asked herself when Tom had made a

funny little grunting sound. (They'd gone up to her bedroom one night when Emma's mum was out on another blind date.) What a lot of fuss about an act that was rather daft when you thought about it!

She certainly didn't feel that tingling that she'd experienced last night when Yannis had walked her back. Emma shook herself. It was ridiculous to compare the two! Tom was her husband. You didn't need chemistry when you had been together for as long as they had. Anyway, there certainly wasn't much room for passion when you had kids.

Or was that really just a convenient excuse? And was that why the fury inside her was reaching boiling point?

The massage was a great idea. She'd never had one before. Mind you, it was a bit of a surprise when a man did it (a rather short one who barely came up to her shoulders). Rather awkward too, having it on the beach with everyone going past. But then, as the masseur's hands worked their way down her spine, Emma closed her eyes and began to forget she was in public view.

Mmm. This was lovely. So relaxing. Then she stiffened. Surely his hands weren't going to go up there? So close to her . . . well, her intimate bits.

Emma froze; at least she tried to, but her body had different ideas. She was beginning to experience a sensation she hadn't had before. Not exactly an orgasm (something she rarely managed to achieve with Tom) but a general, well, letting-go.

'Enjoying yourself?' asked a voice.

Gasping, Emma lifted her head to see Yannis. He was walking past – not stopping, thank goodness – but there was something about his voice and the smile on his face that made her want to curl up and die.

What was happening to her? The old Emma in England wouldn't be having any of these thoughts! As if on cue, her mobile went as soon as she'd handed over the money, reprimanding herself for being so wasteful. Twenty euros would have paid for at least three dinners back home.

'Em?'

Emma's heart began to race. 'Mum! Is everything all right?'

'Stop flapping.' Her mother's voice was crisp. 'I just wanted to know where you'd put Gawain's spare Spider-Man outfit. The others are all in the washing machine.'

'Spider-Man! I want to be Spider-Man!'

It was Gawain. She could just see him now, stamping his little feet in fury. Immediately, Emma was transported back home. Gawain wouldn't wear anything else apart from the red and blue top with matching trousers, just like his hero. 'Try the back of the linen cupboard. It's a bit of a mess; I meant to organise it before I left but—'

'Got it! It's all right, Gawain, you can wear it now. Say hello to Mum.'

'Mummy?' Her son's little voice made her body go limp. 'Where are you?'

This was awful! Her eyes filled with tears. 'I told you before, darling. I'm on an island in a place called Greece.' She was walking through the sea now, feeling the waves slap gently against her ankles. 'I wish you were here. One day, Daddy and I will bring you. Would you like that?'

No answer.

'Gawain?'

Her mother's voice cut in. 'He's run off to play. You just enjoy yourself.'

Enjoy herself? She'd been doing OK, but now Gawain's little voice and her own stupid behaviour last night – coupled with this ridiculous desire to have sex like everyone else – just made her want to go home.

Still, only another day and a half and then they'd be getting the plane back. Frankly it wouldn't be a moment too soon. It had been very sweet of Bernie and the girls to splash out, but she'd had enough of honeymoons to last her a lifetime.

Then a noise above her head made Emma stop, shading the sun with her hand to peer up at the rock above. She'd noticed it before. It was very flat – perfect for sunbathing. In fact, quite a few of the locals sat there. But today there were only two people on it. Jack. And, if she wasn't mistaken, Alice. Lying very close to each other.

What was it Melissa had said? The children were playing football with Jack. Well, it didn't look like football. And Alice's younger brother certainly wasn't there. Emma hurried on. Should she say anything to the girl's mother? Or should she just leave them to it? Emma's heart softened.

There really was nothing like young love before real life got in the way. Who was she to spoil it, just because Tom had spoilt it for *her*.

TRUE HONEYMOON STORY

'We didn't have a honeymoon. My husband went off to Bosnia the next day.'

Mary, now mother of three young children

Chapter Twenty

WINSTON

Winston couldn't get the headline out of his mind: 'Twenty Things You Didn't Know About Winston King!'

So far, the series hadn't come up with anything drastic. The name thing was no big deal. Nor was the fact that he'd been brought up by his grandmother after his parents had died. Or that he spoke fluent Spanish and was allergic to anchovies.

But it was what they were going to run next that was worrying him. In fact, Winston had been so rattled that he'd hardly been able to concentrate during the yoga class.

Would it be the usual stuff about the morals of shooting to kill (the armed forces were always being asked that one)? Or could it be the story behind Nick? And if so, how much of it did they know? They might well have got hold of the inquest report, Winston reasoned. There was nothing he could do about that. But what if they'd interviewed men who'd been with him on that day? It was rare for a Green Beret to talk to an outsider about an incident. There was usually a sense of loyalty that could be stronger than blood ties. But there was always a danger that someone might be persuaded to talk for enough money. Life after the services wasn't always easy.

'Got a bit of a migraine,' he confessed to Melissa after lunch on the terrace when she asked if anything was wrong.

'Poor you.' She reached up and did a little circular motion with both her thumbs in his temples. 'Does that help?'

Not much. In fact, the touch of her fingers made him feel even worse. He loved this woman so much. Adored the way she was different from anyone he'd met before. Scatty one minute yet organised the next. Arty. Maternal (even though she let the kids get away with murder). But above all, vulnerable. He had to protect her.

Yet if everything came out, she'd be hurt all over again. People would talk. They would point fingers. That bastard of an ex-husband of hers would tell her that he knew all along that Winston was a no-good, lily-livered coward.

But even worse, she would think badly of him.

'Think I might go and lie down on the bed for a bit,' he found himself saying. Melissa gave him a surprised look, as well she might. He wasn't the type to lie down like that wimp who was married to Emma. How could a man be so pathetic as to spend his entire honeymoon in bed, alone?

'Look, darling.' She stroked his arm. Melissa was one of those touchy-feely women, he'd discovered, even when she didn't know someone well. At times, it made him feel quite jealous. 'I'm really sorry, but . . .'

He felt a horrible apprehension. Was it to do with Marvyn and whatever he'd said to the *Globe*? Did she know what was going to be in print?

'. . . but I can't come up to the room with you,' Melissa continued, putting her arms around his waist as far as they would go. 'I really ought to go and check if the children are all right.'

Was that all? Relief flooded through him.

'They promised to be back for lunch and they're late.' She bit her lip worriedly. 'Freddie said they were going to play football with Jack.'

Good. So the boy was doing his bit then. 'They'll be fine. You've got to give them some freedom or they won't grow up.'

'You don't understand.' Melissa was shaking her head crossly as though he was the child. 'It's not as simple as that.'

Wasn't it? He would have argued it out but the throb in his temples was getting so bad that he just had to get away; otherwise he'd be sick right there on the spot.

Instead, he only just made it up to Mrs Harrison's loo off

the bedroom, with its pretty pink walls and frilly lavatory roll holder that reminded him of England about twenty years ago. Winston wiped his mouth with a towel. It had been a long time since he'd had a migraine, although there had been times when he'd thrown up after action. There'd been sights there that would make anyone sick.

If that was the kind of thing they ran in this *Globe* piece, it didn't matter. It was the other stuff he didn't want in it. The details from the inquest, for a start.

In an attempt to ease the pain in his head, Winston sat upright on the bed, stretching his head from one side to the other. It was during the right-hand twists that he noticed the photograph. It was the only one here, which seemed a bit odd, since, in his experience, people who were a long way from home generally had quite a few pictures around. (His men certainly had, although he'd been the exception. When someone had occasionally commented on that, he'd given them a short, sharp answer: 'I don't need photographs to remind me of the people who matter.')

This picture, he noticed, showed a youngish girl with shoulder-length hair with her arms around another girl of about the same age. Judging from their clothes, he'd say it had been taken about fifteen or maybe twenty years ago. Winston bent his head further to the left and heard his neck scrunch like little crystals being ground up. Now to the right, where he could see that photograph which was beginning to bug him. There was something about the girl with long hair that appeared familiar. Was it Rosie Harrison when she was younger? Possibly, although she'd changed a lot if that was the case. It wasn't just the hair length; it was the face itself. The photograph showed a girl with a very sweet, innocent look.

If he was right, and the two were the same, that expression had certainly gone now. Mrs Harrison looked as though she didn't suffer fools gladly. Perhaps life had treated her harshly, he mused. Then again, you probably didn't get to run a place like this without keeping your wits about you.

Winston leaned back and closed his eyes, trying to shut out thoughts of the awful newspaper 'exclusive'. Did these people have any idea of the fear they caused when they declared their intention to expose someone? Fair enough if the person involved had deliberately broken the law. But he had tried to do the right thing. God knows he'd tried.

'Nick, Nick,' he found himself muttering. 'I'm so sorry.'

Shut it out. That's what the post-traumatic stress counsellor had said afterwards. Think of something else to replace it. For some reason, Mrs Harrison swam back into his mind, together with her Greek boyfriend. Winston hadn't cared for the cut of his jib. The man's eyes had actually narrowed when he'd seen him on the beach this morning after the yoga class.

He'd been bringing his boat in with the night's catch, and when Winston had raised his hand in greeting, he'd scowled and walked past with his head high. Maybe he didn't like tourists.

The pain was subsiding now. Perhaps he'd go downstairs and find Melissa. The sickening thought occurred to him that it might be one of his last chances to be with her. If – when – all this broke, there'd be a lot of explaining to do. She might not understand.

Making his way down the stairs, Winston passed through the small lounge and nodded at Rosie Harrison, who was vigorously cleaning the windows. She worked hard. He'd give her that.

'I know I've said it before, but we do appreciate you giving up your room,' he began awkwardly, wanting to make amends.

As she whipped round, he realised he'd startled her. Indeed, she looked quite flustered. 'Not at all,' she said, smoothing down her hair. 'We like to keep our guests happy, and besides, it was our mistake. I'm afraid my son might have got the booking wrong. He's still quite young and maybe I gave him too much responsibility.'

Mrs Harrison's eyes met his challengingly. 'But he's a good boy. He told me about you offering him money to look after your stepchildren, but I could have told you that he'd refuse.'

'You paid Jack to take out my children?'

Shit. It was Melissa, standing in the doorway behind him. Winston felt the sweat pouring down his back. Now he'd really had it.

'Only on one occasion,' he blustered.

Melissa's eyes were black with fury. 'The night he took her out on the bike?'

This was getting worse. 'It was only so that we could have some time on our own,' he faltered.

His wife was shaking with rage. Rosie, he noticed, had turned her attention back to the windows. 'How could you, Winston? My kids are part of me. If you wanted to get rid of them, you shouldn't have married me.'

'No. Don't say that!' Winston made to hold her but she stepped back, oblivious to the fact that Rosie wasn't the only one who was staring at her. So, too, was that fisherman, who'd slipped in through a side door.

'Do you two know where my kids are?' demanded Melissa fiercely. 'I've been looking for them everywhere.'

Rosie bit her lip. 'Your son's watching television in the conservatory. I'm not sure where your daughter is.'

The Greek threw back his head and laughed. 'I can tell you that. When I was mending my nets this afternoon, I saw them going into the cove. The one by the point.'

Melissa gasped. 'Oh my God. Quick. Show me.'

Winston tried to hold her back. 'Are you sure that's wise? I mean, they're entitled to some privacy, aren't they?'

His wife rounded on him, her eyes flashing like a wild animal. 'They're kids, Winston. And if you had them yourself, you'd understand.'

Winston hadn't realised how fast Melissa could run as they headed for the beach. It reminded him of a story he'd once read about a mother lifting a car up off the ground and saving her toddler who'd been trapped underneath. 'If that boy has touched her, I will never forgive you for this,' she snarled.

Rosie, on the other side, was panting slightly as she spoke.

'I'm sure Jack wouldn't do anything. He's a responsible boy. They're just friends.'

There was a sharp laugh from the Greek. 'They looked more than friends to me, I can tell you. See! There they are!'

So they were. Sitting together on a rock. Fully clothed. Not even holding hands. Winston's heart leaped with relief.

'Mum!' Alice was very red, or was that just the sun? 'What's up?'

Melissa grabbed her daughter's arm, yanking her away from the kid. 'What are you doing here? You said you were playing football – all three of you.' She spun round furiously to face Jack. 'Did you take advantage of my daughter? Tell me. Did you?'

'*Mum!*' spluttered Alice, appalled.

'Because if you did, my husband – I mean Alice's father – will kill you.'

So she still saw Marvyn as her real husband, did she? Winston felt as though someone had punched him in the stomach. It was just as he'd feared. When someone had been married for over fifteen years, as Melissa had been, it was pretty difficult to take over after just three months.

'We didn't do anything,' stammered Jack. 'We were just talking. We're friends.'

Rosie had her hands on his shoulder protectively. 'If that's what my son says, I believe him.' Her voice was defiant. No longer was she the owner of the Villa Rosa, trying to do everything she could to please the guests. She was a mother, Winston recognised. A tiger ready to protect her young, just as Melissa was.

He had to – grudgingly – admire them both.

'I think we all ought to go back,' he said quietly. Rosie took the lead, striding ahead with Jack and whispering urgently. Alice, on the other hand, refused to talk.

'Don't ignore me,' pleaded Melissa to her daughter, as though it was she who was in the wrong. 'I was only trying to look out for you.'

'That's true,' added Winston but Melissa shot him a furious

look. 'Don't even say anything. This is your fault. If you hadn't tried to bribe that boy to take my kids out, it wouldn't have happened.'

'What?' Alice ran up to Jack, tugging on his arm, two small red spots forming on her cheek. 'Winston *paid* you to be with us? Is that true?'

'Yes. N-n-n-no.' The poor kid was stammering again. 'He just gave me some money the first time – but I wouldn't take anything after that.'

'I thought you *wanted* to be with me!'

'I do.'

Alice burst into tears. 'I hate you,' she said, rounding on Winston. 'I really do.'

'Darling, come back!'

But ignoring her mother, Alice pushed past and raced on up towards the villa. 'Leave her,' said Winston firmly.

Melissa looked as though she was going to scratch his eyes out. '*Leave* her? After what she's just found out? You don't get kids, do you, Winston? I must have been mad to have thought you'd understand.'

She was off, racing after her daughter. Winston's mouth felt dry the way it used to in action, on the few occasions when he'd made the wrong call. If his wife was acting like this now, what was she going to do when the *Globe* did its worst?

'Now she'll never want to see me again,' groaned Jack.

There was a snort from the Greek. 'Teenage love. It is so fickle, is it not?' The man shot him a nasty look, his eyes narrowing. 'It is so strong and it can have such consequences.'

Winston shrugged. 'Suppose so.' He stopped as they reached a part of the beach where there was only space for one person to squeeze past the boats at a time. He gestured to Rosie to go first, and then the boy, polite kid that he was, let Winston go past.

As he did so, Winston froze. 'Would you like to tell me why your shirt is inside out?' he said to the boy quietly.

'We didn't do anything. Honestly. Not . . . not *that*. I promise. We just cuddled and kissed a bit.' Then he glanced at his mother, who was walking ahead with the Greek bloke. He looked up at Winston pleadingly. 'I really like Alice. But I'm worried now that I've ruined my chances.'

Winston nodded grimly. 'And I really like the mother, kid.' Then, without meaning to, he added, 'But I'm worried I've ruined my chances too.'

He slapped Jack on the back. 'Promise me you didn't go too far?'

The boy nodded. 'Promise.'

'Then we'll say no more.'

'Thanks.'

The relief on the boy's face made Winston feel good about himself for the first time since his agent had told him about the *Globe* series.

But now he had to face his wife.

TOP FIVE HONEYMOON HORRORS

- Food poisoning
- Ants on floor of 'luxury' hotel
- Inadequate sex
- Bumping into old flame
- Lost luggage

Taken from a recent honeymoon survey

Chapter Twenty-One

ROSIE

Promising that she'd meet him later that night, Rosie left Greco at the gate to the villa and marched back to the kitchen. Thank goodness Yannis – who'd turned out to be a real asset in the kitchen – had had the initiative to start halving the red peppers for tonight's dinner. They were going to stuff them in a minute: something that took time and care.

When you ran a business like this, there was no room for emotional domestic dramas. Jack had been brought up in the business, she thought indignantly. He knew she needed all hands on deck – and he'd already made them way behind by not being here to prepare lunch, which in turn had made them late for dinner. But even so, she couldn't get her son's distraught face out of her head.

'Give him time to himself,' Greco had advised during their walk back, wearing his man-of-the-world expression. But how long? Her son had been just behind her on the beach but now there was no sign of him. Where was he?

Part of her wanted to run upstairs and see if Jack was all right, but if they didn't get a move on, the meal would never be ready. It was the Greek-themed evening, too, with dancers from the village.

She'd give him ten more minutes and then go and find him. But a few seconds later, she heard his footsteps coming down the stairs.

Rosie's heart fell as she took in her son's red, blotchy face. She'd hardly ever known Jack to cry before. Even as a baby, he had simply sung to himself in the morning while lying in the crib, until she'd picked him up. When, at around the age of four or so, she had explained that his father had died in a tragic motorbike accident before his birth, he'd accepted it in such a calm way that she wondered if he had actually taken it in.

'One day,' Cara used to say sternly, waggling a dark finger at her, 'you will have to tell him the truth. Otherwise, if he finds out, he will never trust you again.'

Rosie had just shrugged, silently telling herself there was no way Jack could find out. It wasn't as though she was ever going to go back to England, not after those terrible things that her father had said. It had been clear too that he had really meant them, otherwise he would have got in touch.

Now, as she looked with dismay at her son's tear-stained face, she felt a sharp chill pass through her. Maybe there was more to it than that horrible scene with the girl. Had Greco gone after him and, out of spite for Winston, seen fit to spill the beans about Jack's parentage, even though he had sworn not to?

'Are you all right?' she asked, looking up at him and wondering when it was exactly that he had suddenly got so much taller than her. Children did that to you. They fooled you into thinking that you were the adult and then suddenly, they not only shot up in height, but arrogantly assumed they knew so much more than you did.

'Yes.' Jack moved away to the sink but not before she'd noticed something.

Her voice was sharp with suspicion. 'Why is your shirt inside out?'

He was turning the tap on full and washing his hands with deliberation: standard practice when you were about to work in the kitchen, although Rosie had a definite feeling that this was more to defer the moment.

She nodded at Yannis to suggest that he might like to step outside for a minute and give them some time on their own. To his credit, the man got the message.

'Jack,' she said softly, taking his hands which were so much bigger than hers. 'Tell me what really happened with Alice?'

He hugged her. A big bear hug that sent enormous waves of relief running through her. So he still loved her, despite everything. Thank God!

'I like her,' he said in words that sounded muffled against her shoulder. 'I really like her.'

Rosie felt another chill pass through her. 'You didn't *do* anything, did you? I mean, nothing serious. She's underage, for a start.'

''Course we didn't do anything, Mum!' Her son's furiously indignant voice made her realise she'd pried too far. Yet she had a responsibility, as both a parent and a hotelier.

'Didn't you have a boyfriend at my age?' Jack was glaring at her, as though all this was her fault.

'Actually, no, I didn't. Your grandfather wouldn't allow it.'

He was chopping figs for the fruit salad now with short, sharp angry actions. Don't slice your fingers off, Rosie wanted to say.

'But you met Dad when you were seventeen.'

Rosie's mouth went dry. 'Yes, I did.'

'That's not much older than I am now.' Jack's voice had a catch in it. 'Did you know he was the one immediately?'

Rosie's voice came out in a squeak. 'I *thought* he was.' Suddenly, without warning, a hot tear slid down her cheek at the memory of Charlie abandoning her.

Instantly, Jack put his arm around her. 'I'm sorry, Mum. I didn't mean to upset you about Dad. Can we just forget this?'

She nodded, grateful for the reprieve, but livid with herself for letting her emotions get the better of her. She *had* loved Charlie/Winston, dammit. And even though she kept telling herself that he meant nothing to her now, she still felt a strange pang every time she saw him kiss his new wife.

After all, he'd been *hers* first.

'The thing is,' said Jack, slicing the last fig with such force that one half skidded off the table and onto the floor, 'Alice won't speak to me. She thinks I only showed interest because Winston offered to pay me.'

He looked down on her, his expression clearly saying *Help me, Mum. Tell me what to do.*

This was exactly why boys needed fathers! Every now and then, she'd had to face male transitional stages, like the time Jack got his bits stuck in a zip when he was ten. But each time, she'd got through it. Until now.

He needed a man around. The irony of his real father's unexpected presence was so sharp as to be almost comic.

'If I were you,' Rosie said slowly, 'I would go and find Alice after dinner tonight and tell her how you feel.'

Jack made an unsure sound. 'Really?'

'Yes,' said Rosie firmly. 'The truth is always best.'

Hypocrite, she told herself as she opened the door for Yannis (who had clearly been listening in, judging from the way he fell back). But it was so hard! Didn't all parents want to make sure that their children didn't make the same mistakes *they* had?

To Rosie's relief, all the guests came to the Greek evening, as well as a group of other tourists who'd been staying at a small taverna at the other end of town. They certainly needed the custom. Takings were down considerably on previous years and they needed a certain number to pay for tonight's buffet and the band.

'We heard your Greek evenings are really good,' said one woman excitedly.

Rosie only hoped that the new blood might help to lighten the atmosphere. She hadn't been at all sure that Winston and Melissa would turn up, and when they did, it was clear they weren't talking.

It was equally clear that Alice wasn't talking to Jack, either, from the way she turned her head away when he approached her at the buffet table. Rosie had to stop herself from rushing over to the stupid girl and asking if she realised what a fine boy her son was.

'We wouldn't have come,' said Melissa meaningfully when she floated up to the buffet table for some salad, 'but we didn't want to let you down. I don't hold you responsible, Rosie, but I do hope you've had a word with your son.'

Rosie felt her cheeks burn. 'Jack has done nothing wrong. They're just kids, Melissa.' She paused, remembering that although most of her guests asked her to call them by their first name, this was the first time she'd addressed Winston's wife like that. 'Don't you remember what it was like when you were a teenager?'

Melissa nodded slowly, artfully brushing aside a strand of dark hair. 'I was only nineteen when I met my first husband.'

There you are then, Rosie wanted to say triumphantly. 'My son really likes your daughter, you know.' She gave Melissa a little nudge. 'Looks like she feels the same way.'

It did, too. The pair were now talking earnestly on the little ledge that ran along the patio, looking down on the beach below. 'Sweet, don't you think?' said Rosie wistfully.

Melissa shrugged. 'I suppose so.'

'He's a good boy, you know,' added Rosie defensively. 'He wouldn't do anything wrong.'

The woman's voice was low. 'It's Alice I'm worried about. She can be a bit strong-minded.'

Maybe because she was allowed to get away with so much, Rosie thought. She had heard the way those children spoke to their mother. Jack would never be so rude. Perhaps that's what came of a loving community like Siphalonia, where the young respected their elders.

The band struck up, interrupting her thoughts.

'Greek music,' called out the plump blonde excitedly, clapping her hands at the other side of the terrace. 'How exciting.'

'Still no husband?' asked Rosie, raising her eyebrows, glad to change the subject from her son and his new girlfriend.

Melissa shook her head. 'Emma says he's feeling better but that he doesn't like the sun or dancing. Sounds like a real bundle of fun, doesn't he? Here he comes.'

For a minute, Rosie thought Melissa meant Tom Walker, but then she spotted Winston getting up from the table by the edge of the patio. Her heart began to pound although it

216

was clear she might as well not be there. Winston only had eyes for his wife. But when he touched Melissa's arm in an affectionate greeting, she appeared to ignore it.

Interesting.

'Shall we dance,' he murmured.

Rosie's heart almost stopped. Those were almost exactly the words he'd used all those years ago at the disco where they'd met. They'd been engraved on her heart ever since.

'You can dance on your own or with someone else if you wish,' Melissa replied coolly. 'I'm going to dance with my son.'

'Actually,' ventured Rosie lightly, 'it's the kind of dance where everyone joins in.'

It was true. The leader of the band was encouraging them all to join hands in a circle. Reluctantly – or so it appeared – Melissa linked fingers with her husband. Somehow, Rosie found herself standing next to Winston.

He gave her a friendly smile and then his eyes travelled to her clothes. Her lavender dress still fitted after all these years. Too late, Rosie wished she hadn't put it on. What are you playing at? she asked herself. Do you want him to recognise you?

Yes.

No.

Don't be daft. Why would he remember a small detail like that?

Everyone in the circle was holding hands now. It would have looked odd if she and Winston didn't. As if reading her mind, he reached out.

A shock shot through her as his fingers closed over her knuckles. This was the hand of the boy she had loved when she'd been not much older than her own son. This was the father of her child. A man who was now married to someone else.

'I'm sorry,' Rosie heard herself saying, letting go. Suddenly, the sense of loss was so overwhelming that if she didn't go now, she knew she might confess everything on the spot. 'I have to tidy up first.'

Before he could say anything, she rushed through the doorway with its curtain of hanging beads and sat down at the huge scrubbed kitchen table, gasping for air. Breathe, she told herself fiercely. Breathe.

After a while, her heart stopped pounding. Through the window, she could see the children who had come with the non-resident couples, dancing along with the adults.

Emma was bending down, talking to one of the little ones. She was missing her kids dreadfully, as she'd told Rosie and anyone else who would listen endlessly.

Uh-oh. Briefly, Rosie forgot her own problems as she observed Yannis walking up to Emma, holding out his hand and swinging her round in time to the loud music, with his eyes firmly fixed on her low-cut top, which was revealing rather more than it should.

Was Emma in control? She'd had rather a lot to drink at dinner, Rosie had noticed. She wouldn't be the first tourist to have underestimated the strength of the local wine and ouzo.

'So, you are here! Hiding from me!'

Rosie gave a little gasp as a warm pair of arms encircled her from behind. Greco laughed delightedly: a deep, throaty laugh that made her tingle. 'You hide like your English Cinderella in the kitchen. Well, no more. Come!'

Despite her protests, he pulled her outside onto the terrace, where the music was just beginning to change. Unable to stop herself, Rosie searched the floor for Winston. He was sitting next to his wife, glumly staring out over the olive groves.

'It has strains of Chopin, do you not think?' said Greco as he put his arms around her.

He was right. It did. Sometimes Greco surprised her, and not just with his bottom smacking. When she'd first gone to his cottage on the shore, she'd been taken aback by the rows of well-thumbed books and alphabetically ordered CDs.

And yet, ever since Charlie had pitched up, she'd felt uncertain about Greco all over again . . .

Meanwhile, Melissa was still pointedly ignoring her husband. It was obvious that she cared for him. Of course she did! She was simply cross that Winston had tried to 'sell' her daughter.

Rosie would have felt the same herself.

'You know,' whispered Greco into her ear, 'I have a surprise for you.'

Please don't let it be a ring! Ever since they'd got back from the mainland, Greco had been strutting around like a cockerel round the island, making it clear to all and sundry that he and the Englishwoman were a couple. Did he really want to make it official? If so, he should have spoken to her first. Besides, she wasn't ready.

'My surprise, she is sitting in the kitchen,' continued Greco with a glint in his eye.

She?

'It was why I had to remove you just now. But we will go back, yes?'

Rosie gasped. Greco was sweeping her off her feet, literally; carrying her through the whooping and clapping, ducking and diving of the Greek dance. Through the beaded curtain into the kitchen with its copper pans hanging from the ceiling.

There at the table sat a small woman with bright, bird-like eyes. Her face was tanned and lined; thanks to the sun, she looked older than she really was. Her arms, as she held them out to Rosie, had sagged with age and she seemed frailer than before.

'Cara!' Rosie gasped delightedly. 'What a lovely surprise!'

Greco stood there; his grin had gone and in its place was a serious expression. 'I call her,' he announced. 'I tell her you are in trouble and that you need her.'

Rosie gave a scared little laugh. 'What do you mean?'

Cara took both her hands and gripped them with a strength that belied her appearance. 'It's all right, my child. I am here now. Greco has told me about this man who has come back into your life. I always told you that the time would come. But do not worry. I will help you to break the news.'

Her hands tightened round Rosie's even more firmly. 'To both father and son.'

HONEYMOON – IN DIFFERENT LANGUAGES

French: *lune de miel*

Spanish: *luna de miel*

Portuguese: *lua de mel*

Italian: *luna di miele*

Welsh: *mis mêl*

Polish: *miesiąc miodowy*

Russian: медовый месяц

Arabic: (*shahr el 'assal*)

Greek: μήνας του μέλιτος

Hebrew: (*yerach d'vash*)

Persian: ماه عسل (*māh-e asal*)

Turkish: *balayı*

Hungarian: *mézeshetek*

Chapter Twenty-Two

EMMA

This time tomorrow, they'd be on their way home! Emma's tummy was abuzz with excited butterflies. She simply couldn't *wait* to see the children. But at the same time she'd almost got used to them not being there.

It seemed more normal now to sleep through the night, instead of keeping one ear cocked, in case Gawain or Willow woke. She'd fallen into the habit of meaningful conversation with people she'd only just met, instead of always watching the children while she spoke. And she'd really enjoyed the painting and yoga classes, which had permitted her time to be herself.

Did that make her a bad mother?

There was something else that really worried her, too. Without the children, she and Tom had hardly anything to talk about.

'Fancy a walk?' he suggested after breakfast, which they'd had in their room (her idea, as Emma had felt too awkward to face Yannis after the night before). 'I know I promised yesterday.'

He spoke as though he was doing her a big favour. They started strolling along the beach, but before long, Emma wished she was on her own. He didn't even hold her hand! Instead he just moaned about the stones that were cutting his feet through his sandals and how hot it was.

Don't be so boring, she wanted to say. Can't you see it's part of the adventure? Why do you want everything to be the same as England?

Then he started asking her questions about the Greek evening the night before, which made her feel so awkward that she bent down to pick up a shell on the beach, ostensibly to add to her take-home-to-the-children collection. But really it was to hide her confusion.

'What was it like then?' he said chattily.

'OK,' Emma replied, hoping her voice sounded normal.

Tom cast her a sideways look. 'Did you talk to the famous Winston King?'

She shrugged, wishing now that she hadn't told him so much. Hadn't she made a vow not to tell anyone? Still, Tom was her husband.

'More to his wife. She's really nice, although a bit soft with the kids. There was a bit of a barney yesterday, apparently, cos her daughter went off with the owner's son.'

Tom raised his eyebrows. 'Went off?'

Emma felt bad about gossiping but grateful at the same time for a chance to steer the conversation away from potentially awkward questions. What if he asked who she had danced with? Then again, it wasn't as though he was there to care.

'Not like that. At least, I don't think so. They just disappeared for a bit. I saw them on my walk, actually, although I didn't say anything to Melissa.'

'What were they doing?'

'Nothing.' She bent down for another shell. A pretty one with a pink edge. 'I think it's rather sweet, actually. At least they know how to show affection.'

The anger slipped out in her voice before she knew it.

'Hey.' He took her hand. 'I know this hasn't been the most romantic of honeymoons but please don't be mad at me.'

Guilt over Yannis had made her upset. Still, it was better for Tom to think she was cross over that, than the other. Not that anything had happened during the dancing. She'd drunk rather a lot – again! But it still wasn't enough to crush that undeniable chemistry: the way her body had literally burned when Yannis had held her hand during the dancing.

Nothing happened, she kept telling herself. Only in her head. And that didn't count, did it?

'Shall we go back to our room?' Tom suddenly suggested meaningfully. He took her hand as he spoke, interlacing his fingers with hers.

Now he wanted it! Emma's heart sank as they made their way back across the sand. This wasn't the way she'd imagined it. Not when her head was still so full of the striking Greek, who had showered her with an attention that no one else had given her for a very long time . . .

Back at the cottage, Tom began to fumble with the zip of her shorts. His naked body against hers was hot and sticky. His movements, never confident at the best of times, made her feel slightly repulsed. He was pumping away, clearly waiting for her to get there. But she couldn't. Not unless . . .

Yes.

Oh God. There it was. That pendulum swinging sensation that took her breath away. She was even crying out loud, something she never did at home. Not because it might wake the children but because Tom never made her feel like doing so.

Tom had rolled off her now and was looking down at her with a self-satisfied smirk on his face. 'So I haven't lost the old magic then?'

It was all Emma could do not to cry. Easing herself out of bed, she made her way to the bathroom. Vigorously, she began to wash herself. How could you? she asked herself in the mirror, trying to wash away the picture of Yannis in her head, with his piercing eyes and goatee beard that she found so strangely attractive. How could you imagine making out with a man you hardly know, instead of your husband?

It was wrong. Horribly wrong!

Then again, hadn't there been a survey in *Charisma* the other week about women who visualised making love to someone else during sex? The funny thing was that Winston King (whose picture Bernie had pinned up in the staff room next to a list of his 'Five exercises-a-Day') had come out second.

By the time she got back to the room, Tom was sitting up

in bed with the air conditioning blaring out noisily. He patted the place next to him expectantly.

'Sorry – I promised to meet Melissa for the painting class near the pool,' said Emma, trying to hide her distressed face as she squeezed back into her shorts. 'Then there's the fishing trip. Are you coming?'

She held her breath, knowing that Yannis was going to be part of the crowd, helping Rosie with the picnic.

'Mind if I don't?' Tom made a little boy face. 'I'm just beginning to feel better and I don't want to get seasick.'

Emma felt a mixture of relief and irritation. 'That's fine,' she said quickly. 'See you later.'

Head spinning, she made her way to the pool, unable to clear her mind. Hadn't she always said there was no excuse for infidelity? Of course she'd never do anything like that. Yet Yannis had looked at her in a way that Tom never did. He made her feel beautiful. Her body melted every time his eyes drank her in, even though she knew it was wrong.

Why couldn't she feel like that with Tom, the father of her children?

Then again, if the price for being a mother was a rather average marriage with pretty boring bedroom routines, surely it was worth it?

Even so, it was impossible to ignore the sexually charged air that hung over the island, what with Melissa and Winston; the French couple; Rosie and the Greek; and now Yannis. She'd just have to ignore it, she decided, and concentrate on what was important. Still, she couldn't help wondering if there was something she had seriously missed out on . . .

Melissa seemed in a sombre mood when Emma reached the pool. Her daughter was with her, too, although obviously not willingly. 'I'm so bored,' she was whining.

'Then give the painting class a go, darling. It's something different.'

Alice scowled. 'Something to keep me away from Jack, you mean. It won't work, Mum. This is *my* life. Not yours.'

'I know,' said Melissa in a weary voice, 'but you're still very young.'

'I'm nearly fourteen! Unlike you.' The girl's eyes narrowed. 'At least I act my age. I've told you before, Mum, just because you wear leopard-print sunglasses, doesn't mean you're fashionable.'

Melissa flushed. 'Shh. We're about to start.'

The artist, a bohemian-looking young woman with a long cheesecloth skirt and yellow beads in her black hair, had given them all a sheet of paper. There was a large box of watercolour tubes and, in front of them, a vase with flowers.

After the demonstration (it looked so easy!), Emma set to with gusto. How wonderful it was to lose herself; to forget about Tom's fumblings and that strange attraction to Yannis.

But Melissa seemed keen to talk. 'Can I confide in you about something?' she hissed quietly.

Emma flushed. 'Of course.'

'Thanks.' Melissa glanced around to check no one could hear. The two of them were sitting on the edge of the painting group and the others seemed very absorbed in their work. 'I haven't known you very long, Emma, but you seem like the kind of person who can keep confidences.'

'I am.' Emma thought of all the things Bernie had told her about her marriage to Phil. Things which she wouldn't tell anyone.

'The thing is, my husband is *the* Winston King. The one on television.'

Emma nodded importantly. 'I guessed that.'

Melissa looked alarmed. 'Winston said you would. I just thought that maybe you might not recognise him with his shades.'

That was daft! Everyone in the UK knew who Winston King was, shades or not. The thought struck Emma that maybe Melissa wasn't particularly bright.

'I mean,' Melissa continued, 'there are other Winston Kings around. I looked them up on Google once. There are over a hundred.'

'Yes, but they don't all look like him, do they?' Emma couldn't help commenting.

Melissa looked scared. 'You haven't told anyone that you guessed, have you?'

'Of course not.' Emma touched her friend's hand briefly in assurance. 'I reckoned you needed your privacy like anyone else.'

'Thanks so much.' Melissa gave her a brief hug. 'The thing is, Winston's a bit upset because the *Globe*'s doing a series of articles on him.'

Emma, who really wanted to go back to her painting – the pink flower she was copying was so beautiful – tried to give her friend her full attention.

'It doesn't say very much,' Melissa continued.

There was the sound of footsteps. Alice was coming up and had caught the tail end of the conversation. 'It doesn't say very much because Winston's boring. Dad says he's a waste of space.'

'Alice!' This time, Melissa did seem annoyed. 'That's very rude.'

She waited for Alice to go back to her painting on the other side of the group. Then she turned back to Emma. 'So far, it's just the usual stuff about the Marines that's been said before. Winston says it's to get people to buy today's paper. But it's tomorrow he's worried about.'

'Why?' Emma whispered, flattered that Melissa felt she could trust her.

Then she nudged Melissa to warn her that the art teacher was coming round now, making small exclamations of praise combined with gentle suggestions. The French couple were there too: their 'flowers' looked more like a pair of nudes entwined in the shape of a nutcracker.

'Because,' said Melissa in such a quiet voice that Emma could hardly hear her, 'my first husband has apparently given them an interview.'

Emma gasped, glancing at Alice, who had given up on the painting and was furiously texting, doubtless running up an enormous phone bill.

226

'What has he said?' asked Emma.

Melissa shrugged. 'I don't know. I've tried to Skype Marvyn but he isn't answering.'

Emma's heart gave a little jump. So she had Skype! Bernie had that on her computer. 'My mum always says that there's no point in worrying about something until it happens.'

Melissa nodded. 'I know. She's right. But it's difficult, isn't it? Still, it's nice to have someone to talk to.' She squeezed Emma's hand lightly. 'Thanks.'

'It was nothing. Any time.' Emma had almost forgotten her painting now. 'Listen, I hope you don't mind me asking, but is it possible to use your Skype? It's just that I'd love to try to contact the kids; I'd give anything to see their faces.'

'Sure. I'd better not lend you our iPad as Winston will want it, but you can borrow Alice's.'

'No way.' The girl had crept up on them again. It was slightly unnerving. 'It hasn't got much battery left and I forgot my charger.'

'Alice! Emma wants to talk to her children.'

'Well, maybe they don't want to talk to *her*, just like I don't want to talk to my mother.'

Emma tried not to show her shock, but Melissa just looked resigned rather than angry. Reluctantly, the girl got it out of her bag. 'Do you know how it works?' Alice demanded, as though Emma was the child and not the adult. 'You can only talk to someone if they're online.'

With any luck, Bernie might be around. She was having the children, Mum had said, so there was an outside chance.

Emma could hardly wait for the class to finish (the teacher had nodded approvingly at her flower!) so Alice could show her how to look up Bernie's Skype address. Within minutes, her friend's warm, chubby face swam into view.

'Emma!' She was eating something. A chip, from the look of the bag next to her. 'What are you doing online? You should be making wild, passionate love on the beach with your new husband.'

Emma flushed. 'Hah!' She went beetroot, unable to look at

Melissa or her daughter, who was sniggering. 'A . . . a friend has lent me her iPad so I can talk to the children.'

Her heart was thumping with excitement.

'Gawain!' Bernie yelled out, swallowing her mouthful. 'Come and look at this. It's Mummy on a special television. No, love. Not like the one that Granny lets you watch all day long.'

There was an 'ahh' sound from Melissa as her little boy came into view. 'Isn't he sweet? What gorgeous blond hair. And is that your daughter sitting next to him? She's beautiful.'

Emma gazed with longing at her little ones, perched on stools at Bernie's kitchen table, making Play-Doh shapes.

Willow was staring at her with her wide blue eyes, as though she didn't even recognise her. The pain made Emma feel sick. But Gawain's voice called out through the miles. 'Mummy!' he was saying, reaching out to her. 'Mummy.'

Oh dear. He was crying. Banging his little arm on the table, the way he did when he was upset. This was selfish of her, Emma realised. Gawain couldn't understand why he could see her but not touch her. She was unsettling him.

'Mummy's going on a boat trip later on,' she said in as light a tone as possible, as though it was quite natural for her to be doing something different away from the children thousands of miles away.

But Gawain was yelling so much now he didn't seem to hear her.

'Maybe this wasn't such a good idea,' said Bernie hurriedly. Even though the screen was getting blurry and out of focus now, Emma could make out her friend's arms wrapped protectively round her son. It should be *her* doing that. 'It's all right,' her friend was saying soothingly. 'Your mummy will be home soon. Let's have another go at telling the time, shall we?'

Teaching him the time? That was *her* job!

Then Gawain's face disappeared and Bernie's swam back into view. 'Don't worry. He'll stop crying when you've gone. Having a good time, are you? Your mum says Tom's feeling better now. Everyone at this end has stopped being sick too.'

That was good. Then she remembered her manners. 'Thank you so much for looking after them and for organising the honeymoon,' she began. What? How did that happen? The screen had gone blank.

'The Wi-Fi reception is shit here,' said Alice scathingly.

'Darling, I've told you before not to use words like that.'

'It's true.' Alice leaped up, snatching the iPad back. 'I'm going for a walk. Yes, I am, Mum. You can't stop me.'

The two women watched the young girl flounce off, texting furiously as she went. 'She thinks she's in love with Jack,' said Melissa quietly. 'I hadn't expected this so soon.' She smiled sadly at Emma. 'There's nothing like your first boyfriend, is there?'

Emma, still aching from the sight of the children, thought of Tom, wryly. Bernie had been right when they'd been at school. She should have had more fun before settling down.

'You've got all this to come,' continued Melissa. 'Make the most of it while your two are young. At least you know where they are. Teenagers are like fleas: always jumping in and out of the house without notice.'

She patted Emma on the arm. 'See you on the boat later tonight. I'm hoping it might distract Winston. Sounds rather good fun; there's going to be a wonderful picnic, apparently.' She smiled warmly. 'Thanks so much for listening. It really helped to talk.'

Emma felt a glow. It was so nice to help others out, even though she didn't think she'd done much. Meanwhile, she didn't feel like going back to the cottage. Not yet. She would have to tell Tom that she'd Skyped Bernie and that Gawain had got upset. Then he'd tell her that she should have left them to it and that might lead to another argument . . .

Instead, she dangled her legs in the pool, thinking about the future. Seeing the children had put life into perspective. It would be all right, she told herself, when she got back into the groove of things at home. The routine with the children; her little job; Mum; Bernie and her other friends. They would all distract her from these silly unsettled feelings she was having about Tom. She watched Rosie walk past with a small, wrinkly-faced woman. Maybe it was natural to have these doubts. They were no more than post-wedding nerves, that was all.

As for Yannis, with his handsome Greek face and his way of looking at her as though she was the only woman in the room, she'd just been really silly. She wouldn't drink tonight, she told herself. Just stick to non-alcoholic punch.

'Excuse me,' said a voice, slicing into her thoughts. 'Is this the Villa Rosa?'

Emma turned round. Even though she had never met a journalist before, she had a funny feeling that this young woman, with her sharp, foxy face and notepad sticking out of her bag, wasn't your usual tourist.

She nodded.

The girl's eyes lit up. 'I'm looking for someone called Winston King. Don't suppose you know him, do you?'

Emma found herself shaking her head. 'He was staying here but he's moved on.'

'Any idea where?'

She shook her head again.

'Well,' said the woman, handing her a plain white business card with a number on it, but no name or mention of a company, 'if you happen to hear, can you give me a ring?' She smiled coldly. 'I'll make it worth your while.'

HONEYMOON FACTS

More than half of all newly-weds are too tired or argu-
mentative to have sex on their wedding night.

National newspaper article

Chapter Twenty-Three

WINSTON

WHAT IT WAS REALLY LIKE TO WORK FOR WINSTON KING

'Self-absorbed, paranoid about privacy and a loner' – that's Poppy Pops' verdict on her old boss.

'He made me book different hotels all over the world to keep his Greek honeymoon destination under wraps,' reveals Poppy. 'But I got my own back by cancelling his reservation. I know it was wrong, but I felt he needed to be taken down a peg or two.'

So the muddle over rooms had been Poppy's fault and not Jack's! Winston reread the opening lines to the feature on his iPad. How dare she?

'He never spoke about his experiences in Afghanistan or Bosnia . . .'

Why should he? He wasn't the only ex-Green Beret to block it out.

'And once, when he'd fallen asleep in his dressing room after filming, I heard him muttering someone's name. I can't say for certain what it was but I always felt that Winston was hiding something . . .'

Winston stiffened, running his eye down the rest of the feature. There was nothing else as far as he could see. But it was enough.

Did these hacks have any idea what damage they did to people, digging into their private lives like this?

It was really unfair, thought Winston angrily. Everyone had a past, didn't they? Frankly, he had a sneaking sympathy for politicians whose earlier lives were keenly scrutinised for anything that might have been at all dodgy. After all, they hadn't known when they were younger that they were going to be in positions of power. Besides, how else could a young man (or woman) learn about life, unless they made mistakes?

His eye was drawn to the paragraph at the end of the offending article.

'Don't miss tomorrow's issue! 'How Winston caught my wife on the rebound,' by Mrs King's former husband.

The rebound? Winston's heart gave a little thud. Melissa's divorce had come through two days before they had met. She'd been vulnerable, certainly.

Was *that* why she'd married him? Not because she'd been carried away, as he had been?

The bedroom door flew open. Hastily, Winston made to put the iPad away. 'Are you coming or not?' Melissa stood there in her white shorts and tee-shirt, her black eyes cool. 'We're meant to be going on the trip now.'

She glanced at the iPad. 'Don't bother filling me in on today's feature. I've already read it.'

'So is it true?' he heard himself say. '*Did* you marry me on the rebound?'

Melissa gave a little laugh. 'It's not *that* you should be worried about, Winston. Let's just hope that Marvyn hasn't told the world that you tried to pay the owner's son to take the kids off your hands. It doesn't make you look like a great stepfather, does it?'

'How would he know that?'

Melissa's cheeks coloured.

Then he realised. 'You *told* him, didn't you?'

She shrugged. 'Marvyn and I might be divorced but we still talk about our children. Now do hurry up. Everyone's waiting.'

Bloody fishing trip! It meant they were all stuck in one boat together for God knows how many hours. There was no chance to go for a long, thoughtful walk on his own, which was what he really wanted to do. 'You don't have to come,' Melissa declared coolly as they walked down to the harbour together, carefully keeping a distance between them.

Clearly, she hadn't forgiven him for paying Jack. Nor had the kids. Instead of arguing, they were presenting a united front for a change. Freddie was following his sister around like a lost dog, sucking up to her, as if trying to make up for the fact that he'd slunk off and got her and Jack into trouble.

Even now, his wife was ignoring his outstretched hand as she stepped into the boat, manned by the grinning Greek fisherman who couldn't keep his eyes off the villa owner.

She was a strange one. He couldn't make her out. There was still something about that photograph in her room that unsettled him. Rosie, he thought to himself. Rosie Harrison. The name didn't seem familiar. Yet there was definitely something about her that was nudging his memory.

'Everyone on board?' the Greek was calling out. 'Fantastic! There are lifebelts in the chest under the deck – see? – but do not look worried. They're just a precaution. The weather, she is fine. We will stop in an hour or so, on a small island which is not inhabited. No tourists go there, so you are in for a treat, I think!'

Emma shuffled over, looking nervous. 'I hope it's safe.'

Melissa, he could see, was giving her new friend's hand a quick squeeze. 'I'm sure it is, otherwise they wouldn't risk taking us all there.'

I'm not sure that's true, Winston almost said, but managed

to hold his tongue before Melissa bit his head off again. If only she'd turn some of her anger towards her children.

Take Alice, who was sitting at the far end of the boat, shooting him filthy looks and texting furiously at the same time. She'd been told not to use her phone so much; the bill would be horrendous. Melissa would pay, of course, but now she was married, her personal settlement from Marvin had gone. So now he, Winston, would have to fork out.

Wistfully, Winston thought back to the day he'd asked Melissa to marry him and she'd accepted, rather fast. *On the rebound* . . . Maybe, he thought, trailing his fingers in the water as they set off, *he* was the naive one.

Winston glanced at Freddie, carving his initials into the wooden box marked LIFEBELTS, next to the French couple (who were snogging as usual). These children were impossible! If only he could persuade Melissa to send them both off to boarding school. It had certainly taught *him* how to behave.

Or had it? There were some things in life that he would do very differently next time round. Winston felt sick again, thinking of tomorrow's paper. It was like waiting for the guillotine to drop.

'Have you got a second?' He looked up to find his wife's new friend squatting next to him. Now what? A request for an autograph? Or for a personal exercise programme? Melissa had confessed to him that she'd confided his identity to this Emma. Another example of his wife's naivety . . .

'Someone was asking for you on the island this morning. She had a notebook poking out of her bag and she looked as though she was on business rather than holiday.'

Winston's skin crawled with fear. 'I'm afraid I said that you had been staying here but that you'd moved on.' The blonde bit her lower lip. 'I hope you don't mind, but something made me think she might be a journalist and I didn't think you'd want that. Not on your honeymoon.'

She glanced down at her shiny wedding ring. 'I'm really grateful to you for finding this. I don't know what I'd have done if I'd lost it.'

Suddenly Winston felt a wave of compassion. 'That's very nice of you. Thank you.'

'Not at all.' She seemed embarrassed now as she lumbered to her feet. 'I'll leave you in peace. I expect you don't get much of that in your job.'

He'd misjudged her. Abashed, Winston watched the woman waddle off. So they were after him! The *Globe*, perhaps, or one of the other papers. Had they found out about Nick?

'Enjoying yourself?'

He looked up to find Rosie Harrison had planted herself next to him. She'd been moving, he'd noticed, from one guest to the other, making sure everyone was all right. Now her startling green-blue eyes were searching his face.

Winston nodded, looking for the right words which would be both polite and accurate. 'It's a break,' he said, looking across to Jack, who was busy handing out tumblers of ouzo to everyone. He worked hard, he'd give him that. Alice could do with getting off her butt and having a holiday job, but Melissa said she was too young. 'Is your son all right?'

Rosie Harrison shrugged. 'Bruised. Alice is still upset because she thinks he was "paid" to be with her. He's tried explaining that he really likes her but she won't listen.' She gave him a quizzical look. 'Quite a stubborn girl for her age, isn't she?'

He nodded. 'Like her mother,' he said, without meaning to.

She was looking at him sharply now. Flustered, he tried to change the subject. 'So tell me, Mrs Harrison, how did you end up here?'

'Rosie, please,' she reminded him.

She was looking away now, over the water towards the small island in the distance, a glow of red creeping over her cheek. 'I went travelling after school and met Cara. She's the other owner of the villa; we're co-partners.'

Interesting! Was she the elderly wrinkled woman in the red headscarf who'd turned up yesterday? Winston felt a creeping curiosity. 'So how many years have you been here?'

Rosie Harrison was getting very red now. 'More than fifteen.'

Winston made a quick mental calculation. So she'd either arrived when she was pregnant with the boy or had got pregnant soon after. He glanced at the Greek fisherman who was sitting at the wheel, his back very straight. Was he the father?

'And where did you grow up?'

His question, innocuous as it was, appeared to nettle her. She was getting up now, smoothing down her shorts (women, in his experience, always fiddled with their clothes when they felt nervous, much as men tended to straighten their ties) and calling out to Jack that they needed some juice over here.

'In the South-West,' she threw over her shoulder.

'Really? I did my training there . . .'

He stopped, his words lost as an unexpected gust of wind tipped the boat sharply to one side, sending plastic tumblers scattering all over the deck. There was a collective gasp, including a little scream from the blonde bride.

The Greek was wrestling with the wheel. 'It ees nothing to worry about,' he yelled out over his shoulder. 'Just a squall, that is all.'

Winston's eyes narrowed at the sky, which had grown quite dark during his short conversation with Rosie Harrison.

The waves were rocking the boat even harder now, tipping them from side to side. He made to take Melissa's hand but she'd already moved towards the kids, who were jumping up and down as though this was some kind of entertainment put on for their amusement.

'You must sit,' roared the Greek oik, 'or you will change the balance on the boat.'

'Mum!' Alice was gripping the edge. 'I'm scared.'

Rubbish. She was only trying to get attention. She was texting one-handed now, no doubt sending a minute-by-minute account to her friends. Then the boat heaved again as another wave hit it, sending him lurching against the blonde bride.

She grabbed him, her nails cutting through into his flesh.

'I'm not a strong swimmer. You don't think we're going to capsize, do you?'

Possibly. Why the fuck hadn't Mr Greek Charmer there distributed the lifebelts? He made for the chest, but as he did so, there was a blood-curdling scream.

'My phone! It's slipped into the water. Help me, someone!'

Melissa was hurling herself towards her daughter. 'Leave it. Do you hear me? Leave it!'

Stupid, stupid girl! She was going to jump in. Oh my God. There was a gigantic splash. 'Alice!' screamed his wife.

But it wasn't Alice. It was her brother who had jumped in, trying to save his sister's phone. Without thinking, Winston kicked off his sandals and dived in after him. The sea was rough, reminding him of a training exercise where he hadn't done as well as the others.

Better on land than the water, his report had read. That was because you knew where you were on firm earth. The sea could be a devil. A demon that might finally finish him and Melissa unless he could rescue the boy.

Where the hell was he? Winston couldn't see anything through the waves, which were buffeting him all over the place. Dimly he could hear Melissa screaming. Or was that the wind? Taking a deep breath, he swam down below the surface of the water, opening his eyes to scan the blue-and-green underworld.

Nothing.

You can't fail, he told himself. This wasn't just about Melissa now. It was about saving a kid's life.

Doing what he hadn't been able to do with Nick.

He rose to the surface, gulping in air and scanning the water in case Freddie had come up without him knowing.

'Can you see him?' Melissa was yelling through the wind. At least, that's what it sounded like. Her face was contorted with fear. She needed him. He couldn't let her down.

Unable to answer, Winston dived down again. Maybe Freddie had hit his head on the side of the boat. If so, he'd probably had it. He'd have been underwater for too long.

Melissa would never manage if something happened to one of her children.

Nor would he.

Up again for more air. Someone was shouting. The Greek. He had a pair of binoculars in his hand and was pointing at a bit of wood that was floating some distance off. Bloody hell. It was Freddie. Winston lashed his way through the waves, imagining that he was cutting swathes through the enemy. He could feel a dull pain in his knee but it wasn't important. All that mattered was getting to the boy who, he could see now, was hanging on to the plank of wood and crying.

Nearly there now. Nearly there.

'It's all right,' he gasped. 'Hang on to me.'

Freddie was shaking his head, still gripping the wood.

'You've got to trust me.'

The same words he had used to Nick came out of his mouth as though they had been sitting there, waiting for a second chance.

'I'm . . . too . . . scared . . . to . . . let . . . go.'

There was another wave coming. A big one. 'If you want to see your mum again, you've got to let me grab you. OK?'

The boy nodded, tears streaming down his face.

'I promise it will be all right.'

Again, exactly what he'd said to Nick. But this time, it had to be true. He couldn't fail twice.

Just in time, Winston took the boy in his arms before the next wave smashed into him. Cupping one hand under his chin and using his left arm to hook under the boy's armpit and round his chest, he began to swim back to the boat, keeping Freddie on his back, his face above water.

It was difficult to see where they were going, swimming backwards like this, but miraculously the waves had started to calm down and the sky was beginning to lighten overhead as though nature had given up its fight.

Through his exhaustion, Winston was dimly conscious of a deep voice calling out, 'We will help you up.'

Greco! Thank God. He was throwing them a rope from

the boat, which was still a way off. 'Grab it,' urged Winston but the boy was too weak. There was nothing for it but to continue holding Freddie while swimming backwards.

'You're here now. Hang on to me,' he heard the Greek say.

Summoning up all his strength, he held Freddie up for the fisherman to grab. Shit, he was slipping. 'Take him, man, can you?' Winston spluttered.

Yes. At last, Greco had him and was hauling him over the side. Then he reached out his arms to Winston.

Ignoring them, he heaved himself up and clambered over into the stern.

Winston hardly heard the round of clapping. It was his stepson he was looking for. 'Are you all right?'

Melissa had a towel around her son and was clasping him to her. The boy was crying into her chest. If he could do that, he was probably OK. Then Freddie looked up at Winston.

'Thank you,' he sobbed.

Melissa's eyes locked with his. 'You did it,' she said, with a look of total adoration. Then she kissed him. Full on the lips. 'My hero.'

TRUE HONEYMOON STORY

'My ex texted to ask if I'd have a drink with him when I got back. I said yes.'

Anonymous

Chapter Twenty-Four

EMMA

Even when Freddie was safely back on the boat, Emma couldn't stop shaking. In fact, it was worse now that the drama was over. Maybe it was shock.

When Melissa's son had gone overboard like that, she'd thought he was just playing around like kids do and would climb back on. But when Winston had dived in she'd realised it was serious.

Then she'd got into a worse state than Melissa, who was just sitting there, horribly quiet, eyes glued to Winston as he swam around, looking for her son.

She'd tried to comfort her new friend. 'It will be all right,' she'd said, taking her hand. But her words came out all wobbly and weren't, she could see, any help at all. The awful thing was that inside, she felt an enormous surge of relief. What if she and Tom had brought the children on their honeymoon and it had been Gawain or Willow out there? She would have gone to pieces. Yet Melissa just sat quite straight, her gaze steadily focussed on the distant black blob that was Winston amidst the waves that had swallowed up Freddie. Not saying a thing.

Alice, on the other hand, was whimpering. 'Is he going to be all right, Mum?'

Melissa's voice could hardly be heard above the wind, but it sounded like 'He's got to be.'

Then, all of a sudden, there they were! Winston swimming boldly through the waves on his back, holding Freddie under his chin.

They were safe! Emma could hardly believe it when – after

that terrifying last slip – Greco helped to yank Freddie over the side of the boat and then Winston clambered up too.

Such courage! Such amazing strength in those muscles . . .

Melissa was crying now as she clung on to her son and husband. Emma edged away, not wanting to intrude. 'Did you find my phone?' demanded Alice, tugging at her brother's soaking-wet tee-shirt.

Little monkey.

Ironically, the waves were beginning to subside and the sun was actually coming out. But they could all have died if the boat had capsized. Emma felt a thrill of panic in her chest. How would the children have managed without her if she had drowned? Tom wouldn't be any good at bringing them up on his own. Mum would help, of course, but it wouldn't be the same. Dear Lord, it made her feel physically sick to think of it.

'You are shaking, I theenk.' For a moment, Emma thought it was Greco talking but then realised it was Yannis. Hadn't someone said he was Greco's cousin? They certainly looked similar.

She hadn't even realised he was on board, but now he was putting a dry towel round her. Until then, she'd hardly noticed that her shorts and tee-shirt were soaked through.

'They were so lucky,' Emma tried to say, although her teeth were chattering so much that the words came out in a muddle. Yannis, whose English was really rather good, seemed to understand her, though.

'Yes. They were.' He nodded at Winston, who had one arm around Melissa and the other round Freddie. 'But he is strong man, I think. Here, take this.'

He handed her a small glass with a golden-brown liquid inside. 'It will warm you up.'

Shaking with the cold and wet, she drank it gratefully. Instantly, there was a rush of heat down her chest. 'What is it?' she asked.

Yannis tapped the bottle beside him. 'A local drink. I think you need another, yes?'

She'd sworn not to overdo the alcohol after last night but this tasted innocuous enough, rather like the aniseed drink she'd had earlier.

'Where were you when all this was happening?' she asked after the second glass.

He shrugged. 'Down below. I was preparing the food for our picnic.' Then he pointed up at the sky. So blue! It was difficult to imagine it was the same one as a few moments ago. 'We will have a good day for it, I theenk, now the gods are not so angry. Look! Here is the island.'

Helping her up, Yannis pointed to the small, surprisingly green piece of land that was approaching. 'We are here. It is time for us to relax.' His warm smile sent a little tingle through her. 'We all deserve it, don't you think?'

The relief at having Freddie and Winston back safely – coupled with a general feeling that they had all escaped – made everyone else heady with excitement, as well as her. Even the French couple, who had hardly spoken to anyone else on the boat but sat there, with their arms around each other, were now laughing and knocking back the wine that was being passed around.

Had she had too much to drink? wondered Emma. If she had, it had only been to calm herself after a pretty scary ordeal. Surely that was acceptable.

'Food is ready,' Rosie Harrison was saying briskly, as though she was one of the prefects at Emma's old school.

She was nice, Emma had decided during the last few days, although there was a certain sharpness to her too. Maybe you had to be like that when you ran a business.

Emma's eyes began to feel very heavy. 'You must eat, I think,' urged Yannis, pointing her towards the amazing feast that had been spread out on a tablecloth on the sand.

There was certainly enough. Plates piled high with little triangular pastry shapes; huge dishes of lasagne; a large platter of crispy sardines with slices of lemon; and those divine bread rolls with nutty seeds that she'd grown to love.

Yet even though Emma's rumbling stomach told her that she was hungry, she could only manage a bowl of salad. The heat made it hard to eat and besides, all she really wanted to do was sleep.

Her mind went back to the many occasions that she'd tried desperately to keep the kids awake when they'd started to nod off in the car. 'Don't – or you won't sleep tonight,' she had urged. Now she felt just the same way herself. It was so hard to keep her eyes open!

'Want to play French cricket?' asked Melissa, coming over. Emma could see her friend glancing at Yannis curiously.

'I don't think so,' she murmured, feeling her head fall onto Yannis's shoulder. Part of her felt distantly embarrassed. The other part felt it was quite natural. They were just friends, after all.

Melissa knelt down next to her. 'Thank you for comforting me earlier on when Freddie was out there. It meant a lot to me.'

Emma squeezed her hand in reply.

'Are you all right?' Melissa's voice seemed to be coming from a long way off.

She tried to nod but her head wouldn't obey. 'I'm just sleepy.'

'Maybe it's the sun. It is very bright here.' She could feel Melissa's hand patting her arm. 'Why don't you move to the shade?'

Dimly, Emma was aware of a hand steering her away from the picnic, towards a little clearing just up from the beach. There was the sound of giggling and someone speaking in a French accent.

'Mum, Mum!'

Emma stiffened. For a minute, she'd thought it was Gawain calling her.

'The kids want me.' Melissa spread out a red tartan rug. 'Why don't you sit here for a bit? Have a little snooze.'

There was silence for a while and then the sound of footsteps padding across the sand, followed by the cracking of a twig. 'Ah, so this is where you are hiding,' said an amused voice. It wasn't Melissa's, as she'd thought, but a man's. The thought occurred to her dimly that maybe Tom had come to find her after all.

No. It was Yannis. The realisation both excited and frightened her. Was he really interested in her, a podgy mother of two? If so, it was, she had to admit, quite flattering. Especially after Tom's earlier honeymoon behaviour.

'Mind if I sit down with you?' he said, putting his head to one side quizzically.

'No. Yes. I'm not sure.' She felt herself blushing furiously.

'Don't be shy.' His hand reached out and held hers. Emma knew she ought to move away but was unable to. Maybe, she thought suddenly, this was the real thing – passion – what she'd wanted all her life and exactly what Tom hadn't given her. Didn't she deserve it? A throb of desire shot through her. If she said no to Yannis now, she might never know what it was like. Was this the drink talking? No. If she was honest, she wanted him. She desired this handsome Greek, partly because his interest made her feel beautiful. Sexy.

'May I kiss you?' he asked softly.

Emma found herself nodding as his mouth came down on hers. Instantly, her entire body burst into flames – or so it felt. So this was what it was like!

'May I?' he asked again. This time, his hands began to move underneath her tee-shirt.

'Yes,' she whispered, feeling as though another woman was speaking. Then she added, almost as though to convince herself, 'Please.'

Emma woke with a start after an erotic dream in which Yannis had been making love to her. She flushed furiously at the thought. Honestly, it was amazing what the mind could do when you were asleep. If she was honest, she couldn't help fancying him. But it went without saying that she'd never be unfaithful to Tom. Besides, Melissa had been with her in the woods, hadn't she? But where was she now?

Making her way out of the clearing, conscious of the taste of drink in her mouth, she made her way down to the beach and the sound of voices. There they all were, gathering around the boat with its little red front and talking urgently. Mrs Harrison's Greek boyfriend was particularly loud, waving his hands around and talking vigorously.

'You've been away for ages,' said Melissa, looking up. She dropped Winston's hand, Emma noticed, but now seized Emma's as though they were old friends. Her face creased with concern. 'You haven't been in the woods all this time, have you?'

'Well, yes.' Emma felt confused. 'You were there. Don't you remember?'

Melissa shook her head. 'Only for a bit. Then I came back here. We had a lovely game of French cricket and then we swam and did some sunbathing. But it looks as though we've got a problem.'

Emma's chest did a funny little flip of apprehension. 'What sort of problem?'

Melissa gestured at the boat. 'The engine won't start. Greco reckons that it's got some kind of rubbish stuck in it . . .'

'Flot Some and Jet Some,' chirped Freddie beside them. 'That's what it's called.'

'Show-off,' spat Alice.

'So what? Just cos you're stupid.'

'No, I'm not.'

'Yes, you are.'

Well, at least things were back to normal! Apart, of course, from the engine. 'But they can fix it, right?'

Melissa shrugged. 'They're not sure. Winston's trying to help – he's rather good at that sort of thing – but they reckon they might need a new part to get it going.'

A new part? Whenever Tom said that about the car, it always meant trouble.

'Problem is,' continued Melissa, tossing back a strand of dark hair in a gesture that Emma was beginning to think might be deliberate, 'no one's mobile is working here.'

Really? Emma got hers out to look but Melissa was right. No signal. Just Willow and Gawain's sweet little faces grinning toothily from her screen saver. So far away . . .

'Greco says that he can send up some flares when it gets darker,' added Melissa lightly as though she was a mother trying to reassure a child, 'but it's possible that if he can't fix it, we might have to stay the night.'

'Cool!' Freddie's eyes were shining. 'Can we explore by moonlight? Do you think we'll find treasure?'

Alice snorted. 'Don't be stupid.'

'I'm not.'

'Yes, you are. I'm not staying here, arguing with a baby.'

'Alice.' Melissa's tone suggested she'd given up before she'd begun. 'Come back.'

But the girl was already off, walking down to the beach where she proceeded to sit down, cross-legged, looking out at the horizon which was a wonderful explosion of apricot and blue. Almost immediately, a figure joined her.

Jack.

'They're all right,' said Melissa quietly, as though to herself. 'I trust her. We've had a long mother–daughter talk.'

Would she and Willow have the kind of relationship where they could do that in years to come? Emma hoped so – just as long as Willow wasn't rude like Alice. Then she realised something with a thud. 'But if they can't fix the engine, we might not get back in time for our flight.'

Melissa shrugged. 'I know. Real bore, isn't it? Still, at least it means Winston can't read the papers yet. Poor man. He's really nervous about the *Globe* piece, although, as I've told him, he has to ignore things like that.'

Emma heard her voice come out like a child's wail. 'But I've *got* to get back. Tom will be out of his mind with worry. We can't miss the plane either. The children and Mum are expecting us. And we can't afford another flight.'

Her friend gave her a sympathetic look. 'Haven't you got travel insurance?'

Emma thought of the shiny blue-and-white EHIC card she'd

248

carefully put in the back of her purse. No need to have anything else, Tom had said. 'I don't know that it covers us for a new flight.'

This was dreadful! It would be so expensive to have to buy two more air fares. They couldn't afford it. Not with the expense of the wedding and the gas bill that was much more than they'd thought it was going to be. But none of this was as important as the immediate problem: the need to get back to Tom. Even worse was the fear of missing the flight home, back to the kids.

At that moment, Yannis came up the steps from the bottom of the boat. He looked straight at her, a soft smile playing on his lips. 'You were wonderful,' he whispered, as he went past. 'Can you get away later?'

Emma froze. 'What do you mean?'

Yannis's eyes went cold. 'Don't play games, Emma. You wanted it as much as me. In fact, you were begging for more.'

Bile rose up in her mouth. Was he telling the truth? She'd had too much to drink, after all. Supposing that erotic dream she'd had about Yannis had been true?

No, it couldn't be. Could it? In her 'dream', she'd been eager. Passionate in a way she had never known herself to be. To be crude, she'd definitely been up for it. Oh my God! What had she done?

'Are you all right?' asked Melissa, in a kind, concerned voice.

She shook her head as a dark pool of terror formed in her chest. 'No, actually, I don't think I am.'

TRUE HONEYMOON STORY

'A couple at the next table insisted on paying for our dinner. They were celebrating their forty-fifth anniversary and wanted to "share their good fortune".'

Amelia, a newly-wed

Chapter Twenty-Five

ROSIE

The trip was fated! She'd had a bad feeling about it from the minute that Yannis had come on board, with the stench of wine about him. Recently, Rosie had decided she didn't care very much for Greco's cousin. Cara clearly couldn't stand him, though, frustratingly, she refused to explain why. Rosie appreciated that he was a great cook, but he had an air of arrogance about him that grated. Just look at how he had turned up a week late, without so much as an apology. Nor did she like the way he was so familiar with the guests, especially Emma Walker.

If it hadn't been for the fact that she was desperate for help in the kitchen, Rosie would have told him where to go.

'Have you been drinking?' she'd asked him sharply before they'd set off on the trip.

He'd shrugged, giving her that lazy smile of his. Here was a man who clearly fancied himself. Hah! It was wasted on her.

Greco, overhearing the exchange, had taken her aside. 'He will be all right. I will keep an eye on him.'

Against her better judgment, Rosie had agreed, but only because she needed help with the picnic. Then when she'd seen him go up the beach and into the copse where the new Mrs Walker had just disappeared, she had felt extremely perturbed.

Should she go after them? Part of her wanted to, but at the same time, it was really none of her business. Emma Walker was a grown woman, and what she did or didn't do was up to her.

Everyone, as she'd tried to tell Cara back at the villa, had the right to choose how they led their own lives. And it was her choice not to tell Jack the truth about his father, even if Cara thought otherwise.

'We'll talk about it when you return,' the older woman had declared.

Much as Rosie loved Cara, she'd forgotten just how dogmatic and insistent she could be, like many Greek matriarchs.

But all this was nothing compared with what might have happened to Freddie. Rosie still felt sick with relief. Supposing the boy had drowned? It wasn't the terrible publicity that worried her (although that would have been awful). It was how his poor mother would have coped.

Losing Jack would be her worst nightmare. Yet Melissa had been so calm, so dignified, as she'd waited, watching her husband scour the sea for him. She'd believed in him, Rosie realised, which was why she hadn't gone to bits. And she had to hand it to Winston. He'd saved the boy, against the odds.

But now, just as everything seemed all right again, the engine had packed in! Rosie hadn't believed it when Greco went to start it, after the picnic. She didn't know much about boats but even she could tell that the spluttering and choking sound wasn't good.

'Mind if I take a look?' asked Winston after Greco had played around with it for over an hour, before announcing that they needed a spare part. 'I might be able to fix it without.'

Greco had scowled. Greek men were not good, Rosie had observed over the years, at letting someone else do better than them.

'Let him try,' she'd said softly, laying a calming hand on Greco's strong brown arm. His heat transferred itself to her and for a minute, she had a lovely warm recollection of last night; a stolen hour after the Greek evening in Greco's little white fishing cottage on the beach.

He'd cooked her a plate of delicious sardines with brown

crusty bread and a glorious crispy salad, accompanied by lashings of red wine. Afterwards, they had lain side by side on the colourful rug that covered the stone floor, leaning against giant cushions in stunning blue and red. Greco might be a fisherman but he had an eye for design.

'I don't want to talk about Jack and Winston,' she'd warned at the beginning of the evening and he'd steered clear of the subject. Instead, they chatted about books and music and some ideas Rosie had for the villa.

Soon, as they lay together, her head in his lap, the talking had stopped, and they had merged as one, right there on the rug.

He'd insisted on keeping the light on, his eyes on her throughout as though to tell her that she was the one that he wanted. No one else.

I've misjudged this man, she thought afterwards. Greco is a good man. He and Yannis might share the same grandmother, but they were cut from a different cloth.

Now, on the boat, she stroked Greco's arm encouragingly, willing him to allow Winston to have a go with the engine. 'Very well.' Her man had shrugged with that almost aristocratic toss of his head which might seem rude to others, but which Rosie knew was a sign of male pride. 'See if you can do better.'

Winston was clearly taken aback by Greco's hostile tone. No wonder! How could he know that Greco was jealous of him?

'I cannot bear to think of you and that man together,' he had growled last night, as they'd cuddled up together.

'I don't question you about your past girlfriends,' she'd pointed out.

Greco had shaken his head. 'But they are not present, right now, are they? Not like that man.'

'But Winston doesn't know! He doesn't remember me.'

Another furious toss of the head. 'That makes it worse. How can a man father a child and not remember the woman he made it with?'

Exactly what Rosie had been asking herself. 'I don't know,' she replied, flustered. 'He must have had several girlfriends since then, I suppose.' She dug him in the ribs, trying to introduce a note of lightness. 'Just like you.'

'No.' Another vehement toss of the head. 'I recall each one of the girls I have been with.'

'But there are rumours of children on the mainland.' It was one of the many things that had been troubling her about her lover's past.

Greco propped himself on his elbow and gazed down at her. 'Those are untruths, put about by women who wanted to be with me. Do you not think that, if I had a child, I would take care of it? I am a responsible man. A child needs a father: that is why I feel so strongly that you should tell Winston about Jack, even though I do not like it. But I can assure you, Rosie, that I am not a father myself.'

His slow, steady gaze took in the rest of her body which had, much to her surprise, sprung back into shape after Jack's birth. Indeed, to look at her flat stomach, you might not think she had ever had a child. 'Yet I would like to be a father, one day.'

Rosie hadn't expected that.

He was stroking her stomach now and then his hand moved lower down, making her feel weak inside. 'I am not asking for an answer now, my Rosie. I simply want you to think about it.'

Think about a baby? Did that include marriage as well? For all his bravado, Greco (like many Greek men) was solidly conventional. Something had fluttered inside Rosie's chest. Marriage to Greco – was that really such an unexpected idea?

'I think I might have found a solution here.'

Winston's clear English voice cut through her thoughts. 'If we can find a piece of metal that can be twisted round this part, we might be able to link these bits – see what I mean? – and that could, with any luck, get it going.'

Greco gave a very slight, almost imperceptible nod of grudging agreement. 'Perhaps. I did, in fact, think of that myself.'

Winston raised an eyebrow. Talk about competitive! They were as bad as each other.

'I have some fishing hooks down below,' Greco announced coolly.

'Great. That might do the trick.'

There was an awkward silence while Greco was gone. She ought to talk to Winston, Rosie told herself. After all, she was his hostess. But what if he asked her more questions about her past? He'd really spooked her out earlier.

'How do you know so much about engines?' she asked politely.

He shrugged. 'The Royal Marines. Our training covered quite a lot of ground.' Then his eyes fixed on hers. 'You said earlier that you came from the South-West. I trained in Plymouth. Did you live near there?'

Yes, she wanted to say. Of course I did, you idiot. Don't you remember me at all? But the words faded on her lips just as Greco came striding up the steps, triumphantly waving a clutch of fish hooks and a strip of rubber. 'This might do,' he said with a look at Rosie which could clearly be translated as, *See, I'm just as capable as this old flame of yours.*

There was a small crowd around them now, watching the two men as they knelt down, side by side, twisting bits of metal. It was almost like a race. Greco was making the sorts of noises she could remember her father making when he'd tinkered with the car at home. But Winston was working steadily and silently.

It was difficult not to admire him.

'If anyone can fix it, Winston can,' Melissa was saying proudly. 'Don't worry, Emma. I'm sure you'll be back in time to get the flight.'

There was a little whimper. 'But Tom will be so worried.'

So would everyone else on the island! A missing fishing boat was nothing short of a world-wide alert in Siphalonia. Poor Cara would be scared witless, Rosie suddenly realised. Hadn't she already lost one daughter at sea?

'Greco knows what he is doing,' she said meaningfully,

partly to support him and partly to try and calm herself. 'Besides, I am sure that someone from the mainland will come out to find us.'

As she spoke, there was a splutter from the engine followed by another. Then a whirring noise which stopped almost as soon as it started. Rosie's heart sank. Then, to her huge relief, it began again. Hesitant at first and then growing increasingly confident.

The Frenchman began to clap, even though his arms were firmly around his wife (did those two ever take their hands off each other?). Someone else followed suit and Emma exhaled a huge sigh of relief. 'Thank goodness for that.' Her eyes filled with tears.

Rosie's eyes slid across to the beach where Jack and Alice had been sitting, talking, for the last hour or so.

Sweet. Yet at the same time, dangerous. What if Jack made the same mistake as she had and went too far?

'Come on, you two.' She waved furiously. 'Quick! They've got the engine started.'

Greco took a mock bow as she spoke, making Rosie wince. After everything she'd thought about leopards changing their spots, this arrogant gesture made him look vain in front of Winston, who was nonchalantly returning to Melissa's side.

'Well done,' Melissa said quietly.

Winston nodded. 'Team effort.' He looked down at Freddie, who had fallen asleep next to his wife. 'It's been a long day.'

'And night,' added Melissa, frowning, looking at Alice as she came aboard. 'Sit with us, can you, darling?'

The girl scowled. 'I'll sit where I like.'

'Don't be rude to your mother.'

Rosie started at Winston's heavy-handed reproach, which reminded her of Dad. Yes, the girl had been rude, but Rosie couldn't help feeling a sneaking sympathy. It couldn't be easy having a stepfather. Supposing Greco started getting heavy-handed with Jack?

Darkness was falling, but the *Siphalonian* was now making steady progress across the bay. The wind was helping too.

Lights were on, she could see, glimmering on the water. Were they from the houses, or were some of the fishermen coming out to find them? Oh my God! There was a little dinghy! She recognised it as belonging to Greco's uncle.

'Are you all right, nephew?' a voice yelled out.

'The engine broke! But all is well. I fixed it.'

That wasn't fair. 'Along with one of our guests,' Rosie added in Greek.

Greco visibly bristled. 'It is clear whose side you are on.'

'Don't be ridiculous,' she retorted, taking care not to use English so as not to embarrass Greco in front of Winston. 'I just don't like it when someone takes all the credit instead of sharing it.'

For a minute, they looked at each other challengingly. Don't look away, Rosie told herself sternly. This is important.

Eventually, Greco shrugged. 'You are right.' Then he called back to his uncle. 'The English helped. Perhaps they are not quite so useless after all.'

There was a loud chuckle.

Rosie nodded her approval. 'Thank you,' she whispered.

Greco looked pleased. 'In fact, he saved a boy from the seas,' he called out. 'We have many tales to tell.'

So they did. Thank goodness the trip was ending well. It could all have been so different.

Meanwhile, Greco was mooring the boat and helping her guests to make the short jump onto the shore.

'I don't know that I can do it,' Emma was whimpering.

Yannis loomed up from the bottom of the boat as though he had been waiting. 'I can help you, yes?'

'Get off me!' Emma was pushing him away furiously. 'I don't want you to touch me.'

Rosie caught her breath. Something had definitely happened there and, if she wasn't mistaken, she wasn't the only one to have noticed.

'It's all right, Emma,' Melissa was saying kindly. 'Winston will carry you, won't you, darling?'

Suddenly Rosie noticed a commotion on the beach. It wasn't

just curious villagers who had come out to greet them. There were lights flashing – camera lights, she realised.

'Mr King! Mr King! Can you give me a comment, please, on a story that's running in today's newspapers?'

Rosie froze. What was going on?

Winston's angry voice could be heard clearly from the jetty. 'I haven't seen the article yet and I do not wish to be bothered. This is a private holiday.'

The voice – a woman's voice – cut through the air. 'Don't you mean honeymoon? Congratulations, Mrs King, by the way.'

Rosie shone her torch onto the speaker. She was a tall, foxy-looking woman with a confidence that rang out through the night air. 'Perhaps you would like to give me a quote on your first husband's allegation that Winston stole you from him.'

'That's ridiculous!' Melissa's voice was furious. 'We were divorced when I met Winston.'

The woman was holding out a microphone. 'But only just. Your ex-husband claims you were on the rebound. There's something else I'd like to ask you, too.'

There was a tense silence. The beach was crowded with locals, Rosie saw, gripped by this drama being played out in front of them. It wasn't every day that the British press descended on Siphalonia.

'Is there any truth, Mr King,' said the woman slowly, 'in the rumours that you have a love child?'

What? Rosie put a hand to her mouth, in an attempt to suppress the little scream that came out.

There was a gasp from Melissa, followed by a loud laugh from Winston. 'You people are disgusting, making things up. You ought to be ashamed of yourself. Now leave, or else I'll call the police.'

Even Greco was waving his fist at the journalist and so were many of the others, including Greco's uncle. Their English might be limited but they understood enough to realise that bad publicity might not be good for the island.

'Did *you* tell the journalist?' Rosie demanded furiously as they left them to it and made their way up the beach.

Greco shook his head. 'Of course not. I would not betray you.'

But he *had* overheard her on the phone to Gemma. Of everyone around them, he was the only one in a position to betray her, possibly out of spite for Winston. Unless it was someone else . . .

Rosie glanced at Cara, who was waiting at the top of the beach, her shawl flapping in the cool evening breeze. 'Do you think it was her?'

Greco shook his head. 'She would not do that.'

'Then who?' hissed Rosie urgently. 'How has someone found out that Winston has a child? And what if someone links him with me?'

He shrugged. Together, as if by unspoken agreement, they searched the beach for Jack. There he was, holding hands with Alice, walking ahead, oblivious to anyone else save the girl he so obviously cared for.

'He must not know about Winston,' hissed Rosie again. 'Otherwise he will never forgive me.'

'Mustn't know what?'

She whipped round. Melissa was standing right behind her. The woman's eyes were flashing.

Rosie felt herself stammering. 'N-n-nothing.'

'*Nothing?*' Mrs King's voice rang out with fury. 'I don't believe you! I want the truth, do you hear? Otherwise I will Twitter and Facebook and do whatever else I can, to make sure that no one else ever visits your villa again. Now *tell* me!'

CELEBRITY HONEYMOONS: WHERE DID THEY GO?

Zsa Zsa Gabor: the Venice–Simplon Express (first time)
Michael McIntyre: the Maldives
Duke and Duchess of Cambridge: the Seychelles
Reese Witherspoon: Belize

Chapter Twenty-Six

EMMA

Emma stumbled back to the cottage, her heart pounding and head whirling. Not just from what had happened with Yannis, but the other thing too. She hadn't meant to listen in on the conversation between Melissa and Rosie just now, but she'd reached the top of the beach and then remembered that she'd left her beach bag on the harbour wall.

So she'd come back to get it, only to hear an angry exchange between the two women.

It was difficult to hear the exact details – not that she was trying, of course – but the words 'Jack' and 'Winston' were clearly audible.

What had happened? Melissa looked terribly upset, and as for Rosie Harrison, she looked as though she had seen a ghost.

Luckily, the bag was still there, so she just grabbed it and walked away as fast as she could. But then, when she got close to the villa, she could hear more raised voices. This time it was Winston and the woman she had seen earlier.

Now, instead of having a notebook poking out of her bag, she had a camera slung round her neck.

'I won't have any pictures!' Winston was yelling. Emma gasped silently as he stepped forward. Surely he wasn't going to hit the girl? Then she realised he was about to rip the camera from her neck until Greco stepped in, holding him back.

'No, man,' he was saying. 'You will make the situation worse, I think. Let us go. Now.'

Then, even though it had been clear on the boat that Rosie's Greek boyfriend and Winston didn't like each other very much,

261

Greco put his arm round Winston's shoulders and was virtually pulling him away as the girl took snap after snap.

Emma only hoped that she wasn't in one of the pictures. She was in enough trouble as it was.

Wrapping her jumper around herself, even though it wasn't that cold, she began to shake as she picked her way across the strange tough grass, towards the cottage.

God, how she hated herself! How could she have been so horribly stupid? She'd vowed to herself that she wouldn't drink on the boat trip and now she'd done something that could never be undone. Something that made her feel dirty, through and through.

Stumbling over a sharp stone, she began to cry silently – and not just because it had stubbed her toe. 'You've been married for one week,' she told herself, 'and already you've been unfaithful.'

Even as she said the words, they felt unreal, as though the situation belonged to someone else. Now she was no better than her father. Why had she done it? Because she'd had cold feet about getting married; had been flattered by another man's attentions; and had had too much to drink.

As for Yannis – she could hardly bear to say his name – she must have been mad. When he'd given her that smug, satisfied smile at the end of the evening, she had felt nothing but loathing for him. Very different from the lust (there was no other word for it) that had taken her over earlier, almost like a body-snatcher.

She was despicable. But then again, so was he.

Creeping into the bungalow, Emma braced herself. It was past midnight but Tom would still be up. He would be pacing the floor, worried out of his mind because she was so late. He might even, she told herself, as her hand shook on the bedroom door, be outside, looking for her. Or . . .

Her heart almost stopped as she took in the snoring mound on the bed. Tom was fast asleep. He wasn't worried that she hadn't come back from what was meant to be a 'day trip'. Or if he was, it wasn't enough to keep him awake.

Tiptoeing into the bathroom, Emma held the shower against her body for as long as she dared, in case the noise of the water woke her husband. Wash it away, she whispered to herself. Make me clean.

But when the warm water turned to cold, she still felt as dirty as ever. Desperately, she rubbed her thighs with the towel. If only she could turn back the clock! She would never have gone on the stupid boat trip. Would never have taken that drink which Yannis had offered to 'steady her nerves'.

Instead, as she slipped into bed next to Tom, whose snores were becoming progressively louder, Emma knew she had crossed a line which could never be rubbed out.

Opening her phone to check there hadn't been any urgent messages from Mum or Bernie, she pressed her lips to the picture of Willow and Gawain on her screen saver.

If she told Tom what she had done, he would leave her. They'd have to share the children (what an impossible thought) and then, if Tom married again, another woman would have them for half the week.

Emma felt sick. That sort of thing happened to other people. Not to her and Tom.

But if she *didn't* tell him, she would have to live a lie for the rest of her life. Every time they celebrated their wedding anniversary, she would think back to that time on the island she'd slept with another man: a man for whom she had felt an irrational drunken attraction.

Suddenly, Tom turned over and took her in his arms sleepily, holding her so tight that she could hardly breathe. He might not stir her body in the way that a virtual stranger had, but he loved her. They shared two children, a bond which was, she could see now, far more precious than cold-blooded sex. 'I'm sorry,' she whispered silently. 'I'm so very sorry.'

Emma's uneasy sleep was punctuated by a dream in which she was swimming along the sea bed, looking desperately for her children. She was calling out for them, even though she

263

was under the water while Tom swam along beside her, refusing to talk or to acknowledge that she was there.

Then he suddenly shot up out of the sea and when she followed him, all she could spot was a small fishing boat on the horizon with three small figures on board. Tom. Gawain. And Willow.

Tom was ignoring her again but the children were waving frantically and screaming. 'Mummy. *Mummy!*'

Someone was shaking her. Who was it? Yannis! '*Go away!*' she screamed. '*Go away!*'

'Emma?'

Dimly, she was aware of Tom's voice. How was that possible? He was on the boat, taking the children from her. Leaving her far behind. She should never have told him the truth . . .

'Emma, wake up! We'll miss the plane if you don't get a move on!'

Slowly, the room swam back into focus. Relief flooded her body as she realised that she wasn't in the sea at all and, more importantly, Tom hadn't stolen away on a boat with the children. Instead, he was stuffing clothes into his suitcase, including her own, without even folding them.

'We've overslept!' He gave her a quick kiss on the cheek. 'Come on, love. Rosie has already been down once to chivvy us along. They're all waiting for us.'

There was no time for another shower, even though her body was still crying out to be washed.

'Did Rosie tell you what happened?' Emma asked as she slipped into her travelling jeans and smudged her mascara in her haste.

'Happened?' Tom repeated, picking up the cases. 'What do you mean?'

Emma hesitated, wondering how much to say, mindful of the dream which might have been a warning to keep mum. 'The engine broke down and we were late,' she said carefully.

'Were you?' Tom was casting an eye over the room in case

they'd left something behind. 'I didn't notice. Flat out, I was.' He gave her another kiss on the cheek. 'Still, the good thing is that I feel a whole load better now.'

If only he'd felt a bit better before, none of this might have happened. But that was no excuse.

'Next time we go away, we'll stick to Britain and take the kids with us,' said Tom as they walked up towards the villa where their car was waiting. 'I'm sorry I was a bit of a stick-in-the-mud during the holiday. Weren't too bored, were you?'

Emma felt herself colour up furiously. Swiftly, she turned away to try and hide it. 'Not really. I had Melissa to talk to.'

Tom gave her a big grin. 'Making friends with the celebrity wives, are we?'

Again, Emma flushed. 'It's not like that. Melissa's really nice.' Then she thought of the argument last night between her new chum and Mrs Harrison. 'I don't think it's very easy for her.'

Tom looked bewildered. 'Why?'

'Oh, you know,' said Emma vaguely. 'Marrying someone famous means you lose your privacy, doesn't it? Some photographer has already turned up to interview Winston, and there's a big piece about him in the *Globe*, apparently, dishing the dirt.'

Tom shrugged. 'They get paid enough. They have to put up with the shit too.' Then he nudged her. 'From the way you're talking about them, you'll be asking them round to dinner next!'

BEEP, BEEP.

Tom broke into a run as the driver hooted impatiently. 'Come on,' he called out. 'The sooner we get there, the sooner we see the kids!'

Emma felt her skin crawling with guilt. What if Gawain and Willow ever found out that their mother had cheated? They'd never forgive her. Just as she had been unable to forgive her father.

At the tiny airport, it was noticeable that Melissa and her children were sitting at a table while Winston was at the bar.

'Perhaps I'll go and chat to him,' suggested Tom brightly. 'It's not every day you have a chance to talk to a bloke on the telly.'

But he was back within a few minutes. 'Moody so-and-so,' he sniffed. 'Didn't want to talk at all. Just sat there, nursing his beer.'

On the plane, Melissa sat with her children while her husband was three rows behind. The plane wasn't full – surely they could have been nearer each other if they'd wanted?

'Looks like they've had an argument already,' remarked Tom, slipping his hand into Emma's. 'I thought, from what you said, that she was all over him for rescuing her son. Do you think something happened afterwards?'

Emma froze, recalling the conversation she'd overheard on the beach. 'I don't know,' she managed to say weakly.

Tom squeezed her hand so tightly that it hurt. 'I'm glad we're not like them,' he said, lightly brushing her cheek with his lips. 'I wouldn't want to be famous if that's what it does to you. Nice and normal. That's what I want.'

It's what I want too, Emma thought miserably. But all she could think about was Yannis holding out that golden liquid, urging her to knock it back. Thank God he hadn't been around when they'd left the villa that morning. She never, ever wanted to see him again.

'Right!' Tom was decidedly chirpy as he heaved the cases off the luggage belt. 'Let's go.'

Melissa and her kids were in front as they went through Customs. This time, Winston was walking next to his wife, although they weren't holding hands. They were talking in low, urgent voices. Emma heard the phrase 'united front' but nothing else. Poor Melissa. She looked really miserable.

'Look!' Tom was leaping up and down, pointing. Instantly, Emma forgot all about her new friend's troubles. Willow and Gawain! They were here with Mum and Bernie, waiting in Arrivals with a huge home-made banner with childish writing in red and blue felt-tip.

'HOPE YOU HAD A GREAT HONEYMOON!'

Emma broke into a run, ducking under the barrier and scooping up Gawain, holding him in her arms and smothering him with kisses. 'No.' He was pushing her away. 'Want Gran.'

Her mother gave her a slightly smug look. 'Don't worry, love. You know what kids are like. He'll be all right in a minute.'

Something was different about him. 'He's lost a tooth! Why didn't you tell me?'

'Goodness me,' clucked her mother, 'there was enough going on without me having to remember every tiny detail.'

'Did the tooth fairy come?' Emma whispered to her son, ignoring her mother.

Gawain shook his head sorrowfully.

'Maybe he'll come tonight,' she suggested, 'if you give me another cuddle.'

Her son shot her a distrustful look. 'In a minute. I'm busy.'

Busy? No guesses where he'd picked that one up from. Mum used to say that when she had been a child too.

Hurt, Emma knelt down beside Willow, who was in her pushchair. 'Did *you* miss Mummy?' she asked softly. But her daughter just sucked on her dummy and stared at her as though Emma was a stranger.

'Little so-and-sos,' chirped Bernie brightly, offering her a piece of gum. 'They're just giving you the cold shoulder cos you left them. Mine did the same when Phil and I went away last summer. Don't take any notice of them.'

She nudged Emma chummily. 'Didn't mind me coming along too, did you? Only your mum was a bit worried about driving on her own.' Then she stopped, her eyes bulging, staring across the Arrivals hall. 'Bloody hell, isn't that Winston King over there?'

'Certainly is,' declared Tom importantly. 'He was staying at our place, can you believe, with his new bride. *And* her kids. Our Em here got quite chummy with them.'

'Why didn't you tell us?' demanded Mum and Bernie at the same time.

'They asked me not to.' Emma felt herself going red. 'It was a secret.'

'Doesn't look like it any more,' snorted Bernie.

Heavens! Just look at the gaggle of photographers congregating around Winston! Poor Melissa looked terrified and even her kids, usually so confident, were hanging on to each other for comfort.

'I've got to help them,' said Emma immediately. 'Wait there, can you?'

Elbowing her way through the crowd of photographers and journalists, she tugged at Melissa's sleeve. 'Can I do anything? Take the children for you?'

Melissa's face was stony. 'I think you've done quite enough, thank you.'

A horrible cold feeling crept through Emma. 'What do you mean?'

Melissa waved a newspaper in front of her. 'Look at this.'

Honeymoon exclusive. Winston's stepdaughter in love with Greek waiter.

Emma gasped. 'How did they know that?'

'Through *you*, perhaps?'

'You think I spoke to that journalist on the island? Of course I didn't!'

Melissa's eyes narrowed. 'I don't believe you. From the minute you met us, you latched on like a limpet. I felt sorry for you then, but now I can see that you're one of those people who just want to be near someone famous. Tell me, how much did they pay you?'

'Nothing,' spluttered Emma. 'You've got it all wrong!'

At that moment, a tall, skinny man with slit eyes and a camera slung round his neck slid in front of them.

'Mrs King. Do you have any comments about your husband's love child?'

'No,' snapped Melissa. 'I don't.'

The skinny man was writing furiously on his pad. 'Then what about Nick Thomas? Do you have any comments?'

'Nick Thomas?' repeated Melissa, clearly confused. 'Who's he?'

At that moment, Emma felt herself being pushed to one

side. It was Winston. His face was livid. Seizing Melissa's arm, he marched her off. 'Get away!' he shouted over his shoulder at the man with the camera. 'Scum like you shouldn't be allowed! Kids, follow us.'

Emma was left, confused, watching the four of them run through the doors and into a waiting black car. It wasn't fair. How could they think she'd betrayed them? Yet at the same time, she couldn't help feeling terribly sorry for Melissa. What an awful thing to happen just after your honeymoon.

'Does Nick Thomas have anything to do with Winston's love child?' she couldn't help asking the skinny man with the camera.

He gave a nasty smile, reminding her of a crocodile in one of Gawain's picture books. 'You'll have to read tomorrow's newspapers to find that one out. Don't miss it, love! It's a great story.'

AFTER THE HONEYMOON

TRUE POST-HONEYMOON STORY

'After we got back, we found our new flat had been burgled. Everything had gone apart from a hideous brown tea set which my new husband's aunt had given us. I've tried hard to break it ever since but have never succeeded.'

Sally, now coming up to her tenth wedding anniversary

Chapter Twenty-Seven

WINSTON

'We need to talk.' Winston reached out for Melissa's hand in the back of the taxi from Heathrow but she snatched it back smartly. It was an action which did not go unnoticed by her sharp-eyed daughter (how much make-up was she wearing, for heaven's sake?), who shot him a smug *see, she doesn't like you any more* look.

Freddie was in the front. Ever since he'd plucked him out of the water, Winston no longer saw him as 'the boy'. It had brought them together. When he'd been the only one to talk to him on the journey back home, Winston had been pathetically grateful.

'Let me at least explain,' he tried again with Melissa.

His wife had her face set away from him. She really did have the most beautiful profile, he observed. Very classical, with a nose that was aristocratic rather than pretty and cheekbones that could have been sculptured. Right now, her gaze was fixed on the passing suburban shops; so different, he reflected, from the sun-soaked white villas and aquamarine sea from the past week. If only they were back in Greece before the journalist had shown up. If only he could turn the clock back.

But that was impossible. Hadn't he tried to do the same after Nick?

'Please, Mellie,' he persisted.

This time, her face turned to him. Those black eyes made him feel like a stranger who had bothered her with an inappropriate request. 'Not now,' she said icily. 'Not in front of the children. Anyway, it's Melissa. Not Mellie.'

Alice – little so-and-so! – gave him another smug smile. He was cornered. Talk about friendly fire! In a way, Winston thought, he'd rather be out in the field than face these two females, regarding him with undisguised contempt.

Giving up, he closed his eyes, and the events of last night flooded back.

They'd got back to the Villa Rosa after the showdown with the journalist. He'd had a shower and changed, wondering where Melissa was. Probably settling the children. Hopefully Freddie would have learned his lesson. You didn't just jump into water like that. Just as you didn't climb trees that were too high. Or send people into dangerous situations before checking it was safe.

At last. He could hear his wife's steps on the stairs now. Fast. Urgent. He wanted her; could feel himself hardening. The fact that his body was behaving as it should made him almost giddy with relief. However, this wasn't the time, dammit. Not after what had just happened.

As soon as they got back to the UK, he vowed, he would put his lawyer onto that journalist. That would teach her to make up tales about some love child.

'It's a pack of lies,' he had said to Melissa as they'd pushed past the journalist on the beach. 'You know what these people are like. Ignore her.'

'All right.' Melissa had nodded uncertainly. 'See you later in the room. There are a couple of things I need to do first.'

Suddenly, the door flew open. Melissa stood there, her jeans still wet from the boat trip; her dark hair spilling over her shoulders. Her face was different. It looked hurt, like it did when she spoke to Marvyn.

A tremor of apprehension passed through Winston like an electric shock, so powerful that he found his knees buckling.

She knew.

He could just tell.

'How could you have brought us here?' she snapped.

This wasn't what he'd expected. 'What do you mean?' he snapped back. 'If you remember, it was your idea to come here. Not mine.'

'But you were keen enough, weren't you? Probably thought it was a great opportunity to introduce me to your son!' She was hissing now, like a furious cat. There had been cats in Bosnia, he recalled irrelevantly. Cats that had hidden in the caves. He'd stroked one once, soothing its arched back before giving it back to the child who had lost it. It had been no substitute for the parents who were gone but at least it had been something.

'My son?' He laughed out loud, dizzy with relief that she had got the wrong end of the stick. For a moment there, he thought she'd discovered the truth about Nick. 'I don't have a son, Melissa. What are you talking about?'

Another flash of the eyes. As she came towards him, Winston felt his muscles tighten just as they had before battle. She had him by his collar now, her face so close to his that he could taste her breath. 'That's not what Mrs Harrison has just told me. Her son, Jack, is yours. You got her pregnant. When she was seventeen!'

The room around him started to drop away. At the same time, the gymkhana rosettes loomed out of the wall at him. Turning round, he stared at the photograph of the two girls he'd seen before. As if by telepathy, two names formed in his head. Rosemary who loved riding. Rosemary and her friend with the blonde hair. What was she called again? Jenny? Gemma?

No. That was impossible. Or was it?

'Rosemary,' he said quietly as though talking to himself. 'Of course. Rosemary.'

'So you admit you know her?' Melissa's voice was trembling. Too late, he realised she'd expected him to comfort her; tell her that it wasn't true.

'Yes. No. I don't know.' As he spoke, he knew he wasn't making sense. He tried again. 'I thought Mrs Harrison seemed slightly familiar when we met, but I couldn't place her.'

Melissa gave a hoarse, slightly hysterical laugh. 'Well, she can place *you* all right. I overheard our hostess talking about you to her Greek boyfriend.' She was spitting out the words like hot coals. 'Turns out that you went out together, when you were training. Don't deny it, Winston!'

Tears were rolling down her face. 'Then you went back to your training, leaving her pregnant.'

'But I didn't know . . .' he tried to say.

'Don't come near me.' She pushed him away. 'I don't want to hear any more of your lies.'

Winston felt his breath coming out in huge gulps. Rosemary from Devon. He couldn't even recall her surname. He'd slept with her, certainly. She'd meant a great deal to him at the time – not something he should probably share with Melissa – but then he'd been transferred.

Could she really have got pregnant by him? And then turned up here, Siphalonia, of all places – where he had come for his honeymoon?

Desperately, he tried to get his head straight, though he was stumbling over the words in his distress. 'If it was the same girl – woman – I didn't know she was pregnant. You have my word on that. Yes, we went out for a month or so.' He paused at the bitter-sweet memory. 'I wrote to her after I left but she didn't write back.' He shrugged. 'It happens in the services. Girls don't want to wait for you . . .'

There was another snort. 'Well, this one did. She tried to find you.' Melissa made a little choking sound. 'Jack even *looks* like you.'

Winston felt his stomach tighten.

'I noticed that, when we arrived,' Melissa added, her voice cracked with emotion, 'although I didn't put two and two together. He has the same eyes. Olive skin. He raises one eyebrow, just like you do. There's a funny little kink on the side of his ears that you have as well. And he does that thing with his hands that you do when you speak. I'm a make-up artist, Winston. I notice these things.'

Really? He had to confess he hadn't been so sharp with his observations. His mouth was bone dry. 'I need to talk to her,' he said.

Melissa nodded, her eyes shadowed with pain. 'Yes. I think you do.'

When he went to find her, Rosie was sitting on a big wooden chair in the kitchen, mug of tea in her hands, staring out of the open window towards the sea. It was too dark to see much but there was, he noticed, a small light a long way off. A boat, presumably. Or maybe a flicker of hope in his imagination.

No one else was in the room, thank goodness. He couldn't have borne trying to explain himself in front of Greco. Or, even worse, Jack.

'Rosemary?' he asked quietly, slipping into the chair next to her.

She raised her head and gave him a rueful smile. 'Charlie?'

He nodded wryly, in acknowledgment. 'My agent made me change my name. It's one of the few things in that newspaper series that's true.'

Instantly, her face tightened. 'So you think they lied about your so-called love child?'

His knuckles clenched under the table. 'Yes. No. I don't know. For pity's sake, Rosemary – Rosie. *You* tell *me*.'

Don't lay yourself open, he could hear his old commanding officer saying. Don't invite trouble. Yet somehow he could tell that this woman was genuine.

'I discovered I was expecting after you'd gone.' Her hands were shaking, he noticed, and her voice quivering. 'My friend Gemma came with me to buy the pregnancy test.' She looked up at him and he suddenly saw the young schoolgirl he had fallen for, hook, line and sinker. 'I was so scared. You can't imagine it.'

He couldn't. But being pregnant and alone at seventeen must have been terrifying. His heart went out to her.

'I wrote to you,' she added quietly, 'but you didn't reply.'

What? 'I didn't get a letter. I promise you. In fact, I wrote to *you* but didn't hear back.'

Her eyes bored right through him. 'I didn't get a letter.'

The two of them stared at each other, neither willing to look away. Both determined to prove they were right.

'OK,' she said reluctantly. 'I believe you.'

'Me too,' gulped Winston. 'I'm so sorry. It must have been really tough for you.'

'Yes and no. But I had Jack, didn't I? I could never regret that.'

He felt a crushing pang of loss at having missed out on so much.

'People were very kind, on the whole,' she added. 'When I ended up here, a wonderful Greek woman called Cara – who's listening from the scullery, by the way – took me in.'

He glanced around nervously, aware at the same time that something was missing in her story. 'Your father. How did he react?'

Her mother, he dimly remembered now, had died during her childhood.

Rosie looked away. 'Wouldn't have anything to do with me after I told him I was pregnant. Still won't.'

That was awful. 'And Jack? What does he know?'

The boy's name sounded different now he knew he was his. Rosie's face softened with what might or might not have been wistfulness.

'He thinks his father was killed in a motorbike accident.' Then her mouth tightened. 'And that's the way I want it to stay.'

Was she that naive? 'But supposing someone finds out?'

'How?'

'These journalists are scavengers.'

'They just referred to a love child, not Jack by name. And if they do, I'll deny it.' Her voice hardened. 'I'll tell him that we went out as teenagers but that was it. I'll make him believe that the newspapers are lying. Don't you see, Winston? I don't want any more to do with you, than you do with us. I'm certainly not after your money.' She folded her arms. 'Jack and I have managed perfectly well without you so far, and we can carry on that way.'

This wasn't what he'd expected. A picture of her son – *their* son – swam into his mind. A nice boy. Well-mannered. Fun. Not boring. Good-looking. 'You've done a great job, Rosie, but a boy needs a father.'

Her chair scraped against the wooden floor as she stood up. 'There are plenty of male role models here, thank you very much.'

Now it was his turn to leap up. 'Like your Greek boyfriend, you mean?'

She might be smaller than him – a lot smaller – but she was glaring up at him like someone who had the upper hand. 'At least Greco can say that he's known Jack from birth, which is more than you can. Get real, Winston or Charlie or whatever you call yourself now. You can't just come waltzing into our lives and start to play mummies and daddies after all this time.'

'But,' he began and then stopped at the sound of clapping. A very small, wrinkled woman in a faded pink-and-blue cotton pinafore was emerging from what he'd previously assumed was a large cupboard by the side of the sink. 'My English, she is not very clever, but I comprehend enough.'

The woman slapped him on the back; she was stronger than she looked. 'Your English gentleman, he is right, Rosie. Your son, he needs to know who hees real father is.'

Rosie's eyes, he saw to his chagrin, were filling with tears. 'Not yet. Give me time. This is all too much.'

He could see that. 'Of course it is,' he said softly. Part of him wanted to give her a quick cuddle to show he understood. 'When you're ready, let me know. I'll come back here and we'll sit down for a chat.'

He'd almost said 'family chat', but that seemed too presumptuous at this stage. Even so, he felt an excited tingle down his spine. A son! He had a fully formed son, who didn't need training or taming like Alice and Freddie. Yes,

Jack had done a few daft things, but you needed to when you were a boy. On the whole, he was a great lad. A son to be proud of. How ironic, he realised, that he'd discovered this now. If it had been a year ago, when he'd been single, there would have been no problem. No one else to explain it to.

'I need to talk to my wife,' he added, finding himself unable to meet either Cara or Rosie's eyes. 'I need to tell her everything.'

The old woman had snorted. 'Good luck.' Then she had wrung his hands like an old friend. 'You will need it, I theenk.'

Winston swallowed hard. 'Yes.' Then he remembered something. 'The dress,' he said, turning back to Rosie. 'The purple dress you wore the other night for the Greek dancing. It looked familiar.'

His voice trailed away with embarrassment.

Rosie's eyes met his gratefully. 'You remembered,' she whispered.

He closed his eyes briefly as the memory of their first kiss suddenly hit him with such force that he almost keeled over. 'I didn't realise I'd forgotten.'

Melissa hadn't taken it well.

'Your Rosie Harrison might not want money now,' she'd snapped when Winston had finished telling her everything, in the room that belonged to his ex. 'But she might well change her mind later on.'

In vain he tried to point out that Rosie wasn't 'his' but he could feel the jealousy rising off her like steam. He could understand that. Wasn't he jealous of Marvyn?

'What about your ex-husband?' he'd asked. 'Are you going to tackle him about those lies? He's more or less implied that I stole you from him before your divorce was finalised.'

'Leave him to me,' she'd announced crisply. 'The same goes for that silly Emma who must have told them about Alice and Jack. I don't know who else could have done. By the time I've finished with her, she won't have any friends left in

Corrywood.' Her eyes had glittered with anger. 'Alice is so upset that she says she won't go back to school.'

Winston shrugged. A change of school might not be a bad thing, especially if it was a long way off. 'What I don't understand, is how they know I had a child.'

Melissa snorted. 'You're so naive, aren't you? Whatever you think, I still believe it was *her*. Rosie Harrison. I told you she'd be after money. The paper probably paid her handsomely.'

'My money's on your friend Emma.'

'Maybe.' Melissa's eyes had shone with tears. 'How could this happen to us, Winston? On our honeymoon, too!'

Winston's mind came back to the present. He couldn't help noticing that Alice seemed quite buoyant. Doubtless she was delighted that he and her mother had had a massive argument.

'Hi, Dad,' she was chirping now into Melissa's mobile. 'We're almost back. Can you come round and meet us?'

Melissa, staring out of the window, didn't even move. Couldn't she see that the girl was doing her best to break them up?

'By the way,' Melissa said coolly as the taxi drew up outside her house (he still saw it as hers, even though they were married), 'I meant to ask you something else. Who is Nick Thomas?'

Winston felt as though someone had just punched him in the solar plexus, leaving him writhing on the ground. 'Why?' he managed.

Melissa's eyes narrowed. 'One of the reporters at the airport mentioned his name.'

His mouth was so dry that he could hardly form a word. 'What did you say?'

'That I didn't know.' Her gaze hardened. 'Is he a friend of yours?'

'Sort of.'

She narrowed her eyes again in an *I don't believe you any more* gesture. 'Well, we'll find out in the papers tomorrow. Something else to look forward to, I suppose.'

Trembling with apprehension, Winston paid the driver and watched the kids race out of the car, towards a man lounging against his sleek silver Jaguar, parked in the drive as though he still lived there. 'Dad, Dad!'

'Hiya, you lot!' Marvyn was beaming with malice. 'Had a good time, did you? Sorry about that crap in the papers, by the way. Some journalist rang me up to ask how I felt about my wife marrying a TV star. I told her I was very happy for you both.' He grinned again. 'You know what these journalists are like. They get it all wrong. Not cross with me, are you, Mellie?'

So *he* was allowed to call her that, was he? His wife gave her ex the sort of look that he'd thought was reserved only for him.

'No,' he heard her say. 'It's not you I'm upset with. Is it, Winston?'

Upset? Winston pretended to check his phone, which had got clogged up with messages during the flight, including one from his producer. That would be nothing when she read about Nick.

TRUE POST-HONEYMOON STORY

'We didn't have a honeymoon. I didn't want to leave my youngest. We had a lovely meal out instead.'

Author, second time around

Chapter Twenty-Eight

EMMA

'Mummy! I need a wee-wee!'

It was so hard to get back into the swing of things, thought Emma as she shepherded Gawain to the loo. To think that she'd spent most of her honeymoon wishing she was back with the children. But they'd been home for two whole weeks now and already Emma was wishing she was back in Siphalonia again. At the beginning of the week, before she'd met Yannis.

'Too late!' sang her son in her mother's voice. 'Gawain's wet myself.' He pointed down to his pants, pleased as punch. Oh dear. He'd been prone to the odd 'accident' before the honeymoon but when she'd got back, Mum had gleefully announced that she'd 'finally got him dry' – as though all it had taken was Emma's absence.

But now he seemed to have regressed.

Mum and Bernie between them had taught him to tell the time. Well, the o'clock bit and the half past. *And* she'd virtually got Willow to sleep through the night by using the 'rapid return' technique from Dr Know's telly programme.

But instead of being pleased, Emma just felt redundant. Clearly she wasn't needed for motherhood, the only job she was qualified for.

Now it looked as though she was going to have to start all over again, at least when it came to potty training. Gawain still kept trying to snatch Willow's dummy, too, as well as referring to himself in the third person – something new. Was it because he'd felt insecure when she was away? Or had her son picked up on her distress, which she'd been trying desperately to hide from Tom?

'What's wrong, love?' her new husband had asked when they'd finally fallen into bed on the first night back and he'd held out his arms to her. (Now he was back in his own home, Tom seemed perfectly well, without any sign of sickness.)

'Nothing,' she'd replied swiftly, turning her back to him. 'Sorry. It's more comfortable this way, after the plane.'

As she spoke, Emma crossed her fingers. Lies were wrong, as she often told Gawain. Especially, she added to herself, when you were grown up.

'Still upset about that stuck-up Melissa woman?' he'd asked gently, reaching out and stroking her shoulders.

Normally, Emma would have welcomed his touch, but now it was a hideous reminder of her own unforgivable behaviour.

'Yes,' she'd sighed, seizing the excuse he had just handed her on a plate. 'I *am* upset about Melissa. It's not fair. I *didn't* talk to the papers, whatever she said, even though I could have done. I'm not like that.'

She'd buried her face in the pillow. As if she didn't have enough to cope with! How awful that someone as important as Winston King and his wife hated her! What would happen when she went back to school in September? Would Melissa blank her, tell everyone else not to talk to her?

'Willow still has nappies, so why can't Gawain?'

Her son's voice cut into her thoughts, yanking her back to the present. Grabbing the cloth she kept behind the loo, especially for this purpose, Emma began to mop up. 'Because you're a big boy.'

Just as she was a big girl, she reminded herself. Too big to get drunk and do things with a man she didn't know while her husband was ill in bed. Emma found herself digging her nails into her left arm. The pain felt good. She deserved it. No. She deserved far worse. Before her honeymoon, Emma had felt nothing but scorn for people who moaned about feeling guilty over an affair (usually on those daytime chat shows that Mum was addicted to). 'Then don't have one,' she used to say out loud.

But now she understood how easily it could happen and how the self-loathing grew and grew inside, until it threatened to suck you up and suffocate you.

'Mummy!' Gawain was tugging at her impatiently, his little legs dangling over his toddler step. 'Wipe bottom.'

'Wipe *my* bottom, *please*,' Emma retorted automatically, aware at the same time that regressive baby talk and bad manners was nothing compared with infidelity. If only, she thought, while searching for a clean pair of Spider-Man pants, she could confide in someone.

But she didn't dare. Mum would only say 'I told you so'. Bernie, for all her loud talk, would be shocked. And as for confessing all to her new husband, she couldn't even go down that road. He'd never forgive her. Indeed, he'd call her (justifiably) a hypocrite for condemning her dad and yet doing it herself. Maybe – what an awful thought – it was in the genes.

No, Emma told herself as she heard a tired cry from the children's bedroom, indicating that Willow had woken up too soon from her morning nap. She'd just have to get on with it. Pretend it had never happened.

Lying was the only way to save her marriage.

'Let's go to the park today, shall we, children?'

Emma forced her voice to sound bright, even though she felt exhausted. There were only so many things you could do with an active four-year-old and a toddler who was running into everything. Since Willow had learned to walk, the house had turned into a danger zone. Every table corner was a possible hazard, and every step just one call away from Casualty.

For the last month or so, since getting back, she'd been trying out different things to keep the kids amused. Drawing, cutting and pasting at the kitchen table. (Her wax crayoning had improved vastly after the classes in Greece. And the shell animals they'd been making, from her honeymoon collection, had gone down a treat.) That wasn't all. They'd been watching educational DVDs. Visited the kids' indoor gym on its half-price day. Gone swimming. And then, of course, they'd had the usual rota of pre-school friends round, although that wasn't always a great idea. It turned out that Gawain wasn't the only four-year-old to be regressing when it came to bladder control. 'I'm so sorry,' grimaced the mother who was known as Too Many Kids Mum because of her addiction to pregnancy. She'd taken the bag of wet pants and shrugged. 'It's only started since the last one was born. I think it might be jealousy.'

But now Emma's *Keep Gawain occupied during the holiday* ideas were running out. In fact, it would be a relief when school started next week.

'Don't want to go to the park,' Gawain frowned. They'd been playing cars on the kitchen floor since breakfast and tempers were becoming decidedly frayed.

'Ducks,' declared Willow, her little face breaking out into a broad smile.

Emma clapped her hands with delight. 'Yes! Clever girl! We'll take some bread to feed them.'

Willow nodded with that bright enthusiasm you rarely saw in an adult. If only she could bottle that for ever! 'Come on, Gawain. You'll like it when we get there.'

Bundling her son into his little coat (it was one of those bright but nippy late August days), Emma shepherded him towards the door. 'Wait there until I get Willow's pushchair,' she instructed. Honestly, it was like a military campaign getting them both out of the house! On the other hand, thank heavens for routine. It was the only way to block out those awful memories which kept coming back into her head.

Her lust. The drink. The need to be truly desired in a place where everyone else seemed to be 'at it' . . .

'Come on. Walk nicely,' she pleaded with Gawain, who insisted on walking precariously, one foot in front of the other, along the side of the pavement. 'Gawain! I said not near the road! If you don't stop, you can't go on the slide.'

The slide was his favourite, but she could already see from the park gate that there was a long queue. This place got really busy in the summer holidays, stuffed with parents (either the bored variety or the over-enthusiastic) plus a sprinkling of au pairs, who were more interested in yabbering away on their mobiles than looking after their charges.

'It's my turn!'

'No, it's not, it's *my* turn!'

Those voices sounded very familiar . . .

'Melissa!' Emma came face to face with the tall, slim, dark-haired woman who was trying to stop Alice and Freddie from clambering onto one of the kids' swing seats.

Her breath caught in her throat. This was the first time she'd seen her 'friend' since that awful scene at the airport. All through the summer holidays, Emma had been keeping her eyes peeled, mentally preparing the speech she kept going over and over in her mind.

But now she was right in front of her, it all went out of her head.

'Oh. It's you.' Melissa turned her back on Emma. 'Stop it, you lot. You're both too old to play on the baby seats. Why don't you go to the pitch and putt instead?'

'That's for saddos.'

'It takes one to know one.'

Goodness. They weren't easy, were they? 'You might like it when you're doing it,' suggested Emma brightly, going into work mode.

'We don't need any advice from you.' Melissa's sharp voice was so different from the kind woman who had befriended her in Siphalonia. 'Why don't you concentrate on your own lot?' She threw a disdainful glance at Gawain, who was tearing towards the roundabout. Willow, meanwhile, was straining vigorously from the confines of her pushchair, uttering loud cries of 'Out, out.'

'I just wanted to say,' stuttered Emma, keeping one eye on Gawain while lifting Willow into the tyre swing, 'that I really wasn't responsible for talking to that journalist. You've got to believe that, Melissa. Can't we just be friends again?'

There was a short silence. Emma was aware of being

scrutinised. Even Alice seemed to be looking at her as though appraising her. 'I'm sorry,' Melissa said finally. 'I've learned that you can't always trust people. Come on, you two. We're going.'

Emma watched them leave with a sinking heart. For a moment there, she'd thought Melissa was going to give her a brief hug and say that of course she knew Emma wouldn't have done such an awful thing. But instead, she'd seen something in those eyes that she hadn't seen on holiday in Greece.

Pain. Mixed with fear. Did it, Emma wondered, as she gently pushed Willow on the swing, have anything to do with that last newspaper story about Winston, the day after they'd got back from Greece?

The one about Nick Thomas.

When Tom had read out bits from his paper, she'd had to admit that it didn't sound as though Winston had behaved very well in the Marines.

Poor Melissa. Maybe she was finding out, too, that married life wasn't all it was cracked up to be.

'Push, push!' Willow was now demanding.

Emma did as she was told. Uh-oh. Instead of sitting quietly on the roundabout, Gawain was trying to climb all over it. It was so difficult to be in two places at once when you had two kids under five.

'It's OK! I'll stop him.' Bernie's cheery voice rang out across the park.

Apprehensively, Emma watched her friend sprint over and lift Gawain up, tickling him. 'Got you, you little monkey. Now if you behave yourself, Auntie Bernie will get you an ice cream.'

Why didn't he laugh like that with her, instead of grizzling all the time? Was it possible that he'd bonded with Bernie – as well as Mum – while she'd been away?

'Hello, stranger.' Bernie's voice had an edge to it. 'Hardly seen anything of you this summer. Where've you been hiding yourself?'

Indeed, Emma hadn't called round, hadn't even rung to

suggest that Bernie came over for a coffee. The truth was that if she spent time with Bernie, she might just find herself telling her about Yannis. (Even his name made her feel sick!)

On the other hand, Bernie was her friend, wasn't she? Maybe she should take the risk. 'Actually, there's something I wanted to ask you . . .'

Bernie beamed. 'Me too.'

'You first,' said Emma quickly, losing her nerve.

'No, you.'

Gawain was tugging at her jeans. 'No arguing,' he said bossily. No guesses where he'd picked that up from! Clearly Mum had had a hard time when they'd been away.

Bernie gave him another tickle. 'Actually, I was going to ask if you wanted a bit of extra cash when term starts. They need someone to help with the after-school club. I can't do it cos I agreed to help Vanessa in her shop two nights a week. Quite excited, I am, about that! Fancy myself as a fashion advisor, I do. But I did suggest to Gemma that *you* might be able to do it if your mum was able to have trouble here.'

'You seem to have it all sorted out for me.' Emma heard the words coming out of her mouth more sharply than she'd intended.

'What's up with you?' Her friend gave her a worried look. 'Ever since the honeymoon you've been like a cat on a hot tin roof. Is everything all right?'

If Bernie's voice hadn't been so kind and understanding, Emma would have managed to stay silent. But the sympathy, combined with her exhaustion, eroded the last part of her defences.

Just as well that Gawain was back on the swings again.

'Oh Bernie.' Hot tears rolled down her face as she clung to her friend. 'I've done something awful. And now I don't know what to do . . .'

She felt better afterwards. 'Nothing like a good cry to let it all out,' Bernie had said, giving her a big hug before she and the kids set off for home. 'And don't worry. I won't tell a soul. You can trust me.'

What would she do without a friend like that? One Bernie was worth more than a million Melissas. The woman wasn't worth bothering about. As for Yannis, Bernie was right. There was no point in dwelling on what she should have done. The best thing to do was to block it out and get on with her marriage.

Meanwhile, Emma felt quite excited about the after-school club opening. They could certainly do with the money. Maybe she'd drop in on Mum on the way home to sound her out.

'Hello, you two!' Mum opened the door with a delighted beam, bending down to tickle Willow under the chin and ruffle Gawain's hair. 'Give Gran a kiss then.'

Gawain flew past her. 'Can we have tea in front of the telly?'

Clearly they'd been allowed to, when she'd been away . . .

He was rifling through the cupboards too. 'Gawain wants a chocolate biscuit, Gran.'

Chocolate biscuits? Another no-no on the list she'd left her mother.

Willow, meanwhile, was straining in her pushchair, desperate to get out. If she did, it would take ages to coax her back in again. 'Actually, Mum, I've come for a favour.'

Emma felt rather bad about always asking her mum to help out. Then again, she didn't seem to mind. 'Is there any chance you could have the kids for two afternoons a week when term starts? Only there's a job going in the after-school club and we could do with the money. I should be back here by sixish.'

Mum looked as though she'd just been given a present. 'I'd love to. Although I have to say that if Tom wasn't just a garage mechanic, he'd be able to provide better for his family.'

Not again. 'Please, Mum. Can we let that one go, just for once?'

Mum shrugged. She really did look good for her age, Emma

thought. Her blonde hair – natural like her own – made her look much younger than fifty-two, and she was wearing a new lipstick (a pale orange) which suited her better than her usual rose. 'OK. By the way, a letter came for Tom this morning. Don't know why it got sent here, unless whoever posted it thought you two still lived with me.'

She put the letter in Emma's hand excitedly. 'Look at the frank mark. Come from a newspaper, it has.'

So it had. Maybe Tom had won something in one of those competitions he was always entering. Yes! Her heart beating with excitement, she pulled out a cheque. *Two hundred pounds!* It must have been *some* competition. There was a chit with it too.

Payment for reader tip.

She stared at the writing.

So it had been *Tom* who had tipped off the newspaper about Alice and Jack. He'd told them what she had told him in confidence. And he'd asked them to send the money to her mum's address so she wouldn't open it. How could he?

'Won some money, has he?' demanded Mum, staring at the cheque.

'Looks like it,' said Emma dryly.

'What did he do to get that, then?'

'I'm not sure of the details,' said Emma grimly, watching Gawain finish the packet of chocolate biscuits. 'But I'll find out more when he gets home tonight.'

TRUE POST-HONEYMOON STORY

'Seven weeks after we got back, I found myself expecting
a honeymoon baby.'

Mary, now pregnant with her third

Chapter Twenty-Nine

ROSIE

The Villa Rosa was virtually empty now, apart from a skeleton staff and a couple who always returned every September. 'We like to wait until the schools are back,' the wife said each time as though she hadn't said it the previous year, and the year before that. 'Nice and quiet, don't you think?'

Too quiet, thought Rosie. Jack was still barely speaking to her, save the odd phrase like 'I'll be late from school' or 'I can't work in the kitchen today.'

She didn't blame him. Any teenager had every right to be angry if his mother had lied to him for the past fifteen and a half years.

Now, sitting on the terrace overlooking the sea, Rosie reflected on that awful scene after Charlie – so hard to call him Winston! – had finally left the island, along with his bride and her two ghastly children.

'You've got to tell Jack,' Greco had said gently but firmly, putting his arm around her as they stood watching their guests' taxi scattering dust down the lane as it headed for the airport. 'Now that Winston and his wife know, you owe it to your son to come clean. Otherwise they might write to him themselves.'

He'd squeezed her bottom. 'That's no way for a boy to find out about his father, is it?'

He was right, but the prospect of breaking the news to Jack was so daunting that Rosie could feel her skin breaking out into a cold sweat. 'Do you know where he is?' she asked, her mouth so dry with nerves that she was almost unable to speak.

Greco smiled wryly. 'Sitting in my boat, nursing his broken heart. He's just had to say goodbye to his girlfriend, hasn't he? So I suggested he might like some space.'

This man never failed to take her by surprise. Not only was he bright but he was also kind.

Greco understood, just as she did, that poor Jack was devastated over Alice. She'd felt exactly the same when Charlie had left her at the age of seventeen.

And now she was going to have to break his heart again.

Slowly, Rosie peeled away from Greco's comforting arms and kissed him lightly on both cheeks. She slipped on her blue canvas beach shoes and began to walk down to the shore where the *Siphalonian* was anchored.

It was a pretty boat with a red hull and white woodwork which Greco painted every year, after the onslaught of the sun, wind and storms that it valiantly fought its way through. 'My boat is my escape,' he'd murmured to her the other evening when she'd asked if he was ever lonely. She'd been touched by his reply. 'She is my wife. My child. When I am with her, I feel safe.'

Jack, it seemed, felt the same. There he was, sitting cross-legged on deck, staring out at the impossibly blue water with its slivers of green and the odd flash of a silver fish.

She called out to him. Would he mind if she joined him? It was worth the risk. She kicked off her canvas shoes and swam the short distance to where the boat was anchored.

'You can always write,' she said, once she was squatting down next to him. 'To Alice, I mean.'

Her son had nodded, his face set on an unseen spot on the horizon. 'We use Facebook nowadays, Mum. Letters are so uncool.'

She shrugged, thinking of the letter she had sent Charlie: a letter he had denied receiving. Rosie steeled herself. 'There's something I've got to tell you.' She could taste bile in her mouth now. This was even harder than she'd thought. 'You know how strange things happen, sometimes?'

Jack was still looking at the horizon. It was so difficult to know if a teenager was listening. The next bit would soon tell her. Rosie took a deep breath.

'I actually met Winston before this summer. It was when I was quite young and living in the UK.'

Her son's face whipped round. She definitely had his full attention now. 'No way!'

He was grinning as though this was one of those happy coincidences instead of one that was going to change the course of his life. It's not too late to come up with another story, Rosie told herself.

'How did you know him, Mum? And why didn't you tell me before?'

His eyes were open, waiting. She hesitated. Briefly, Rosie thought of Greco and of Cara who was sitting waiting for her in the kitchen. They were right. She owed Jack this, whatever the consequences.

'I met him at a dance,' she replied, ignoring his last question. 'We . . . we fell in love.'

That was important. He needed to know it was that and not just lust. Jack wasn't grinning now. He had his head to one side in that uncertain position he adopted when he wasn't sure about his maths homework.

'So what happened?'

'He . . . he had to go back to his training camp.' She could leave it there; she didn't have to tell him the whole story. But the words were spilling out now, in a flood of relief, and at the same time, a searing, burning guilt. 'I wrote to him but he didn't reply. I needed to tell him something, Jack. I needed to tell him I was pregnant.'

Just as she spoke, a large bird flew by, screaming as it landed on the water. Jack was frowning. 'What did you say?'

This was awful! Forcing herself, she squeezed the next sentence out. 'I needed to tell him I was pregnant,' she repeated softly.

Jack leaped to his feet, staring down at her. His eyes bored into hers and his fists, she could see, were clenched by his side. He didn't look like a youth any more. He looked like a man.

'So I have a brother? Or a sister?'

She shook her head. Jack ran to the side of the boat and grabbed the railings. For a minute, she feared he might throw himself over. Scrambling to her feet, she joined him. 'Please don't say you had an abortion,' he was muttering.

'No.' She put an arm around him. 'I didn't.'

His face was shining. 'Then I *have* got a brother or sister. It's what I've always wanted. It's OK, Mum. There's someone else at school whose mum had a kid before she got married. She was really young too.' Then he stopped. 'Did my dad know about this before he died?'

Yes. All she had to say was yes. But lies were too complicated. They had a way of forcing themselves out of the woodwork over the years. She'd started. She had to finish.

'Jack, love.' She took both his hands. '*Winston* is your dad.'

'*No!*'

At first she thought the howl came from the large bird which had now flown onto the handrail next to them. Then she realised it was Jack, bending double as if racked with pain. He was glaring at her now with a fury that reminded her of someone else's face. Her own father's.

'You've been lying to me all these years! You told me my dad was dead, killed in a motorbike accident. You even told me the date – November the twelfth! Every year we say a prayer for him!'

That had been the priest's idea. Rosie had been unable to find a reason to turn it down, despite Cara's disapproval. 'I'm sorry, I'm so sorry.'

There was a crack as her son brought down his hand on the handrail, frightening the bird so that it flew off, squawking madly. 'Is that why he came here? To check me out? To see if I'm the kind of son he wants after all these years?'

'No, it wasn't like that.' She reached out her hand but he angrily pushed it away. 'Winston didn't write back to me all those years ago because he didn't get my letter.'

There was a disgusted sound. 'Or so he says.'

'It was as big a shock to him to find us here as it was for me to see him. You've got to believe me.'

Jack was regarding her now with the disdain that she'd seen on Alice's face when talking to Winston. But worse. 'Why should I believe anything you say? Fuck off, Mum. I never want to see you again.'

Then he'd leaped off the side of the boat and swum to the shore. She'd followed him, of course, but although they were so close to the beach, he got there before her. 'He'll come back,' soothed Cara when she eventually returned to the villa, dripping wet, both from her tears and the sea. 'My daughter, she was the same at that age.'

But your daughter didn't come back, Rosie almost said. For two agonising hours, she waited for him to return. Then, just when she was about to call the police, the door swung open and Jack stomped in with sand all down his legs and shorts.

'Get off.' He pushed her away as she went to greet him; marching instead to the sink and washing his hands before starting to prep the veg for dinner. 'I don't want to talk to you, Mum. Got it?'

It would pass, Cara said. And maybe it might have done, if not for the next instalment of Winston's life story which the *Mail* ran the following day.

WINSTON'S SHAME

Winston King has built his reputation on being a fearless Royal Marine. But the truth is very different.

Four years ago, Winston was in charge of escorting convoys through Afghanistan. It was an operation fraught with dangers – and one that demanded great care. Winston, then known as Charlie, allowed one convoy to pass through a route renowned for landmines.

Tragically, part of the convoy was blown up, leading to the death of Nicola Thomas, a 36-year-old Wren with whom Winston was in a relationship at the time.

298

In an official report, Winston was exonerated from blame for the incident. It was claimed that, in the circumstances, the risk was justified.

However, both the mother and sister of Nick Thomas still feel very bitter towards Mr King. 'He should have waited for confirmation that the route was clear of landmines,' says Pamela Thomas, Miss Thomas's 72-year-old mother. 'If he had, my Nicola would still be alive today. It makes me sick to see the man on our television screens every morning, telling us how to get fit. It's about time everyone else knew the truth about him.'

Rosie had read the newspaper article with a mounting sense of dismay. During her long heart-to-heart with Winston, she'd been taken aback to find that he seemed a decent, honest sort of man. He had really appeared shocked that she had been pregnant. Unless he was a very good actor, he hadn't received that letter.

Nor did he seem the kind of man who would carelessly allow a convoy to cross dangerous territory without making the right safety checks.

She couldn't help wondering how he would be taking the news, back in the UK. Part of her wanted to email him and tell him that she was sorry he was having such a tough time. The sensible part told her to forget it. His wife might take it the wrong way, interpreting it as a move to get him back. Besides, why should she worry herself about Winston King?

Because he was Jack's father, that's why. Rosie closed her iPad quickly. There was no reason for Jack to read the papers. Like most teenagers, he was far more interested in Facebook. With any luck, he might not see this. Her son had only just found his father. It didn't seem fair that he should be turned against him.

After all, as Cara kept telling her, there were usually two sides to a story. The problem was knowing which one was true.

Now, as Rosie scrubbed down the patio table, making a start on all the post-season jobs that she did at this time of the year, she still couldn't get rid of that feeling of unease.

If Jack had read that final story about his father and the Wren, he hadn't mentioned it. 'Best leave sleeping cats lie,' Cara had said, nodding toothily to make her point.

Rosie couldn't be bothered to correct her. There were more important things to worry about.

Meanwhile, there had been one email from Winston, asking her to let him know if he could 'do anything'.

I think you've done more than enough already, she'd emailed back. *We don't need your help. On the other hand, if you want to email your son, that's up to the two of you.*

Did they keep in touch? she wondered as she scrubbed the table harder, letting out her anger and fear. If so, that was another thing that Jack was staying silent about.

Suddenly she felt a warm breath on her neck, followed by a pair of strong arms around her. Before she knew it, Rosie was being lifted into the air. 'Please,' she laughed, breathless. 'Put me down!'

Reluctantly, or so it seemed, Greco did so. 'Leave this,' he declared, gesturing towards the bucket and scrubbing brush. 'Come on the boat with me.'

It was tempting. Since she and Greco had got together, they had made several wonderful boat trips. Sometimes it seemed it was the only time they could have together, away from prying eyes and Jack's sullenness.

'Not now,' she said, nestling her chin on his shoulder. 'I need to be here for when Jack gets home from school.'

Greco gave her a comforting squeeze. 'I think he may be some time. I saw him at the bar when I was coming over here.'

Her heart filled with unease. That was another thing her son had started to do, since the summer. Drink. All the other teenagers did it but she still didn't like it.

'It's just a stage,' said Greco softly. 'He'll get through it.'

But would he? Rosie wondered, looking out over the horizon where the sea merged with the sky in a dramatic indigo-blue line.

And even if he did, what about her? Would she get through

it too? A memory of Winston's mouth on hers in that crowded dance hall came back to her. As clear as the carved heart on the leg of the patio table, in its teenage capital letters.

ALICE LOVES JACK.

The girl must have done that, before she'd left. However hard she scrubbed, the heart wouldn't come out. And why should it? There was something about your first love that could never go away.

Maybe, Rosie admitted to herself, that was why she was still unable to banish her own memories, especially now they had been rekindled.

In fact, after this summer, could anything ever be the same again?

ADVICE FOR TODAY'S NEWLY MARRIED BRIDE

Start as you mean to go on – providing it's *your* idea.

Stash a secret pile of 'running away' money in case things get tough.

Be selective with your past history.

Never be rude about his mother, even if *he* is.

From Charisma's *bridal special*

Chapter Thirty

WINSTON

'Where are my football boots, Mum?'

'Who's hidden my laptop? I know it's you, Freddie. Give it back or you'll never see your football boots again!'

'Buck up, you lot! You're going to be late!'

Winston paused, mid-exercise, to shut the door of the spare room which Melissa had allowed him to convert into a gym. He should be at the television studio now. Not listening to this awful pre-school argument that went on every day with minor variations.

Sometimes it was homework that went missing. Or one of the children – usually Alice – would kick up a fuss because her jogging bottoms were still in the wash. It made his head ring. But worst of all was the discovery that Melissa, whom he'd first thought so sweet, turned into a harridan when it came to getting the kids off in the morning. It had certainly shown him a new side of her.

Still, thought Winston, looking out of the window at the row of neat suburban gardens backing an identical row of spacious Edwardian semi-detached houses (so boringly smug compared with the colourful life-on-the-streets view outside his London flat), his new wife would probably say the same about him.

Sweating, and not just from the exercise, Winston sat astride the rowing machine that he'd brought down from his place, along with a few of his other possessions, and grabbed the handles, working himself up to the maximum speed. Sheer hard graft was the only way to block this all out.

'Who's moved my car keys?'

'Don't blame us, Mum! Look after your own stuff!'

Faster. Faster. Winston's hands tightened. Thankfully, Melissa was going to do a makeover at the other end of town after the school run. It meant that, for a few hours at least, they wouldn't have to pussyfoot around each other all day, with the kind of polite distance that he'd always abhorred in couples who had little to say to each other.

What had happened to those lovely long conversations they used to have, not to mention the warm, melting kisses?

Winston stopped rowing. The truth was that it had never been the same since that bloody newspaper series.

Melissa might just have been able to cope with the news about Jack. As she reluctantly said, it wasn't always easy for a man to know if a girlfriend was pregnant. But it was the story about Nick that had really done it.

If only he could have hidden it. For one mad moment that day, Winston had considered the possibility of shredding every copy in the land, along with each iPad, like the fairy-tale character who had banished all spinning wheels from his kingdom.

If only.

Instead, Winston had woken up the morning after returning from Greece to find Melissa studying her iPad with a frown on her forehead.

She'd glanced at him and then at the Google news item headed 'Winston's Shame'. 'Do you want to tell me what happened?' she'd said in a voice that was scarily devoid of emotion.

He'd felt a catch in his throat. 'Yes, I do.'

Bracing himself, he'd propped his pillow up next to hers. She'd edged slightly away.

Not a good sign.

Winston took a deep breath and began to talk.

'I'd had girlfriends before you,' he began.

She gave a short laugh. 'I think Jack is proof enough of that, don't you?'

Ignoring the barb, he carried on. 'But none of them lasted, partly because of the nature of the job and partly because I didn't feel ready to be committed. But then, one day, a new Wren was posted out.'

Melissa cut in. 'Nicola Thomas,' she said quietly, glancing at the iPad with its picture of a young woman in formal uniform and hair knotted back in a bun, staring out at them both.

'Nick,' whispered Winston. 'She was known as Nick.'

A look of hurt passed over Melissa's face. 'She was pretty,' commented his wife, chewing a wisp of hair like a child. It was a vulnerable gesture which, he'd noticed, she often made when describing how Marvyn had betrayed her.

Now it was his turn. Betrayal could also mean *not* telling someone something, couldn't it?

'She looked a bit like you,' he added, wondering too late if it was wise to admit this. 'She had dark hair with a hint of red, although it was shorter than yours. She was easy to talk to. And there was something different about her.'

Melissa's lips tightened. But he had to go on. Not just for her, but for himself. 'She was good at her job, too. Nick was a nurse in the Wrens. She was passionate about saving lives. If there was a risky operation, she was always up for it. It was what she'd been made for. That's what she used to say.'

Now his wife was edging further away. As she did so, his hopes plummeted even lower. 'That was how *you* felt too, wasn't it?'

He nodded. 'One scorching hot day, when our lungs were full of dust and our uniforms soaked with sweat, I was asked to lead a convoy carrying medical supplies to some men who had been injured. We all knew it was dangerous.' He groaned inside. 'It was a route that was still being cleared of landmines. I was told that it was virtually free but that if I wanted to be certain, we needed to wait forty-eight hours.'

The silence hung heavily between them. 'We didn't have forty-eight hours, Melissa. Those injured men needed help urgently. I might have held off if . . .'

'If Nick hadn't pushed you.'

He looked at his wife gratefully. He could see it now. Nick tugging at his sleeve as he stood in the tent, poring over the maps. 'I can't stand here doing nothing,' she'd said fiercely, as though he was a coward.

Sometimes, he wondered if Nick should have been a man. She had enough balls, and there was a certain boyish look about her. But there was also a vulnerable side, a tender one that only he knew about. A picture of her lying next to him in bed flew into his mind. That was definitely not one to share with his wife.

'It was my decision, of course, but the rest of the team wanted to go too.' He took another deep breath. 'So we went.'

Getting out of bed, he began pacing round the room. It was easier to make his confession on the move: it made him feel like he was doing something.

'At first, we made great progress. The cars didn't hit any of the usual obstacles like rocks, and, thank goodness, we didn't come across any snipers.'

Melissa gave a little gasp. 'It must be scary knowing that someone could take a potshot at you any time.'

Winston shrugged. 'The strange thing is that there's no time to be frightened. You're too busy keeping your wits about you and making sure everyone is doing what they should.' He paused by the foot of the bed. It had a pink counterpane: too girly and frilly for his taste. Had it been here when Marvyn had been married to Melissa? He didn't like to think of that, any more than he liked to dwell on that hot, dusty day in Afghanistan.

'Go on,' she urged.

Winston wanted to look Melissa in the eyes but couldn't. Turning round, he addressed the wall. There was one of those black-and-white studio family portraits there, showing a younger, gappy-toothed Alice standing behind her little brother. Her hands were on the kid's shoulder and she looked as though she was about to throttle him.

Quite possible.

Next to it was a slightly faded space and a picture hook, suggesting there had once been another photograph there. Marvyn and Melissa, perhaps. Maybe a wedding photo. He wouldn't blame Melissa if she wished it was still there; that Marvyn hadn't gone off and – more crucially – that she hadn't met him, Winston.

'I felt lucky that day.' He laughed. 'So did Nick. She told me before we set off that fortune favoured the brave. It was one of her favourite phrases. Far better to risk one's life by helping others than lead some boring life in an office like her sister.'

He glanced down at the iPad and the interview with Nick's family. 'Whatever that says, I can tell you that Nick's sister hardly ever saw her; she couldn't even be bothered to come round when we were back on leave.'

Melissa's voice had an impatient edge. 'What exactly happened on that day, Winston? I need to know.'

Focus on the wall. On the faded space. 'I was in a jeep behind the car carrying Nick and another Wren. We were nearly there. Then suddenly there was the most almighty noise.'

As if on cue, a shout came from Alice's bedroom next door. 'Get out, Freddie! You're not allowed in here!'

Wasn't it possible even to make a confession in peace? Winston carried on speaking, louder and steadily. It was the only way. If he allowed himself to waver, he would crumple. 'Nick's car was engulfed with flames. It was like one of those scenes you see on television.'

Even as he spoke, it didn't feel real. 'I didn't think. All I can remember is leaping out of the jeep and running towards Nick's door, which was buckling in the heat before my eyes.' He shuddered, putting his hands up to block out the mental image.

'Inside, I could see Nick staring at me. She wasn't screaming. Just looking at me, waiting, trusting. Certain that I would get her out. But I couldn't.'

He was weeping, dammit. Weeping tears that he'd kept in

for all this time. Dimly he was aware of Melissa putting her arms around him. 'It's all right,' she whispered. 'It's all right.'

Unable to stop himself, he rounded on her. 'No, it's not!'

She drew back as though he'd hit her. 'Don't shout at me, please.'

He was tempted to point out that the children did it all the time. 'I'm sorry. But don't you see? I *couldn't* get Nick out. I failed her. And even though the official report cleared me, saying that I'd made the convoy decision for the "greater good", the guilt and the smell of that burning flesh will stay with me for life.'

He sat on the edge of the bed now, head in hands.

'What happened to the other Wren?' asked Melissa quietly.

'She was thrown clear. Don't ask me how. There's no rhyme or reason in war.'

'Mum, she's hurting me!

Freddie burst through the door, closely followed by his sister. Ignoring him, they leaped onto the bed.

'Get off, Alice!'

'*You* get off!'

Then the girl turned and gave him a nasty look. 'I've been reading about you on Facebook. My dad says it's *your* fault that someone died.'

Melissa's voice was quietly reproachful. 'Alice! Don't be so rude!'

'Well, it's true, isn't it?'

The din was so loud that he almost didn't hear his mobile ring. But he could see the name flashing on the screen. His agent.

Leaving the bedroom, Winston headed downstairs for some peace and quiet. Melissa's sitting room wasn't to his taste with its red and green rugs and squashy blue sofas. They'd get a place of their own soon, they'd told each other during the honeymoon. They needed that. It was important for them to create something together. Now, as he perched on the edge of a stiff-backed chair that had once belonged to Marvyn, it all seemed horribly irrelevant.

'Winston.' Tara's voice was politely distant, faintly

condemning. 'I presume you've seen the news. Look, there's no easy way of putting this. The producer has been trying to get hold of you. It might be best if you didn't go into the studio for a few days. Wait until the fuss has died down.'

Not go into the studio? He felt as though he'd been punched in the chest. 'What about the programme?'

There was a short pause at the other end. 'Don't worry. They've got someone else to step in for you.'

His pulse quickened. 'Who?'

'A new face.' Tara was talking quickly, attempting to make light of it. No 'darling' or 'sweetie' this time, he noted.

Clearly this was serious.

'He's quite young,' she added.

'How young?'

'Twenty, twenty-one. Don't worry! He won't be as good as you. No one can be, whatever Poppy says.'

'You know she admitted to messing up my honeymoon?'

'And did *you* know she's the producer's niece?'

No, he hadn't.

'I might as well tell you. This new chap they're trying out is her boyfriend. I know, I know. But my hands are tied. The producer is insistent. Just sit it out. It's the only thing to do.'

Was it?

'Definitely.' His agent sounded like Melissa did when she was trying to get the kids to do something they didn't want. 'Have another honeymoon. Use the extra time to be with your new bride and her children. OK?'

That had been a few weeks ago. Since then, Melissa had been very quiet. Yes, she understood, or so she said, but he didn't believe her. Meanwhile, she was taking more and more make-over jobs, both locally and in London, while he was passing the time by working out, house-husbanding and 'babysitting'. Every now and then he found himself turning on the television and watching this skinny kid running *his* show. Incredibly, the critics loved him, and so did the mums and grans, who saw him as a pin-up son.

'Piss off, Freddie!'

As for the kids, they were so noisy that he had a permanent headache. Thank heavens school had started now.

The phone! He seized the landline with the desperation of a man who was utterly bored.

'Winston?' Tara rarely had to say who was calling. Her voice did that for her.

'Any news?' he asked hoarsely.

'I'm afraid there is.' Her flat tone gave him the news before she spoke. 'The decision has finally been made. They've terminated your contract, Winston. And before you ask, they're entitled to do so. There's a small clause about a presenter's conduct – either past or present – bringing the programme into disrepute.'

'I see.' He was already pulling on his jogging jacket. Out. He needed to get out. In the kitchen, he could still hear Melissa yelling something about missing shoes.

'If it makes you feel any better,' his agent was adding, 'they weren't going to renew next time anyway. The general feeling was that they needed someone younger . . .'

His fingers pressed the red button, terminating the call. He could always blame poor reception, but the truth was that he simply couldn't take it any more.

'Hiya, Winston!'

The man on the doorstep virtually walked right into him. Marvyn! 'Kids ready for school?'

The bloke was looking around as if he still owned the place, instead of having reluctantly 'given' it to Melissa as part of the settlement. 'Said I'd do the school run today for Mellie as she's under the weather.'

Marvyn fixed him with a disdainful sneer. 'All this nasty publicity over your sordid past has got her down. I have to say, I was never out of work myself. Never allowed myself to be, not when I had a family to support.'

Winston felt his muscles tightening. 'Don't worry. I can look after my wife.'

There was a nasty laugh. 'Can you? Not if you believe all

310

your hate mail on the net. Personally, I rather like your successor. And do you know why?' His face hardened. 'Because he's not under the same roof as my own kids.'

That was it.

'You can keep them, especially your spoilt brat of a daughter.' Pushing past him, Winston strode into the street, breaking into a jog. As he ran, he switched on his phone. He hadn't wanted to make this call. But now there was no alternative.

TRUE POST-HONEYMOON STORY

'We had to live with our in-laws for the first six months. It was hell.'

Angela, now living three hundred miles from her husband's family

Chapter Thirty-One

EMMA

'How could you?' Emma had yelled at Tom after she'd discovered the payment slip from the newpaper. 'How could you have sold a story about my friends?'

He'd just come home from work, still in his greasy navy blue overalls and with oily hands that he was washing now under the kitchen tap, even though she'd told him time and time again to do that in the bathroom instead of mucking up the sink.

The children had been having their tea, Willow reluctantly strapped into her high chair, banging her spoon on the food tray, while Gawain (who'd been sitting quite nicely on his booster seat for a change), leaped up on seeing his dad.

'Lift, Dad! *Lift!*'

Tom had scooped up his son – now his overalls would stain Gawain's sweatshirt – and given a shrug. 'It wasn't a story, love. Just a tip-off. The paper runs a little box every day, asking readers to send something in that might be worth publishing.'

'That doesn't mean you have to stoop to its level!' she'd spat back, furious at his lack of remorse. 'And it wasn't just a tip-off. It was a betrayal. I told you in confidence about all that Winston stuff. I was trying to divert you when you were feeling poorly. And now you repay me by making me lose a friend!'

Two little red spots appeared on each of his cheeks. Good. So he knew he was in the wrong. 'These celebrities set themselves up in the public eye, love. They get paid enough.'

'Well, not now. Winston hasn't been on telly since we've got back.'

313

Tom's cheek spots were crimson now. 'That's not my fault.'

'How do you know? I suppose you somehow found out about Winston being Jack's dad, did you, and told the paper about that too?'

'What?' She had seen he was genuinely perplexed. 'No way. I was as surprised as you to read about that.' He reached out his hand. 'I'm sorry, Em, but I thought it was a harmless way to earn a bit of spare cash after the wedding.'

Turning away, she'd pulled Gawain out of his arms, despite his little hands hanging onto those filthy overalls.

'Dad Dad!'

In vain, she'd tried to get her son to sit down at the table. 'Well, it *wasn't* harmless,' she threw out over her shoulder. 'Like I said, Melissa isn't talking to me any more, and I don't blame her. Now go and change, cos to be honest, I don't want to talk to *you* at the moment either.'

She'd ignored him for the next few weeks, quietly seething inside. Part of her anger, Emma knew, was because she felt guilty herself. It was all very well Bernie advising her to 'put it behind you', but she wasn't made that way. She'd been unfaithful during their honeymoon and Tom had caused problems with someone else's marriage.

They made a right pair.

Just as well that she had the kids – and the after-school club – to distract her. In fact, she was really enjoying her little extra job. Unlike her lunchtime duties, this was more relaxed. All she had to do was make toast for the children (who came from both the primary and secondary schools) and put out some toys and games for the younger ones. The older kids had a special quiet corner to do their homework.

'I'm doing a project on animal behaviour,' one of them told her.

Hah! They ought to come and do some research at her house, then.

Sometimes, they asked for a bit of help, even though they were meant to do it on their own. 'Mrs Walker,' asked a little girl with a patch over her eye one evening; 'what does Con

Fid Ent mean?' The kid frowned down at the sheet of questions in front of her, sucking her pencil. 'You've got to say what these words mean. I've done some but I don't get them all.'

'You know,' she said, pulling up another small chair and inviting the little girl to sit next to her. 'When I was your age, I couldn't swim.'

The girl's eyes widened. 'Really?'

Emma nodded. Even now she felt embarrassed to admit it. 'My dad used to take me down to the swimming pool every Sunday.' A lump swelled up in her throat. It had been their special time together. 'Gives me a chance to have some time to myself,' Mum had said.

'But,' she continued, talking more to herself than the little girl now, 'I was too scared to leave the shallow end. I didn't have the confidence, you see.'

She was conscious now of a couple of other children listening in. 'What happened, miss?' asked a big kid with round red cheeks.

'My dad told me that we can do whatever we want.' Her voice grew soft at the memory. 'He said that our minds can be like magic. You have to believe and then it works.'

She could almost see Dad right now, standing waist-deep in the water and holding his right hand up in the air. 'So he pretended to wave a magic wand. I was really into magicians then. Dad and I used to watch a conjuring show every Friday night on telly.'

Emma paused again, remembering how they'd snuggle up together on the sofa, her head on his shoulder. Thick as thieves, her mother used to say. 'So I believed him.'

The little girl with the patched eye drew in her breath. 'Cool. So did you swim to the deep end then?'

'Not immediately. It took a bit of time. But I did make a start by doing a few kicks.'

When she had learned to swim properly, Dad had gone out and bought her a pair of roller skates. 'You're spoiling her,' Mum had grumbled.

'So what?' Dad had retorted. 'What's the point of having a kid if you can't give her stuff?'

How was it possible, Emma thought now with a lump in her throat, for a father and daughter to have become so distant? Why oh why had he betrayed Mum and her like that? But who was she to talk?

'I can do the next word on the list! I can do it!' The little girl with the covered-up eye was jumping up and down with excitement.

Emma glanced down at it. *Forgive.* There it was, in black and white, as though someone had written it down especially for her. 'It means make up,' babbled the little girl. 'My mum's always saying that my sister and I have to do that when we're fighting.'

Getting up from the child-sized chair and adjusting her elasticated skirt, Emma patted the little girl on the shoulder. 'Your mum's right. Arguing isn't nice. Now, who'd like some toast?'

There was a wave of excited 'Me!'s as she headed for the kitchen. 'Emma!' called out one of the other helpers. 'Can you make some for my table too?'

'No, thanks.' A cool, confident voice rang out. 'I don't want *her* to make me anything.'

Was that Alice? She hadn't noticed her there in the other homework corner. Unable to stop herself, Emma felt her cheeks burning, making it look as though she was in the wrong. The other helper was staring at her curiously. 'Something I ought to know about, here?'

'My mother says that she isn't to be trusted.' Alice's words rose above the din around them.

The helper was giving her a really funny look now. 'It was a misunderstanding,' Emma muttered. 'How many pieces of toast did you say you wanted?'

Somehow she got through the rest of the session, but all the time, she had her eye on the door. Would Melissa pick up Alice and Freddie, or would it be Winston? Should she say something or just keep quiet?

'Always be true to yourself, love.' That had been one of

316

her dad's sayings. He might have been a hypocrite, but there was no reason why she had to be one too. So as soon as Melissa came through the door, with her hair tied back in a really clever knot and her face beautifully made up, Emma made her way over, heart pounding with apprehension.

'*You?*' Melissa's face said it all. 'What are you doing here?'

'Working. Can I have a word?' Emma took her to one side. 'I've been waiting for the right moment to tell you this.'

Melissa's glossy lips tightened. 'Tell me what?'

'It was Tom that did it.' Emma gave a quick look around to check no one was listening. 'I'm so sorry. He texted the paper and told them some of the stuff I'd told him about you and Winston and the kids . . . I know I promised not to tell anyone, but I didn't think my own husband counted.' To her embarrassment, she felt her eyes well with tears. 'I'm beginning to think I don't know him as well as I thought.'

Something gave in Melissa's beautiful dark eyes. 'It's not always easy to know what someone is really like.'

She turned to go but Emma caught her by the arm. 'I miss . . . I miss talking to you. It was really nice having you on holiday. You were so kind to me, lending me that medicine and including me in things. I'd like to think we can be friends.'

Melissa hesitated.

'It's not cos you're famous,' Emma added hastily.

'Hah!' There was a wry smile. 'Not any more.'

Of course. There was a new presenter now, wasn't there? Mum loved him, but personally Emma didn't think much of his exercises. They didn't push you like Winston's had done. Not that she'd given them a fair chance.

'It's because I *like* you. So can we? Can we be mates?'

Melissa smiled. When she did that, she was a different person. 'Maybe. I suppose it's nice to know you're here to look after my two at after-school club.' She glanced at Alice, who was hogging the computer, despite the queue. 'Poor things. They've been through so much recently. Perhaps you could keep a special eye on them, to make up for everything else. OK?'

*

Well, that was something, at least. She'd got things straight with Melissa, even if it had meant dropping Tom in it. Mind you, it served him right. He shouldn't have done what he had, just as she shouldn't have allowed the drink and sun to go to her head . . .

Feeling a bit uneasy, Emma finished tidying the after-school club along with the others and began walking back to her house, where mum was looking after the kids. There was a definite chill in the air: autumn was beginning to set in already. They'd been married now for two months and already they were in trouble. Every time Tom kissed her, she felt so horribly guilty.

'Thank goodness you're back.' Mum opened the door with Gawain in her arms before she had a chance to get the key out. 'What was in that blue bottle in the bathroom? There wasn't a label on it.'

The blue bottle? Emma felt a cold fear go through her. That was the one that Rosie Harrison had given her, wasn't it? She'd brought it back from the villa by mistake, forgetting to give it back. 'Something to stop you being sick. Someone lent it to me in Greece when Tom was ill. Why?'

Mum jerked her head at Gawain. 'This one's only gone and climbed on a stool to take a swig.'

'What?' Emma felt her chest tighten with fear. 'Where were *you*?'

'Trying to get Willow onto the potty.' Her mother's tone was defensive. 'It's not easy being in two places at once.'

She knew that. But that was part of a mother's job description. Still, this wasn't the time for blame-throwing.

'What are you doing?'

Emma was rifling through the kitchen drawer, trying to find the travel file she'd put together after Bernie's surprise wedding present. There it was. A printout of their flight itinerary and, crucially, a mobile number.

'Ringing Rosie, the woman who runs the villa.' She glanced through the door of the lounge to see Gawain playing happily with his cars. He looked all right but you never knew. 'With any luck, she'll tell me what's in it.'

318

Her heart still beating furiously, Emma listened to the continental tone. The phone call would cost a fortune but this was more important. What time would it be there? Eight o'clock. She could just imagine Rosie sitting out on the terrace with a glass of wine, snuggling up to Greco, with Yannis perhaps, in the background.

Don't let *him* pick up the phone. Don't.

'Villa Rosa. May I help you?'

The lilting sound of Rosie's voice filled her with relief. 'It's me, Emma. You know. My husband and I spent our honeymoon with you. He was ill . . .'

There was a slight change in the tone. 'I remember.'

'Look, I'm sorry to bother you, but . . .'

Briefly she explained what had happened. 'Jack gave it to us,' she went on. 'He said you swore by it.'

'It's all right.' The voice now had changed from cool to reassuring. 'It's only flavoured water.'

'I don't understand.'

'Nor did I at first.' There was a laugh. 'It's one of Cara's recipes. Remember? She's the co-owner and a good friend of mine. When Jack was young, it was a little trick of hers. She says that if children *think* they're getting something to make them better, they often get better on their own. In other words, it's psychological. Works on adults too – especially the ones who are hypochondriacs, if you don't mind me saying.'

Emma could have cried with relief. 'Thank you so much.'

'Not at all.' There was a slight hesitation. 'Actually, it's funny you should ring. Jack and I may be paying a visit to the UK soon. I was just looking up flights.'

Really? Perhaps that was so Jack could see his father. Poor Melissa! That wouldn't be easy for her. 'If you come to Corrywood,' she said carefully, 'I do hope you'll come round for a cup of tea.'

Now why had she said that? Immediately Emma regretted her invitation, made out of politeness and relief about the medicine. Rosie might say something about Yannis in front of Tom . . .

319

'Thanks, but we're actually going to Devon. Anyway, it was nice to chat. Do keep in touch.'

Devon? Emma couldn't help feeling curious as she went back to the kitchen. Maybe Jack and his dad were going to meet up out of the public eye.

Still, the important thing was that Gawain was all right. But how weird to give someone something that wasn't medicine at all! This Cara was either a bit touched or really rather clever . . .

'That's all right then,' said Mum, casually, when she gave her the good news.

'Not really,' said Emma awkwardly. 'I don't want to criticise, but you need to watch the kids all the time to make sure nothing happens to them.'

Her mother slammed the teapot down on the table. 'If you don't trust me to look after my own grandchildren, you can always find someone else.'

Oh dear. Now she'd offended her.

'Want chocolate biscuit!' Gawain was grabbing the packet on the side before she could stop him.

'Not before your meal, love.'

Too late! Brushing the crumbs off him, she had a sudden yearning for chocolate herself. Unable to resist – despite her new healthy eating regime since Greece – she popped a little piece in her own mouth. Ugh!

Mum rolled her eyes. 'What's wrong now?'

'This biscuit.' Emma eyed the rest suspiciously. 'It's off.'

'Mine's all right.'

'It tasted, well, metallic to me . . .'

Emma heard her voice trail away as her mother's eyes hardened. 'Metallic?'

Then her eyes fell to Emma's stomach. It was flat. In fact, she'd actually lost some weight in the last few weeks, thanks to the protein diet. It was true that the period she'd had after coming back from honeymoon had been very light, but that wasn't anything unusual.

'Do you think you're pregnant?' asked her mother sharply.

'What does Preg Nent mean?' chirped Gawain.

Why was it that kids only overheard stuff they weren't meant to?

'It's possible, I suppose.' Emma clutched the chair as her mind went back. Tom . . . Yannis . . . The recent change in her pill – at her doctor's suggestion – because she'd been getting so bloated.

'Sit down, love.' Her mother was clucking. 'A honeymoon baby? How on earth are you going to manage with three? Honestly, Em. Talk about being careless . . .'

TRUE POST-HONEYMOON STORY

'After the honeymoon my new husband was posted to Brussels. I stayed in London for my job. It's a great recipe for marriage!'

Gail, still happily commuting

Chapter Thirty-Two

ROSIE

Dear Rosemary,

How are you doing out there? I get some news from Gemma, of course, and often think about you and your little boy – although he's not so little now, is he? It seems hard to think that it was all so long ago. I don't know where the time goes!

I'm writing an old-fashioned letter because I can't get the hang of these emails, and sometimes it's better to put things on paper rather than a computer where it's so easy to say something you don't mean to, don't you think?

Anyway, excuse the rambling, but I'm also writing for another reason. I'm aware that you and your dad haven't seen eye to eye for a while, but I thought you ought to know that he really hasn't been at all well. In fact, he may well have written to you himself and told you – if so, please excuse me for interfering – but I had a funny feeling that your mum would want me to say something.

If you do decide to come over and pay him a visit, you are very welcome to stay with us. I know Gemma would be thrilled to see you – she and her little family come down to Devon whenever they can. The boys love digging sandcastles on the beach and they've given my husband a new lease of life. I am sure your dad would like to see Jack too.

Hope to hear from you soon.
Much love,
Sally

*

Rosie had read and reread the letter several times since it had arrived out of the blue a few days before. No one ever wrote to her from England: she and Gemma always emailed. But when she read the name 'Rosemary', she was taken back all those years to the confused, scared teenager whose father had thrown her out of the house.

'What's wrong?' Greco had asked, noticing her expression.

They were having breakfast on the terrace, overlooking the vineyards dropping down to the sea. Yannis had made a delicious concoction of honey and yoghurt, which seemed to be a rather perfect ending to the half-hour that she and Greco had just spent in bed. Now that the final guests had left and the villa was closed for the usual winter clean-up, Rosie could afford to take some time off in the last of the warm autumn sun.

She glanced down at the letter again with its beautiful sloping writing in proper ink. 'It's from my friend Gemma's mother, Sally. She lives near my dad – in fact, she was a friend of Mum's – and she says . . .' She hesitated slightly, still not sure of her emotions. 'She says he's ill.'

Greco sat forward, his handsome face concerned. 'Then you must go and see him at once.'

'You don't understand.' She stood up and walked towards the edge of the terrace, where tubs of bright red and orange geraniums were still cascading down. 'When I was pregnant with Jack, Dad said he never wanted to see me again.'

A pair of arms wrapped themselves around her and she leaned back into his warm, reassuring body. Over the last few months, Rosie had learned more about this body – and Greco's mind – than she could ever have thought possible. Both were full of surprises.

'People change, my loved one,' he murmured. 'It is normal for the old to look back and regret their mistakes. We will do it one day ourselves.'

Rosie gulped, trying to concentrate on the line of trees between the terrace and the sea to stop the tears from welling up in her eyes. 'Sally implied that Mum would want me to go back and see him. She also said that my father would want to see Jack.'

'Exactly.' Gently, Greco spun her round so she was facing him. 'You do not need to worry about the villa. Cara and I will look after it, will we not?'

He addressed his remark to the figure asleep on the chair in the sunny corner of the terrace. It was Cara's favourite morning position. Every now and then, the older woman would have unexpected bursts of energy and insist on cleaning the kitchen floor because 'no one else does it as I do'. Then she would have a long nap before waking up with renewed vigour.

'Of course we will look after the villa.'

So she wasn't asleep after all. In fact, Cara was sitting upright now, like a little bird, her beady eyes looking round her. Greek matriarchs, Rosie had noticed, gave the appearance of being ancient with their crinkly tanned skin, but then they surprised you with their sharp minds and observations. 'It is right for Jack to see his grandfather and show respect, however badly your father has treated you both. It is also important that the boy sees his own father. You must not let history repeat itself. The two of them need to build a relationship just as *you* need to rebuild one with your own surviving parent.'

Then, as if exhausted by her speech, Cara sank back into her chair and closed her eyes. On the other hand, that might just have been her way of saying 'No more arguments'.

Rosie glanced up at Greco, who gave her a wry smile. 'What Cara says must be done,' he said, gently tilting her chin up to his face as he often did when he was about to kiss her.

'And you can keep that kind of business to your own room,' came the voice from the chair.

Rosie moved away, embarrassed, but Greco laughed out loud. 'She is right. Come, let us take a walk.'

She knew what he had in mind. A walk along the beach often ended up with something more, provided that no one else was around. Rosie didn't know what had come over her since that time in Athens. It was as though Greco's touch had unleashed something in her that she hadn't known existed.

Winston had helped, too. Although she didn't like to admit it, the sight of him fawning over Melissa had proved that any hope she might have had of them reconciling was gone for ever.

It made Rosie even more determined to carve a new future for herself.

'I can't,' she said, tucking the letter into her trouser pocket. 'Go for a walk, that is. I have so much to do now, so much to organise.'

Greco gave her a meaningful look. 'So you are going, then?'

'Yes. I suppose so.' The words didn't seem to match the reality of the situation. 'Provided Dad wants me to.' She gave a short little laugh. 'I'll have to ring him, I suppose. Knowing my father, he'll tell me not to bother.'

'Then just go,' called out the voice from the chair. For a woman of her age, Cara had sharp hearing. 'Turn up at his doorstep with Jack next to you. Your boy will soften the hardest of hearts. Your papa will be a fool if he does not want to own a grandson such as that.'

But what about school?

'He can catch up on his education,' said Greco, as if reading her mind. 'Cara is right. You must go. Come.' He placed a hand in the small of her back, sending electric tingles down her spine. 'I will help you make arrangements if you like.'

A week ago she would never have thought they'd be standing here. It was all so different! So cold, too. Rosie and Jack huddled, shivering, outside Gatwick airport, scanning the people milling in and out of the doors with trolleys laden high with suitcases.

It wasn't just England that had changed, she thought to herself, looking around at the billboards advertising everything from a quiet night's sleep at a hotel chain to immaculate teeth.

It was her as well. She was older. Wiser. More Greek, at times, than English.

'The people look different,' observed Jack while texting at the same time (to Alice, perhaps?). 'Paler and really stressed out.'

Rosie let out a silent sigh of relief. It was one of the first proper sentences her son had spoken to her since she'd told him about his father back in July. Even when she'd explained that she was going to see her own dad in the UK and that she'd like it if he came too, Jack had simply shrugged as though she'd suggested a trip into the main town on the island.

Then she'd tentatively added that he might like to combine the trip with a visit to his own father in Corrywood, which was about three hours from Grandad's home in Devon. 'Whatever,' he'd said, although the fleeting expression on his face suggested a mixture of apprehension and excitement.

So she'd booked their tickets and asked Gemma's mother if they could take up her kind invitation to stay for two weeks. 'Please don't tell Dad,' she had written to Sally. 'I'm concerned that he might try and stop me coming.'

Once her mind had been made up, she really wanted to go, partly because of something that Greco had said. 'If you don't and he dies, you may feel guilty for the rest of your life. Trust me, my Rosie, I know what I am talking about.'

And now, finally, they were here. But where was Gemma?

'So sorry we're late!' Rosie felt someone hugging her almost before she actually saw her old friend.

'I can't believe you're here after all these years! Jack, let me take a look at you! You've grown since the last pictures Mum emailed. Wow! You're going to break a few hearts!'

Resisting the temptation to say that he already had, Rosie gave Gemma a big hug back. 'And I can't believe how you look exactly the same! Still blonde and beautiful!'

'Hah! I wish.' She smoothed down her jacket self-consciously. 'Wait till this is off and then you'll see what three children do to your waistline – not to mention another one on the way.'

'How are you feeling?' asked Rosie excitedly, stopping Gemma from picking up her bags.

'Great, thanks.' She took in Rosie approvingly. 'Love your tan! Right. Ready, everyone? I can't wait for you to see the boys. They're in the car now with Joe, but I warn you, they're all high as kites with excitement about meeting "Mummy's special friend and big grown-up boy". And they've got half-term fever too!'

Of course! How well she remembered this lovely time of year with the trees turning into a blaze of burnished copper and yellow ochre. She and Gemma used to go for long walks as teenagers, crunching through the leaves or ambling along the beach with her friend's old dog, wondering if either of them would ever, ever find a boyfriend!

'Have you seen my dad?' Rosie asked quietly as they reached the car park.

Gemma's beaming smile faltered. 'I caught a glimpse of him the other day, coming back from the surgery when I was staying with Mum.'

Rosie felt another prickle of unease. Sensing her anxiety, her old friend laid a comforting hand on her arm. 'Look, there's no point in worrying. You'll be there soon enough. There they are!' Gemma waved her hand. 'We're here!'

Immediately, two little boys flew out of the car towards her, their apple-red cheeks reminding Rosie of Gemma when she'd been younger.

'Auntie Rosie, Auntie Rosie!' called out one, reaching out for her hands and swinging round her legs. 'Is Greece called Greece cos it's greasy? My brother says it is, but I think he's wrong!'

Rosie laughed but before she could reply, Jack had stepped in. 'It can be greasy if there's an oil slick in the water.'

'What's an oil shlick?' asked the second little boy, who was just a bit smaller than the first.

'Slick,' corrected Jack kindly. 'It's when oil gets into the water, usually from a boat.'

Arm in arm, the two women watched their children carry

328

on their animated conversation as they shepherded them into the enormous people carrier. 'They get on so well,' Gemma whispered excitedly. 'You're right. We should have brought them out to see you, but to be honest, there's never been the right time.' She laughed. 'I always seem to be pregnant, don't I, Joe?'

Rosie took in the stocky, dark, good-looking man at the wheel. Of course, she recognised him from photographs, including the wedding pictures (an occasion she hadn't attended in case she bumped into her father), but now she could see, from the looks they exchanged and the way they lightly touched each other, that they really were as suited as Gemma had said.

For a second, she felt a touch of envy. No. That wasn't fair. Didn't she have Greco? Yet they didn't have the shared background that Gemma and Joe had. And, more important, she and Greco didn't have a child together. A quick picture of Winston shot into her head. There was something about that which bound you together, whether you liked it or not.

Carefully, Rosie climbed into the seat next to a sleeping toddler, thumb in mouth. Gemma turned round, beaming, from the front. 'Heaven knows how we're going to manage with four!'

Joe gave her a quick kiss on the cheek. 'We will. Now, let's get on, shall we? Sally will have dinner ready and I know she can't wait to see you.'

Rosie adjusted her watch as Joe drove through the suburbs and then open countryside. It was getting darker. Too late, she told herself, to call on an old man whom she hadn't seen for sixteen years and who didn't know she was coming. Far more sensible, surely, to wait until the morning.

'It's *so* lovely to see you again, dear,' enthused Sally for the millionth time. 'Although you'll have to excuse me for calling you Rosemary, still. I just can't get used to the Rosie bit.'

They were having breakfast in the large, airy kitchen that overlooked the sea. As a child, Rosie had loved coming here.

Her parents' little bungalow, with its view of the street outside, wasn't nearly as exciting. It didn't have the nooks and crannies of Gemma's house where you could play hide and seek. And more importantly, after Mum had died, it didn't have the laughter.

'It's so lovely to have my grandchildren down for half-term as well as my children,' Sally added, glancing fondly at Joe, who was trying to encourage the youngest to eat a mouthful of boiled egg. 'My son-in-law is so good with the children.' She dropped her voice. 'Gemma tells me you have a handsome Greek boyfriend.'

Rosie flushed, hoping Jack hadn't heard. Of course he knew about Greco, but every now and then she got the feeling that he was rather embarrassed about Mum 'dating'. It couldn't be easy.

'Jack is very good with little ones, isn't he?' Sally carried on, dabbing her mouth with a napkin. Rosie had forgotten how Gemma's mum could talk for England. It was probably to make up for her friend's father, who had always been a rather stern, forbidding figure, keeping mainly to himself in his study.

They both looked down the table to where Jack was helping the older two boys make a boat out of the empty cereal packet. 'I'm worried about how Dad is going to react,' Rosie whispered.

'Nonsense!' said Sally, sounding rather less assured. 'If he's any sense, he'll be thrilled to see you. At his age, you have to let bygones be bygones.'

But Dad had been older than Mum and Gemma's parents. That generation could, as she knew from Cara, be very stubborn, not to mention narrow-minded when it came to babies born out of wedlock. 'When are you going to go round?' Sally asked, sensing her hesitation.

Rosie glanced at her watch. Ironically, now she was here, she wanted to put it off. 'The curtains are usually drawn mid-morning,' Sally added. 'I reckon he has a nap then. You might as well go now rather than later. Don't wait to say goodbye to Gemma. She's still feeling nauseous in the morning, poor thing.'

The palms of Rosie's hands began to sweat. 'Go on,' she could hear Greco and Cara saying. She couldn't come all this way and then chicken out.

'You know,' said Sally softly, 'you've done a great job with your son.'

'Really!' Rosie flushed at the praise. 'It's not easy being a single mum.'

Sally put her head to one side sympathetically. 'I'm sure it's not.'

'And I'm always trying to stop him making the mistakes that I did.'

Sally reached across for her hand. 'We all do that. But when you get to my age, dear, you realise that you don't do them any favours that way. They have to make those mistakes themselves in order to learn. In fact, as your dad would probably hate to admit, we keep on making them. That's why we have to learn to forgive others . . .'

'What if Grandad doesn't want to see us?' demanded Jack as they walked along the front towards her old home. The tide was out and someone was throwing a red ball to a black dog along the wet sand. There were some boats there too, stacked up after the summer season. They reminded her of the boat where she and Winston had found privacy, sixteen years ago.

'I don't know,' she said truthfully. 'I suppose we can at least say we've tried.'

Jack shrugged, pulling up the collar of the warm jacket that Joe had lent him against the wind. 'Loads of people have kids nowadays without being married.'

His words might sound mature but his voice was tinged with hurt. Had she been right to tell him the truth about her father's likely reaction? Maybe. Maybe not.

'Attitudes were different in his day,' she added tentatively.

Jack began texting furiously as though he didn't care. 'My

philosophy teacher says that. But I think it's stupid. No one should judge anyone else.'

Rosie gave him a brief hug. 'Does that include you and me?'

To her relief, instead of moving away, he hugged her back. 'Yes. Sorry, Mum. I didn't mean to be mean to you over the last few weeks. It's just that it's been . . .'

His voice tailed away. 'Too much to handle?' she suggested. He nodded. Then she stopped outside a small black gate. The path beyond it was lined with neatly planted wallflowers. In front of them stood a brick bungalow with lace curtains and a white front door with a brass knocker in the shape of a mermaid.

For a moment, Rosie was unable to speak. It was as familiar as if she'd been here last week. Nothing had changed. Dad might not be well but somehow he had continued to keep things exactly as he had when Mum had been alive. As they went round the side, she half-expected the smell of a newly baked Victoria sponge to come floating out of the back kitchen door.

Mum would be opening it now with her cheery smile and saying . . .

'What the hell do you think you're doing here?'

Both Rosie and Jack stopped in their tracks as an old man with thin white hair and stretchy blue braces over a moth-eaten green jumper stood on the doorstep, waving his stick at them. 'Get out before I call the police!'

He jabbed his stick in the direction of the sticker by the door. 'Can't you read? It says *No cold callers*.'

Rosie felt for Jack's hand and squeezed it reassuringly. 'It's all right, Dad. It's us. Rosie. Rosie and Jack. Your grandson,' she added, just in case he was too confused to remember. He certainly looked frail enough. Her heart contracted as she took in his thin legs and hunched-up shoulders.

'I know it's you.' Dad's eyes narrowed. 'You're the spitting image of your mother. What do you mean by calling in like this, unannounced? Think you can turn back the years, do you?'

Then his gaze transferred itself to Jack. 'And as for bringing along your coffee-coloured bastard . . .'

There was a gasp. Not just from Rosie but from Jack too. 'Come back,' she called. But it was too late. Her son had torn down the path, slamming the gate behind him.

'How dare you!' Rosie spluttered with rage. 'You stupid, stupid old man! I've come all the way back because someone said you were ill. I thought you'd have changed your mind, but now I can see you're as stubborn and nasty as ever!'

Her back was sweating so much now with the heat of her anger that she was almost dripping. 'You don't deserve me and you certainly don't deserve a fine young grandson like my son! Mum would be ashamed of you, but luckily she'll never have to face you, because frankly, when you die, you won't end up in the same place as her!'

With that, she turned on her heel and ran down the path. 'Jack,' she called out. 'Jack!'

Feverishly, she scanned the street. There was no sign of him. Running down to the beach, she couldn't see him there either. Her chest grew tight with fear as she looked up at the cliffs. What if he had done something stupid?

Go back to Sally's house first and get some help, said the voice in her head. Yes. Of course. That would be more sensible. Racing along the roads, she burned with fury, both towards her father and herself. She might have known. Some people never changed and she'd been a fool to expect her dad would.

'You've just missed him.' Gemma met her at the door, her sweet face creased with concern. 'He came in, grabbed his bag and tore off. What happened?'

Rosie couldn't help it. She burst into tears.

'What's wrong, Auntie Rosie?' One of Gemma's small boys tugged at her coat. 'Do you need a plaster?'

She tried to smile to reassure the child but it was no good. 'Did he say where he was going?' she managed to blurt out.

There was a slow nod. 'Corrywood.'

Corrywood?

Gemma bit her lip. 'To see his dad.'

TRUE POST-HONEYMOON STORY

'When we got back from our honeymoon, the photographer rang to say her hard drive had broken and all our wedding pictures were lost. I was distraught until my husband pointed out that no one could take away the memories in our heads.'

Alex

Chapter Thirty-Three

WINSTON

'Morning, everyone!'

Winston smiled broadly at the motley class in front of him, with their assortment of shorts and tee-shirts. Inside, his heart was sinking. How was it possible to fall so far so fast?

Was it really only a few months ago that he'd been earning a lucrative living on television? *Work Out With Winston* had been the programme on everyone's lips! The entire female population had followed his buttock- and breast-firming exercises, from grandmothers to teenagers.

Now he was running a local authority class in Corrywood village hall, a place he had never heard of before he'd met Melissa. And although he kept telling himself that a job was a job and that the glitz and trappings of his old life didn't matter, he found, to his surprise, that he missed it.

'They don't want me any more,' he'd told Melissa after making that grovelling phone call to the upmarket gym he used to work for in London before *Work Out With Winston*. 'The manager was perfectly blunt. Said his clients wouldn't want someone whose name had been sullied.'

He'd swallowed, hoping for an understanding word of comfort from his new bride. But she'd just given him a disappointed look. 'You've got to see it from their point of view, Winston. They didn't have the training you had. All they can see is a man who sent an innocent woman down a road that wasn't safe instead of waiting to check it was clear.'

Winston winced. Only someone who'd been there could really understand.

Meanwhile, he had to support his new family somehow.

Of course Melissa had maintenance for the children until they were twenty-one, but her personal allowance from Marvyn had stopped on her marriage to him. So she was far worse off than she would have been if she'd stayed on her own.

But on the plus side, he had Jack. Every now and then, Winston found himself saying the words 'I have a son' inside his head with a mixture of amazement and excitement.

'Aren't you even going to request a DNA test?' Melissa had demanded, rather insensitively, he'd thought. But no. He wasn't. Anyone could see Jack was his son. He looked like his mother in some ways, but in others, he had features that reminded Winston of himself at that age, and his much-missed, departed grandmother.

He and Jack had been been emailing, gradually getting to know each other a bit. Winston knew now that Jack loved skateboarding as well as riding his scooter. He learned that the boy loved languages but hated maths at school (just like him). The kid was clearly popular with girls (another similarity!) and kept asking him how Alice was. And he also discovered that the boy's favourite food was pizza, which Yannis, the chef, had taught him to make.

Even better, it wouldn't be long until he was here. 'We're coming to the UK to see my grandad!' the boy had emailed last week. There had been a big exclamation mark after 'grandad' plus a smiley face, indicating the boy's enthusiasm. 'Shall I text when we're there?'

'Of course,' he had replied instantly. 'We'll go to this smart pizza place in town and you can give me your verdict.'

His mind had been reeling ever since. So Rosie was paying her father a visit, was she? He only hoped the old man had mellowed a bit. It made his blood boil to think of how he'd treated her all those years ago. Or was that because he felt guilty himself, at not being there? Maybe a bit of both.

Suddenly, Winston became aware of a sea of women, ranging from teenagers to grannies, all looking at him expectantly. He'd been so busy going over the last few weeks in his mind that he'd almost forgotten why he was here. That wouldn't do. He needed this job, even though his earnings were peanuts compared with his previous salary. If nothing else, it was better than sitting in Melissa's house, making desperate phone calls to old contacts who didn't want any more to do with him.

Besides, he loved his work. It was great to see the change it made in people's bodies, and their outlook too. There was a great deal to be said for the happy hormones that came from exercise.

'Right, everyone,' he grinned, rubbing his hands together and flexing his abs. 'Let's get going with a warm-up, shall we?'

'That was great,' said a really skinny woman after class. She was wearing a tee-shirt emblazoned with PAULA AND JILLY'S AU PAIR AGENCY. 'I can't believe that I've actually been to a class run by *the* Winston King.' Then she turned to her friend. 'Can you, Jilly?'

The hall treasurer – who was also in the group – seemed pleased, too. 'Great attendance figures. You've got most of the women in Corrywood turning up to see what you look like. Mind you, the test will come in the following weeks when the celebrity novelty wears off.'

So now he had to prove himself. And why not, thought Winston as he walked back through town with a spring in his step. He'd done that before and he'd do it again. In a way, it was a relief that everyone knew about Nick. It didn't take away the pain of his guilt and loss, but at least he didn't have to worry about any more secrets coming out.

'How the mighty have fallen!'

Winston stepped sideways as the passenger door of a metallic-grey Jaguar opened, almost knocking right into him. Marvyn's smug face grinned up at him. There was, he noticed, a cheap-looking blonde in the driving seat, whom he recognised from class. 'Dawn here says you were quite good. But it can't be the same as telly, can it?'

The cheap blonde gave him an apologetic smile.

337

'It's a job,' said Winston defensively, 'and I enjoy it.'

Marvyn's smugness turned into a leer. 'It's not going to keep Melissa in the life she's been accustomed to, is it? As for my kids, just make sure you remember whose they are, will you? Hear you've been playing football with Freddie. It's *me* he plays with. Not you.'

Then he slammed the door shut and the car drove off, leaving Winston to stare after him. '*It's me he plays with. Not you*.' For the first time since he'd met Marvyn, Winston began to feel a sneaking sympathy. Of course the man had been the architect of his own misfortune (better not tell Melissa that her successor was in his class), but it couldn't be easy knowing that another man was living with your kids.

After all, he felt a similar antipathy to Greco, who had known his son since childhood – something that he, Winston, could never reclaim. All his good humour from the class began to melt away as he made his way up the hill to Melissa's house. His mobile bleeped to announce a text, but in his present state of mind, he couldn't be bothered to check it. As he reached his front door his phone beeped again. This time he looked at it.

ON MY WAY TO CORRYWOOD. JACK, it said in capital letters.

That was it. No time or meeting place. *Great*, Winston texted back, his heart pounding. *When?*

But there was no reply. How would Jack know where to go? Then he realised. Of course, Alice would have given him the address. Maybe he was more interested in seeing her than him. Even so, he felt a flutter of anticipation. His son was coming to see him. His son!

'What time is he coming?' demanded Melissa when she got home. Her career as a make-up artist was really taking off, just as his was failing. How ironic that it had been her experience on his show that had helped resurrect her career.

'I don't know,' he said, opening the oven door to check on supper. When his wife was working a full day, it was his turn to cook the evening meal. He'd suggested that one, and Melissa had seemed pleasantly surprised. Obviously this wasn't something Marvyn had done. One up on him, then.

'I've made soya shepherd's pie,' he announced, adding a little more cheese so it bubbled nicely on top.

Alice, just back from holiday club at school, groaned. 'Not another veggie dish. Can't we have proper food?'

Vegetarian *is* proper food, Winston was about to say but then stopped himself. She might have a point; at least where his son was concerned. 'I wonder what Jack likes to eat?' he asked, wondering at the same time how many fathers would ask that question.

'Does it matter?' remarked Melissa, a touch sharply. 'When you turn up without much notice, you eat what you get.'

Just what he, Winston, had always said about Alice and Freddie. They should finish what was on the plate in front of them. Yet somehow it was now important that Jack should enjoy his meal.

'I just want him to feel welcome,' he said, putting on the kettle.

'It seems to me that you're making rather a lot of fuss,' retorted Melissa sharply. 'No tea for me, thanks. I had a latte at the station.'

By the time it got to eight o'clock and there was still no sign of Jack (he'd been right – Alice confirmed she'd given him the address), Winston began to get worried. If only he knew which train he was coming in on, he could have met him.

But when he tried to ring Jack's mobile, it went through to answerphone. By nine, he was pacing up and down with anxiety. 'Now you know how I feel when Alice is late home from her friends,' remarked Melissa, feet up on the sofa as she watched television.

'He's never been in the UK before,' retorted Winston, perhaps a touch too defensively. 'What if he's got lost?'

Melissa flicked channels. 'All he has to do is ask.'

He moved closer to her. 'Are you OK about him coming?

339

I mean, I know it's been a lot to get used to, with him and Rosie, but I thought you'd understand, being a mother yourself.'

His voice tailed off as she gave him a withering look. 'The difference is, Winston, that you knew I had children before you married me. I certainly didn't know about Jack. In fact, it turns out, as Marvyn says, that there's quite a lot I don't know about you . . .'

'Hang on.' Winston sat bolt upright on the sofa. 'What did you say?'

Melissa sighed. 'Well, it's true, isn't it? I don't know much about you . . .'

'Not that bit. The Marvyn bit.' Winston felt himself going cold. 'Have you been discussing me with *him*?'

Melissa coloured. 'I do need to talk to the father of my children, you know. When you have kids, you can't just cut off all contact. That would be irresponsible.'

'I can see that.' Winston struggled to be reasonable. 'But I don't like the idea of you discussing me behind my back.'

Melissa stood up and moved to the chair next to the sofa. It was a pretty chair, covered in a Cath Kidston fabric, which Marvyn had apparently given her a few years ago as a birthday present. 'I don't do anything behind your back, Winston.' The emphasis on the 'I' suggested that he did. 'In fact, I was waiting for the right opportunity to tell you something else.' She shrugged. 'It's not great timing but I might as well come out with it. My boss has asked me to do Billy.'

Winston let out a low groan. She was going to do the make-up for Billy the Kid – the skinny youth who had taken over his slot? Poppy's boyfriend.

'I know it's hard.' Melissa looked more sympathetic. 'But I can't afford to turn work down now that you're . . .'

She stopped. 'Now that I'm not earning what I was,' said Winston, completing the sentence for her.

There was a reluctant nod. 'I won't do it if you don't want, but . . .'

Again, she broke off her sentence just as Winston's phone

rang. 'Jack!' He felt relief flooding through him. 'Where are you? The station? Hang on. I'll be down in a minute.'

Leaping up, he grabbed his car keys from the table. 'I want to come too,' called out Alice, who must have been eavesdropping.

'You've got holiday homework to finish,' said Melissa firmly. 'You'll see Jack soon enough.' She glared at her watch pointedly.

The traffic lights were red, and just as they changed to orange, a far-too-thin woman in joggers nipped across, waving merrily. From the writing on her sweatshirt, it was Paula of Paula and Jilly's Au Pair Agency, who had signed up for every one of his classes.

Nodding back tersely, he drove on through town and down to the station, heart in his mouth. Was this silly? A few months ago, he hadn't even known he had a son, but now Jack's existence gave a completely different meaning to his life. Of course, he couldn't expect to pick up the pieces just like that and be a full-on dad. But he could at least be there for him when he wanted him to be. Like now.

But where was he? Winston scanned the station. There were a couple of teenage girls, speaking urgently into their phones. A mother with six kids, trying to stop the seventh from running off. A bohemian-looking woman with her hair done up in feathers, next to a younger girl with tattoos down her arm. And then he saw him. A tall, slim boy with wavy brown hair and tanned complexion looking anxiously around. Winston pulled up in a parking bay and waved at him. 'Jack! Over here!'

The boy broke into a run. 'Hi. Thanks for coming.' His eyes were bright but he was shivering. Instantly, Winston was jolted back to the time he had run away from school. 'Does your mum know you're here?'

There was a shrug. 'Sort of.'

Sort of? Winston was reminded of the *Unknown Call* that left no message. Had that been Rosie?

341

'Hop in.' He watched Jack take in the Audi convertible with wide eyes. 'We'll chat on the way. In fact, we'll stop off somewhere first so we can have a good talk before getting home.'

Winston couldn't believe it. He'd come across racism at school, naturally. In his experience all kids got bullied anyway regardless of nationality. A friend of his had been nicknamed Dirty Bacon because he was called Graham (gray ham, as he'd later explained).

Kids could be very cruel. But adults should know better. Especially grandfathers.

'I'm so sorry,' he said when Jack told him, in a clipped voice that suggested a great deal of hurt, what Rosie's father had said. Coffee-coloured bastard? That was unforgivable.

Jack looked away. 'It's all right.'

But it wasn't. It wasn't all right at all. 'Have you rung your mother to tell her you're here?' he asked.

Jack shook his head.

'Then we must do so.'

Reluctantly, Jack got out his phone. Winston went to the bar to buy them both another orange juice, to give him some privacy, but when he returned, the boy was still talking in monosyllables. Yes. No. Don't know. 'She wants to talk to you,' he said eventually, passing the handset over.

'Winston!' The delight – or rather relief – in Rosie's voice propelled him back over the years, reminding him of how she had sounded when they had fallen into each other's arms after a gap of an entire twenty-four hours. 'Thank goodness you've got him! I was so worried.'

'Don't be.' He gave Jack a reassuring smile that he would have given his mother if she'd been sitting next to him. 'He's fine.'

'Has he told you? About my father?'

'Yes.' This time, Winston couldn't keep the anger out of his voice. 'I feel like coming down there and giving your dad a piece of my mind.'

'Don't.' She sounded scared. 'It would only make it worse. You don't know what he's like. I shouldn't have bothered coming over to the UK. It's only that my friend's mum said he was poorly.'

'Then at least you've tried.'

He could almost see her nodding. 'Thanks.'

It was so easy to talk to her – much easier than it had been on the island with Melissa around. Now it was like reassuring an old friend. 'It's too late for Jack to come back,' he added. 'Is it all right if he stays here for a couple of days?'

As he spoke, he watched the boy's face. To his delight, it lit up. 'OK.' Rosie's voice was hesitant. 'It will give me time to go down to my father's house without him. Try once more.'

That was decent of her. Many daughters wouldn't bother. 'When are you flying back?'

'Not for another fortnight. I've got permission from Jack's teachers.'

Winston felt another leap of hope in his chest. 'Then would it be all right if I took him up to London to see some sights?'

There was a slight pause. Had he pushed it too far? When Rosie's reply came, it was cool. 'If Jack wants that.' Then, after another pause, she added, 'Provided Melissa doesn't mind.'

'Don't worry,' he said firmly as if to brush away his own misgivings. 'She won't.'

'There's just one thing.' Rosie dropped her voice. 'Jack can't hear me, can he?'

Fortunately, Jack was investigating the pool table. 'No.'

'Please keep an eye on him and Alice. I don't want things to go too far.'

He was with her on that one. 'Absolutely not.' They might, he thought, as he said goodbye, be a married couple, concerned for their teenager's wellbeing. It was quite a nice feeling.

'Shall we go now?' he said to Jack. 'You must be starving. I've made a shepherd's pie.'

His son made an apologetic face. 'I'm really sorry, but I'm vegetarian.'

Yes! Winston beamed. 'Me too. It's soya.'

The two days turned into a week. 'We need more time,' Winston had said to both Melissa and Rosie (separately, of course). 'There's so much to do!'

There was, too. Thanks to Corrywood's half-term, there weren't any classes at the hall, so he was able to take the kids to the London Eye, the Natural History Museum and the Victoria and Albert Museum. If Jack hadn't been there, Winston would have bet his last penny that Alice would have whined her way round. But because she was so desperate to make a good impression in front of her boyfriend, it improved all the family dynamics.

'You seem to have enjoyed yourselves,' remarked Melissa with an obvious touch of jealousy when she got back from work.

'We did,' breathed Freddie. 'It was cool.'

Jack, his face flushed, possibly from a day of hand-holding with Alice (it had seemed churlish to stop them), couldn't stop talking. 'There's loads to do here,' he enthused, laying the table for dinner without being asked. 'Thanks so much for having me.'

See, Winston wanted to say to Melissa. Look how well-mannered my son is. Laying the table and saying thank you. Mind you, he couldn't take any credit. Rosie had done a great job.

'He seems very happy,' he told Rosie during what was becoming a regular evening phone call to report on how Jack was. Even though Jack rang her too, Winston felt it might be nice for Rosie to get a full picture. Teenagers, he was beginning to learn, tended to speak in one-word sentences on the phone. 'But how are you doing?'

There was a small sigh at the other end. 'My father's allowed me to go in and talk to him.'

Big of him, Winston wanted to say.

'But he's so unfriendly and cold.' Rosie's voice faltered and he felt sorry for her. 'He keeps telling me that he's managed fine without me so far and he doesn't need anyone coming to see how he is now. It's as though I left of my own accord rather than being kicked out. The trouble is that he really is quite ill. He's got prostate cancer and it might have spread.'

'That's tough. I'm sorry.' When Winston put down the phone, he was aware of Melissa watching him. 'You two seem pretty pally,' she remarked, taking a large slurp of red wine.

Winston shrugged. 'As you're always saying, it's important to talk when you have a child.'

Melissa took another slurp, her eyes fixed on him. 'I wonder how she managed without you before. By the way, Billy the Kid sends his regards.'

Winston stood up. It wasn't like Melissa to be spiteful. Jack's arrival seemed to have made her snappier.

'Rosie's happy for Jack to stay an extra couple of days,' he added.

Melissa raised her immaculately groomed eyebrows. 'Why doesn't that surprise me?'

'So I thought I'd drive Jack down to his mother's on Monday after my class.'

'Can't he stay longer?' Alice's voice came from behind the door – she must have been listening.

'Don't be silly,' snapped Melissa. 'You've got school to go to and we've got work. He can't be here on his own.'

Jack's face appeared behind Alice's. 'Actually, I don't really want to go back to Devon. I can make myself useful here. I can cook and I'm great at housework. I do a lot for my mum at home.'

Winston couldn't help it. His chest was puffing up with pride. Melissa drained the wine bottle. 'Looks like I don't have much choice.' Her eyes stared at him stonily. 'You know, Winston,' she said, softly but dangerously, 'I sometimes wonder if you know how to be married.'

He had to wait until they had time alone before tackling her on her latest cruel comment. 'What did you mean by that?'

he'd demanded when they'd gone to bed that night, each moving to their own far side of the bed.

'You don't know how to share things, Winston.' Her voice rang out clearly in the dark, as if she'd been practising the words. 'You've been on your own so long that you don't realise that some decisions – such as having your son to stay – need to be taken together.'

'But—' he began.

There was the sound of her turning over. 'I don't want to talk about it now. I'm tired. Goodnight.'

Nor did she want to talk about it the next day, or the day after that. So much for sharing!

The following Monday, Winston waited until the kids had gone to school before telling Jack about the thing on his mind. 'I've got to go somewhere after my class. Will you be all right on your own today?'

The boy nodded. 'Sure. I can do some gardening if you want.' He looked out of the window. 'Looks like it needs a bit of tidying up.'

Great. Winston drove to his class so he could make a quick getaway. Luckily the traffic down to Devon wasn't too bad and he was there by the middle of the afternoon. Don't let Rosie be there, he told himself. And please don't let Gemma (whose number he'd got from Jack) let on. 'I don't want anyone else to know,' he'd explained when he'd rung to get the old man's address.

As he turned into the road, he recognised the bungalow in its neat row of similar properties, each with their lace curtains and tidy gardens. Poor Rosie. He could imagine her all too well, as he rang the front doorbell, a terrified seventeen-year-old, leaving home with a baby inside her. Where had he been?

'What do you want?' The old man at the door scowled. 'Can't you read?' He pointed to the sign with his walking stick. 'No cold callers . . .'

Then his voice trailed away. 'Hang on. You're that bloke that used to be on the telly, aren't you? The one that did those exercises. I used to watch you. Not that I could do them

346

myself, mind you. You were good. Much better than that skinny kid they've got now.'

Winston cut in. 'Actually, I'm a bit more than that. I'm your grandson's father.'

The old man's jaw dropped. 'Yer what?'

'It's a long story.' Winston held out his hand courteously. 'How do you do, sir? We've never met before but I am aware that you've never approved of me. Perhaps we ought to start again. Mind if I come in?'

TRUE POST-HONEYMOON STORY

'My husband and I divorced within a year. Sometimes you need to get married to know it won't work.'

Anonymous

Chapter Thirty-Four

EMMA

Tom was ecstatic when Emma's pregnancy was confirmed.

Ironically, he viewed 'his' honeymoon baby as a sign of his virility, strutting around with his chest puffed out with pride. 'Shows we've still got it in us, doesn't it?' he announced to everyone, from the postman to his mates in the pub when they went for a Sunday lunch 'celebratory' drink.

Emma felt as though she was going to be sick, and not just from the usual morning nausea.

'Mummy, Mummy.' Gawain's little face stared urgently up at hers as they all sat in the family area, along with Bernie and her husband, plus some mates of Tom's from the garage. 'What's a honeymoon baby? Does it come from the moon?' He frowned. 'Cos Granny says babies come out of eggs.'

There was a burst of laughter followed by a round of clapping. 'He's a bright one, your lad,' said Phil admiringly.

'Me bright,' repeated Gawain, beaming. The regression to baby talk didn't show any sign of going away, Emma thought dejectedly.

'Very bright,' slurred Tom, on his fourth pint courtesy of his garage friends, who kept buying the rounds. 'Takes after his dad.' Then he added quickly, 'And his mum too.'

Hah! Emma caught Bernie's sympathetic eye. She hadn't been particularly bright over Yannis, had she? Nervously, she took a sip of orange juice. If only she had stuck to non-alcoholic drinks in Greece . . .

'Do you have any idea whose it is?' hissed Bernie when they both went to the loo together, Emma leaving Willow in her mum's arms. (They'd invited her along as last night's date had been a particular disaster. The man in question had turned out to have an 'understanding' wife who 'didn't mind' him seeing other women. Mum had soon told him where to get off.)

'No,' Emma admitted quietly. 'I've already told you. It could be either of them.'

Bernie put down her packet of crisps to give her a quick comfort hug before anyone else came in. 'Now don't go all guilty on me and confess everything to Tom. Trust me. He wouldn't understand. Don't look like that, Emma. I know you're not the deceitful sort, but . . .'

Emma broke away, talking furiously to her reflection in the mirror. 'What I did in Greece was unforgivable.'

'Don't be so hard on yourself.' Bernie was trying to make it better, bless her. 'There were reasons, weren't there? You had too much to drink.' She looked ruefully at the glass of vodka and coke in her own hand which she'd brought into the Ladies with her. 'It makes you do things you shouldn't.'

It certainly did.

'Want my advice?' Bernie's voice turned bright and sunny, suggesting this mess could be solved after all. 'Forget about it. *Pretend* it's Tom's. After all, from what you've told me, there's a fifty-fifty chance it might be his after all. Believe me, you won't be the first not to know for certain. And you won't be the last.'

At that point, one of the other garage wives came into the Ladies, causing Bernie to stop suddenly. 'You've been in here ages. OK, are you?' She gave Emma a sympathetic look. 'I had the sickness real bad with my fourth.'

Four? 'How on earth does she manage?' whispered Emma to Bernie as they went back to their table.

'She doesn't,' Bernie hissed back. 'Despite that parenting class they run at school.'

'What's that?' asked Mum, her spirits only slightly mollified by her second glass of Chablis.

'We were just talking kids,' said Emma quickly, aware that

350

the loo woman's husband was sitting opposite, soothing a grizzling baby and trying to stop a snotty-nosed toddler from nabbing someone else's crisps. 'Anyone seen our Kerry?' he kept saying, looking wildly around. 'And Josh too? They were here a minute ago.'

Emma's mother snorted. 'On the slot machines by the Gents. If you don't stop them, they're going to smash that thing.' She gave a meaningful glance at her daughter. 'See what you've let yourself in for?' she muttered. 'I found it hard enough with just one.'

Bernie put an arm around her shoulder. 'She'll have us to help, won't she? Now my two are older, I'll have more time on my hands. We'll all muck in. Whoops!'

Emma caught the glass just as Willow's chubby little arm was about to knock it off the table. Mum was right. How *was* she going to cope? Not just because she'd have another little one to look after but because, despite Bernie's reassurances, there was no way she could go through life not knowing if this baby was Tom's or not.

She'd just have to find the right time – and courage – to tell her husband the truth.

Meanwhile, there was something else she needed to do. Something that had been preying on her mind, ever since they'd got back from Greece.

If he hadn't put his address on the letter inside the wedding card, Emma wouldn't have known where to have found him. She certainly couldn't have asked Mum. The word 'Dad' wasn't allowed any more.

But ever since she had been stupid enough to have gone with Yannis, Emma had begun to realise there were two sides to a story.

Yes, she had been drunk at the time. If she hadn't, none of that stuff would have happened. But if she was being truthful, maybe she'd *allowed* herself to be seduced because she'd been cross with Tom on so many different levels. She'd felt railroaded into marriage for a start. He'd known perfectly well that she hadn't particularly wanted to have a wedding but he'd pushed her.

Then there was the sickness thing. Tom could be a bit of a hypochondriac. Even at home, if he had a cold, he claimed it was flu. And he could have made a bit more of an effort on their honeymoon *after* he'd stopped being ill.

Did she need more excuses? Yes. Take the sun and all that sex going on around them. That's right, Emma told herself. Sex. Might as well come clean about it. She'd felt as though she'd been missing out; something that Tom's own pitiful performance at the end of the week had demonstrated.

Emma shivered, hating herself. Why had her body been more aroused by Yannis – a man she barely knew – than her own husband?

'Some women find it exciting to make love to a stranger,' Bernie had said soothingly when she'd confided in her. 'Maybe it was a release, too, after all that pressure of the wedding.'

Possibly.

The whole thing had got her thinking about what Dad had said, when he'd left Mum. 'It's not just because of Trisha,' he had declared, referring to his fancy woman from the office.

'I don't want to hear,' she had retorted, cutting him off. But now, after all these years, maybe it was time for Emma to find out what he'd meant.

Should she have called to say she was coming? Emma had made the forty-minute drive from Corrywood and now she parked outside a tidy, semi-detached house and nervously smoothed her navy fleece jacket down over her bump.

No. Why should she give him time to make up an up-to-date defence? Emma needed to see her father face to face, to read what was behind it.

Dad worked nights. She knew that from Bernie's dad, who worked at the same factory. So with any luck, she might just catch him in. She glanced at her watch. An hour. That was all she had. Then she needed to get back to collect Gawain from nursery and Willow from Mum's. 'I just need to get some more clothes now my waist is getting bigger,' she'd fibbed when Mum had asked her where she was going.

Another lie. It was scary how they could grow.

Now, as she walked up the tidy stone path, she noticed the car in the drive – a very clean white Volvo with a newish registration. No shortage of money there, she noted, her lips tightening. Poor Mum was still struggling on benefits and the odd cleaning job. It wasn't fair.

A figure was looming towards her through the glass door. Emma felt her heart in her throat. What if it was *her*? Trisha. She hadn't thought about that. Her mouth went dry. If it was, she'd tell her exactly what she thought of a marriage breaker. She'd . . .

'Emma!' The older man standing in front of her was so much thinner than she remembered. His hair was tinged with grey. He was slightly stooped, too. Yet despite this, he was still a good-looking man for his age. That look of pure delight in his eyes took her sharply back to the time she'd learned to swim with his help. There was no disguising it. He was thrilled to see her.

'Emma!' he repeated, tears shining in his eyes. 'Is it really you?'

'Don't think I forgive you,' she repeated. They'd been sitting in what he called 'the sitting room', rather than the lounge. (So he'd got posh, had he?) Him in a modern grey leather chair and her on the matching sofa. There was a glass-topped coffee table in front of them spread with women's magazines. Trisha read the same ones as her mum, Emma noticed with a pang.

On the mantelpiece was a collection of photographs. She'd taken a peek when he'd gone out to put the kettle on. Some of them made her cross, like the ones of Dad and Trisha on a cruise. He'd never taken her mum on one. The others, of her as a child building sandcastles on the beach, made her want to cry.

There was even a framed cutting of her wedding report,

which had come out in the local paper during their honeymoon.

'Don't think I forgive you,' she said, once again. 'I just want to know how you could have done it. Left us.'

She glanced down at her bump. 'I could never leave my kids, and I know Tom couldn't either.'

Dad's eyes never left hers. 'I didn't want to go, love. Your mum made me.'

That old excuse again! 'She made you because you had an affair with Trisha in the office!' Emma exploded.

Dad smiled sadly. Then he stood up and went over to one of the pictures of her as a child. She must have been about six or seven then, thought Emma, glancing at it. She could remember that red scooter all right. It had broken after a few weeks but Dad had fixed it. He'd been able to fix anything, until he'd gone.

'Did Mum ever mention Keith?'

Keith?

Slowly, the memory came back. 'Wasn't he our next-door neighbour? He was married to Auntie Jean.'

She wasn't a real auntie, of course, but she'd acted like one. When Emma was little, she'd been in and out of their house all the time, making toffee and Halloween decorations. Keith and Jean hadn't had children of their own, so they'd liked it when she'd come round. Then Jean had died, and later, poor Keith had moved away.

'He went because I found out about them,' said Dad gruffly, putting the picture back on the mantelpiece.

'Found out about them?' she repeated slowly.

Dad nodded. 'Your mum confessed it had been going on for years, even when poor Jean was alive. They saw each other when you and I went swimming on Sundays. Said it was because I didn't show her enough affection.' His mouth twisted with pain. 'Said I wasn't as good in . . . in the bedroom as Keith.'

No! Emma jumped to her feet. This couldn't be true! 'You're just saying this,' she stammered.

Dad shook his head. 'If you don't believe me, ask her.'

It didn't make sense. 'But Trisha . . .'

'Trisha was a shoulder to cry on.' Dad sat down again and tried to take her hands, but she was having none of it. 'Please try to understand, Emma. I know you're happily married to Tom, but imagine if you weren't. Think what it might be like to be with someone who doesn't show you any affection and who has been unfaithful. I'm not saying that what I did was right, but I want you to know the reasoning behind it.'

Emma felt numb. If it wasn't true, why would he invite her to ask Mum? Unless it was a double bluff. That was it. He was banking on her not telling.

'I don't believe you!' she spat. 'You're just telling more lies like you did before. No, don't say anything more. You'll just make it worse.'

She felt sick, hardly able to look at this man who had ruined all their lives. 'Do you realise the consequences of your actions?' she said sadly. 'We could have been a proper family if you hadn't left us.'

'Don't you think I haven't told myself that every day?' Then he looked down at her bump. 'I would have loved to have been a grandad. A proper hands-on one. Don't think I'm prying, but are you expecting again?'

She nodded, unable to say anything.

'That's wonderful. You must both be thrilled.' Then he leaned forward hungrily. 'Have you got pictures of Gawain and Willow? See, I know their names through Bernie's dad, but I'd give anything to meet them . . .'

Wait. This was too much. Too fast. 'I don't know.' Stumbling to her feet, she pushed past his embrace towards the door. 'I need to think about this, OK?'

Then, unable to look back, she rushed down the path and towards the safety of her car.

'Mrs Walker, Mrs Walker! I don't like peas. Can I have one without?'

'Mrs Walker, he's got more on his plate than me!'

'Mrs Walker! My mum forgot to give me my packed lunch.'

'Mrs Walker, why is water wet?'

It was the week after she'd seen Dad but Emma still couldn't get it out of her head. Nor had she found the courage to tell her mum what Dad had said about her and Keith. Besides, it was a lie, wasn't it? Mum wouldn't have done anything like that. It was Dad, trying to make excuses for his own bad behaviour.

Instead, Emma had desperately tried to block it all out by concentrating on the kids and Tom and work – which was particularly busy this week, as the kitchen for the secondary school was out of action and they had to feed extra mouths. Thankfully her morning sickness was dying down a bit, although they'd had to find her a bigger kitchen pinny to take in her expanding waistline. Everyone knew now. One of the teachers even asked if she was having twins.

And *still* she hadn't summoned up the courage to tell Tom the truth. She'd thought about it after the first scan but when she'd seen the look on her husband's face as he held the black-and-white picture, she couldn't find the words.

Coward, she told herself. Just like Dad. Except that her sin was different, wasn't it? She'd done something silly, just the once, because she'd had too much to drink. Dad's was deliberate, long-term deceit.

Was there a measurement for calculating degrees of infidelity? Or was she just kidding herself?

'Excuse me, but is it possible to have a vegetarian dish?'

Emma did a double take. This lad was a dead ringer for Rosie Harrison's handsome boy in Greece.

'I'll see what I can do.' She took in his coffee-coloured complexion, which she'd put down to a tan at the time but could now see was possibly mixed race. 'What's your name, love?'

'Jack.' He gave her a handsome smile. 'I remember you from the island.'

So it *was* him! Emma recalled her conversation with Rosie on the phone. 'Thought you were going to Devon with your mum.'

The boy turned to look at a girl sitting beside him. Alice, Emma realised. 'She's there but I'm staying here for a bit so I can see my dad.'

Of course.

Emma felt a catch in her throat. What if Yannis had boasted about his 'conquest'? Siphalonia was a small island. People were bound to talk. Jack might have heard something. He might tell Alice, who might tell her mum, who might tell someone else . . .

Racing back to the kitchen, Emma grabbed Bernie, who was helping herself to a spare veggie burger. 'That kid, whose mum owned the honeymoon villa, he's here! What if he says something about you-know-who?'

Bernie picked up her spatula as though it was a weapon to ward off any evil. 'Then you deny it, don't you? More peas, love?' The last comment was addressed to the bright kid in glasses. 'Sorry. All gone. How about chips instead?'

By the end of October, Emma had decided that maybe Bernie was right. Much as she disliked lying to Tom, perhaps it *was* better to keep quiet about Yannis.

How could she risk him leaving her? Did she really want Gawain and Willow to grow up in a single-parent family as she had, as a teenager? Seeing Dad had really brought that home.

Fear of losing Tom suddenly made her appreciate him all the more. What had seemed irritating, like his heavy snoring or fastidiousness about drying the cutlery even though the dishwasher had done it, now appeared comforting.

What was it the song said? Something about 'You don't know what you've got till it's gone.'

It was true. She loved Tom. He was the only one she wanted. It had been a terrible, terrible mistake . . .

Nor would she tell Mum that she'd seen Dad. What was the point? There was too much water under the bridge now. Perhaps she should count her blessings.

'Mind if I go out with the lads tonight?' Tom asked one evening. It was nearly Halloween and she was helping Gawain to carve out a pumpkin.

''Course not.'

'Don't do the nose, Mummy. Gawain wants to do that.' Her son was getting increasingly bossy as her waistline expanded. Perhaps he could sense the new rival growing inside her. She patted it gently. Poor little thing. It wasn't its fault that she didn't know who its dad was.

Willow meanwhile was into everything.

'Not the knife!' She grabbed it just in time. Parenthood was like negotiating your way through a maze of potential dangers. Frankly, it was a wonder that there weren't more accidents.

'Sure you can manage?' asked Tom, standing there, clearly desperate to go.

She tried to make a joke out of it, patting her stomach again. 'If I can't manage with two, there's no hope!'

After he'd gone, Gawain started to fall asleep over the pumpkin and Willow, bless her, did the same. Bliss! She could get both children to bed and sit in front of the television, feet up on the sofa, watching some soppy drama.

It was, as chance would have it, about a father and daughter reunion. Emma's attention began to wander to the letter that Dad had sent, just after her visit, asking if she would consider bringing the children over.

Give me some time, Dad, she'd written back. *I'll think about it.*

At the moment, it was too much. If she did take the kids, Gawain would be bound to blab it out to Mum and then there'd be all hell to pay. She hadn't even told Tom about the visit in case he opened his mouth.

Another deception. Where did it end?

Emma must have fallen asleep, because the first thing she heard when she woke was the door slamming. Briefly, she thought she was still dreaming.

'*What the hell were you thinking of?*'

Sleepily, she sat up, feeling the baby kick as she did so. Rubbing her eyes, she saw her husband standing before her. His eyes were wild and red.

'What do you mean, Tom?'

He sat down opposite her, his face drawn with anguish. 'Why don't you tell me?'

A cold fear shot through her. Never before had she seen Tom like this. At the same time, she could hear Willow crying, closely followed by Gawain.

'You've woken the kids,' she said nervously.

'*Whose* kids, Emma?' he roared. 'Are they really mine, or might they be someone else's, like that one in your stomach?'

He jabbed a finger towards her. Emma's body froze and the baby went still as though it knew something momentous was happening.

'Who told you—' she began.

'So it's true!' Tom flung back his head as a wail came out of his mouth. 'Phil was right.'

Phil, Bernie's husband? She'd told him?

'It's not the way you think,' she began.

'I don't want to know any more.' Tom was pulling her to her feet. 'Get out. All of you. The kids too. I don't want to see any of you again.'

GOT YOU!

A couple on honeymoon who burgled a pensioner's house, were jailed for four years.

Recent newspaper headline

Chapter Thirty-Five

ROSIE

It was November already. Bonfire night! Rosie hadn't expected to stay this long in England. A fortnight was surely enough time to pay her dues to her old father.

But then circumstances had forced her to change her plans.

Rosie still felt furious when she recalled that horrible scene where her father had called her son a . . . No. She wouldn't even say those words out loud.

Afterwards, when she had marched back to tell him what had happened as a result, her dad had expressed a mild regret. 'Stormed off, you say? Well, I can't help that. You used to do the same when you were his age, I remember. But you always came back again.'

Then, with a flicker of concern in his eyes, he had added, 'Got to his father's place safely, has he?'

'Yes,' she'd replied tersely, thinking of all the panic calls she'd made to Jack's mobile that had gone straight through to answerphone. She had thought the worst, worked herself up into a real state before Jack had finally called.

He'd refused to pick up her calls after that, though, until the following day. 'Are you all right?' she'd demanded, anger fuelled by relief.

'Stop fussing, Mum. Of course I am. Dad says I can stay up here for a bit.'

For a boy who'd only just met his father, he seemed to have slipped into the 'Dad' bit rather easily. What did that mean? That he'd craved a father figure all along?

Certainly he sounded quite happy – not at all like the upset boy who had rushed off from his grandfather's cruel greeting.

'At least here I'm with people who want me,' he added in a more biting tone.

Rosie had gripped the mobile. 'You're wanted down here too. I miss you. And Gemma's children love being with you.'

'Yeah, but Grandad doesn't, does he?'

She'd winced at the raw hurt in his voice. 'You will come back in time for our flight, won't you?'

'Whatever,' he muttered.

So she'd spent the rest of half-term making the most of Gemma's company and spending a couple of hours every day with her father, because Sally had been right. Dad wasn't very well.

'Heart trouble on top of the cancer. Not much they can do about it. One of those things. Waterworks problem too.' He patted the bag at his side. 'Charlie the catheter, I call it. Bit of a nuisance, but they say that at my age, you're more likely to die *with* prostate cancer than from it. Got a few problems with my liver, too.'

More than that he wouldn't say, but there was no doubt that he was quite frail. It took him an age to get up and put the kettle on. 'I can do it myself, thanks very much. I'm not dead yet.'

Gradually, over the next two weeks, she'd learned to ignore his harshness. Age had changed *her* too. Instead of being cowed by him, as she had been as a teenager, she realised that bullies like Dad soon gave in, if challenged.

'You shouldn't have sent me away when I was pregnant,' she'd finally said, the day before they were due to fly home. Jack would be back tonight and if she didn't say what needed to be said, there might not be time. They were sitting in his lounge with the late autumn sun shining weakly through the lace curtains, which needed a good wash. (Not that she was going to interfere unless she wanted her head bitten off.) 'I was only seventeen. Mum wouldn't have done it.'

His eyes had flickered. She'd struck a nerve there. 'You shouldn't have got pregnant,' he sniffed.

'It happens sometimes. Anyway, I wouldn't change it for

the world.' She got out her iPad. 'Jack's a fine boy. You hardly got a chance to look at him. Take a glance at some of these pictures.'

He waved his hand dismissively. 'I don't do all that new-fangled technology. Photographs should be held – not seen on some kind of screen.'

Then Rosie thought of the photograph album she'd slipped in her bag at the last minute, before leaving Greece. 'He looks like you, you know.'

'Hah! With that colour?'

'You could see it right from babyhood,' she continued, ignoring him. 'Look.'

Before he could protest, she'd placed Jack's baby and toddler album on her father's lap. The resemblance really was amazing. Jack might have Winston's colouring, but he had his grandad's nose and that way of holding his head to one side, as though asking a question.

Her father snorted again. 'If you say so.'

'I do,' she was about to reply but then her phone had rung. *Jack*. Getting up, she made an excuse to go into the old-fashioned galley kitchen with the calendar on the wrong month and the loaf of bread that was growing mouldy on the side.

'Hi! Are you on your way down now?'

'Actually, Mum, I've got something to tell you.'

Rosie leaned against the fridge door, closing her eyes. Part of her had been expecting this. 'Dad says I can stay on if I want.'

'But what about school?'

'That's the thing. Can you talk to Gemma's husband?' She could hear the pleading in his voice. 'See if I can go to Corrywood for a bit? It would give me a chance to get to know Dad. Please.'

It was the 'please' that tore her heart. What, she wondered, staring at the dirty plate on the side of the sink, had happened in those two weeks? Was it possible that Winston, damn him, had taken her place in his affections?

'How long is a bit?' Rosie asked quietly.

There was a short silence. 'Maybe until Christmas?'

Christmas? That's crazy, she started to say, but then stopped as Dad appeared at the door, stick in one hand and catheter bag – which needed emptying – in the other. She had gone through much of her life without a mother and at the age of seventeen had had to make do without either parent. Perhaps her son deserved some time with his father now – time he should have had when he was younger.

'OK,' she heard herself say, while rapidly thinking through the practicalities. The flight would have to be changed. She'd need to talk to Cara and Greco, not to mention Jack's school. And she ought to talk to Winston, too, and Melissa. Would she mind, Rosie wondered fleetingly, about her husband's love child (as the papers put it), taking up residence for three months?

'I've got things to do here too,' she added. 'I'll have to ask Sally if I can stay on with her.'

As she spoke, she looked at Dad. Was she imagining it, or was that a brief flicker of pleasure on his face? If so, it had gone before it could be properly identified. 'I also want to talk to Winston,' she added. 'Is he there?'

There was the sound of someone speaking loudly in the background. A woman. 'They're busy at the moment,' said Jack quickly. 'Look, I've got to go. Thanks so much, Mum! It would be really cool if Joe agrees to take me on at Alice's school. And it will be a great chance for me to see what an English education is like, won't it?'

Nice try. She knew why he really wanted to stay. It wasn't just because of Winston – it was because her son was in love! What right did she have to put a halt between Alice and Jack? Especially after what had happened to her.

Dad hobbled over to the kettle just as she slipped the phone back into her pocket. 'So you won't be shooting back to this Greek place after all, then?' He sniffed, wiping his hand on his sleeve before putting the same hand in a rusty tea caddy. 'We'll have more time to talk then. Fancy another cuppa, do you?'

*

Yes, Joe had said, after he'd made some enquiries. Jack could stay at school until Christmas, although he'd need to work hard. The curriculum was different from the one he was used to, but it wasn't the first time that they'd taken in children on a temporary basis.

Of course, Sally had said. She'd love Rosie to stay on. It would be company, and it would give her a chance to see her father, wouldn't it?

'Isn't it great?' Gemma had enthused on the phone. 'You can come up to Corrywood and see us at weekends. It will give you a base to visit Jack.'

But Rosie wasn't sure. It was too much change, too fast. Not long ago, she and Jack had seen each other all day, every day. She missed him. Just as she missed Greco, who had sounded most put out when she'd rung with the news.

'You are not coming back for three more months?' She could just see him tossing his head with indignation. Almost hear the sea splashing against his boat with the waves spar-kling in the sun. 'You wish to spend some time with Winston, I suppose.'

'No, it's not like that,' Rosie tried to explain, aware of the thin wall between the guest room and Sally's bedroom. 'I'm only going to be in Corrywood at the weekend. I'll be spending the rest of my time with my dad.'

'Pah! The one who threw you out?'

'You were the one who encouraged me to go,' she reminded him. 'Like you said, he's old. I may not have this chance again. Talk to Cara. She will understand.'

There was the sound of shuffling as though Greco was moving to another place. Perhaps he wasn't on the boat after all. Maybe he was at the villa, leaning over the terrace wall and admiring the olive grove. She felt a lurch of homesickness.

'Our Cara,' said Greco quietly, 'she is here for a reason.'

Rosie sighed. 'I know. She thought I needed her and now I am gone.'

'No. It is not like that. She tell me the truth now. Her

nephew's wife, she threw Cara out. Said she is interfering old lady.'

Rosie gasped. 'That's awful. May I speak to her?'

'No. She has pride. Me too. You stay in your England, Rosie. We will manage without you.'

Then he had rung off. Bruised, Rosie resisted the temptation to ring back. If Greco wanted to act like a child, that was up to him.

Now, four weeks later, their communication was only in the form of brief texts. Greco didn't do email, and when she rang him, he failed to pick up. Meanwhile, her weekday visits with Dad were growing easier and longer. They had fallen into quite a pleasant routine. She would arrive in the morning with the paper and a bag full of shopping (no more mouldy bread) and they'd do the crossword together over a cup of tea. Then she'd do some washing for him – grudgingly he'd agreed to that – and a bit of cleaning after lunch, while he had an afternoon nap. After cooking him a bit of supper she'd head back to Sally's.

The evenings were more difficult. Lovely as Sally was, Gemma's father was more austere and dinner was very formal. Rosie often thought, with longing, of the balmy evenings on the terrace at home, in Greco's arms, with fairy lights strung above them. Still, if he couldn't accept what was happening in her life, he wasn't worth it, was he?

She missed Jack too, dreadfully. 'Are you sure he's all right?' she asked Winston on more than one occasion during their increasingly regular *let's talk about our son* calls. Although she'd gone up to Corrywood twice to visit Jack, it had been difficult. Gemma's terraced house was already bursting with three small boys and there was little privacy to talk. When she'd taken Jack down to the local pizza place, it had been full of single dads, trying desperately to talk to their kids. And so far, there hadn't been an invitation from Melissa and Winston, where Jack was still staying, to go over there. Not even for coffee.

Until now, that was. *R u cming up ths wkend?* Winston had texted when Dad was having a nap one bright November

366

day. *If so, wd u like to spend bonfire nt with us? There's smthing gng on at the schl.*

Yes, she had texted back after checking that Gemma could put her up. She'd love to. And now, here she was, at Corrywood station, waiting for Winston and Jack to collect her. Gemma would have done it, but she was busy cooking for the firework spread and Joe was up to his eyes in organising the display.

Rosie was beginning to feel like a teenager all over again, waiting to be picked up. It was cold, too, but a rather nice brisk cold, with the sky lit up by pink swirling stars and bursts of sparkling silver trails. Other families and schools had started their fireworks early, reminding her of childhood bonfire nights in Devon. It had been so exciting!

'Mum!' Rosie was jolted out of her reverie by a tall boy waving at her from the road outside. Jack! She'd only seen him two weeks earlier but he seemed different now. A new jacket, she noticed. Rather nice. Brown suede. Had his father bought that? She should have been pleased but instead she felt slightly cheated that Jack could allow Winston to slip into his life so easily.

Running towards her, Jack gave her a big hug. That was better. 'I've missed you,' he said, his breath warm on her cheek.

'I've missed you too,' she managed, as he dragged her to the car. Melissa was in the front seat, eyeing her coldly. Uh-oh. Winston's invitation had clearly come from him alone and not from both of them.

In the back, she could see Alice, done up to the nines with heavy black smudgy lines round her eyes and a skirt that was surely guaranteed to give her hypothermia. Her brother, Freddie, was digging a packet of sparklers into her ribs.

'Get off, Freddie!'

Some things never changed.

'Welcome!' Winston gave her an uncertain smile from the driver's seat. 'Had a good journey? Jump in. We're going straight to the display.'

The conversation in the car might have been stilted if it hadn't been for Alice and her brother.

'They're *my* sparklers.'

'No, they're not. They're mine.'

'Piss off, Freddie!'

'Alice!'

This last remark was from Jack. 'Thank you,' said Melissa coolly, turning round briefly. She really was very beautiful, Rosie thought, although she looked a bit thinner than last time. Then she added, 'Your Jack is very good at keeping my daughter in line.'

'Mum!' whined Alice. 'You're *so* embarrassing!'

What did her son see in this girl? wondered Rosie exasperatedly as Winston pulled up in the school car park. Still, parents couldn't choose their children's friends, could they? Just for a minute, she thought of Dad and his reaction to Winston. Maybe it wasn't easy for any generation.

'You're here!' squealed one of Gemma's little boys, running towards her clutching a torch and wrapped up in a woolly hat and gloves. It was difficult to tell which one of Gemma's lot he was in the dark, but Gemma was close behind. She watched those three like a hawk.

'Come and have a mulled wine,' said her friend, grabbing her by the arm. Rosie looked back at Jack, who was holding hands with Alice and heading off towards a group of teenagers. Both Winston and Melissa had melted into the crowd, no doubt relieved to be free of their pick-up duty.

'It's been so weird without Jack,' said Rosie wistfully as she watched Gemma juggle her children with 'Not another drink!' and 'Hold my hand!' and 'Not near the bonfire!'.

'I can imagine.' Gemma clucked sympathetically. 'Any chance he might go down and see his grandad again?'

'No way. Jack's furious with him.'

'You can see why. I remember when—'

'Mummy, I need a wee-wee.'

Gemma groaned. 'Why is it that you can't have a conversation for more than one minute without someone wanting to join in?' But she said it in a laughing way rather than an irritated one. 'Can you hang on to these two for me? I won't be long.'

Rosie took a small warm hand in each of hers. She would have liked more than one child . . . Still, she was lucky to have Jack.

'Hi. Are you new here?'

She looked up to see a rather good-looking, shortish man hovering nervously nearby. He was holding hands with a small girl with long blond plaits and a pink fluffy coat.

'My name's Matthew. This is my daughter Lottie.' Then he glanced down at the boys. 'Which class are yours in?'

Rosie laughed awkwardly. 'Actually, they belong to Gemma and Joe Balls.' She looked across at the bonfire where her own son was chatting to some other teenagers. It hadn't taken him long to make friends, she observed with a mixture of admiration and hurt. 'My boy is nearly sixteen. He's over there.'

'With your husband?'

Was she imagining it, or was this kindly-faced man chatting her up? 'Actually, I've never had one.'

It felt curiously liberating to tell the truth after years of pretending to be a widow in Greece.

The man was looking really keen now. 'I'm a widower and . . . yes, Lottie. What is it?'

The girl was tugging at his hand impatiently. 'I want a burger from the stall over there.'

'Of course, princess.' He gave her a regretful look. 'Maybe see you around later?'

Rosie nodded just as Gemma came rushing back. 'Sorry. There was quite a queue. Was that our Matthew I just saw? Chatted you up, did he? Poor man is always looking for a wife. He did have someone – a lovely woman who went back to Canada – but now he's really lonely.' Then Gemma stopped as though an idea had just occurred to her. 'Actually—'

Rosie cut in before she could speak. 'Don't even think about matchmaking. My life is complicated enough as it is.'

The boys were still hanging on to her hands. 'We want a sausage! We want a sausage!'

They were so sweet! 'I'll take them,' Rosie offered. Feeling pleased to have a job, she made her way to the burger stall. There was a long queue. 'There's another over there,' said someone. So there was.

'Don't let go,' she instructed the boys as she threaded her way through the crowds. 'Is Daddy coming too?' she heard a little boy asking his mum. 'I don't know, Gawain,' said a blonde woman, who also had a pushchair in tow.

Wasn't that Emma, the bride from last summer? But before she could say hello, a particularly bright firework lit up the sky, casting a great umbrella of light over the whole playing field. It only lasted for a few seconds but it was enough to make Rosie gasp.

Not because it was so beautiful – because it was, with its pink trails entwined with blue and silver rain – but because of what it had revealed.

Melissa. At the edge of the car park. Tall, beautiful Melissa, with a man's arms around her.

Someone who – she could almost swear – wasn't Winston.

But before she could even take in the implications, her phone rang. Greco. Greco?

'It is me. I am 'ere.'

The noise around her was so loud that Rosie could hardly hear. 'Can you say that again?'

'It is me. Greco. I am in England.'

This time, there was no mistake. 'Why? Where?'

'To see you, my Rosie. But there is problem. Big problem. The police, they have got me.'

A chill passed through her as she clung on to the boys, who were beginning to wriggle madly. 'What do you mean?'

'Eet is complicated. Please come and help me, Rosie. Quick.'

HONEYMOON HOMILY

If a husband suggests a second honeymoon, he's probably having an affair.

If a wife suggests a second honeymoon, she's probably not getting any sex.

Anonymous

Chapter Thirty-Six

WINSTON

Winston was looking for Melissa in the bonfire crowd – where on earth was she? – when he caught sight of a distressed Rosie stumbling towards him, with a small boy in each hand. 'Have you seen Gemma? I need to find her urgently to give these two back.'

Instantly he knew something was wrong. Her eyes were wild and a tendril of blond hair had escaped from under her pink woolly hat which he almost felt like pushing back for her. 'Greco has just rung. He's in trouble.'

Greco! The name took Winston back to those hot, heady days of the honeymoon. Melissa had been more loving then, although he should have seen the signs when the children had arrived – signs which had been confirmed since he'd moved in to Corrywood. He was never going to be part of this family. They had made their roots long before he had come into their lives. It was a losing battle.

'What's wrong with Greco?' Winston asked reluctantly. He hadn't cared for the man then, and there was no reason to change his mind.

But perhaps, he thought, looking at Rosie, who really was rather lovely in a completely different way from Melissa, he was ever so slightly jealous . . . It didn't seem right that this Greco had seen more of his own son over the years than he had. Or that he now had the girl whom he, Winston, had fallen in love with so long ago.

'He's been held at Customs,' Rosie was babbling in distress. 'Something about being given something without him realising.'

That old chestnut! Winston let out a groan. 'Drugs?'

Rosie shook her head vehemently. 'Greco doesn't do that sort of stuff.'

How often had he heard that before?

'He wants me to go there. To Heathrow.' Rosie was gasping now. 'But I don't know how at this time of night.'

'I'll take you,' he heard himself say. 'I know a good lawyer, too. We can ring on the way.'

'There you are!' Gemma came rushing up, her face etched with concern. 'You weren't where I left you. I've been looking for the children everywhere.'

She sounded cross, Winston noticed. 'I'm sorry.' Rosie was crying and Winston felt hurt on her behalf. Couldn't her friend see something was up? 'I was looking for you too. I've had a call and . . .'

He'd leave them to it while Rosie explained. Besides, before he could take her anywhere, he needed to find Melissa and fill her in on what was happening. She must be somewhere, he told himself, threading through the crowd round the bonfire. Ah! There was Alice. Holding hands with Jack.

'Seen Mum anywhere?' he demanded, shouting above the noise around them.

A firework flew overhead with a hissing sound, lighting up her face. He could see the girl smirking. 'She's talking to Dad.'

Really? He hadn't known Marvyn was here. 'Tell her I've had to take someone somewhere as an emergency,' he said quickly. 'I'll ring her. OK?'

If Winston was forced to admit to a weakness, he'd have said cars and bikes. The latter was great for getting about town, but after *Work Out With Winston* had taken off, he'd also treated himself to an Audi convertible. Its four-wheel drive was brilliant in weather like this and it gathered speed smoothly. It felt as though he was doing forty instead of seventy.

He might not be earning what he used to but this was one luxury he was determined to keep.

The motion, as they shot down the motorway, soon rocked

Rosie to sleep. Best thing, Winston observed. It gave him time to think too. Not just about Melissa, who was being so off and distant at the moment, or her daughter, who had made it clear she loathed his presence, even though her brother (still grateful perhaps for the boat incident) was much nicer. But about himself as a father.

Over the last few weeks, since his son had been here, Winston had noticed things that he hadn't done before. Alice and Freddie weren't the only ones to leave the fridge door open, or take a bite out of the cheese before putting it back, or store goodness knows how many mugs in their room, or leave lights on after they went out. Jack was just the same. Had he been too hard on his stepkids?

He also felt aggrieved when Melissa told Jack off for any of the above. She seemed to be stricter on his son than she was on her own kids, and it wasn't fair.

Just as it wasn't fair that Rosie's father should be racist towards his own grandson. Still, Winston told himself as the rain began to fall gently on the windscreen, he'd sorted that one out, hadn't he?

He hadn't told anyone that he was driving down to see Rosie's father. It had been his intention to tear a strip off the old man, but it hadn't quite worked out that way.

Instead, Rosie's father had welcomed him in with open arms. It had been the first time, since the damning *Globe* piece, that fame had worked in his favour.

'I miss your programme,' the old man had said after he'd invited him in. 'Like I said, the skinny kid doesn't compare to you.'

Winston had been determined to be polite but firm. 'You seem very keen on making judgments, Mr . . .'

'Call me Derek. Sit down, will you? Cup of char?'

'No thanks.' Winston remained standing to give himself the advantage, looking down at Rosie's dad, who had slumped down, stick by his side, on a chair that had seen better days. 'I'm here about my son. You upset him, you know.'

The old man nodded. 'I'm sorry if I hurt the lad. Didn't mean anything. You've got to understand that it's different for my generation. We say it as it is.' He squinted up at Winston. 'The lad *is* coffee-coloured, just like you.'

'Maybe.' Winston was struggling to retain his composure. 'But that's no reason to call him a bastard, is it?'

The old man shrugged. 'That's what we called it in my day, though I accept I should have held my tongue a bit more.' He glanced over at a tortoiseshell-framed black-and-white photograph of a pretty woman, looking sedately out of the frame. She was wearing a dress that reminded Winston of photographs showing his own mother in the Sixties. 'My wife always used to say that.'

Winston glimpsed an opportunity. 'What do you think your wife would say if she was here now?'

The old man sniffed, looking out through his grimy lace-curtained windows as if avoiding Winston's eyes. 'She might welcome the lad in, I suppose. My wife loved kids.' There was another sniff. 'Would have liked more, we would have, but we only got the one.'

'Then shouldn't you treasure Rosie?' Winston sat down opposite Derek, taking in the old man's mottled purple hands. 'Your family's come back to you, Derek. Given you a second chance. Don't you want to take it?'

The old man's eyes grew watery. Winston held his breath. 'Could do,' he finally admitted gruffly. 'If the lad comes round again, I'll see him.' He snorted. 'But don't push him into it, mind. He's got to visit of his own accord. If he really cares, he'll give me a second chance too.'

Now, as Winston took a left towards the airport, he wondered if he'd been right to obey the old man's edict. He'd heard, through Jack, that Rosie visited her father regularly but his son still refused to go down. It was stalemate. As Nick used to say, when describing her own difficult mother and sister, if you can't make peace at home, it's no wonder that we can't make peace in the rest of the world.

In fact, perhaps he ought to . . .

'Are we here?' Rosie's voice broke into his thoughts. She didn't sound sleepy. Maybe she was one of those people who was able to wake up just like that with a snap. He was the same.

Greco, he suspected, was one of those lazy, stretch-in-the-bed yawners who would make love first thing, seeing it as a natural part of his morning routine like coffee and shaving.

'Almost. Where did he tell you to go?'

'Immigration.' Rosie's voice faltered. 'Goodness knows where that is. Suppose we'll have to ask when we get there. Did you get hold of your lawyer?'

'Yes.' Winston kept his eye on the road. Rufus's father had handled his grandmother's affairs. It was Rufus who had advised him not to respond to the *Globe* series in the summer. 'Leave it alone and they'll find another story,' he had said.

He'd been right.

'He's meeting us there,' Winston told Rosie as he headed for the short stay car park.

She nodded gratefully. 'Will he be awfully expensive?'

Yes, but there was no need for her to know that. He'd let her down enough in the past. This was one way he might be able to make up for it. 'Don't worry about that. Not at the moment.'

Helping Rosie out of the car, Winston glanced at the text messages on his mobile. Rufus was already waiting. Jack was back at home. Nothing from Melissa.

Briefly he placed his hand in the small of Rosie's back to steer her. Instantly, an unexpected bolt of energy shot through him.

'Don't worry,' he said, trying to sound normal. 'We'll sort this.'

Despite his words, Winston soon found that the situation was much graver than he had feared. Greco was seated in a small, plain room without windows in front of a metal-legged table on which were five wooden figures, beautifully carved. Next to him was Rufus, and on the other side, a thick-set bulldog of a policeman with a tape recorder beside him.

'Have you seen these figures before?' The policeman fixed a relentless gaze on Rosie. She nodded. 'Greco makes them. He sold similar designs to various shops when we were on a trip to Athens recently.'

Greco was nodding enthusiastically. Yet he looked tired and Winston noticed that his hair was slightly greasy and that he was shivering in his thin white cotton tee-shirt. Not such a lothario now, he thought with satisfaction.

'You see,' he was saying. 'I told you. They are just ornaments that I make from driftwood on the beach.'

Carefully, the policeman picked one up and removed a tiny loose panel in the back. Rosie and Winston gasped as the man then pulled out a small packet of white powder. 'They also seem to have another use,' he snapped.

Greco spread his brown hands out on the table. 'I do not make this hole. I tell you, I sell these figures to the French couple who stay on the island last summer. When they leave, they give them back and ask me to post them because they cannot fit in their luggage. I forget so they ring again. I plan a surprise trip to my friend Rosie so they ask me to bring the figures with me at the same time.'

'A surprise trip?' repeated the policeman suspiciously.

'That ees what I say.' Greco jerked his head in Rosie's direction before scowling at Winston. 'I wish to see that she is happy.'

The policeman's eyes narrowed. 'This French couple. Were they meant to meet you?'

'Yes.' Greco was nodding again. 'At Arrivals. But they are not here. I tell you the truth, I promise.'

Suddenly, Winston had a memory of a light flashing from the bungalow where the French couple had stayed.

'Officer,' he began.

'Superintendent, actually.'

'Apologies.' He tried again. 'I was in Greece last summer and I recall a French couple. They acted very strangely.'

'Yes,' Rosie cut in. 'They kept themselves to themselves and . . .'

She blushed furiously.

'Go on,' said the superintendent.

'And they weren't shy about showing their affection outside,' she added.

Alfresco sex, Winston almost added. He'd seen them himself. Quite disturbing, actually.

'To divert attention perhaps?' suggested Rufus sharply. 'Do you have any photographs of them by any chance?'

Greco shook his head.

'Wait!' Rosie spoke up. 'I have. On my phone. It was during one of the evening barbecues. Look.'

She handed her mobile over. The superintendent's eyes flickered. Then he handed her a file.

'Recognise any of these?' he asked.

Winston watched her turn the pages, breathing in her perfume. Fragments of a sixteen-year-old memory he didn't even know he still possessed suddenly came back to him. Her smell . . . her touch . . .

Rosie stopped. 'That's her! I think.'

Winston nodded.

The super glanced at the picture on the phone and the one in the book. 'And that's the man,' added Rosie, turning over another page.

'Does this mean I am free?' asked Greco, tossing his head. 'I tell you I am innocent.'

'Not yet.' The super's eyes grew steely. 'There are still several unanswered questions, such as why this couple failed to turn up at the airport – if indeed, there was any such arrangement. Meanwhile, you're not going anywhere.'

Greco shot Rosie a desperate look. 'Can you not do something?'

'We can apply for bail in the morning,' said Rufus.

Rosie reached for Greco's hand. As she did so, Winston felt a knot in his stomach. 'So he has to stay in a cell overnight?'

The super nodded. 'Arrangements will be made.'

'But that's not fair.' Rosie was hanging on to Greco's hand. Would Melissa be as loyal to him?

'Rosie,' said Winston quietly. 'It will make it worse if you fuss. Come on. Say your goodbyes and then let's leave them to it. Jack will be wondering where we are.'

He spoke, he realised, as though they were a normal pair of parents with a teenager at home. And for a minute, as he shepherded a weeping Rosie back to the car, he found himself wondering what life would be like if they had been a real family . . .

After dropping Rosie off at Gemma's, Winston made his way back to Melissa's place. His predecessor's stamp was on it in so many ways that it was impossible to relax. Thank goodness he hadn't rented out the London flat but had kept it, in case the market improved. Maybe, if things didn't work out, he could go back there for a few weeks . . .

The house was silent and dark. Melissa hadn't even left a light on for him. Padding silently up the stairs, instinct made him glance into Jack's room. His boy – lying there, his eyes closed, his chest rising and falling.

Then he saw a foot poking out from the side of the bed. A girl's foot, unless Jack had taken to wearing bright pink nail polish. His stepdaughter was in bed with his son!

Winston's first reaction was to yank off the duvet. 'Go away,' murmured Alice sleepily.

'What the hell do you two think you're doing?' hissed Winston.

Jack was awake now, sitting up and putting his arm protectively around the girl. They were both fully dressed. That was something, at least.

'We didn't do anything.' His son was glaring at him as though it was him, Winston, who was in the wrong.

'We were just having a cuddle before going to bed,' pleaded Alice. 'Honestly. We must have fallen asleep. Please don't tell Mum. She'll kill me!'

Were they telling the truth? Winston thought back to the

time he had almost been expelled from school for slipping out to see a girlfriend. That had been innocent too.

'We'll talk about it in the morning,' he growled. 'Meanwhile, Alice, get back to your own bed.'

Exhausted, he couldn't tell if he'd done the right thing. Too much had happened tonight for him to be sure. He began to peel off his clothes for a brief shower in their en suite. As he did so, Winston's eye fell on the mobile that had been left on the vanity unit.

Melissa's.

Don't do it, he told himself, but unable to stop, he checked the last number.

Marvyn.

From the timing, he could see that his wife had made the call at one a.m., some three hours earlier.

There was a text too. His heart racing, Winston opened it. It was from Marvyn.

Miss you.

Followed by three kisses.

Sweating, he selected Sent messages.

Miss you too, it said. Four kisses.

Winston felt sick as all his worst fears shone out from the screen in front of him. So he was in the way, was he? Well, not for long.

Now wide awake with shock, he hastily got dressed again, flung some clothes in a case and headed back out to the car. He'd explain to Jack later, but at the moment, he just had to get out of that house.

Dawn was breaking over London when he arrived. What a relief it was, to drive down the familiar streets with the early-morning stirring of stallholders and suited men and women rushing off to work! Anonymity. That's what he needed, Winston told himself, opening his front door and setting down his case.

Peace and quiet. Away from the complexities of a marriage which he had, with hindsight, made too soon to a woman who hadn't got over her first husband. As for Jack, he could still see him. He'd bring him up here, in fact. Maybe offer him and Rosie a spare room for the time being so they could spend some time together.

Meanwhile, the answerphone light was flashing, demanding his attention. Melissa? Rosie? Rufus?

'*You have two messages.*'

'Winston? Are you there?'

My God. It was Nick. At least, it sounded just like her.

'This is Pam, Nicola's mother. I've been thinking a lot about you since the summer. I'd appreciate it if you could call me back.'

Still reeling from the voice, Winston played the message again to make sure he had got it right.

'I'd appreciate it if you could call me back.'

What did she want? Hadn't the woman ruined his life already with her newspaper interview?

Unnerved, Winston played the second message.

'Mr King?'

The voice had an American drawl. 'My name is Kurt. I work for CBS in New York. I wonder if you'd care to give me a call. There's something I'd like to discuss.'

TRUE POST-HONEYMOON STORY

'After our honeymoon, we both caught measles from our nine-year-old bridesmaid.'

Sandra, recently married, and now fully recovered

Chapter Thirty-Seven

EMMA

'Don't say you've left him,' Mum had said when Emma had turned up on the doorstep, clutching Gawain's right hand. By her side was a slumbering Willow in the buggy, a bag slung across the handle, bulging with trainer pants and winceyette pyjamas, which she'd hastily packed before leaving.

The sound of Tom yelling at her – making both kids burst into floods of tears – still rang in her head.

'You silly little fool.' Mum's voice was kinder than her words. 'Better come in then. I'll put the kettle on.'

Shepherding the children inside, Emma sank miserably into one of Mum's two plastic kitchen chairs. Willow was still asleep in the pushchair, thank goodness, and Gawain was nodding off against her shoulder.

She waited until he was asleep before telling Mum what had happened. When she got to the bit about Yannis, Mum had gasped and Emma knew, from the burning on her cheeks, that she had gone bright red.

'Tom might be dull but he's a decent man, Em. How could you have done something so bloody daft?'

Gawain stirred and then sat bolt upright as though he hadn't been asleep at all. 'What does "bluddy daft" mean, Gran?'

'It means that someone has done something stupid, love. Here, have a chocolate biscuit.'

Emma was about to say she'd been trying to reduce his sugar intake to stop him being so hyper, but what was the point? It didn't seem important any more.

'Going off with some complete stranger,' continued Mum, pouring an egg cup of whisky into each of their coffees. 'You must need your head examining.'

'Shh,' said Emma urgently. If Mum wasn't careful, Gawain would grow up hating his mother for wrecking the family; just as she had with Dad.

'I'd had too much to drink,' she said quietly, pushing the whisky coffee away. 'And I was nervous about having got married.'

Her mother snorted. 'You're meant to have nerves *before* the wedding. Not after.'

Gawain began twisting her hair round and round. It was a new habit of his, picked up from pre-school, and it hurt. 'What are nerves, Mummy?'

'Things that get ripped to shreds if people do daft things,' said his grandmother tersely.

This wasn't fair. 'You're the one who always said that Tom wasn't good enough for me,' shot Emma.

Her mother shrugged. 'One husband is better than none when you've got two kids under five *and* one on the way.'

Her son was wriggling now on her lap, bored with twisting her hair. 'Gawain is going to be five soon.'

'Not till after Christmas, love. Then you'll have to start being a big boy, won't you? Now what do you want Granny to get you?'

'A swing!' Gawain's eyes lit up. 'Like the one at school.'

Her mother gave a little laugh. 'Then let's hope you'll be back home by then. You won't be able to fit a swing into my little patch.'

Gawain stuck his thumb in his mouth: another habit he'd picked up from his baby sister since the honeymoon.

'Want to go home *now*.'

Emma looked at Mum. 'We can't. Not yet.'

There was a sigh. 'All right. I suppose you can stay here for a bit, although it will be a squash.' She gave Emma a shrewd glance. 'But if I were you, I'd go and find your old man in the garage first thing tomorrow and put things straight.

Trust me. Life's no bowl of roses when you're a single mum. I should know.'

But Tom wasn't in the garage. Or so they said.

'Sorry,' sniffed the youth who worked with him. 'Gone out on a job.'

He said it in such a deliberate, staged way that it was obviously rehearsed. So Tom had told him to keep her away, had he? Emma negotiated the oily patches on the garage forecourt and made her way to Corrywood School, feeling scared, sick and angry. She was going to be early for work, but that was good. It would give her time to ask Bernie why on earth she'd ratted on her.

'I'm sorry.' Her so-called friend ran towards her as she took her coat off. 'Phil promised not to say anything but the drink must have loosened his tongue.'

'That's no excuse.' Emma rounded on her, realising at the same time that this was exactly why she had gone too far with Yannis. Perhaps they *all* drank too much to 'relax' from the strain of parenting. Well, from now on, she wasn't going to touch a drop. 'I told you my secret in confidence. You weren't meant to blab to anyone.'

Bernie's eyes widened. This was obviously serious. 'But I didn't think Phil counted. I tell him everything. Don't you do the same with Tom?' Her hand flew to her face as she spoke. 'Sorry. Obviously you didn't tell him that stuff about Yannis or else this wouldn't have happened, but . . .'

Emma walked away in disgust to start laying out the tables and chairs ready for the first lunch sitting. If only Tom had given her time to explain she'd been drunk. But even so, something told her he still wouldn't have understood. She couldn't blame him. She doubted she would have either, if it had been the other way round.

'Mrs Walker, can I sit at another table? I don't like Billy any more.'

'Mrs Walker, my mum's given me a note to say I can't eat vegetables.'

Whoops! Here they came. Emma braced herself as Year One came flying in to take their places with all their usual demands.

'I've lost my lunchbox again, Mrs Walker!'

'Please, please, may I sit next to Daisy? She's my best friend now!'

Maybe, Emma told herself as she attempted to make everyone happy, she'd try again with Tom. Perhaps she'd call round this evening and take the kids with her. Surely he'd be missing them by now? And besides, he couldn't really believe that Gawain and Willow weren't his.

Could he?

But the house was dark and cold. Empty too.

'Where's Daddy?' asked Gawain in a small voice as she opened up.

Emma struggled to restrain Willow, who was fighting her pushchair straps. 'I don't know.'

'Yes, you do.' He was tugging at her arm.

Why was it that kids always knew when you were fibbing?

'You know everything, just like Jeeves.'

She couldn't help smiling, despite what was happening.

'Want my Spider-Man outfit.' Gawain ran up the stairs. 'And want my . . .'

He stopped at the sound of the key in the lock. Emma froze. Tom was home!

'Daddy!' Gawain yelled, flying down the stairs.

Her husband stood there, looking up at her. Not in his usual greasy garage overalls but in his jeans and yellow striped jumper that she'd given him last Christmas. He seemed different. More attractive, somehow, although she couldn't say why.

'Hello, little man!' To her relief, he scooped up his son and held him for a few minutes before putting him down. Then he gave her a horrible cold dismissive glance. 'What are you doing here?'

He spoke as though she had no right to be in her own home.

'I wanted to talk to you.' Coming down the stairs, she tried to take his arm, but Tom stepped away. There was a smell of stale beer on his breath. 'Please, I want to explain.'

'I've already heard all I want to.' He knelt down next to Willow, doing 'round and round the garden' circles in the palm of her chubby little hand.

'The children are yours, you know,' whispered Emma.

Tom's eyes, red and raw, locked with hers. 'Sure?'

'Of course I am. They both look like you, don't they?'

He was observing them now, as if taking them in for the first time. 'Yes.' Then his eyes hardened as he transferred his gaze to her bump. 'But that one isn't.'

'We don't know,' said Emma desperately. 'It could be. But you see—'

Tom's voice cut in. 'I don't want to see. Don't you realise? Whatever you say now can't mend what you've broken. We're finished, Emma.'

This couldn't be happening! He was the father of her children. Without him, their family wouldn't be the same.

'Daddy!' called out Willow, holding out her chubby arms. 'Play, please.'

Play, please? It was the first time she'd heard her daughter use that phrase. Any other time and she'd have hailed it as a milestone. But Tom was shaking his head. 'Another day, poppet.' Then his eyes turned to her, narrowing. 'What do you want to do then? Come back here – I can go to Phil's – or stay at your mother's?'

She couldn't face the idea of being in the house alone, not right now. 'I'll go back to Mum's for a bit,' she said in a quiet voice.

'Daddy come too!' Gawain, sensing something was up, was clinging to his father's legs.

'I'll see you at the weekend, son.' Tom knelt next to him, ruffling his hair. 'We'll do something fun together. Just you and me and Willow.'

Gawain's face fell. 'Not Mum?'

Tom shook his head. 'No. Just the three of us. You'll see. It'll be great.'

And that was how the weeks went by. Tom arrived on Mum's doorstep every Saturday morning and took both children out for the day, coolly declaring that he'd bring them back by teatime.

'Please let me tell you what happened,' she said at first, but each time, he gave her a disappointed look.

'I don't want to know the sordid details.'

So she'd given up. If it wasn't for the fact that she wasn't talking to Bernie, she might have got Phil to act as a go-between. Then again, he'd already done more harm than good. It was a joke in their crowd that Phil was as thick in the head as Bernie was big-boned.

'How long do you think you're going to be stopping with me?' asked Mum one Saturday afternoon. They were sitting in a cafe on the high street, Emma watching all the couples going by with their pushchairs and baby slings. It wasn't until now that she realised how much she'd taken that family-ness for granted. Saturdays were the worst. She felt so lost without her nearest and dearest around her. The growing lump seemed like an imposition. At times, she hated it. At others, she felt desperately sorry for it.

'I'm not really sure,' said Emma, stirring her latte and watching the brown sugar lump dissolve in circles. Unlike the others, this baby had given her a sweet tooth. 'I'm sorry if we're in the way.'

Her mother rifled through her bag for her lighter. That was another thing: Mum had started smoking again, and even though Emma had dropped heavy hints about it not being good for the kids, she carried on doing it. Still, it was her house.

'I just don't feel ready to be on my own yet,' added Emma quietly. 'I'm sorry, but—'

'Hello.' They both looked up at the sound of a once-familiar voice. Emma's heart took off at a hundred to the dozen as she absorbed the man with thin silver hair, slight stoop and pale blue eyes. *Dad!*

Frantically, she looked at her mother, who was sitting very still with two small red spots on her cheeks. 'Ted,' she said in a thin voice. Then her eyes darted to his side. Thank heavens, Emma thought, that he wasn't with Trisha.

'Bit of a coincidence, this.' Dad looked as though he would like to pull up a chair. 'I don't usually come here. How are you, Shirley?'

The red spots on Mum's cheeks grew brighter. 'OK. Yourself?'

He nodded. 'Very well, thanks.' He glanced at Emma. 'Having a break from the kids, are you? Some mum and daughter time?'

The envy in his tone was almost palpable. Emma nodded, shooting Mum a look to say *Don't tell him about Tom and me.* Thankfully, she seemed to get the message.

'I'll be off then.' Her father was smiling hard in the way that people do when they don't want to show their pain. A few weeks ago, she wouldn't have cared, but something tugged now in her chest. Then he held out his hand to Emma, giving it a quick squeeze. 'Give me a ring sometime, love. I'd really like to see the children one day. I'd like to give them some Christmas presents too.'

There was a grunt from Mum's side of the table. 'That would be a first.'

Dad was nodding. 'Yes. There are things that we all should have done earlier, aren't there, Shirley? Or maybe not done at all. Still, as they say, it's never too late.'

Then he was gone, swallowed up in the crowd of early-December shoppers. Emma continued to stir her coffee even though it was cold; more to give herself something to do while she braced herself for the question that had to be asked. 'What did Dad mean about doing things earlier or not at all, Mum?'

Her mother's hand was shaking on her bag clasp. 'How am I meant to know? Maybe he was talking about going off with that tart.'

'Or do you think he meant Keith?'

The words were out of her mouth before she could take them back, but the effect on her mother's face was instant. 'What are you talking about? Keith who?'

Emma felt herself shaking. 'Wasn't he a neighbour?'

'So?' Mum was staring at her stonily. Too late, Emma realised she'd made a dreadful mistake. Dad had lied about his mistress, hadn't he? He'd probably lied about Keith too.

'Nothing,' she said. 'It was just something that Dad said when I went to see him.'

Her mother's face set. 'You went to see your father?'

I have every right, Emma wanted to say, but the pain on her mother's face instantly made her guilty. 'I'm sorry, Mum. He sent me a wedding card and I felt I owed him.'

Mum got up, wrapping her coat round her. 'You don't owe him anything. Trust me. Now let's get out of this place. I need to buy some more fags.'

The run-up to Christmas was getting hectic. Gawain and Willow had both made their lists for Santa, sitting on Granny's sofa in front of the quiz programme that she was addicted to.

'Daddy says we can do another list with him on Saturday,' announced Gawain brightly. 'He says Santa is going to come twice this year.'

Their son had stopped asking when they were going back home now. Instead, both children seemed to have accepted that they saw Daddy all day on Saturday instead. How adaptable they were at this age! Far more so than adults.

Meanwhile, she ached for Tom. Yearned for his arms at night. Missed the familiarity of not having to say something, because they were comfortable with each other's silences. As for his irritating habits, like leaving clothes on the floor or lights on, they seemed like trivialities in comparison with not having him at all.

'He won't listen to my Phil,' said Bernie one day at work. 'Put those roast spuds out of reach, please. I don't want to be tempted. Phil's tried telling your Tom that you didn't know what you were doing but he won't listen.'

Emma turned away. Since Tom had thrown her out, she'd still refused to talk to her 'friend' apart from the odd phrase that had to be said at work like 'More beans, please'.

'Mrs Walker, Mrs Walker!' A little girl with plaits came rushing up to her indignantly. 'Sam won't talk to me cos he says I kicked him under the table, but I didn't. It was an ax idn't.'

Bernie gave her a look over the kitchen counter as if to say, See? We ought to teach kids to make up: set an example.

If she thought she was falling for that one, she was mistaken. In the meantime, Emma had carried on working extra hours at the after-school club to give Mum some money towards their living expenses. Despite being tired ('This baby of yours is a big one!' the midwife had declared at her last antenatal), she still loved it – especially when one of the kids asked her to help with homework.

'You're good at this,' said one of the other helpers approvingly when she'd been helping a little boy with his reading. 'Just like a proper teacher.'

Hah! In her dreams . . .

Every now and then at work, Emma would see Melissa coming in to pick up Alice and Freddie. Since they'd sorted out that horrid misunderstanding over the journalist, she'd been very sweet to her. 'How are you doing?' asked Melissa one evening, glancing at her stomach.

She busied herself with tidying up crayons, hoping Melissa wouldn't ask about Tom.

'Fine, thanks.'

'Your husband must be very proud.'

Emma started to nod and say that yes, he couldn't wait to have a third. But instead, she found tears filling her eyes. 'Actually, we're having a bit of a break.'

'No!'

Now it was the other woman's turn to look moist-eyed. 'So are *we*, at the moment.' She glanced around. 'Winston's gone back to London. But don't mention it to anyone, will you?'

Emma shook her head vigorously. 'Of course not. I'm so sorry. Do you think it will be, you know, permanent?'

Melissa shrugged. She looked thinner, Emma noticed. It didn't really suit her. 'I don't know. What about you?'

Emma's mouth went dry. 'I don't know either. He won't talk to me.'

'Tell you what.' Melissa touched her arm in that pally way she used to do in Greece. 'Why don't I give you a make-up lesson as a bit of a treat, to cheer you up. No, I insist. Come round to my place one day next week.'

When Tom brought the children back after his next visit, he handed her a piece of paper with Gawain's loopy childish handwriting.

'It's their list for Santa,' he said briefly as they flew through the front door with Gawain yelling, 'Granny, we're back!'

Emma had glanced at it. There were the usual impossible expectations like a swing and one of those motorised model planes that were far too expensive. And then, right at the bottom, were the words I WANT MY DADDY.

The lump in her throat was so big that she could hardly breathe.

'Maybe,' said Tom quietly, studiously avoiding her swollen stomach, 'we ought to have Christmas dinner together. For the kids' sake.'

'Maybe this is your chance to get Tom back,' suggested Melissa brightly when she gave Emma that promised make-up lesson just before Christmas.

'I don't know,' replied Emma doubtfully, looking round Melissa's stunning bedroom with its lemon walls and pictures of the children on the dressing table, along with one of her ex-husband (whom she'd seen fleetingly at school) but none, surprisingly, of Winston. 'I did something, you see, that he can't forgive.'

Melissa traced a thin grey-green line underneath her left eye and then her right. It made her look rather striking, even though Emma would never have thought of using that colour herself. 'You'd be surprised what you can forgive when there are children at stake,' she said quietly.

Emma glanced at her friend's closed expression in the mirror, which also reflected the huge bed behind, with a lovely rose-patterned chintzy ottoman at the end of it, and the chest of drawers with a pot of fat blue hyacinths on top. Did that mean she was ready to forgive Winston? Or her *first* husband? It was hard to tell and Emma didn't feel able to ask.

'Thank you so much,' she said when Melissa had finished and a new Emma stared out from the mirror.

'Think you can remember how to do it?'

Emma nodded. 'I'll try.'

'I'll write down some instructions to help.' Melissa gave her a little kiss on the cheek. 'Good luck.'

Emma flushed. 'You too.'

On Christmas morning, Emma spent ages getting ready. 'Bloody hell, what have you done to your face?' demanded Mum when she finally emerged from the bathroom. 'Don't rub it off, love. It's quite nice. Just that it takes some getting used to.'

Tom's expression, when he let them in, showed that he was surprised by the new-look Emma with her glossy lips and curled eyelashes, even though he didn't say anything. Meanwhile, the house itself looked as though it had had a makeover. So tidy and clean! Almost as though someone had been round to sort it out.

Tom? Or a new girlfriend? 'Men don't hang around long,' Mum had warned. 'If you want to get him back, you'll need to act sharpish.'

Gawain, who'd shot upstairs to his old room, wouldn't

stop jumping on his bed. 'It's bouncier than my one at Granny's,' he called out.

Her mother, whom they'd had to ask too, of course, rolled her eyes. 'Then you're welcome to come back to this one, pet. Give me some peace again.'

'Do you need a fag, Gran?' Gawain called.

'Not inside if you don't mind,' said Tom, heading for the back door. 'I need us all to go outside together. Em, cover Willow's eyes. I'll do the same with Gawain.'

Em? He hadn't called her that since that awful night when Phil had spilled the beans. Her heart leaped with hope. Then the five of them, including Mum, who was muttering something about smoking and human rights, went down the little side path into the garden.

'A swing!' gasped Gawain. 'A real swing!'

Racing across, he leaped on it. Next to it, on the bright blue plastic frame, was a toddler-sized bucket seat. Willow wriggled out of Emma's grasp, squealing with delight.

'That must have cost a pretty packet,' said Mum sharply.

Tom shrugged. 'I've been doing overtime.'

For a bit they stood there, watching the children. An onlooker might have mistaken them for an ordinary family, thought Emma wistfully. Was it too late? Judging from Tom's coolness towards her, the answer was yes, despite her earlier optimism.

Eventually, they went back into the house. 'I need a double whisky to warm myself up,' Mum grumbled. 'Don't be so stingy with that bottle, Tom. Give it to me.'

By the time it came to the turkey, Mum was well and truly sozzled. 'Not for me, thanks,' said Emma, putting her hand over the glass when Tom offered her some wine.

He shot the bump a distrustful glance. 'Of course. Can't let anything upset your baby.'

Emma bit her lip. 'It's not just because I'm pregnant. I've decided never to drink again. Alcohol made me do things I regretted.'

He hesitated. 'I've done things I regretted too, like telling the paper about Winston King. But there are some sins that are beyond forgiveness.'

Wait, she was about to say but was interrupted by the sound of the doorbell ringing. 'Santa!' screamed Gawain who was now really hyper. 'Maybe he's coming a *third* time!'

Willow was clapping her hands as Tom, who had gone to investigate, came back with a pile of presents, each with a neatly written gift tag. 'They were left on the doorstep,' he said suspiciously, giving Emma a distrustful look. Then he added in a whisper. 'From your fancy man, are they?'

She turned over the label on top and took a sharp breath. *To Willow, with love from Grandad.*

'They're from Dad,' she said, embarrassed.

Mum, her face flushed from a combination of whisky and wine, gave a short laugh from the sofa where she'd been dozing. 'Thinks he can make up for lost time, does he?'

Gawain frowned. 'How does time get lost, Daddy?'

'Good question.' Tom jerked his head in Mum's direction. 'Maybe you'd better get her upstairs, Em, and let her sleep it off.'

He was right. Mum was well and truly out of it now, mumbling incoherently as Emma led her into the bedroom she had once shared with Tom. Everything was the same, she noticed with a pang. The yellow rose bedspread. Her dressing table. The clothes that she'd left behind in the wardrobe. It was almost as though she'd never gone.

'I'm sorry,' slurred Mum as Emma pulled back the sheets.

'It's fine. We all have too much to drink sometimes.'

'No. I'm sorry about Keith.'

Emma's heart thudded. 'What do you mean?'

'If I hadn't gone with Keith, your dad wouldn't have gone off. I didn't love him, you know. He was just there.'

Then she was out, fast asleep, snoring with her mouth open. So Dad had been right! Mum *had* had an affair first. Scarcely able to believe it, Emma stumbled her way downstairs. Tom had put on a DVD and both Gawain and Willow were sitting in front of it, mesmerised.

'I'm going out now.' Tom rose to his feet awkwardly.

Emma felt a stab of alarm. 'Where?' she asked, knowing at the same time that it was none of her business.

He was looking decidedly shifty. 'Promised someone I'd meet them.'

A chill cut through her. So he *had* got someone else! 'What about the children?' It was her last card and, despite hating herself, she had to use it.

He looked down at the pair glued to the screen. 'They seem happy enough.'

'But *I'm* not,' she said softly. 'I miss you, Tom.'

Then it happened before she knew it. His lips came down on hers. Hard. Purposefully. Meaningfully. He kissed her in a way he had never kissed her before and, just as surprising, her own body was reacting too.

She fancied him! Much more than she had ever done when they'd been together . . .

Then he broke away, muttering something about having to go, and was out of the door before she could stop him.

Emma was left staring through the window as Tom broke into a run down the street, out of sight. What did that kiss mean?

And – more worryingly – who had taught him to snog like that?

BEDDING IN ON HONEYMOON

Honeymoon bliss is a myth! Couples are most unhappy during the first year of married life when they are still getting to know each other. They are happiest after they have clocked up forty years or more.

According to a recent survey

Chapter Thirty-Eight

ROSIE

Looking back over the previous weeks, Rosie couldn't believe how much had happened. That terrible experience with poor Greco in Customs was still fresh in her memory. If it hadn't been for Winston and his hotshot lawyer, Greco might be in prison.

Of course, he had been very naive. 'Didn't you think it was odd that this French couple asked you to bring the figures back with you?' one of the policemen had demanded.

Greco had shrugged. 'No. It was part of the service.'

Rosie could see his point of view. In a culture where neighbours did things for each other as a matter of course, Greco's actions weren't as daft as they seemed. Besides, he was a fisherman. He spoke as he thought and wasn't well versed in the subterfuge of a drug-driven world.

Even so, the police might not have believed him if she and Winston hadn't identified the French couple from the ID shots. Shortly afterwards, they'd been tracked down in Notting Hill and arrested.

Rosie felt like jumping in the air with relief. 'We did it!' said Winston, giving her a high five when she told him the good news over coffee in London before Greco flew home. The touch of his skin gave her a tingly, unsettling feeling. Not a good idea, she wanted to say, glancing at Greco's sulky expression over his latte.

'So you're not going back to Greece yet?' continued Winston casually.

Greco stiffened.

'I'd like to,' Rosie said quickly. 'But Dad needs me. He

really seems to be mellowing and keeps talking about lost time. Besides, I need to be near Jack.'

She stopped, not wanting to say any more in front of Greco, but the truth was that you only had to look at her son's shining face to see what a difference it had made to have a father in his life. How could she take that away?

'You will come home soon, I hope,' Greco had said, when she saw him off at the airport at the end of November.

She nodded. 'I'll stay just until the new year. Look after Cara for me and keep an eye on the villa, won't you?'

Swiftly, he'd bent down to kiss her, watched by a rather envious-looking middle-aged woman at Departures, and for a few seconds Rosie felt herself being transported away from the hustle and bustle of Heathrow. Greco really knew how to kiss!

They continued waving until she could see him no more. Feeling deflated – surely a good sign if she was serious about him? – she threaded her way back through the crowds towards the underground sign.

Then her mobile rang. Her heart lifted. Was it Greco, at his departure gate, with a final goodbye?

Winston.

'I didn't want to tell you in front of Greco but things have changed.' His voice sounded tight. 'I've moved back to London. Alone. Jack really likes his school and wants to stay until the end of term. So I've persuaded Melissa to let Jack stay with her in the interests of his education. Meanwhile, I'd like to see him at the weekends if that's all right with you.'

Rosie's head whirled. Did that mean that he and Melissa had separated, or was Winston's move precipitated by work? And where did that leave her? She wanted to see Jack at weekends too. It didn't seem right that other people were organising her son's life.

'I've got a job in a London health club,' he added. 'And there's a guest room in my flat if you'd like to stay.' There was a moment of hesitation. 'You could bring your father up too if you want.'

Rosie snorted. 'That's very kind but he'd only be terribly

rude – he's like that with everyone. And anyway, he's not really well enough to travel. It's best that I stay with him to make the most of the time he's got left.'

Winston's voice softened. 'You're a good daughter. What exactly is wrong with him?'

Rosie took a deep breath. It was only at her last visit that Dad had come clean. 'Cancer of the liver amongst other things. It's inoperable, apparently. They've already done what they can.'

'I'm sorry.'

His voice felt strong, like a hand to hold on to. 'Thank you.'

'Tell you what. Why don't you and Jack come up this weekend? We could do some museums. The National Portrait Gallery has got an exhibition on.'

Rosie felt a burst of excitement. 'That would be lovely – provided Jack's OK about it.'

'He is. I've already spoken to him. If you ask me, he and Alice might just be cooling off, which is probably just as well.'

'Really?' Part of her was relieved but she was also concerned for Jack. Who had hurt whom? She needed to call him, make sure he was all right. There was nothing more painful (well, almost nothing) than unrequited teenage love.

She should know.

'I'll text later to make arrangements,' said Winston. He seemed to add something else – about Dad? – but she was walking down to the underground now and the signal had faded out. As Rosie stepped onto the tube, surrounded by people with heavy cases and rucksacks, or others like her who had just seen off loved ones, a thought struck her. Winston had spoken to Jack about staying on at Melissa's before he'd discussed it with *her*. It made her feel pushed out and jealous.

Even more confusing, she and Winston had just had yet another conversation about their son, like any pair of parents, and it had felt disturbingly normal.

'Gemma's mum says you've got a boyfriend,' said Dad with a *what's going on?* look in his eye, when she went down to see him soon after her conversation with Winston.

400

He was sitting in a G-Plan armchair with frayed arms and an old red tartan rug draped over his knees, even though it was a bright day outside.

Rosie nodded, resisting the temptation to say that she was a grown-up woman now and that boyfriends were her own business.

'A Greek boyfriend,' said Dad, adjusting his spectacles. They had a bit of sticking plaster on the side, saying 'Short distance'. The other pair with 'Long distance' taped to them was on the side table, along with a copy of the *Daily Express*, which she had bought at his request.

'A Greek boyfriend who was arrested by the police,' added Dad with a warning tone in his voice.

Sally could be quite a gossip. Gemma must have said something to her mum, who in turn had passed it on. How many others knew?

'Not exactly,' said Rosie quickly, getting up to refill Dad's mug of tea. 'It was all a bit of a misunderstanding.'

Her dad made a clucking noise of disapproval in the back of his throat. 'I must say, you do pick 'em. First a coffee-coloured bloke who leaves you up the duff, and then some Greek fella with a criminal record . . .'

Enough was enough. 'That's not fair, Dad. Winston may not have been around when Jack was growing up – just as you weren't – but he is shouldering his responsibilities now.'

Dad winced. 'I'd do the same if the lad let me.'

Had she heard correctly? 'Can you blame him for not coming down? You were very rude to him.'

'I know, I know. Don't go on.'

'You were the one who brought it up. As for Greco . . . my Greek friend . . . he's entirely innocent and he doesn't have a record. He's gone back to Siphalonia now, which is where I'm returning after Christmas.'

Her tougher stance seemed to be working. Now Dad was looking like a child who knew he'd stepped out of line. 'Have you *got* to go back to Greece, love?'

This was so hard! An unkind dad was much easier to leave

than one who was giving her this *I need you* stuff. 'Sorry, but I must,' she replied more softly. 'It's my job. But Jack and I will stay for Christmas and we'll have lunch together.'

Even as she said it, she wondered whether Jack would agree.

'The lad will come too?'

Rosie nodded uncertainly. If necessary, she'd make him – as far as you could make a nearly-sixteen-year-old boy do anything. 'Now let me get on and make you this cuppa. Got any more tea bags, by the way?'

He sniffed. 'If you were here more often, you'd know where I keep them. Under the stairs. And be careful you don't knock over your mother's china.'

Only Dad would keep tea bags under the stairs instead of in the kitchen cupboard! Still, at least it had an interior light. Rosie fought her way through all the rubbish to get to the box marked 'TEA/COFFEE' sitting on top of a cardboard box stuffed with packets of (out-of-date) biscuits.

He needed looking after. It was all very well the nurse from the surgery coming in every now and then, but it wasn't enough. She'd have to arrange some regular help, maybe talk to Sally to see if she knew someone. Ouch!

Rosie tripped over another cardboard box that was in the way. It fell over on its side, spilling out paperwork. Exasperated, Rosie began to shovel it all back in. There were gas bills going back years. Old Christmas cards too and . . . and envelopes. Addressed to her. Opened envelopes with postmarks that went back to the summer before Jack had been born.

Her heart racing, Rosie sat down on the rubbish around her and pulled a letter out. It was dated a month after she'd left for Europe and it had a foreign stamp that she didn't recognise.

Dear Rosemary,

I still haven't heard back from you. Does that mean you have forgotten me already? I hope not. I think of you every day. I cannot get you out of my mind. In my sleep, I stroke your hair and kiss you. If this sounds like twaddle, please ignore this letter so I can get on with my life, leaving you to get on with yours. But if you feel half of what I do, then write back, dearest Rosemary. Somehow we'll find a way to meet up.

Love Charlie

Stunned, Rosie stumbled out of the under-stairs cupboard and into Dad's lounge. 'About time,' he mumbled, barely looking up from his paper. 'My mouth's parched. How long does it take to make a cup of char?'

Trembling furiously, she held out the letter in front of him. 'Why didn't you give me this, Dad? Why have you kept this and the other letters from Winston for all these years?'

Dad gave the bundle a cursory glance. 'Can't remember. It was so long ago. You did remember to put in three sugars, didn't you? The nurse says I need to keep my strength up. Got any more of that cake that Sally made, have you?'

What an appalling old man! They might be related, but she'd had enough. 'I've been wrong about you.' Rosie grabbed her coat, tucking the letters carefully into the pockets. 'You let me think that Winston left me in the lurch. But instead, he was waiting for me. Jack could have had a father to bring him up.'

Dad's hands began to slowly tear a strip from his newspaper. He used to do that during their teenage arguments, she remembered. 'You weren't here,' he said slowly. 'You just went. I didn't know where to send them.'

'Gemma knew! She told you where I ended up. And I wrote after Jack was born. Remember? You could have sent them then.'

He was tearing up another page now. 'I thought it was too late. 'Sides, I didn't like the sound of him. I didn't realise he was a decent enough bloke until I met him . . .'

Wait! 'You *met* him? When?'

Dad was tearing up a third page now, scrunching it into a ball. 'He came down here a while ago. After I'd been rude

403

to the lad. Told me I should have known better. Nice bloke, he was.' His milky eyes met hers regretfully. 'You didn't tell me he was that bloke on telly that did exercises. I told him I liked him better than that whippersnapper they've got in his place.'

Rosie held out a hand to steady herself. Dad was unbelievable. If he wasn't old and ill, she'd tell him what she really thought of him. But now he had her over a barrel. She had to be nice to him because his time was running out.

'I'm going back to Sally's now,' she said, forcing herself to sound civil. 'And I'm going to spend the afternoon reading all these letters that I should have been given years ago.'

His face was on hers, watching. Saying nothing. 'I'll be back tonight with your dinner,' she added, 'and I don't want to say anything else about this, ever again. In return, I'm going to bring Jack and Winston down here for Christmas lunch – *if* they will come – and you are going to be on your best behaviour to both of them. Got it?'

He nodded, relief washing through his eyes. 'All right.' As she went through the door, she thought she heard him say something. It sounded like 'Thank you'.

How could he? Rosie asked herself, shaking her head as she walked down Dad's little path towards the gate. She would never have hidden anything from Jack. In fact . . . whoops! she almost collided with a small, dark-haired woman in a blue uniform carrying a small case. 'Sorry.'

The woman beamed at her. 'You must be Derek's daughter. He's been talking non-stop about you since you arrived. You live in Greece, don't you? He's very proud of you, you know. And his grandson.'

Were they talking about the same person? 'Actually, I'm glad I've seen you,' said Rosie, glancing at the net curtains, which now looked less grubby since she'd washed them. 'I wanted to speak to Dad's doctor but he wouldn't let me.' Lowering her voice, in case he was listening at the window, she added, 'Isn't there *anything* they can do for Dad?'

The nurse gave a sympathetic grimace. 'I know catheters

aren't very pleasant, but a lot of people put up with them. There are worse things—'

'It's not that,' broke in Rosie. 'It's the heart trouble. And the cancer of the liver.'

The nurse frowned. 'I don't know anything about that.' Putting down her case, she drew out a folder. 'I'm not really meant to say – patient confidentiality and all that – but as you're his daughter, I think it's all right. No, there's nothing here.'

This didn't make sense. 'Not cancer of the prostate either?'

'No.'

'And the catheter . . . ?'

The nurse gave another smile. 'It's not always easy for old people to get to the loo in time. Especially when they live on their own. If you ask me, dear, that's what he's really got wrong with him.' She patted Rosie on the arm. 'Loneliness. When did you say you were going back to Greece, then?'

'Your dad kept the letters for all those years?' exclaimed Gemma when she rang that night. 'Have you told Winston yet?'

'No. I'm still not sure that I will.' Rosie was lying on the bed in the spare room that used to be Gemma's. It didn't seem like sixteen years since they had both been sitting on it, playing teenage records and talking about boyfriends. Downstairs, Sally was cooking supper. She was too old to be living in bedsit land. But what else could she do at the moment?

'And you can't go too hard on your dad because he's ill, like Mum said. She wrote to you, didn't she?'

Rosie had already discussed this with Sally after coming in. 'That's because Dad told her. She thinks it was to get me back. He's lonely.'

'Poor man.' Gemma was always able to see the other side. 'Poor you, too.'

Rosie swung her legs over the bed and went towards the window overlooking the harbour where she and Winston had spent their last evening together. 'It's Jack I feel sorry for.'

'Don't,' said Gemma decisively. 'He's had a great childhood and he's grown up to be a very well-balanced boy. By the way, you've heard the gossip about Winston and Melissa, have you? She's gone back to her first husband.'

So it was definite. Rosie had thought that they might have made up. Now she felt a little thrill that this wasn't the case.

'I heard Marvyn's a real heel,' continued Gemma excitedly. 'No one likes him, although I shouldn't say that. Mind you, someone told me that he decided to get her back because he was jealous when she married Winston. And she agreed because she felt the children needed to be with their real father. Reading between the lines, I don't think your Winston was as under-standing as he could have been when it came to the children.'

Immediately, Rosie felt defensive. 'He's not *my* Winston and actually he's very good with children. We're all meeting up in London this weekend to go round some museums.'

'Ah. That's lovely. Actually, I was thinking. Got anything planned for Christmas? Mum and Dad are coming up and we wondered if you'd like to join them. Bring your dad, if you like – and maybe Winston.'

It would be better than just the four of them. A noisy family crowd with Gemma's lot might hide any nasty comments from her father. 'I don't know if Dad's up to the journey,' Rosie began. 'He might not have heart trouble or cancer but he's quite frail.'

'My parents can give you a lift. Dad's just bought a huge people carrier. Says it's for his new hobby (did I tell you he's into fossils now?) but Mum says it's for the grandchildren. Go on, Rosie. Think about it. It would be so nice to spend Christmas with you just before you go home.'

They had a great day. Rosie was right. The sheer numbers round the festive table – goodness knows how they all squeezed in – made it difficult for Dad to be his usual sarky self. Instead, he managed to pull a cracker *and* make some reasonable conversation with Winston, about what it was like to be on telly. He also spoke to his grandson, who was on his right.

('Tell me what they teach you at your new school, lad. Bit different from Greece, I'll wager.')

'Jack's going back to his old school next week,' said Rosie, giving her son a warm *it's all right* smile. 'But he'll write, won't you, Jack?'

Her son nodded uncertainly before shooting Winston a glance. Rosie felt a tremor of unease. Jack was going to miss his father. 'You'll have to visit us, all of you!' She looked around the table, taking care to include Winston. Since Greco had left, they'd had some lovely outings together, taking in the London sights. Often they'd been mistaken for a family. If it wasn't for the fact that she and Jack spent the nights in the spare room, she might think they were one.

'Visit you?' repeated her father. 'Reckon my travelling days are over. 'Sides, my days are numbered, aren't they?'

Rosie had decided not to tell her dad what the nurse had told her. It would make him feel stupid; she knew that. Better to play along with it until the time was right. 'Then we'll come back next year to see you,' she added. 'When the holiday season is over for us.'

'Mum, he's kicking me!' protested one of Gemma's small boys.

'No, I'm not! It's him!'

The toddler started to cry just as the doorbell went. 'It's Shirley,' said Gemma, leaping up. 'She used to help me with the boys when they were really small, and between you and me, she's been having a bit of a tough time, so I suggested she came round for a piece of Christmas cake after lunch. She was a bit worried about spending too much time with her own family. Funny that it was her daughter, Emma, who went to your villa, Rosie. Small world, isn't it? You must know her too, Winston.'

'The blonde bride,' he muttered, sending Rosie a conspiratorial look. She gave him a sympathetic smile. It couldn't be easy for him here, amidst so many unfamiliar faces.

'Hello everyone!' Shirley, wearing a rather short red skirt, beamed at them all. She looked flushed and stank of whisky.

'Sorry I'm a bit late, but I was having a nap after my own dinner. I've got to say, it's a relief to be away from my lot. It's a nightmare with my daughter and her husband at the moment.'

Winston found himself unable to warm to this woman. He leaped up. 'Please, take my seat. I was about to make my excuses anyway. I need to visit my . . . to visit someone anyway.'

Melissa? Who else could it be? Rosie felt irrationally disappointed that he hadn't told her. 'Thank you so much for a delicious lunch.' He kissed Gemma on both cheeks, which made her friend flush. 'You must bring the boys up to London sometime.'

Jack cut in. 'It's really cool, and Dad's got this great place, right next to a skate park.'

Dad! It gave her a pang to hear him use the word. Winston was looking at her now. 'May I have a quick word?'

Blushing, she hurried out into the hall, closing the door behind them just as she heard Dad say, 'So where do *you* live then, Shirley?'

'Look.' Winston was taking both her hands and looking straight down at her. Every bone in her body was on fire. She felt weak, just as she had done as a teenager.

'I've got something to tell you.'

'I've got something to tell you too.' She couldn't hold it back. She hadn't been planning on telling him, not wishing to make him feel awkward, but now, after a couple of glasses of wine and the intimacy of sharing Christmas lunch with her son, she couldn't hold it back. 'Dad kept your letters.'

He frowned. 'What letters?'

'The ones you sent me after you left. He didn't give them to me, but I found them. You were telling me the truth, Winston. You did write to me. I'm so sorry I doubted you.'

His eyes misted. 'I'm glad you finally know the truth.'

Rosie gulped. He was nearly crying. This meant as much to him as it did to her. They were standing so close now that they were almost sharing the same breath. 'Do you ever,' he said quietly, 'wonder what might have happened if we'd each received the other's letters?'

She nodded, unable to speak.

Then he put both his hands on her shoulders, making her body pulse. 'It's not too late, Rosie. There's still something between us. I can feel it. Don't go back to Greece. We could start again – here – with our son.' His words tumbled out, not allowing her to cut in. 'Please, Rosie. Think about it. That's all I ask.'

'Wait,' she said urgently. 'What was the thing you were going to tell me?'

He gave her a warm, melting look. 'We've already said it. I love you, Rosie. I loved you before and now I love you again.'

He moved even closer. There was a surge of warmth as their lips met briefly, throwing her back to that very first time at the youth club disco.

And then he was gone, striding down the path towards his sleek car, leaving her dazed and confused. Her mobile vibrated.

Greco.

Feeling dreadful, she let it click into answerphone. Was it possible, she asked herself, to love two men at the same time?

TRUE POST-HONEYMOON STORY

'Six months after our honeymoon my mother-in-law still calls me by my predecessor's name.'

Karen, just about married

Chapter Thirty-Nine

WINSTON

Christmas had never been a big deal for Winston. At school and university he had often stayed with a friend's family (his grandmother had declared the holiday 'too short' for him to come back to the West Indies). Later, in the Royal Marines, he had always volunteered to remain on duty; frankly it was a relief to forget that he didn't have a family like everyone else. Until he'd met Nick, of course.

'When we're home,' she used to say fondly, nuzzling his neck, 'we'll have to visit my mum and sister, but after that, we could have time on our own.'

Time that they'd never had.

But now life was looking up – even though he hadn't, to be honest, *meant* to say that he loved Rosie. The words had just come out of his mouth and then it had been too late to take them back. Truth be told, he was feeling confused. Was his declared love for Rosie part of a misguided, nostalgic desire to find a part of his life that had been good? Or was Rosie really the one?

Maybe. Still, he *had* meant it when he'd said that it would be nice to be a proper family like Gemma and Joe's. He'd enjoyed lunch at their place. Those two really loved each other, even though it was crazy with all those kids.

It had been great, too, really great, to spend some time with his son. His *son*! Those words still gave him a thrill. Indeed, he found himself using them with pride to complete strangers. 'I'm buying this for my boy,' he'd enthused to the bored shop assistant when he'd purchased an expensive, garish sweatshirt as part of Jack's Christmas present, hoping it was the kind of thing that sixteen-year-olds wore.

Luckily, it was. 'Cool, Dad,' Jack had enthused.

'There's another under the tree,' he'd added. 'It's rather breakable.' He swallowed back the emotion in his throat. 'Leave it until after I've gone.'

His father would have approved of the gift, Winston told himself, as he thanked Gemma and Joe for their hospitality and made arrangements to meet up with Jack the following day.

This, together with Rosie's kiss (she'd definitely reciprocated!), had almost made him forget that there were still some more loose ends in his life that needed tying up.

'I need to visit someone,' he had told Rosie.

What he hadn't added was that the person in question wasn't expecting him.

Is this really the right thing to do? Winston asked himself, drawing up outside his wife's house. Everything looked exactly the same, he noticed. Someone else must have clipped the yew hedge just as he used to. It was as though he'd never left.

The speech that he'd prepared during the last few weeks now seemed stupid as he knocked on the door. Maybe it would be best if he just turned round and left . . .

'Winston!' The boy's face at the door broke into a grin. 'Hi! Mum's inside.' A worried look passed across his face. 'With Dad.'

So Marvyn was here! Then again, what had he expected? That daydream where the bastard had gone off again with someone else, leaving Melissa to realise that she'd loved Winston all along, now evaporated as Freddie led him into the sitting room.

There they were – Melissa sitting upright on the sofa, looking beautiful. She was holding a flute of champagne and wearing a silver necklace that he'd never seen before around her elegant throat. Marvyn was standing beside her in a navy jacket and beige trousers (the standard uniform around here), glaring at him.

'What do you want?'

'Marvyn.' Melissa placed a hand on her first husband's arm. 'That's rude.'

Marvyn was virtually snarling, reminding Winston of a sniffer dog they'd had once that had turned nasty. 'How dare you intrude on a family day!'

Winston resisted the temptation to say that legally he still *was* family, even though Melissa had filed for divorce. 'I was just passing so I brought round some presents.'

Alice, who'd been sitting with her back to him, texting furiously, now looked up. 'You can put them under the tree,' she announced coolly, as though he were a lowly Victorian manservant.

Winston braced himself. There was so much he could say. So much he could ask. Such as, how could Melissa have played around behind his back – and with her ex-husband at that? But now, as he placed the presents at the foot of the enormous Christmas tree decorated with blue and white lights with matching bows, the truth finally dawned.

He'd been used. Melissa hadn't really loved him; she'd accepted him on the rebound. In reality, she was still in love with this awful man. If it hadn't been for him, Winston, Marvyn might still have been with his mistress. There was nothing like a bit of jealousy to make someone change their mind.

'Well, it was nice to see you, but I must go now,' he announced as if they had invited him to stay.

Melissa's beautiful dark eyes were on him, her expression unreadable. 'Good idea,' snapped Marvyn. Alice didn't even bother looking up from her phone which, judging from the packaging around her, was brand new. She'd already got through two during the time he'd been with her mother.

'Can you stay for a kick-around?' asked Freddie hopefully. 'Only Dad can't—'

'I'll see you to the door,' said Melissa quickly, but Marvyn had leaped to his feet.

'I'll do it.' It was almost like being frogmarched out of a

building that he'd broken into. They crossed the hall with its wooden floor which Winston had varnished when he was living here. 'If you ever,' said Marvyn, his voice low and threatening, 'come here again, I'll sue you for harassment. Got it?'

Enough was enough. Winston swung round, his eyes blazing. 'Just make sure you don't mess her around again, do you hear me? You're lucky to have a family. Look after it more carefully from now on.'

The look in Marvyn's eyes showed he'd struck a chord. Horrible man! It took every ounce of strength not to punch him, but instead, Winston forced himself to back off.

As he started the engine, he looked up at the house. Was he imagining it, or was that Melissa at the window? Almost immediately, she disappeared.

'It's not working,' Melissa had said when she'd announced she wanted a divorce, a few weeks ago. Maybe she was right. But he'd needed this visit to be certain, and now he was. Glancing down out of habit at his left wrist – it seemed weird not to have his father's watch on – Winston drove slowly out of the drive and towards the motorway.

One down. One to go.

Back in November when Winston had first picked up the message on his answerphone, he'd felt a mixture of shock, fear and excitement. Nick's mother? What did she want?

Mrs Thomas had been brief when he'd rung back. Would he come round, she wanted to know. There was something that she wanted to talk about.

So Winston had driven to the address in Harrow (a place he used to come to quite regularly for school matches) and found himself outside a neat terraced house in a pretty cul-de-sac with a green patch in the middle and a willow tree. It was just as Nick had described.

As he rang the bell of this modest house, Winston wondered what would have happened if Nick had stayed here. Would she have married and be living near here with two children? Would she . . .

He stopped himself as a shape loomed up through the glass door. A small, white-haired woman with a doughy face and an unexpectedly kind smile greeted him. 'Thank you so much for coming,' she said. 'Please come in.'

Winston found himself being led into an L-shaped room with parquet flooring. Beyond that, he could see, was a small garden with a little wooden bench in the corner; again, just as Nick had described it. His first thought was that his old love was everywhere. On the mantelpiece. On the top of the piano. On the low pine side unit along the wall. Pictures of a toothy, skinny, dark-haired Nick in a green school uniform, smiling shyly at the camera. Pictures of a teenage boyish-looking Nick looking more confident in jeans, lounging against a farm gate. Pictures of Nick in a nurse's uniform, proudly clutching a certificate. And pictures of Nick wearing her kit.

Her presence was so vivid that he almost had to put out a hand to steady himself.

His second thought was that Nick's mother had brought him here to castigate him even further. Why else would she have that stack of clippings from newspapers and magazines on the coffee table in front of him? The top one bore a stark black headline: 'How Many More Lives Will Be Lost Before Someone Sees Sense?'

'Please sit down.'

'Thank you, Mrs Thomas . . .'

'Do call me Pam, won't you? Would you like some tea?'

'No, thanks.' He glanced again at the cuttings, steeling himself for yet another inquisition.

'I've been reading them again.' She spoke as though it was some kind of secret vice. 'My daughter didn't want me to, but I felt I needed to after speaking to the vicar. There was a line in one of these interviews that really touched me.' She reached out for the one on top. 'May I read it to you?'

Once more, he braced himself. '*When you lose a soldier, you live with it for the rest of your life.*'

She lowered her glasses. Her eyes were a silky dark brown.

Just like Nick's. 'That's what you said to a journalist back in the summer, wasn't it?'

He nodded, remembering the crowd of hacks who had bombarded him and Melissa at Heathrow after their honeymoon. Pam seemed to be studying him intently. 'Why didn't you check that the path was clear before allowing my daughter down it?' she said softly.

They'd been through this so many times, both at the inquest and during interviews. But this woman deserved better. For a second Winston closed his eyes. He was there. Back in Afghanistan. With Nick. Some dust from the road had got into her eyes and he was gently wiping it out with a handkerchief. The sun was so hot that it was hard to think straight. The constant dry crackling of distant guns was growing nearer. Children were playing – actually playing – on a bomb crater a few yards away, despite their warnings. Time was running out.

'It seemed like a risk worth taking for the greater good,' he said softly. 'Now I can see that it wasn't.'

Her eyes hadn't left his. 'You said before that Nick was aware of the risk. Are you sure of that?' She glanced at the pictures. 'This was her first military posting, Winston. She'd been nursing in England until then. Yes, she wanted adventure, but I'm not entirely sure that she realised how much danger she was putting herself in until she actually got there.'

There was a hint of a desperate sob in her voice. 'I need to know,' she said, sensing his hesitation. He could see now where her eldest daughter had got her steeliness from. And her compassion.

Winston addressed his words to the teenage Nick in the tortoiseshell frame. 'I told her the odds. She said . . . she said that she wanted me to chance it. "We can't not do anything."' The words were engraved in his mind. 'That's what she said.'

'But did she die in vain or did she make a difference?' Pam bit her lip. 'I watched a programme the other month about a father whose son was killed in Afghanistan. He went back to see what it was like. I want to do that one day. I need to know, just as he did, if her life helped someone before it was snatched away.'

He could answer that one all right. 'Nick,' he replied, his voice firmer now, 'was the kindest yet most efficient nurse I have ever come across. During the short time she was with us, she helped countless men with her gentle words and her skill. Children too.' He paused, remembering. 'There was one little boy whose arm had been blown off.' He could see her now, kneeling next to him, speaking soothingly and stemming the flow of blood. 'She saved his life, and afterwards, she went with him to find his family.'

That was something else he had been proud of: the way his men had done their best to bring torn families back together.

The older woman smiled. 'I can't tell you what that means to me, Winston.' Then she reached out to touch his arm. 'My other daughter is still very angry with you, but that is because she needs someone to blame. I've had more time and also I have my faith.'

She reached up to her throat and touched the small gold cross around her neck. 'I also got in touch with the other Wren – the one who survived. She told me how courageous you were. How you put your own life at risk by trying to get my daughter out.'

Automatically, Winston reached up and touched the jagged scar on his neck.

'I want you to know,' she continued, 'that I don't hold you responsible any more, Winston.'

He swallowed hard. 'I don't know what to say.'

'You can tell me that you will visit every now and then. You're my last link, you see.' Pam's voice wavered slightly as she picked up the teapot.

I'm forgiven, thought Winston with a wave of relief. She's forgiven me. He felt dizzy with gratitude.

'Now tell me, do you take sugar? I'm afraid that was something Nicola didn't tell me, although she did mention that you have a penchant for Bourbon biscuits. Or would you rather have a sandwich first?'

She gestured towards the tea tray with its plate of beautifully cut triangles. 'Please, help yourself.'

He faltered. 'I'm sorry. I can't eat ham. I turned vegetarian after . . . after Nick.'

Pam nodded, biting her lip again as though reading his mind. 'A biscuit then. By the way, how is your new marriage going?'

He almost choked at the unwelcome change in subject. 'Not great.' A huge lump suddenly grew in his throat, not just because of the large crumb that had lodged there. It would be easy to make some kind of general pleasantry, but after the frank conversation they'd just had, Winston felt he owed it to Nick's mother to be honest.

'Things are difficult, actually.' He stirred his tea. 'Melissa says I don't know how to be married.'

Pam's voice was stern. 'And is she right?'

Winston had been over this so many times in his head that he no longer knew the answer. 'Possibly. I've been on my own for so long that I probably don't know how to share. I like to do things my way.'

Nick nodded at him through her mother's eyes. 'Recognising something is half the battle, don't you think?'

All that had been six weeks ago. Since then he'd paid her two more visits and spoken to her several times on the phone. She was easy to talk to. Conversation usually revolved around Nick, although he had to get used to the way her mother referred to her daughter as Nicola. Sometimes they spoke about Pam's life, which centred around the church and an amazing charity scheme called Talking Books, where volunteers such as Pam recorded news items onto memory sticks for the blind.

Pam was always asking questions too about Winston's life and the fill-in jobs he'd been doing in London gyms to earn some money. He told her more about Melissa – and also his son. She encouraged him to accept the Christmas Day lunch invitation from Gemma so he could spend time with Jack.

'Come on over to me afterwards,' she'd suggested. 'It will be nice to have the company. My other daughter has chosen to go abroad with friends.' The hurt in her voice was all too clear. And no wonder. Christmas was a time for families.

'We haven't seen eye to eye recently,' she added.

'Because of me?' Winston suddenly twigged.

'She doesn't approve of us meeting,' Pam admitted. 'I'm afraid she's still coming to terms with all her emotions.'

I know the feeling, thought Winston. But maybe it was time to change. So somehow he found himself sitting on the edge of Pam's soft pink velour sofa and telling her about his visit to Melissa that afternoon.

'This first husband of hers sounds like a bully as well as a philanderer. It's a fact of life that some women don't realise they're under someone else's thumb until it's too late.'

There was a quick glance at the photograph on the piano of a stern, dark-haired man with a moustache. So that's where Nick had got her dark looks from. They hadn't got on, Nick had confided soon after they'd met. 'It was one of the reasons I joined the Wrens, I'm afraid. He's a control freak. I had to get away.'

'My husband died of heart failure, soon after Nicola,' added Pam.

'I'm sorry.'

She looked away. 'Thank you. But marriage isn't always a bed of roses. In our day, we kept going. It wasn't always the right thing to do.'

Interesting . . .

'More Christmas cake?' She held out the plate, as if eager to change the subject. 'Go on. It needs eating. Now tell me about your new job. Is it going all right?'

Winston nodded enthusiastically. The opening at a swish health club in Chelsea had come at just the right time. It wasn't so much the money as the boost to his self-esteem. 'Great.'

'But it's not the same as television?'

She was beginning to know him. 'I really miss all that,' he

admitted. 'I loved the adrenalin; the knowing that you were doing it live, so you couldn't afford to make mistakes.'

Another nod. 'We took your career from you, my other daughter and I. If it hadn't been for those articles where we criticised you, you might not have lost your contract. No, don't deny it. I'm sorry.'

'Don't be.' He was being gracious here and they both knew it. 'Remember what Nick used to say?'

'Never look back,' they both said together in one voice. And then, rather to his surprise, Winston found himself in her arms, sobbing like a baby for the first time since it had happened.

Not just for Nick, or for Melissa and Rosie and what might have been. But for his parents too, a grief which he hadn't been allowed to let out as a child, because his grandmother and housemaster had told him to 'be brave'.

Maybe, Winston suddenly realised, courage was the ability to show you were actually as fragile as everyone else, inside.

'It's all right,' said Pam soothingly. 'Let it all out. I understand. There's just one thing I would say. Don't go rushing into another relationship on the rebound.' She patted his hand. 'Allow yourself time to think.'

Just after New Year, Winston went to Heathrow to see off Jack and Rosie. He was really nervous about seeing her again after that Christmas kiss and he could tell she felt the same.

'Can we have a few minutes to ourselves?' he said quietly.

Rosie nodded tightly. 'Jack, do you mind going over to that magazine stand and getting me a paper? Thanks.'

Then she turned to him. 'We'll have to be quick. I haven't told Jack about us.'

Winston's breath caught in his throat. 'So there *is* an "us"?'

Her eyes darted to the news-stand and back to him. 'I don't know. I need more time.'

He put out his hand to touch her arm. Surprisingly, this time, he didn't get the electric shock he'd had before.

'Something's happened,' he admitted. 'I've had a job offer

from an American television channel. I'm not sure I'm going to take it, but it would mean moving to California.'

'California?' Her eyes widened.

'I know. It would mean you giving up the villa, of course, and a complete change of education for Jack unless he went to boarding school in England.'

'Boarding school?' She stepped back. 'Give up the villa? Do you really think you can just come back into my life and change everything?'

Too late, Winston realised he'd rushed her. Just as he'd rushed Nick. He couldn't help it. If there was one thing he'd learned in the Royal Marines, it was that life could be here one minute and gone the next. You had to make each minute count. 'There's no need to make a decision now,' he said.

Rosie stared at him sadly. 'I think I've already made it. I'm sorry, Winston. You're asking too much of us.'

'Then forget it,' he said quickly. 'I'll turn down the offer.'

'You don't want to.' She shook her head. 'I can see it in your eyes.'

She was right. He *did* want to go to the States, but he was also prepared to give it up for her. At least, he thought he was . . .

Then, before either of them could say anything, Jack came running up. That was parenthood for you, Winston realised. Constant interruptions just when you needed to say something important.

'You will come and visit, won't you, Dad?' the boy said as he hugged him goodbye.

Winston remembered the advice Pam had given him about leaving all options open. 'Of course I will. Or you might want to come here, if you prefer.' He glanced at Rosie. 'Both of you.'

Awkwardly, he made to hug her. As he did so, he caught sight of Jack's face, watching. Was that approval or not? It was hard to tell.

'Look,' he whispered, helping her with her case to check-in. 'I'm sorry about what I said about boarding schools. I get it completely. I have no right to interfere with the way you bring up Jack – you've done a great job. I just want you to know that I'm always here if you want me, wherever either of us end up.'

She looked at him as though working out if he meant it or not. 'OK.' Then, as an afterthought, she added, 'Thanks.'

Jack flung his arms around him again. 'Thanks for Grandad's watch, Dad. I'll always look after it.'

He nodded, unable to say anything. 'It was good of you,' added Rosie quietly. 'I know how much your father meant to you.'

Then they were off: Jack waving until Winston couldn't see him any more. Moist-eyed, he turned to see the girl at the information desk eyeing him sympathetically. 'That's my son,' he said, with a huge lump in his throat.

'I thought he might be,' she replied. 'I could see the likeness.'

Yes! Winston took the underground back, feeling a curious buoyancy despite the emptiness in his chest. Other people recognised them as father and son too. It lent an air of authenticity to something that wouldn't have seemed real this time last year. The first thing he would do on getting home, he decided, was email Jack. Not a sentimental *I'm missing you* email but a chirpy one with some jokes. The type they used to tell in the Royal Marines, just before going into action.

He'd need to email Rosie, too. But what would he say? Did he love her or not? Maybe Pam had been right when she'd said he'd allowed his Christmas emotions to get the better of him. Otherwise, why had he felt that gap between him and Rosie just now at the airport?

Life could be so confusing at times.

The flat seemed empty when he let himself in. It would be odd not having Jack here at weekends any more. After switching on Classic FM, Winston turned to his computer.

INVITATION.

Intrigued, Winston read on. It was a call for a reunion with his old batch. They were meeting up later in the spring. Did he want to go?

Do it! said Nick in his head. You've hidden away from your old friends for too long.

Automatically, he RSVP'd yes. As he did so, another email came up. This was from someone else in his old batch. The subject heading was *Urgent*.

DESPERATELY SEEKING A HOME

Barney is a retired sniffer dog who was going to be rehomed this week. Unfortunately, his intended new owner has had to go into hospital and is likely to be in for some time. Barney needs someone to look after him. Can you help?

There was another email too. From Karl at the American television station.

Had any more thoughts about our latest offer, Winston? We've hung on for as long as we can but we need an answer. Now.

TRUE POST-HONEYMOON STORY

'I was seventeen and six months pregnant when we got married. Now, after thirty years, my husband's still my best friend.'

Amanda, mother of three

Chapter Forty

EMMA

The January back-to-school panic helped to distract Emma from the confused thoughts that woke her up at five every morning, even earlier than Willow, who had finally learned to sleep through the night.

Every time she opened her eyes, she reached across for Tom and – for a split second – wondered where he was. Then it would all come flooding back. His absence felt like a gaping hole in her chest, made worse by the fact that she had caused it in the first place. How horribly ironic that it had taken her husband's absence for her to understand that they'd been much better suited than she'd realised.

They might not have had the passion she'd experienced with Yannis on the island, but she and Tom had been comfortable together. They knew each other's little ways – silly things like her not driving on motorways or him always putting his left sock on first. There was a lot to be said for that.

And – this was the deal breaker – they had two children together. No one else could ever be a substitute.

As she lay there, steeling herself to lumber out of bed and get the children ready for their first day after the Christmas holidays, she felt the baby launch an even bigger kick than usual. *It's not my fault*, it seemed to say.

Poor little mite. Emma placed both hands on her swollen stomach, remembering how Tom had loved to do the same when she'd been pregnant with Gawain and Willow.

But this one was going to grow up without a father. Emma felt gripped with apprehension. She'd have to make sure, as

Rosie had done, that she did a good job. After all, Jack, on the whole, was a credit to her.

'Mummy, Mummy!' called out Gawain, bouncing onto her bed, dressed as usual in his Spider-Man costume. 'Is it my birthday yet?'

He'd been asking that ever since Christmas. 'No, love.' She shoved up a bit in the bed to give him room. 'Not till next month.'

'*Next month?*' His little face crumpled with disappointment. 'But Gawain can't wait that long.'

Despite herself, Emma laughed. She could remember saying the same to Dad. He'd promised her a red bike for her eighth birthday and it had seemed like an age until the day had finally come. 'You'll have to wait, love.' She glanced down at the bump. 'All good things take time.'

'But Gawain wants Daddy to be here now.' Her son's eyes were brimming. 'It was on my Christmas list but Santa didn't get it right, naughty man.'

Emma's heart contracted. At the same time, the bump lurched. Luckily, it diverted Gawain. 'How does the baby do that?' he demanded.

She needed to think about that one. Tom had told them they were going to have another brother or sister right at the beginning, before Bernie had spilled the beans. She'd thought Gawain had accepted it. Willow was too young to have taken it in.

Still, at least his question had got them off the *Where's Dad?* subject.

'My tummy's like a swimming pool inside,' she said, smiling encouragingly. 'The baby swims around until it's ready to come out.'

His face cleared. 'Like Gawain and Dad? He's taking us to the pool on Saturday. He said so.'

Really? Tom hadn't told her that. Welcome to the world of shared custody. During the last few weeks, Tom had been coming over every Saturday morning at ten o'clock on the dot to take the kids out for the day, always telling her where they were going 'in case of emergency'.

What he did in between those Saturdays was anyone's guess, although she had an uncomfortable feeling that it might have something to do with that surprise kiss he had given her on Christmas Day. A kiss that hadn't been repeated. A practised kiss.

'Come on now,' she said, finally getting out of bed. Mum's spare wasn't as wide as her old bed at home and it was quite creaky too, especially with her extra weight. 'Let's get you out of your Spider-Man costume and into your school uniform.'

Gawain ducked out of her grasp. 'Want to wear *this*. And want Daddy to come home. *Now*.'

'What's all that noise?' called Mum up the stairs. Since Christmas, she'd got increasingly shirty about them all being here, making constant remarks about fingerprints on the wall and the kitchen being too small for everyone.

Mum was right. It would make more sense if they moved back to the family home and Tom found somewhere else to live. That was something she'd have to talk to him about. To be honest, she'd been putting it off, preferring to be with Mum for some company.

But now that was wearing thin. Mum had got really secretive, often putting down her mobile suddenly when Emma came into the room. The other Saturday, she had gone out for the day saying she was 'seeing a friend', leaving Emma to kick her heels without anyone else around. It had felt really weird.

'Sorry,' Emma called down. 'I'm just trying to get Gawain dressed for school. You couldn't give me a hand with Willow, could you?'

There was a grumbling noise and the sound of footsteps coming up the stairs. 'When I was your age, I didn't have any help, not even when I was pregnant . . .'

She stopped suddenly, as if knowing she'd said too much.

'But when you were expecting me,' said Emma slowly, 'your mum was alive. You said she was always around.'

Mum turned her back, heading towards Willow's cot in

427

the corner. She was getting too big for it now, but there wasn't enough space here for a toddler bed. 'Not always,' came the reply. 'By the way, is there any chance you three can make yourself scarce next Sunday? Only I've got some guests coming round.'

If she was still talking to Bernie, Emma would have confided in her. But the longer she held out against it, the more difficult it was to accept her friend's original apology. Instead, they spoke as little as possible at school, restricting it to 'One plate with no beans' or 'Smaller portion, if you please.'

Then, a few days after her strange conversation with Mum about the mystery guests ('none of your business whom I ask round'), she was putting out lunch for the large table at the end when there was a terrific noise behind her, followed by a shocked silence and then a scream.

'Bloomin' heck!' yelled Bernie. 'Quick, someone!'

Horrified, Emma took in the little girl lying on the ground next to a chair on its side. 'Abigail pushed her,' spluttered a small boy indignantly, his mouth full of baked beans. 'I saw her. It's cos Sophie kicked her. I saw that too.'

'Who's got their first aid certificate?' called out one of the other dinner ladies frantically.

Emma gulped. 'I have.' She'd taken it when she'd been pregnant with Gawain: the supermarket had sent all its employees on a course and they'd seen it, she was ashamed to say, as a chance to have a day away from the tills.

Bending down over the little girl, whose eyes were closed, she tried to remember. Tilt the chin back to check the airway was clear. Seemed to be. Check the pulse. Yes. Place in recovery position. Whoops. She was being sick but at least her eyes were opening now.

'It's all right, love,' she said soothingly. 'You've just had a nasty fall.'

There was the sound of running feet. Gemma Balls! Thank goodness for that. 'We've called an ambulance.' She knelt down next to Emma and the child. 'Hello, Sophie. Had a bit of a bump, have we?' Then she turned to one side, whispering, 'Someone needs to ask reception to ring Sophie's parents.'

'I'll do it.' Emma jumped to her feet.

By the time she was back, Sophie was sitting up and chatting, although she was very pale. The ambulance men were there too. After she'd gone, there was a hushed silence in the canteen. 'Better try and distract the kids,' said Emma to Bernie.

Her old friend nodded. 'How about ice cream faces?'

'Brilliant.' It was something they usually did at the end of term. Bernie would place jelly beans onto slices of Arctic roll to make faces; the kids loved it. Within a few minutes, there were 'oohs' and 'aahs' and then the usual squabbling as though nothing had happened.

'That's better,' said Bernie, leaning over the counter. 'Phew. I'm exhausted from the shock.'

Emma handed her some empty platters. 'Still, it looks as though she's going to be all right, doesn't it?'

Bernie's expression was rueful. 'Do you mean the kid or us?'

'Both, hopefully,' said Emma quickly. It had been a relief, she realised, to talk normally to her friend during the crisis. Life was short: that little girl's accident could so easily have been something worse.

'I've missed you,' said Bernie, reaching for her hand. 'And I'm really sorry about telling Phil. I shouldn't have done.'

'No.' Emma began to scrub down the tables as the children lined up for the duty teacher. 'It's me who should have told Tom.' She moistened her lips. 'Do you . . . I mean, has Phil said . . . It's just that I wondered if Tom was seeing . . .'

'Anyone else?' Bernie said.

Emma nodded, her mouth dry with apprehension.

Bernie's face was sombre. 'Tell you the truth, Em, Phil did say that one of the girls behind the bar took a shine to your Tom the other week. Passed her number to him, she did. But I don't know if he did anything about it.'

So that explained the kiss. Well, if he could get over her

as easily as that, Emma told herself, Tom obviously hadn't cared for her much in the first place.

What were they going to do all day on Sunday? It was raining, so the park was out. 'I want to go roller skating,' insisted Gawain.

That wouldn't work. They'd done it a couple of times when Tom had been home, but who would hold Willow while she was with Gawain? It needed two people to be there.

She was still trying to make up her mind when her mobile went. It was a number she didn't recognise. 'Hello?'

'Emma?'

Her pulse began to race. There was only one man apart from her husband who could make her do that, and he was also the only other one who had broken her heart.

'Hello, Dad.'

'Look, I know this is short notice but I . . . we . . . wondered if you would like to come to Sunday lunch today. Bring the kids, of course. And Tom too.'

'He's not here,' she said flatly.

'I see.' There was a short pause. 'Well, can you and the children still come?'

'OK.' The acceptance was out of her mouth before she could take it back or even justify it to herself.

'We're going to see Grandad,' she told Gawain as she dressed Willow, giving up on her son, who was still glued into his Spider-Man ensemble. 'But don't tell Granny.'

'Why?' Gawain's face shone with indignation. 'It's wrong to tell lies.'

'It's not exactly a lie; it's just keeping a secret.' Oh dear, it was so hard teaching right from wrong.

Gawain nodded seriously, putting a finger to his mouth. 'Spider-Man does that too.'

The only reason she was doing this, Emma told herself as they stood on her father's doorstep, was for the children. Her separation from Tom had taught her how important it was to maintain family ties.

'Emma!' Dad scooped her into a big, warm hug. 'And this must be Gawain and Willow.' His eyes looked suspiciously bright. 'At last! Come on in. We've got ice cream for pudding; it was your mum's favourite when she was your age.'

It wasn't until she went into the sitting room and saw the cards on the mantelpiece that she realised. It was Dad's birthday. A special birthday.

'I wasn't expecting you to remember,' said Dad, slightly embarrassed. 'It was more that I didn't want to reach fifty and still not be in touch with my grandkids. Milestones like that make you think.'

Emma could see that. The second thing she noticed was that *she* was there. Trisha, the woman who had broken up her parents, if Mum's story was to be believed.

'I'm so glad you came.' The tall, elegant woman with grey hair smiled and held out her hand. Ignoring it, Emma scooped Willow up and sat on the sofa. Seeing Dad was one thing but being friendly to this woman was another. 'Ted's been like a cat on hot bricks since he saw you last. All he does is talk about you.'

Was she jealous? Or just being welcoming? It was hard to know.

Lunch was a bit tense, with Trisha trying to make conversation and Emma ignoring her. Luckily, the kids provided a distraction.

'I only eat food that's red and black,' declared Gawain.

'Since when?' retorted Emma.

'That's what Spider-Man does,' he replied, ignoring the question.

'What a bright little boy,' declared Trisha.

If she thought she could endear herself by being obsequious, the woman was mistaken.

'Emma,' said Dad quietly when they'd all finished. 'Can I have a quick word in the kitchen?'

Furiously she followed, taking in the square room with its huge range down one side.

'If this is to tell me I've got to be nice to your wife,' she began crossly, putting Willow down, 'then—'

'It's not.' Dad pulled out a chair for her to sit on. 'It's about Tom. I'd hoped you two might have made it up by now.'

Dad *knew*?

'Tom came to see me the other week after I wrote to him.'

'You wrote to him?' gasped Emma. 'Why?'

Dad looked wistful for a second. 'Because I didn't want him to make the same mistake that I did. So I talked to him about forgiveness.'

'Hah! You're a fine one to talk.'

'Poured out his heart, he did,' continued Dad, as though she hadn't spoken. 'Thought I'd understand as I'd been divorced myself. He loves you, you know.' Then he glanced at the bump. 'But there are some things that a man's pride won't let him accept. It was the same for me when your mum fell . . .'

He stopped suddenly. Emma's blood ran cold as she remembered something that her mother had started to say the other day. 'Mum got pregnant?' she whispered. 'After me?'

Dad nodded.

'No!' Emma leaped up. 'Then where is . . .'

Her voice tailed off as Dad shook his head.

'She got rid of it?'

'Actually, she miscarried.'

'Keith's child?' she whispered.

He nodded. 'I'm sorry, love. I didn't mean this to all come out. The point is that I can't stand by and see my daughter suffer. Tom's a good man. Is there anything I can do to help? Talk to him again, perhaps?'

She shook her head, still wondering whether to believe what her dad had just said. 'He'll never forgive me.'

'Mummy! Trisha's got a Spider-Man DVD.' Gawain tugged at her hand impatiently. 'Come and watch it. *Please!*'

'In a minute, love.' She turned back to Dad. 'Actually, there *is* something you can do.'

He looked hopeful. 'Yes?'

432

'You can be here for the kids. They need a male figure in their lives, someone extra now they only see Tom on Saturdays.'

Her father's eyes were wet again. 'That's the best present you could have given me.'

'Talking of birthdays,' she added, 'you can come to Gawain's party next month if you like.' Then she dropped her voice. 'Mum will be there. Better not bring Trisha if you don't mind.'

She wouldn't say anything to Mum, Emma decided. Otherwise there'd be a scene. She'd just let Dad arrive and then see what Mum said. Maybe then she'd be able to tell from their conversation exactly what had happened all those years ago. After all, she and Tom had agreed to have the party in their own home: it was up to them whom they invited. Not Mum.

'Rather you than me,' said Bernie, impressed when she confided in her. 'Pregnancy seems to have done something to you. Or is it being on your own?'

Bernie was right. Both had made her bolder, braver. Yes, she was a single mum, and yes, she had done something stupid to cause that. But if Rosie Harrison, back on the island, had managed on her own with a young son for all those years, then so could she.

Meanwhile, Gawain was getting feverish with excitement. By the time his birthday actually arrived, he was almost hysterical, bouncing around with his 'NOW I AM FIVE' birthday badge.

Tom came to pick them up. He'd decorated the house beautifully, Emma had to say, with 'Happy Birthday' balloons and streamers. He'd also – without telling her – bought their son a Spider-Man pedal car. 'It will have to stay here,' Emma told Gawain. 'There isn't room at Mum's.'

Tom looked awkward. 'I was going to talk to you about that,' he began but then the doorbell rang and the first of the guests arrived.

By the time Mum got there, they were well into Pass the Parcel, or Piss the Parcel as Bernie called it, because so many kids wet themselves with excitement. But Emma kept glancing at the clock.

Where was Dad? Maybe he'd decided not to come without Trisha. If so, it was his loss. Meanwhile, it was really odd having Tom next to her, helping out as though they were a normal couple. Some of the other parents who had stayed to help were clearly curious.

At last, the doorbell! 'I'll get it,' Mum called out before Emma could move. Uh-oh . . .

'What are *you* doing here?'

'Actually, I was invited.'

Emma listened through the half-closed lounge door with trepidation.

'After what you did to me with that woman?'

'Come on, Shirley. You know there was more to it than that.'

There was a brief silence. 'Not here,' she heard her mother whisper. 'And you'd best not be saying anything. I'll only deny it any road.'

Emma bent down as a sudden pain shot through her. Then another, making her gasp out loud.

'Are you all right?' Dimly she was aware of Tom's footsteps and his arm around her.

'She's started,' gasped Bernie, pointing to a trickle of water.

'I can't have!' Emma's voice rang out above the Pass the Parcel music. She stared up at Tom pleadingly, willing him to do something. 'It's too early. Far too early!'

TRUE POST-HONEYMOON STORY

'After the honeymoon, my (separated) parents reunited.
They said that seeing us get married made them want
to start again.'

Anonymous

Chapter Forty-One

ROSIE

March in Greece was often beautiful. If you were lucky – as they were this year – the temperature was mild and you could wear shorts and a tee-shirt. Small purple bougainvillea buds were already beginning to form on the tree climbing up the villa in preparation for summer.

Like many other house owners on the island, Rosie had paid one of the local builders to give the villa a fresh lick of white paint.

If only she could do the same to her own life. Gloss over those feelings for Winston which just wouldn't go away.

Even so, she told herself, sweeping the rooms as part of her general spring clean, it was so good to be back in Siphalonia! It wasn't just the sea; it was the people too. She'd lost count of the hugs and the 'Welcome backs' that she and Jack had been showered with on their return.

'I thought, maybe, you would remain in England,' sniffed Cara who, despite Rosie's instructions to take a rest, had insisted on donning a brown headscarf and wielding a broom alongside her.

Rosie swallowed hard as she pulled out one of the beds to reach the dust that had got to the far corners. They'd been through this so many times since she'd come back in January, but it seemed that, like Greco, Cara was still in need of re-assurance. 'I've told you,' she declared, shaking her duster out of the window, '*this* is my real home.'

Judging from the contented nod, Cara finally seemed to believe her. Just as well she couldn't read the doubts in Rosie's head. However hard she tried to dismiss Winston's face from her mind – how dare he presume to turn their lives upside down with his suggestion of America and boarding school! – it kept coming back again. His persistent texts and emails didn't help. Apparently the Americans were so keen to have him that they'd extended their deadline.

'It is my home too,' said Cara quietly. 'My nephew's wife, she does not want me there any more.'

Rosie stopped herself just in time from admitting that Greco had told her this already. Cara was fiercely proud. It must have taken a lot for her to confess that.

'*I* want you,' she said simply, kneeling down and putting her head in the old woman's lap. They sat for a minute in silence as Cara gently coiled her hair round a finger, rather like a small child. When she had turned up here destitute, all those years ago, the old woman had acted as the mother that Rosie could barely remember. Now it was her turn to look after Cara.

'My daughter, she would have been like you. If that man had not taken her.'

Rosie stiffened. Cara's daughter was a subject that had always been taboo. No one spoke about her, which was unusual in a place where local gossip was the backbone of day-to-day living. All she knew was that Elena had been lost at sea in a boating accident.

'He took Greco's boat one night,' continued the old woman, almost in a sing-song voice. 'Without permission. He took advantage of my daughter and then she drowned.'

'Who?' Rosie asked intently.

This was the first time that Cara had gone into detail over Elena's death. On previous occasions, she'd darkly alluded to Greco as being responsible in some way. But Rosie knew that couldn't be true. Greco was a good man. At least, he was now . . .

Cara gazed out of the window towards the sea, where a yacht with a white sail bobbed in the distance. 'Greco did not know his boat had been taken – he was away at the time. We had to keep it all secret. That is why she had to live on the mainland.'

Poor woman. She really was losing her marbles. 'But you said she drowned,' corrected Rosie softly.

Cara's fingers were twisting her hair more fiercely now. 'Drowned in grief. Lost! Yannis took advantage of her and then refused to recognise the child.'

'Yannis?'

Cara nodded. 'A son needs a father, even a part-time one. It is why I told you to tell Jack and his father the truth. Naturally, I offered to bring up my grandson, but Elena, she had pride. She moved to Athens, away from the whispers. It is why I visit so often.'

Rosie could hear the smile in her voice. 'My grandson is married now. I call him my nephew to avoid scandal but he knows the truth. He loves me. Yet it is his wife who does not want me any more.'

'And Elena?' She had to ask.

The hands fell away from her hair. 'My daughter died from a broken heart although the doctors said different.' There was a little sigh. 'I thought that God had sent you here, with Elena's soul inside you.'

How tragic! Yet this was the way that life went, Rosie realised, as she wrapped her arms around the older woman, rocking her back and forth in comfort. People loved each other but all too often lost each other too. If they were lucky, they found someone else to ease the pain. A new love. Or maybe an old one.

So that explained why Cara and Yannis refused to speak to each other. What a horrible man. And he'd been over-familiar with Emma Walker on the boat trip back in the summer. She'd had a word with him about that afterwards, warning him that familiarity with the guests was out of bounds.

'It is none of your business,' he had declared with a toss of his head.

Still, she told herself, it was essential to think like a businesswoman if she was to survive. According to the accountant, the Villa Rosa was in danger of closing down if she couldn't think of a way to bring in more money. She had to do *something*. It went without saying that she couldn't trouble Cara with any of this.

'Mum?'

There was a thud of feet coming from the back door. (Why did teenagers stamp instead of walk?) Rosie only hoped Jack hadn't skived off again. She might be glad to be back here in Siphalonia but her son hadn't settled. The term in that English school had made him increasingly critical of his teachers on their small island. He'd also taken to hanging out with his friends much later than she would have liked. It had led to some rather loud rows.

'Back already?' asked Cara sharply.

Jack shrugged, flinging his bag on the floor. 'Our teacher let us off early.' He threw a challenging look at his mother. 'Told us to finish the lesson on our own.'

'So why didn't you?' demanded Rosie, picking up his bag, which was in her way.

'I did.' Her son glared at her. 'I was quick and that's why I'm back. You don't trust me, do you?'

He grabbed his bag out of her arms, but not before she'd noticed something poking out of the top. A packet of cigarettes.

'It is natural for a boy to smoke at his age,' soothed Greco, massaging her back as they lay in bed, later that day.

Maybe in Greece, thought Rosie. But she didn't like it. Jack was, as usual, out with his friends, and although she couldn't help worrying about what he was doing, it did give her and Greco some time to themselves.

That was another thing. Ever since they'd got back, Jack had talked constantly about Winston. Anyone could see that Greco didn't like it at all.

'It is also natural for a boy to argue with his mother,' continued Greco, his hands moving downwards. Rosie felt herself melt. Her mind went back to that horrible scene in the airport with Winston when he'd suggested America and boarding school. Such a contrast to the other end, when Greco had been there to meet her; picking her up and twirling her around. 'I have missed you, my *omorfi*.'

Beautiful woman? Rosie had felt a warm glow running through her, but at the same time, she still couldn't stop thinking about Winston.

'Jack misses his father too, I think,' added Greco now.

The melting feeling evaporated, replaced by defensiveness. 'He's bound to, isn't he?'

Greco was sitting up. The moment had gone. 'And you, Rosie. You miss Winston too?'

She looked away, unable to meet his eyes. 'I've told you before. I have to stay in touch. He's the father of my son.'

'Pah!' Greco got out of bed and put on his boxers. 'Your Jack managed quite well without him all these years.'

'Yes.' Angrily, she flung on her jeans. 'But now he knows he exists, it's different.'

Greco caught her hand. 'And is that why you are always talking and emailing?'

He glanced at her laptop as he spoke. There, for all to see, was the tab that showed she'd been Skyping Winston just before Greco had turned up unexpectedly an hour earlier.

'We have things to discuss,' she said lamely. 'You just have to trust me.'

Greco shook his head. 'I would like to, Rosie. But when I was in England, I saw a different woman. And I do not know which one you are.'

This wasn't fair. 'I'm *me*,' said Rosie desperately. 'Or at least I'm trying to be.'

Greco gave her a disappointed look. 'Goodbye, Rosie. I will see you around.'

The door slammed. Rosie sank down onto the edge of the bed with its crumpled sheets. What had she done? And, more importantly, what should she do next?

The phone call from school came a few days later. Jack had been missing lessons. 'I'm not learning anything,' her son retorted. 'It's not like Corrywood.'

Rosie tried to contain her exasperation. 'It's bound to be different. You're just taking time to adapt back to normal life.'

Jack glared at her. 'Dad said you'd say that. He also said that education is really cool in Britain.'

So that was Winston's game! He was trying to take her son away, tempting him with stories of jolly boarding-school life back in the UK.

'Of course I'm not,' protested Winston when she tackled him furiously on Skype. 'In fact, I told him that he ought to stick it out on the island until he was able to apply to university. I was going to talk to you about that. Have you thought about a British uni?'

'If he's going to keep skipping classes, he won't be going anywhere,' she pointed out.

Winston, who appeared to be in gym kit, judging from his bare arms – such muscles! – nodded. 'Point taken. Would you like me to talk to him?'

Why not? It wasn't as though she was getting through to their son any more. To her surprise, Rosie felt a certain comfort in knowing that she didn't have to shoulder all this on her own.

'I've got to go now to take a class. But I still need to talk to you about tying up the final loose ends for our project. You haven't told anyone yet, have you?'

She shook her head, remembering how cross Greco had been when he'd seen her open laptop. 'No.'

'Thanks. Down, Barney. I said down!'

Despite her earlier anger, Rosie couldn't help smiling as a large brown springer spaniel with adorable floppy ears clambered up onto Winston's lap. He virtually filled the screen. 'How's he getting on?'

'Great. He's brilliant company too. Jack's really excited about seeing him.'

That was another thing. She'd promised Jack, when he'd been so upset at leaving Winston, that he could visit at Easter. It had seemed the right thing to do, although the prospect of losing her son every holiday for the next few years gave her an empty feeling.

'Why don't you come too?' suggested Winston suddenly.

His offer took her by surprise. 'I'm not sure. But thanks anyway.'

'Chat at the weekend then?'

'Sure.'

As she signed off, there was the creak of a floorboard outside her room followed by light footsteps going downstairs into the kitchen. 'Cara?'

The old woman must have got into her favourite chair by the stove rather quickly.

'You were listening, weren't you?' said Rosie indignantly.

Cara shrugged. 'It is all very well finding the boy's father, but he is not right for you. I know it.'

'Actually, it's not what you think . . .'.

Cara waved her away. 'Please. No excuses. I know you.' Those dark beady eyes bored into her. 'Tell me everything.'

So Rosie did. She told Cara about Winston's suggestion that they move to California. About Jack going to boarding school. And she even confessed about the kiss.

Cara's wrinkled face was inscrutable. 'You love him?'

Rosie took a deep breath. 'I find it hard to separate my feelings now from the ones I had when I was seventeen.'

The old lady's beady eyes were still fixed on her. 'If you really loved this Winston, you would give up the world for him.' She reached out and took Rosie's hands in her gnarled ones. 'Tell me. If Greco asked you to sail across the world with him, would you go?'

'Yes.' The word shot out of her mouth. 'Provided that Jack came too.'

There was a gleam of triumph in Cara's eyes. 'And *why* would you give everything up for Greco?'

'Because the real me – the one that *isn't* seventeen – can't imagine life without him.' Again, the words came out of her mouth without Rosie even needing to think about it. 'He makes me laugh and he makes me feel good about myself. But now he's still ignoring me and it's horrible.'

Rosie looked down from the terrace at the sparkling sea below. 'Besides, I know that he wouldn't want to sail away. Not ever. He loves Siphalonia as much as I do.'

Cara nodded, clearly satisfied. 'Then that is your answer, is it not? You love the place as well as the man. Two is better than one, I think. But perhaps you should ask your son what he thinks. He is home early again.' She rolled her eyes. 'On that computer again. It will fry his brain.'

Her old friend had a point: both about Greco and about her son.

'Why bother knocking if you're going to come in anyway, Mum?' Jack demanded angrily, looking up from his desk.

Because she was his mother, that's why.

'Are you working?' She shot a meaningful look at the screen.

'No. I'm looking at porn.'

Very funny. 'Can I see?'

Jack scowled. What, she wondered, had happened to that fresh-faced, smiley son from last summer? 'It's private.'

Just like her letters that Dad had hidden from her many years ago. 'Fair enough. There's just one thing I need to ask you, though.'

His face went all uncertain. 'Is it about what Dad said to you at the airport? I heard him, Mum, so don't deny it. He wanted you to go to America with him.'

Shocked, she went to put her arms around him. 'I'm not leaving you, Jack. Or the villa.'

A wave of relief passed over him. 'Really? I mean, I like Dad but I'm still getting to know him. These things take time.'

Wow. Her son really was growing up.

'What about Greco?'

'He's cool.' Jack grinned. 'And he makes you happy, Mum. I like that.' Then he turned round back to his laptop. 'You can look if you want.'

Curiously, Rosie took in the first line of the email.

Hi, Grandad.

'Dad suggested it,' said Jack, shrugging as though it didn't mean much to him. 'He said I might find it easier at first than talking. So he's set Grandad up with a computer and showed him how it worked. He's quite good, actually, considering how ancient he is.'

Rosie wasn't sure whether to laugh or be angry with Winston for interfering. 'I asked Dad not to tell you,' added Jack, ''cos I didn't want you to think I was being disloyal. Grandad threw you out, didn't he, when you weren't much older than me.'

'He was also rude to you,' pointed out Rosie.

'I know, but Dad says that if you don't learn to forgive, you only end up hurting yourself.'

Just what Cara was always saying. She went towards Jack for a big hug, and to her relief, he hugged her back. 'I don't think it's disloyal to me,' she said. 'Your grandad's getting on now. It's right that you make up.'

Jack's shoulders literally sank with relief. 'We make jokes about Charlie.'

'Charlie?'

'That bag thing that hangs at his side to collect his pee.' He grinned. 'Grandad's really funny about that. I give him girlfriend advice, too.'

'Grandad needs girlfriend advice?'

'Sure. Grandad's dating someone.' Jack roared with laughter. 'Can you believe it? At his age?'

Incredibly, it turned out to be the blonde bride's mother, Shirley. He'd called her up after meeting at Gemma's over Christmas lunch, Dad admitted when she tackled him on the subject during one of their now twice-weekly Skype calls. 'She says what she thinks and I admire that,' he told her. 'Charlie doesn't seem to put her off either. I get up to her place once a week on the train and she comes down to me at the weekends, providing she's not in the hospital.'

Alarm bells began to ring. 'Is she ill?'

'It's her grandson. Born prematurely, he was. Touch and go at the moment.'

Poor Emma. Rosie hadn't known about that. 'Isn't all this travelling too much for you?'

There was a throaty chuckle. 'Shirley's given me a new lease of life. So when am I going to see *you* next? And the lad?'

'He's coming over at Easter to stay with Winston,' she said carefully. 'But I'm not sure if I can make it. Our season will be starting then.'

There was a short silence at the other end of the phone. 'It would be nice if you could come.' His voice sounded gruff. 'But only if it doesn't put you out too much.'

How things had changed! This time last year, she would never have imagined she would be talking to her father. But age, as Cara was always saying, made you put your priorities in order. Perhaps it was time that she did the same.

Tomorrow might be a good time to start.

'I need to talk to you,' she called out.

Greco was dragging his boat in from his early-morning fishing trip. The sun was glinting on the water and he had that faraway look on his face. The sea, he often said, transported not just your body but also your mind.

Kicking off her shoes, she waded out to meet him. It was low tide and the waves were shallow.

'What is it?'

Greco's eyes were cool; since that last argument, he'd been ignoring her. Go and find him, Cara had said. Tell him how you really feel.

'It's about Winston,' she said, climbing into the boat and taking a seat next to one of the nets.

Greco turned his back. 'I thought it might be.'

She stood up again, putting her hands on his broad waist, feeling the heat course through her body. 'It's not what you think. Winston and I have been talking a lot on Skype because

445

he has a business plan to save the villa. It's not been doing well, but Cara doesn't know because I don't want to worry her. Winston suggested expanding it as a creative arts summer centre. He'll run exercise classes and we'll also have another artist. We're going to start a cookery school as well, and we'd like you to have a studio, to sell your figures.'

Greco swung round and she tried not to look at the mass of curly brown hairs on his chest, or else she would get distracted. 'And who is going to provide the money for this?'

'Winston.'

'Hah! He is clever, yes. He knows it will put you in his debt.'

'No. It's a gift, he says, to make up for all the years he didn't support Jack.'

Greco shook his head. 'That's what he says.' Then his eyes grew fierce. 'Don't you understand, Rosie? It is *you* he wants. This arts centre is just an excuse for him to see you.'

It was no good. She had to come clean. 'You may be right. But I know now that it's not what *I* want.'

She leaned her head against Greco's damp chest. 'It's you. Only you. Yes, I was in love with Winston once, but that was a different me. A younger one. Winston and I will always have something between us because of Jack. But it's not what you and I have.'

Slowly, a pair of thick arms wrapped themselves around her. 'Is that true?'

'Yes.'

His eyes bored into hers. Unable to breathe, she held his gaze. They locked together firmly, as close as any pair of bodies.

'I love you, Rosie,' he murmured.

And then, before she could say any more, Greco's mouth came down on hers. A flash of Winston's passionate kiss came to her. Only then did Rosie realise that at last she knew. Finally she understood, for certain, who it was that she really loved.

TRUE POST-HONEYMOON STORY

'My husband put his back out on honeymoon lifting my suitcase. He had to have an op when we returned.'

Kate, never knowingly underpacked

Chapter Forty-Two

WINSTON

'Sit. Sit, stay. Good boy!'

It was amazing how easily Barney had taken to his new home, thought Winston, as he raised his arm to throw the ball across the park. 'Fetch!'

Off he went, haring towards the little wood at the side, ears flapping in the wind, before returning once more to drop the ball at his feet. Winston could swear that the dog was grinning from ear to ear.

'You're the best thing to have come into my life for a long time,' Winston whispered, kneeling down next to him. 'Know that?'

Ever since he'd replied to the *Desperately Seeking a Home* email, Winston's life had taken an upturn. It was amazing what a dog did for you! It wasn't just that you had to go outside, whatever your commitments or indeed the weather (spaniels needed plenty of exercise!). There were also the other dog walkers you met, who'd instantly befriend you.

The responsibility of looking after someone else apart from himself, together with Barney's rather surprising but very flattering admiration (he followed Winston around constantly), made him feel a whole lot better about life.

'I can't wait to meet him properly!' Jack said last time they spoke on Skype, waving his arms excitedly. In the background, Winston could see the boy's bedroom in Greece with the view to the sea through the window. He could even make out a boat. Greco's, perhaps? With Rosie on it?

'Can you see me, Barney?' Jack continued, his face right up to the screen. 'Look, I'm here!'

'It won't be long,' Winston had promised. Indeed, it was already March. Soon he'd be able to spend time with his son during the school holidays.

His son! The phrase was getting more familiar now but it still hadn't lost its sparkle.

'Come on, boy, back we go,' he told Barney. 'Time to get to work.'

Barney padded along obediently by his side, out of the park and up to the main road, where he sat without being told. That was the amazing thing about having a retired dog. He'd been fully trained years ago; all Winston had to do, as the handler had explained, was to use the same commands like 'sit' and 'stay'.

'He could do with a bit of a rest,' the handler had added. 'This dog has seen some sights, I can tell you.'

Winston could believe it. When he'd been in the field, they'd relied on dogs like Barney to save lives. It was incredible how they could lead the way to a hidden bomb lying beneath the rubble, capable of exploding at any minute.

Was Barney finding it as difficult as he had? wondered Winston, as he got out his door keys. 'You'll adjust to normal life in the end,' he told him, rubbing the dog down. 'Just as I have.'

It was true, even though he'd had some pretty big false starts. Like Melissa. And then Rosie.

'If you don't mind me saying,' declared Nick's mum when he'd found himself discussing his personal life yet again over one of their increasingly regular Sunday lunches, 'Melissa might have been using you as a stopgap while she got her own feelings in order.'

Just what he'd thought. But, as he'd pointed out to Pam, he wasn't entirely blameless. He'd been a bit hard on Alice and Freddie, especially at first, until he'd had a taster of what it was like to be a father himself.

'As for Rosie,' continued Nick's mother. 'The past is like a pair of comfortable old slacks. You sometimes have to accept that they've had their day.' She'd patted his hand. 'Don't think

I'm being flippant. It's time to move on, Winston, for both of us. I've taken a part-time job at a charity shop. It will get me out of the house more. Now tell me, what did you decide about America?'

It was a week later. Barney was sitting by the bedroom door, waiting for Winston to change into his gym kit. The invitation to run his old class at the smart London club had come as a welcome surprise back in January. 'You've been missed,' said the manager.

But what about the backlash against him for his so-called 'irresponsible' behaviour in Afghanistan, as the papers had called it?

'People's memories can be quite short,' the manager had pointed out. 'Besides, it looked as though there were two sides to that story.'

He had had Nick's mother to thank for that. Shortly after that long talk at Christmas, she had approached one of the women's magazines and asked if they'd be interested in a story she had to tell them. It came out under the headline 'Why I've Changed My Mind About Winston King'.

It had been a moving piece, describing how she'd got to know him better now. It ended with the words '*If Nick is looking down, as I believe she is, I am certain that she would want us all to see Winston as the brave man that he really is.*'

The amazing thing was that the papers had all picked up on it.

'The Quiet Hero!' trumpeted the *Globe*, as though it hadn't laid into him the previous summer.

'Why We Should All Love Winston!' screamed *Charisma* magazine.

'Winston's Courage!' enthused another glossy.

It had made him feel embarrassed but vindicated at the same time.

Barney gave a short bark, bringing Winston back to the present. 'You're right. We've got to get going.'

450

One of the stipulations Winston had made before accepting the club job was that Barney could come too. In fact, Barney had been one of the reasons Winston had turned down the American television offer. 'But I want him to be there when I come to the UK for university,' Jack had protested when he'd run the job idea past his son. 'Besides, I don't want you to go so far away.'

That had decided it.

In fact, Barney proved to be a great ice breaker at the club, especially with the class of special needs children who came once a week for gentle exercise. This had been Winston's idea: he'd never have thought of it if he hadn't spotted a child in a wheelchair at the Corrywood after-school club when he'd gone to pick up Alice and Freddie last year.

The new course, arranged with one of the local schools, proved to be a great success. In fact, Winston reminded himself as he jogged through the London streets with Barney on the lead, there was a special needs class today.

That was the best thing about his new life: there was always something happening – like the reunion for his old Marine batch which was coming up.

As Nick's mother said, you had to look forward. Not back. And there was no doubt that his plans for developing the villa as an arts centre were really exciting. It would also give him the excuse to spend summers in Greece with his new family.

Gym was challenging today, especially the last class. The children were, as their accompanying teachers called it, 'de-mob happy' with the Easter holidays coming up. It had been difficult to keep their attention. Winston was used to helping them move at their own paces in their own inimitable style. But today they just wanted to play with Barney.

'Can I take him home?' pleaded one little girl with Downs Syndrome as they made their way out to reception to be collected.

Winston knelt down next to her, showing her how to stroke the dog's coat the right way. 'I'm afraid not,' he said gently. 'But you can see him every time you come here.'

'That's really kind.' He looked up to see a tall, very glamorous redhead reaching out for the little girl's hand.

'Don't I know you from somewhere?'

'Sure. I was the deputy producer for *Work Out With Winston*.' She pressed a card into his hand. So she was the senior exec producer now! 'We're having a bit of a rethink for the morning programme. Give me a call.'

'Your Majesty! Good to see you!'

Winston had forgotten the backslapping, not to mention the nicknames that were part of the slapstick in the Royal Marines. The 'Majesty' bit had come on day one of training, when some wag had taken the mick out of his public school accent and surname. At first he'd been embarrassed by the label, but soon decided it was better than some of the other nicknames that were handed out in a spirit of bonhomie.

'You too, Weasel,' Winston retorted, pumping the hand of a thin, wiry bloke who'd been extremely adept at wriggling his way through tunnels.

It was a no-partners reunion, for which he was grateful. It gave them all the chance to have some frank conversations with people who really knew what it had been like out in war zones.

Anyway, there was no one he could have brought if the invitation had included a plus-one.

'So you're a married man now, I hear,' said Weasel, thrusting a drink into his hands. 'Join the crowd! Did you hear that the wife and I are expecting our fourth?' He beamed as though he was pregnant himself.

'Congratulations.' Winston swallowed hard. 'Actually, Melissa and I aren't together any more.' Knocking back the whisky in one, he thought of the decree absolute which had fallen through his letter box that very morning.

Weasel's face promptly turned to one of sympathy. 'Sorry, mate.'

'Don't be. We weren't right for each other: not at this stage of our lives, anyway. I didn't get her kids.' He looked around.

452

'And she didn't get all this stuff – the mess it left me in.'

Weasel looked into his glass. 'Nick was a great girl.'

'Yes. She was.'

For a moment, they stood there in silence.

'So you're going to be back on telly then?' Weasel's voice was admiring. 'Read about it in some magazine. The wife's quite excited. Says she's missed you.'

Winston had had hundreds of emails saying the same thing. It looked promising, said his producer excitedly. He could hardly believe it had all happened so quickly after that chance meeting with the senior exec producer at the gym.

'And I'm also investing in an arts project in Greece,' he added. 'Yoga, cookery, painting – the works.'

Weasel nodded, impressed. 'Looks like you won't have any spare time for what I was going to suggest then.'

Instantly, Winston's ears pricked up with curiosity. 'Tell me.'

'I've been asked to set up a new project to help ex-servicemen get over traumas.' As he spoke, a bell rang, indicating they should take their seats at the huge dining table, laid with glasses and shiny silver cutlery; so different from the tin mugs they used to swig tea out of in the field. 'I'm looking for a part-time co-ordinator,' added his friend as they took their places. 'Funnily enough, we were thinking about including some exercise and art therapy.'

'Tell me more,' said Winston, shaking out his stiff white napkin. 'Sounds interesting . . .'

Winston left the dinner early, partly to get back to Barney – he didn't like leaving him for too long – and partly to mull over Weasel's proposal.

He knew Nick would approve. Only someone who had been on the edge, as his old mate had put it bluntly, could help someone in a similar situation. There might even be enough funding to send clients to 'this place of yours in Greece' for a week as recuperation.

Then, as he passed the news-stand by the tube station,

Winston's eye was drawn to a headline: 'French Couple Jailed for Ten Years After Drug Smuggling Scam'.

Grabbing a copy, Winston scanned it as he walked down the escalator. It was them! And it looked like Greco hadn't been the only naive foreigner to be taken in.

The couple, who lived in London, regularly travelled abroad to dupe innocent locals into sending over significant quantities of cocaine to the UK. They frequently indulged in excessive displays of 'alfresco sex' in order to create embarrassment and divert attention from their drug business.

Had Rosie seen the news? he wondered. Probably. But it would be a good excuse to call tomorrow morning, just to hear her voice.

As Winston put the key in the lock, he could hear Barney barking excitedly from the kitchen. There was another noise too. Skype. He must have left his iPad on.

It was Jack. But it was midnight in Greece. What was up?

'Hi.' His son's face swam into view. 'Everything OK?'

'Sort of.'

He could tell from the hurt look on the boy's face that it wasn't. 'No, it's not. Tell me.'

'It's just that . . . well, Mum's getting married. To Greco.'

Winston felt his heart lurch. 'And how do you feel about that?'

'A bit weird, to be honest. It would have been all right before . . .'

Winston knew what he meant. Before Jack had known Winston was his dad.

'And now you feel torn,' he said, completing his son's sentence for him.

Jack nodded. 'I don't want you to think I'm being disloyal.'

'Of course I don't.' Winston forced himself to sound as though he meant it. 'It's fine for you to like Greco – love him, even, as a stepfather.'

'But I love you too, Dad. I know we haven't known each other that long, but it feels like for ever.'

Winston gulped. 'I know it does. And I love you too.' It was so hard with the screen between them. He leaned forward as if he might be able to jump across the miles. 'Look, we want Mum to be happy, don't we?'

The boy nodded.

'And Greco's a good sort. So you'll have two dads.'

He had to push those generous words out.

'You're really all right about it?' Jack's face was beginning to clear with relief.

Winston crossed his fingers: an old childhood habit from school, when telling a porkie. 'Sure I am.' There was a pawing at the screen. 'Now why don't you say goodnight to Barney and then we'll have a proper chat in the morning.'

HONEYMOON HOMILY

If you plant rosemary in your garden when you return from honeymoon, you will be happy for the rest of your lives.

Anonymous

Chapter Forty-Three

EMMA

When Gawain and Willow had been born, they had been placed almost immediately in her arms, rooting for her breasts. Tom had hovered proudly, telling her how much he loved her and what a clever girl she was.

But this one scarcely looked like a baby at all. It was no more than a tiny scrap, lying in a plastic incubator, its life dependent on spaghetti tubes. It had been a whole month now and still she wasn't even allowed to pick him up. All she could do was stare at him.

And will him to live.

'It's too early!' Emma had cried out at Gawain's birthday party. 'Help me, someone!'

But Bernie's distraught face, not to mention Tom's shocked expression, had confirmed the severity of the occasion.

'Will someone get an ambulance?' Mum had demanded.

'I'm on it already.' That was Dad speaking. Dimly, in the panic, Emma registered that he had turned up, at her invitation, only a few minutes earlier.

The pains were coming regularly now in waves.

'Is Mummy poorly?'

Gawain's voice forced her to smile brightly from her position on the floor. 'Don't worry, darling,' she tried to say, reaching out to touch him. 'Everything's all right. It's just the baby coming.'

His little face shone. 'Cool. Tell it to hurry up, cos then it can help me blow out my candles.'

Emma looked around for Tom. She couldn't see him, even

though he'd been there a few seconds ago. He'd probably left in disgust.

'I've put some things in a bag for you,' said his voice behind her, reassuringly. Instantly, she felt better. 'A nightdress and some other stuff. Don't worry about the kids. Bernie and your mum will look after them. They'll carry on with the party, otherwise Gawain will be disappointed.'

There were murmurs of 'I'll help too' from some of the parents who'd stayed with the children. 'Come on,' Mum was saying brightly. 'How about Grandmother's Footsteps?'

Amidst the excitement, she heard the screaming siren from the ambulance outside. Was that for her? It didn't feel real. 'I don't want to be on my own!' she called out.

'You won't be.' Tom took her hand. 'I'm coming too.'

Maybe they'd be able to give her something to stop it.

'It will be all right,' said Tom, holding her hand in the back of the ambulance.

'Your first, is it?' asked the kindly paramedic.

Emma, in between contractions, was about to answer 'Our third' but then stopped. How did she know it was an 'our'?

Tom, she noticed, remained silent.

When they got to the hospital, it was a blur of white coats, green coats, trolleys, machines plugged into her body and faces peering down at her, assuring Emma that they were all doing everything that was humanly possible.

'Why can't you stop it?' she called out as the contractions grew faster and stronger.

Tom's voice floated above her. 'It's not possible, love. Just hang on in there.'

Love? He'd called her love! Gratefully she reached out for his hand. 'How's Dad doing?' chirped one of the nurses.

Don't, Emma wanted to say. But instead, she gasped as an overwhelming urge to push took hold. 'It's all right. You can do it now,' said someone else. 'This one's in a hurry to get out, isn't it? Here it comes!'

There was a silence. A silence which seemed to last for

ever. Then a cry. A thin cry that pierced the air. 'SCBU,' said a voice. 'Quick.'

From the bed, Emma tried to see what was happening. 'I want to hold it,' she called out, realising as she did so that she didn't even know if it was a boy or a girl.

'I'm sorry, love,' said one of the kindly older nurses. 'Your little one needs special care. You'll be able to see it shortly.'

'What is it?' she asked hoarsely.

'A boy, love. With bright red hair.' She glanced at Tom, who was still stroking Emma's hand. 'Just like Dad.'

That had been a month ago. Since then, both she and Tom had virtually lived at the hospital, taking it in turns to sit by little Scott, named after Sir Walter, whose books Emma had always loved.

It was incredible how you got used to being in a place like this. It was another world, full of kind, clever people who saved others' lives while the rest of life went on outside. Emma was staggered by how nice everyone was, from the team caring for Scott to the cheery tea lady and the young girl at the hospital shop.

Mum too had been amazing about looking after Gawain and Willow, bringing them in when allowed, to peer at their new brother through the window of the SCBU unit.

'Why can't they just wrap him up and bring him home?' Gawain had demanded, as if Scott was a parcel.

'Because he needs lots of looking after,' Mum said. 'When he gets home, you can help everyone if you start being a big boy again.'

Amazingly, it had worked! Almost overnight, Gawain stopped sucking his thumb and trying to steal his sister's dummy. He even stopped referring to himself in the third person.

But the best thing – if something good could come out of this – was that she and Tom had grown closer, partly through the uncertainty over whether Scott would be all right and then, as he grew stronger, over whether there was any mental or physical damage.

There was no doubt he was Tom's. Everyone commented on the mass of red hair. Yet, as if in silent agreement, neither she nor Tom felt able to raise the subject. When people congratulated Tom on his third child, he smiled and said yes, it was amazing, but they weren't out of the woods yet.

Nor was she, Emma thought. Scott might be Tom's but that didn't mean her husband had forgiven her.

Finally the day came when they were allowed to actually hold him in their arms. 'You first,' offered Tom as the nurse gently lifted Scott out of the incubator, wires still attached.

Every inch of Emma's body was yearning to take him. 'No,' she said firmly. 'You.'

She'd done the right thing. Emma could see that as her husband gazed tenderly down at the tiny mite in his arms. 'He's squeezing my finger!' Tom looked across to her. 'He's got guts, this one. A real fighter.'

Emma waited as the nurse slipped out to give them some privacy. 'What about us?' she said quietly. 'Are we going to be all right, Tom?' Her eyes misted as her husband handed her son over to her. 'I'm so sorry,' she said, looking down at Scott and then at Tom. 'It didn't mean anything. It was just the once.'

He winced.

'Once too many,' she added quickly. 'I know that. But I love you, Tom. I really do.'

He went very quiet. Then he put his arm around her. 'I pushed you into marriage, even though I knew you didn't want it.'

'I do now.' All those things which had irritated her about Tom had faded. The last few weeks had proved how well they worked as a team.

'Me too.' Tom's voice was low and gruff. 'This little chap has a lot to look forward to. A brother and a sister – and two parents. All under one roof.'

It was going to be all right! Emma could have cried with joy. And then they heard it. A bleep from one of the machines attached to Scott. Scared, they looked at each other.

'Maybe one of the wires has just slipped off,' said Tom nervously. But a nurse was rushing in, taking Scott from them. There was a bluish tinge to his upper lip which hadn't been there before.

'Everyone out, please,' said one of the doctors, rushing in. 'Sorry. That includes the parents.'

They'd been waiting in the side room for ages when the door finally opened. Emma's heart leaped and then sank again.

Dad.

He'd been visiting right from the beginning, staring at his grandson through the glass window. Usually he texted to see if it was 'convenient' which, Emma knew, was code for 'Will your mother be there?'

Today, he had just turned up, unannounced. 'My poor girl,' he said when he found her in floods of tears. 'Come here and let me give you a hug.'

Emma might be a mother of three, she told herself, but there was still something very comforting about being hugged by your dad.

'So what's going on?'

They explained what they'd been told, or rather, as much as they understood. Something about little Scott's lungs still being too immature to cope on their own. The bleep had warned the staff, luckily before it was too late.

But his breathing still wasn't as good as it had been before and a specialist had been called in.

'You know,' said Dad, holding her hand, 'when you were little, you had double pneumonia and were in hospital for three weeks.'

Really? Mum had never mentioned that.

'In those days, visiting hours were very strict.' His eyes took on a distant look. 'Your mother and I were only allowed to see you for an hour a day. It almost broke my heart.'

But she had gone for years not seeing him; all because Mum had lied about what had really happened. If it wasn't for the fact that she was here and Mum was holding the fort at home, Emma would have had a right old go at her.

461

'When you got better, we treated you like a precious china doll! We were both terrified that you might get ill again. But one of the nurses at the chest clinic where you were checked up gave us a good piece of advice. She said, "Kids are stronger than they look."'

He patted her hand just as the door tore open. Gawain and Willow! And Mum with an elderly man, supported by a walking stick. 'I got your text, love,' she began and then stopped.

Emma waited with bated breath.

'Hi Ted,' said Mum casually.

Emma stared. She'd expected Mum to lash out, make a scene like she had at the birthday party.

'Nice to see you, Shirley.' Her dad nodded at the man with the walking stick. 'How are you doing, Derek?'

'Fine, Ted. You? How's Trish?'

What on earth was going on? Emma looked from one to the other. They all seemed so civil, and they knew each other's names!

'Are we going to the swings again, Grandad?' piped up Gawain, tugging at his sleeve.

'Swings, swings,' chanted Willow.

Emma's mother gave her an embarrassed look. 'Your father has been helping out with the children every now and then while you've been in here,' she shrugged.

'Only when she came down to visit me,' added her companion. 'I'm Rosie's dad, by the way.' His handshake was firm. 'Derek. Nice to meet you.'

Then the door opened again. This time, a different doctor walked in. 'Mr and Mrs Walker? We have some news now.'

'So let me get this right,' said Bernie, helping herself to one of the chocolates in the children's ward. 'Sorry. I can't resist. Your mum and dad have made it up?'

'Kind of.'

Bernie was now rearranging the Get Well cards. There had even been one from Winston, which the nurses, who were all glued to his new programme, had oohed and aahed over.

462

'And you and Tom are OK?'

'Seem to be.'

'Good. So that book of mine worked, did it?'

'What book?'

'Just something I found in the library about how to revitalise your marriage. Had quite a juicy self-help section on kissing properly, actually.'

So that explained it! Trust Bernie to put her nose in it again!

'But most important, little Scott here – who gave us all such a shock – is actually going home soon?'

Emma, who was giving Scott a bottle of expressed milk, nodded happily. They'd been lucky, the consultant said. He was doing remarkably well, given that he'd been premature. But not as premature as she'd thought.

'Turned out that I was three weeks pregnant when Tom and I got married. I just didn't know.'

Bernie let out a slow whistle. 'Bloody hell, Em. That was winging it.'

She didn't need reminding, thank you very much. And she was grateful for the door opening at this point. Probably one of the nurses with . . .

'Surprise! Surprise!'

It was Gemma from school with – goodness! – a tiny pink bundle in her arms. 'I heard you were still here so thought I'd pop in to say hello.' Her eyes rested on baby Scott. 'I'm so relieved everything went all right for you.'

Emma found her manners. 'Thank you for the lovely flowers. And congratulations!'

Gemma beamed. 'I was beginning to think Lucy would never come along! She was two weeks late, you know. We're being discharged tonight and the boys can't wait! I only hope she's prepared for all those little fingers that are just dying to prod her.'

Emma, wishing she could be as laid-back as Gemma, knew exactly what she meant. She only hoped Gawain and Willow would be gentle with their new baby brother.

'Did you hear about Rosie?'

She'd sent a card too.

'No. What's happened?'

'She and Greco are getting married!' Gemma was beaming again. 'Isn't that lovely? We're going to the wedding in the summer and later, when the season has finished, she's coming over here for the christening.'

Gemma laid her cheek against her baby's. 'Rosie's going to be Lucy's godmother, along with my other great friend from uni. Isn't that nice?'

'Mummy, Mummy! Why is God putting water on Scott's head?'

Emma tried not to giggle as her son's words echoed round the church. They weren't a particularly religious family, but Gemma's reference to Lucy's christening had made her think. Luckily Tom agreed. The vicar did it as part of the main service. Mum was there with Rosie's dad. So too was Dad with Trisha. The two women had nodded at each other and she only hoped they'd remain civil. Bernie and her husband were godparents. She and Tom had asked one of the SCBU nurses too.

'And why is Scott wearing a dress?' demanded Gawain hotly. 'He's not a girl.'

Somehow they got through the service and back home, where Bernie had helped her prepare a buffet (and scoff half of it too). Mum and Trisha were on opposite sides of the room. Fair enough.

'Is Charlie all right?' demanded Gawain.

'Who's Charlie?'

Mum's boyfriend looked across from the table where he was piling a plate high with sliced ham. He patted his trousers. 'That's my catheter bag. I nicknamed it Charlie and it seems to have stuck.'

There was a throaty laugh from Mum's direction. 'In more ways than one, eh, Derek?'

'Go quite well together, don't they?' observed Bernie wryly, helping herself to another spoonful of cranberry sauce. 'Surprising really, isn't it? Your mum's happier than I've ever known her.'

So was Dad. It was so good after all these years to have everyone in one room, putting their disagreements to one side for one special day. They were blessed, Emma told herself, as Tom gave her a wink from the kitchen door. Truly blessed.

'Going to a wedding, are you?' Bernie, who didn't miss a trick, picked up the silver-and-white invitation from the mantelpiece. 'Rosie and Greco? Siphalonia? Isn't that the place where we sent you on honeymoon?'

Emma had meant to put that away. The last thing she needed was for Bernie to bring up a reference to Yannis.

'Yes, but we're not going.'

Bernie's eyes opened. 'Because of . . .'

'Because of Scott,' said Tom smoothly. He took his son from Emma's arms and held him, while reaching out for her hand.

'Mum's going,' added Emma, flushing. 'Derek asked her. You did know, didn't you, that he's Rosie's father?'

Bernie, wide-eyed, was taking it all in, no doubt to distribute it around Corrywood later on. 'Actually,' she said, nudging Emma in the hips, 'Phil and I were thinking of going to a holiday camp in Dorset this summer. You know – a traditional bucket-and-spade place. They do great fish and chips. Fancy coming too?'

TRUE POST-HONEYMOON STORY

'After the honeymoon, my new husband got made redundant. So I handed in my notice and we blew our savings on a backpacking trip round South-East Asia.'

Marion, now settled in Surrey

Chapter Forty-Four

ROSIE

Weddings were big affairs in Greece. Rosie had been to more than she cared to count, during her years in Siphalonia. They were always raucous, joyous celebrations, involving great quantities of food and drink from the minute that an engagement was announced, right through to the end of the wedding reception, where the couple would be showered with rose petals and money.

And now it was *her* turn!

'You will make a beautiful bride,' said Cara, pins dangerously poised between her yellow, gappy teeth as she knelt at Rosie's side, weaving her magic. In truth, Rosie had initially wanted to buy a British designer dress which she'd spotted online, but hadn't wanted to offend Cara, who insisted on making her wedding gown. 'You are my adopted daughter,' she had declared firmly. 'It is only right.'

Now, as Rosie viewed herself shyly in the mirror, she was glad she'd agreed. It wasn't just the proud, self-congratulatory grin on Cara's wizened brown face. It was also the cream silk dress itself, with its nipped-in waist and Grecian neckline, which would go down well on any London catwalk.

'Beautiful bride?' she repeated, smoothing down the skirt and wondering if that really was her in the mirror. 'A rather old one, I think.'

'Tsk,' scolded Cara, smacking her hand lightly for touching the material. She put another tuck in the side. 'Nonsense!'

Like any self-respecting Siphalonian woman, Cara had an ability to speak while threading a needle. 'Look at you! You do not seem your age. Besides, better late than never for both of you. It's not as though Greco is a spring cockerel, as you say in England.'

Cara was attempting to learn English phrases from Jack's new iPad (a present from Winston) in order to impress the British guests. She was right, Rosie conceded. Most Greek men were married by their early thirties at the latest. Indeed, the majority of Greco's friends had grown-up children by now.

Her mind went back to their argument in March and that wonderful make-up kiss afterwards. Soon after that, Greco had suggested a moonlight trip on the *Siphalonian*.

'I have a favour to ask,' he had said casually, tossing her one of the smaller fishing nets. 'There is something caught inside, I think. Can you help me find it?'

Surely not . . . Yes! Her heart beating and her mouth dry, Rosie reached down and disentangled a glinting diamond ring which was neatly tied to the net with a piece of string.

'You will marry me, I think.'

It was a command rather than a question, but before she could reply, Greco lifted her up and twirled her around in the middle of the boat. Around them, the water sparkled with the reflection of the stars above.

'You will be Mrs Greco Angelis?'

This time, it *was* a question. Greco's handsome face stared down at hers, waiting. That confidence, Rosie was beginning to learn, was only skin deep.

'Yes,' she said clearly, only realising as she said it, how right it felt. 'Yes, I will.'

Of course, she'd had to run it past Jack first.

'Just as long as you're happy.'

She'd hoped for a more demonstrative response.

'Our life won't change.' She tried to cuddle him but he stepped away. 'We'll still stay in the villa.'

'But I can't be here for ever, Mum.' His words sent a shiver through her. It was so hard being a mother. You looked after them every minute, every day. And then, before you knew it, it was time for them to spread their wings.

Now that Jack was so friendly with his dad, always on Skype to him, Rosie wondered if her son had secretly hoped they might have become the family they could have been.

Why did families have to be so complicated? Even Gemma seemed to have misgivings.

'You don't think your backgrounds are too different?' her best friend had asked with a worried furl on her forehead when Rosie had broken the news about her and Greco on Skype the following morning.

'Because he's a fisherman, you mean?' Rosie had waved her hands dismissively. 'Not at all. In fact, he's more educated than I am. We spend hours reading in the evening before we . . .'

'Don't go there!' There was the sound of a baby crying in the background. 'You'll make me jealous. This one is definitely going to be the last. Joe and I are so exhausted, we've forgotten how to do you-know-what any more!'

Rosie hoped that wasn't true, but even if it was, those two definitely had a solid relationship. When Gemma had first told her, some years ago, about this sullen, rude man who had become her boss at Corrywood School, Rosie had really felt concerned for her. Then, when Gemma had confessed they'd become an 'item', she'd been worried for her friend. But those months in England had shown Rosie how well suited they were, and what a decent, honourable man Joe was.

Just like Greco.

'Is that my lovely god-daughter?' she cooed as little Lucy loomed into view, all snug and wrinkled in the pink Babygro she'd sent over.

'She doesn't smell so lovely, right at this moment,' joked Joe, who was holding her in his arms. 'But she can't wait to come out to Greece to see her Auntie Rosie get hitched.'

Rosie giggled. Not just because Lucy was making such delightful baby faces at her but because Greco had now come into the room and was tickling her. Rosie only hoped he hadn't overheard their earlier conversation.

'I am looking forward to meeting you,' he said gravely to the baby.

'Same here,' said Gemma keenly. 'Actually, Greco, I'm dying to ask how—'

'Sorry, but we have to go.' Rosie didn't want to be rude but this wasn't the time to start interrogating her new fiancé. 'We've got guests arriving and I still need to check their rooms. I'll call next week. Bye!'

Since then, thought Rosie, watching her dress taking shape in the mirror, thanks to Cara's skilled hand, there had been several more excited Skype conversations with Gemma. Was Jack getting used to the idea, she wanted to know? (Possibly, although he spent a lot of time in his room on the computer.) Had she heard about Winston's new television show? (Yes. It was even being screened over here.) Did she know that Melissa had remarried her love-rat of a first husband? (Yes. Winston had told her himself.) And finally, did she know Emma, or the blonde bride as they couldn't help calling her, had had a little boy? A honeymoon baby.

They'd given birth in the same hospital.

Rosie had felt a jolt of apprehension, recalling how Yannis had come striding proudly out of the copse during their island boat trip last summer, flamboyantly doing up his shirt with a rather drunken Emma stumbling by his side. 'Very premature,' Gemma had added, 'but it looks as though they're finally out of the woods. Spitting image of Tom, his dad, with bright red hair.'

Phew! That was all right then. Rosie breathed a sigh of relief. Yannis had walked out on them a few weeks before, without so much as a day's notice. The man had got a job in one of the big hotels in Athens, apparently. Well, good riddance! After hearing from Cara what Yannis had done to her daughter, Rosie had found it hard to stomach his presence at the villa. He might be Greco's cousin and they might look alike with their dark hair, aquiline noses and proud manner of bearing. But that was as far as the similarity went.

'I do what I like,' he had declared, eyes narrowing. 'I know more about you than you realise. As you English say, walls have ears.'

What did he mean by that? But he'd flounced off before she could tackle him.

Fortunately, she and Cara had managed to find another chef, not just for the villa but also for the cookery courses which were part of their new summer entertainment programme. Greco had also offered to do wood-carving demonstrations in the little gallery that was to house his figures.

Already bookings were up – especially during the month that Winston was coming over to run his summer special workout, during his programme's August break.

'A whole month!' Jack had said when she'd told him, his face breaking out into a big grin. 'Cool. I'll take Dad fishing and we can . . .'

Rosie had listened to her son gabble excitedly about all the things he intended to drag Winston to: things that most boys wanted to do with their fathers.

'You were right,' she said now to Cara.

'About the waistline?' Cara was eyeing her creation with an approving look. 'I told you so.'

'About Jack and Winston. A boy *does* need his father.'

Smugly, Cara tied the white satin bow behind her back. 'And a father needs his son.' She eyed Rosie squarely in the mirror. 'He also needs to be friends with his child's mother. It makes life much easier.'

'We are friends,' protested Rosie, aware as she said so that Greco still prickled every time she mentioned Winston's name.

'You need to do something that shows Greco he does not need to worry any more,' said Cara, spitting out the remaining pins into the box with gusto. 'In fact, I have an idea . . .'

The wedding would be a mixture of English and Greek traditions, Rosie and Greco had decided. They would get married in the small church built into the cliff over the sea, and Rosie's dad – who was, incredibly, coming over from England – would

471

give her away. Afterwards, there would be a massive reception on the terrace of the Villa Rosa. The paying guests would be invited too.

And now the day was here! Cara had woken her with a sweet honey drink, clacking and fussing and shooing away anyone who dared interfere with the dressing of the bride.

Jack had spent last night with Winston ('I'd like some time with Dad') and her own father had arrived yesterday morning, along with Shirley, who was as excited as her own daughter had been when she'd come here last year. 'This is paradise, isn't it, Derek?'

There was only one person missing. Someone whom Rosie often thought of, even though it was becoming increasingly hard to remember the precise details of her face.

'Your mother would have been so proud,' said her father, standing beside her outside the villa, awkwardly stiff in what looked like a new suit. Before them, the baker's pony, its mane plaited, was pawing the dusty ground impatiently, waiting to take them to church in a cart festooned with red ribbons. He wiped away a tear. 'I'm sorry, love. For everything.'

'Me too.' She put out her hand. 'This is a new beginning, Dad, for all of us.'

As the cart made its way up the hill, Rosie took in the familiar faces, cheering and throwing flowers: the woman who ran the small local supermarket; the postman; one of Greco's fishing friends; some of the mothers from Jack's school. So many people who had shown a complete stranger such love and care when she had turned up, pregnant and alone, seventeen years ago.

Was it wrong to wear cream, considering she was meant to be a widow? she had asked Cara. The old woman had grinned. 'You really think they believed that story?'

It made their acceptance even more reassuring.

'Nearly there,' said Dad nervously, gripping her hand. It had taken a lot for him to come over here; she knew that. A day's journey for an old man who wasn't particularly strong was a big ordeal.

472

'Shows how much he wanted to be here,' Shirley had declared, knocking back last night's welcome drinks. ''Sides, I'd have dragged the old so-and-so here if he hadn't.'

Dad had definitely met his match there.

'Not too late to change your mind,' her father added as the cart came to a halt. Around them was a sea of yet more locals, all waving and cheering.

'I don't want to, Dad!' Rosie said, turning to him and taking his gnarled old hands in hers. 'I love Greco. He's fun. He talks about things that I didn't know about before. He and Jack get on really well. He's . . .'

She'd been about to say the word 'sexy', but there were some things you couldn't say to your father.

'I'd like to get on with him too,' said her father slowly. 'I just hope your lad has really forgiven me for that stupid stuff I said.'

'I'm sure he has,' said Rosie, hoping this was true. 'He said you were emailing now. That's a start. And now you're here, you can build on that.'

For a brief moment as they sat in the cart, holding hands, they seemed frozen in time. Never again would she be right here, with her father, about to marry the love of her life, who had been living right here all the time, under her nose.

'I think we'd better go now.' Rosie gave her father's rosy-veined cheek a quick kiss. 'Are you ready?'

It was a short walk down the aisle of the little white church where Jack had been christened as a baby. She could see him now: a young man in his stiff collar and white shirt, standing at the front next to Greco. All three men had their backs to her, straight and erect.

Jack. Greco. And Winston.

That had been Cara's bright idea. 'Why don't you suggest to Greco that he asks Winston to be a best man as well as Jack? It will show him that you do not have feelings in that department any more.'

Rosie wasn't quite sure of the logic in that, but Greco seemed to have been reassured. 'So you do not care for this

473

Winston after all.' He had given her a shrewd look. 'A bride would not want to marry a man if her lover was there too.'

There was nothing like Greek passion, or reason! 'I've told you,' she'd said, standing on tiptoes to plant a kiss on his lips. 'Winston is not my lover. But he *is* the father of my child and now he's an investor in the villa. It would really make me happy if everyone got on.'

She was standing next to Greco now, in the middle of her men. Three men who had changed her life in very different ways. Slowly, she reached out for her future husband's strong, warm hand while holding out her other to her son, to show that she would always love him too.

The priest stood in front of them. For a second, there was a silence, punctuated only by the sound of the waves outside. And then he began . . .

It was nearly midnight but still none of the guests showed any sign of leaving. 'It is the mark of a good party,' declared Cara approvingly. They'd certainly had a great time so far. The food had been mouth-watering (the new chef was even better than Yannis) and her English guests had been stunned by the plate-throwing. Luckily, not literally.

'Won't someone get into trouble, Mummy?' one of Gemma's boys said out loud, which had made them all laugh.

They'd loved the money stuffing tradition too. 'Shall I give my pocket money?' asked the eldest sweetly. 'I don't mind. I want to give them a present too.'

They'd even had the 'baby rolling' tradition, where they'd had to roll, giggling, on a mattress on the terrace, to symbolise fertility. Poor Jack, who had his arm round one of the local girls (his relationship with Alice seemed to have fizzled out, judging from the reduced mobile phone bill), had looked rather embarrassed by that. 'Don't worry,' she had whispered afterwards. 'You're the only son I want.'

But now Greco was getting impatient. 'We must go soon,' he murmured, dancing close to her on the terrace, making her body tingle with expectation.

'We will,' she assured him. 'But there are still some guests I have to talk to.'

Reluctantly breaking away, she headed towards Sally. It was so nice of Gemma's mum to have come over. 'Wouldn't have missed it for the world,' she assured her. 'In fact, we're going to take the opportunity afterwards to have a little trip round some of the other islands. It will be nice to have some time with my grandchildren.'

Gemma got the feeling that Sally was secretly relieved to get away from her stiff, academic husband who was 'too busy' to join them.

'By the way,' added Sally brightly, 'there's a little parcel for you inside, on the reception desk. Don't confuse it with the wedding present. My husband did a big clear-out of the garage the other week and found some things that belonged to you.'

That wasn't surprising. She'd spent more time at Gemma's house, after Mum had died, than in her own house.

'Not much,' continued Sally brightly. 'Just a jumper and some books and an old letter. It's actually addressed to someone else, but it has your name and contact details on the back. Do hope it wasn't too important . . .'

The lantern-studded terrace began to blur. Surely not, Rosie thought . . . Glancing back, she could see Greco talking to Winston, slapping him on the back in a friendly, manly way. There was just time. Swiftly, she made her way to reception and began sifting frantically through the presents. There it was. A carrier bag bearing a well-known British shop name.

Rosie's chest thumped as she took out the blue jumper in a style which had been very popular in her teenage days. A book of poetry, too, with her mother's name written in the front. And a letter. Addressed to one Charlie King.

Crouching on the floor, her wedding dress spread out about her, she began to read her loopy schoolgirl writing.

Dear Charlie,
I've got something really difficult to tell you. I'd much rather talk face to face, but I don't know where you've

*gone, so I'm hoping that if I send this to your base, you
will get it before too long. There's no easy way of saying
this . . .*

*I'm pregnant. And I'm scared. I need you here with
your strong arms around me, telling me it's going to be
all right. Dad is going to go absolutely mad when he
finds out. He wants me to go to university and I want
to go too. But I can't get rid of your baby, Charlie. I
just can't.*

*If I don't hear anything back from you, I'll presume
you don't want anything to do with me. But I know
you're not like that.*

Rosie read and reread the letter before standing up and walking
down to the sea, away from the music on the terrace. So
Winston hadn't received the letter, just as she hadn't received
his. He hadn't lied. He hadn't abandoned her. Because he
simply hadn't known about Jack.

Now was the time to put the past behind them, Rosie told
herself as she ripped up the letter into small, thin strips and
watched them flutter into the sea like confetti. After all, Jack
had his father now. And she had Greco. At some point, she
might tell Winston about her own letter going astray, but not
now. Maybe later.

'Where have you been?' Greco asked when she returned.

'I needed to see the sea,' she replied truthfully.

He kissed her full on the lips, to the delight of one of
Gemma's boys. 'That's rude, isn't it, Mum?'

'Not if two people love each other,' smiled her friend.

Jack and her dad, Rosie noticed, were sitting next to each
other, talking. Her dad seemed to be explaining something,
and Jack looked as though he was listening.

'Ready?' asked Cara, handing her the fruit.

'Instead of a bouquet, we throw a pomegranate,' explained
Rosie to her English guests. 'Whoever catches it will have a
baby within the year.'

There was a roar of approval. Greco's arm was on hers, impatiently. 'Here we go,' she called out.

The pomegranate soared into the air. 'Good throw, Auntie Rosie,' called out one of Gemma's boys. 'Whoops. Watch out, Mum!'

Gemma had caught it! More to protect little Lucy than anything else. 'That's all I need,' she said, rolling her eyes. 'Still, you don't really believe in that sort of thing, do you?'

They were going now. Greco's arm was around her shoulder as everyone called out their farewells. She stopped briefly to give Jack a big hug, and then Dad. Winston was hovering. She hesitated.

'It's all right,' Greco whispered. So she brushed his cheek, feeling . . . feeling precisely nothing more than friendship.

Winston looked at her steadily, his hand on their son's shoulder. 'Do you know, I forgot to ask you something.'

Rosie's heart almost stopped. 'What?'

'Where are you going for your honeymoon?'

She thought of Greco's small fisherman's cottage with its rows of books and big comfortable bed, which they'd decided to keep as a bolthole from the villa when they needed time to themselves.

'Home,' she said, nestling into her new husband's shoulder. 'We're spending our honeymoon at home.' Then, glancing up at Greco's loving face for reassurance, she added, 'It's where we belong.'

TRUE POST-HONEYMOON STORY

'In our day we didn't have wedding lists. We ended up with three teapots, four salad bowls, three toasters, four trays and two Teasmades.'

Ethel, still using one of the teapots thirty years on

Chapter Forty-Five

WINSTON

'Down, Barney! Down!'

What had got into him? Maybe, thought Winston as he prepared for the morning's filming, he was still unsettled after the summer. Nick's mum had been great at looking after him while he'd been away in Greece, running his course.

But Barney had been gratifyingly exuberant when Winston had returned, leaping up to slobber him with kisses.

'Had a good time, did you?' asked Nick's mum, after he'd thanked her and given her the presents he'd brought back, including some of Greco's figures which were, he'd checked, reassuringly solid. This time, they didn't contain anything they shouldn't.

'It was wonderful to spend some time with my son,' he said.

Pam nodded approvingly. 'I hope one day you'll bring Jack here to meet us.'

Winston hugged her, noticing, as he did so, Nick smiling at him from a silver-framed photograph on the sideboard. 'I'd like that. He's going to put Exeter University down as his first choice, you know.'

He was unable to keep the excitement out of his voice.

Pam shot him a shrewd glance. 'And how does his mother feel about that?'

Winston thought back to the conversation he'd had with Rosie before he'd left, about the letter she had sent him all those years ago. No one seemed to know how it had ended up in the downstairs cupboard, although Gemma had confessed that she 'vaguely remembered leaving the letter with her mother to post' as she had to rush off to choir 'or something'.

'I'm not certain – it's so long ago. I'm really sorry, Rosie.'

It would have been easy to have fallen out with her friend over it, Rosie had admitted to Winston. 'I almost didn't tell you about it, and then I realised that we'd already had too many secrets. As Cara says, maybe all things are meant.'

Maybe. Maybe not. Deep down, Winston knew that the young Charlie wouldn't have made a very mature father, but he still couldn't help feeling wistful at the same time at what he'd lost.

'Rosie's quite keen that we have some father–son time,' he now told Pam. 'Of course, Jack will go back to Greece during university holidays, and I'll be there in the summer to run my course again.'

Nick's mum was smiling at him in a sideways manner – her youngest daughter used to do the same. To his surprise, Winston found Nick's memory reassuring rather than painful. 'Sounds as though you've wrapped everything up quite neatly.'

Winston grinned. 'Put it this way, I feel much more optimistic about life than I've done for a long time.' Then he caught himself. 'I'm sorry. I didn't meant to be disrespectful.'

'It's all right.' She caught his hand. 'You've given me a new lease of life, Winston. I look forward to your visits – and yours too, Barney!'

So did he. Perhaps, Winston told himself as he sat at the dressing table waiting for the make-up artist to arrive, he'd ring Pam after the programme and suggest Sunday lunch.

Maybe, he thought, glancing at his iPad and rereading the email that had just arrived from Greco, he might tell her about this. Funny, he hadn't put Greco down as an email man, but he'd clearly underestimated him. In more ways than one. The email was couched in formal terms, more like a letter.

Dear Friend (I call you that now),

There is something I must tell you. Rosie thinks it comes best from me. My cousin Yannis – who I do not care for – has been bragging to a member of the family that he made a great deal of money from what he called 'the famous exercise man in Britain'.

> *I am afraid that he overheard my Rosie on the Skype
> to her friend Gemma last year. He was the one who told
> the newspapers that you had a love child, although he
> did not know it to be Jack.*
>
> *I give you my heartfelt sorrow that a relative of mine
> has acted in this way. It goes without saying that I will
> now have nothing to do with this cousin who has brought
> dishonour on my wife and a family friend. Apparently
> this is not the first time he has acted shamefully, and
> somehow managed to keep it hidden.*

So that explained it! Winston leaned back in his chair, mulling it over. Until now, neither he nor Rosie had been able to understand how the papers had known that she was the mother of his child. Still, at least they'd managed to keep Jack out of the publicity glare.

'Hiya!' A small girl with bright pink streaks in her blond hair bounced into the room. 'Sorry I'm a bit late. Weren't expecting me, were you? Thought not. Gwenda's off sick – up the duff, between you and me – so you've got yours truly instead. The name's Toni, by the way. That's with an "i" and not a "y". Who's a lovely boy then?'

Still dazed by Greco's email, Winston thought initially that the last bit was directed at him. But then he saw the girl – now she was closer, he could see she was more of a woman – kneeling down and stroking Barney. The dog (traitor!) was rolling on his back, legs in the air, waiting to be tickled.

'He normally only does that to people he knows,' said Winston, taken aback.

Toni grinned. 'I have that effect on animals. Now, let's get you ready then.' She stood behind his chair. In the mirror in front, he watched her assessing his face with a grave authority that seemed at odds with her entrance and appearance.

Without warning, her fingers ran lightly over his cheekbone and eyebrows, like soft butterflies.

The effect was electrifying.

Why? This girl with her in-your-face friendliness wasn't his usual type. She wasn't like Nick. Or Melissa. Or Rosie. But maybe that wasn't such a bad thing . . .

'Don't think I'm being over-familiar,' she chirruped. 'I like to *feel* people's faces before I do them.'

Briefly, Winston had a mental flash of Melissa doing his make-up on the day they'd met. Strange. The memory didn't hurt as much as it used to.

'Right,' she announced. 'Got it. Going to watch are you – Barney, isn't it? My dog does that too.'

Winston felt that spark of interest growing. 'What kind do you have?'

'Red setter. Quite mad but I adore him. So does my son.'

Really? 'How old is he?'

'The dog or the son?' Toni beamed. She had a nice smile. Rather an infectious one. 'They're both ten. I got Roo when Jake was born. Thought he might be company for us both.'

He glanced in the mirror at her bare left hand.

'I've got a son too,' said Winston, settling back into the chair. Wow. This woman's hands were like magic. The others had never started with a head massage. 'He's called Jack. He lives with his mother in Greece but he's coming over for the next school holidays to see me and his grandad.'

'Cool. There's nothing like kids, is there? Keep you on your toes, that's for sure.'

Then she stopped. Without needing to look in the mirror, Winston knew she'd found it.

The ugly raised scar.

Visible proof that he'd tried – so hard – to save Nick from that inferno before being pulled away by one of his men.

'I think we'll leave that.' Toni's voice was soft. 'I don't believe in covering things up. They're a sign of having survived something, aren't they? After all, if you can get through one problem in life, you can get through another.'

'I agree.' He faced her fully and squarely in the mirror. 'Look, I know this might sound a bit forward. But I was wondering. I know this great place near here that does coffee. They take dogs too . . .'

POST-HONEYMOON NOTES

NOTICE IN CORRYWOOD SCHOOL NEWSLETTER

We are delighted to announce that Mrs Emma Walker (mother of Gawain and Willow, who are current pupils) will be helping to run the new school crèche. Baby Scott will be amongst the first intake! Meanwhile, we welcome her husband Tom as our latest recruit to the PTA. A real family affair!

FOURTEEN-YEAR-OLD GIRL RUNS UP £5,000 IN iTUNES CHARGES

A teenager from Corrywood has landed her parents with a hefty bill after using her dad's iPad to download music. ' Her new boyfriend borrowed it without her permission,' declared father Marvyn, who now plans legal action against the nineteen-year-old (unemployed) youth.

Extract from the *Globe*

TEXT FROM GEMMA TO ROSIE

Cnt believe it! Am pregnant agn! Must hve been that pome-granate. Wll Skype later. Still in shock. Bt nice shock!

POSTCARD FROM DEREK TO JACK

Dear Jack,
Thought you might like this postcard from Devon. See that ice cream place on the front? We'll go there

*when you come over. Don't know about you, but I'm
quite partial to a 99. So's Shirley. Give my love to Mum.
   Love Grandad*

TEXT FROM ROSIE TO GEMMA

*I dn't believe it either. I'm pregnant 2! Greco over moon.
Jack surprisingly xcited. Wants a baby sister . . .*

To Winston@winstonking.com from Melissa@onmyown.com

*Thanks for letting me know your news before anyone else. I
appreciate it. Marvyn and I have split up for good this time.
He went nuts over something that Alice did and blamed me.
It was the last straw. I feel much more optimistic about the
future now. Hope you do too. No hard feelings? All the best,
Melissa*

CHARISMA EXCLUSIVE

Our undercover reporter can reveal that Britain's favourite
exercise guru is getting married again! Winston King is set to
tie the knot with single mum Toni after yet another whirlwind
romance. We can only wish them luck and hope it will be
second time lucky for both of them!

   Rumour has it that they will be honeymooning on a remote
Greek island. Watch this space . . .

MORE TRUE HONEYMOON STORIES

'We stayed at a small hotel in the Lake District where dinner was included. Another couple went somewhere else to eat one night and the owner – who was just like Basil in *Fawlty Towers* – threw them out when they returned. They had to find somewhere else to stay.'

Kim, who's never been back

'My husband was keeping our honeymoon destination a secret – but an aunt blew it at the reception. He was upset but I was relieved. I was able to pack the right clothes!'

Diana, now married for seven years

'We missed our plane for our honeymoon in Paris. It was my fault, but my new husband has never once blamed me. I'm not sure I'd have been so forgiving . . .'

Angela, married for nearly six years

Do you have a honeymoon or post-honeymoon story to tell? If so, email janeyfraser@gmail.com Or Tweet @janey_fraser. For details of competitions and writing tips, visit www.janeyfraser.co.uk